TOWERS

IN THE

MIST

TOWERS

IN THE

MIST

ELIZABETH GOUDGE

HENDRICKSON PUBLISHERS

Towers in the Mist

Hendrickson Publishers Marketing, LLC
P. O. Box 3473
Peabody, Massachusetts 01961-3473

ISBN 978-1-61970-632-3

TOWERS IN THE MIST. Copyright © 1938 by Elizabeth Goudge. Copyright renewed 1965 by Elizabeth Goudge.

First Hendrickson Edition Printing — July 2015

Library of Congress Cataloging-in-Publication Data

Goudge, Elizabeth, 1900-1984
    Towers in the mist / Elizabeth Goudge. — First Hendrickson edition.
      pages ; cm
    ISBN 978-1-61970-632-3
    I. Title.
    PR6013.O74T69 2015
    823'.914--dc23

             2015007397

DEDICATED TO

My Father

Here now have you, most dear, and most worthy to be most dear Sir, this idle work of mine; which, I fear, like the spider's web, will be thought fitter to be swept away than worn to any other purpose. But you desired me to do it, and your desire to my heart is an absolute commandment.

Philip Sidney.

THE AUTHOR

ELIZABETH Goudge, born at the turn of the 20th century in England, was a gifted writer whose own life is reflected in most of the stories she wrote. Her father was an Anglican rector who taught theological courses in various cathedral cities across the country, eventually accepting a Professorship of Divinity at Oxford. The many moves during her growing-up years provided settings and characters that she developed and described with great care and insight.

Elizabeth's maternal grandparents lived in the Channel Islands, and she loved her visits there. Eventually several of her novels were set in that charming locale. Her mother, a semi-invalid for much of her life, urged Elizabeth to attend The Art College for training as a teacher, and she appreciated the various crafts she learned. She said it gave her the ability to observe things in minute detail and stimulated her imagination.

Elizabeth's first writing attempts were three screenplays which were performed in London as a charity fund-raiser. She submitted them to a publisher who told her to go away and write a novel. "We are forever in his debt," writes one of her biographers.

CONTENTS

NOTE

IT is impossible to live in an old city and not ask oneself continually, what was it like years ago? What were the men and women and children like who lived in my home centuries ago, and what were their thoughts and their actions as they lived out their lives day by day in the place where I live mine now? This story is the result of such questions, but I would ask pardon for the many mistakes that must have been made by a writer as ignorant as I am. Three mistakes I have made knowingly. The Leighs are an imaginary family, whom I have set down in the house at that time occupied by Canon Westphaling. The book of manners for children, quoted in Chapter Three, is a real book, and is to be found in the South Kensington Museum, but it is later in date than the date of this story. Worst of all, I have been guilty of bringing Philip Sidney up to Christ Church several months too early.

CHAPTER I

MAY-DAY

SPRING, THE SWEET Spring, is the year's pleasant king;
Then blooms each thing, then maids dance in a ring,
Cold doth not sting, the pretty birds do sing:
  Cuckoo, jug-jug, pu-we, to-witta-woo!

The fields breath sweet, the daisies kiss our feet,
Young lovers meet, old wives a-sunning sit;
In every street these tunes our ears do greet:
  Cuckoo, jug-jug, pu-we, to-witta-woo!
    Spring, the sweet Spring!

THOMAS NASHE.

1.

THE first gray of dawn stole mysteriously into a dark world, so gradually that it did not seem as though day banished night, it seemed rather that night itself was slowly transfigured into something fresh and new.

So shall I be changed, whispered a dirty, ragged boy who lay on a pile of dried bracken, two books beneath his head for a pillow, within a gypsy tent, and he sat up and grinned broadly at the queer gray twilight that stood like a friend in the narrow doorway. He had been awake for an hour or more, waiting to welcome this day, and now it had come upon him unawares, stealing into the world as though it were something quite trivial instead of the most important thing that had ever happened to him.

He got up and went to it, tucking his two books under his arm and picking his way cautiously over the recumbent forms of the six children and five dogs who had been his bedfellows through the night. . . . And a wild wet night it had been, the last of the stormy nights that usher in the spring, or he would never have exchanged a sweet-smelling and wholesome ditch for the vile stench of the suffocating tent.... To come out of it into the new day was like plunging head over heels into a clear bath of ice-cold water.

It had been dark when the gypsies arrived at their camping place the night before and the boy had seen nothing of it but the smooth trunks of the beeches lit by the glow of their fire, and the javelins of the rain that spun by in the night beyond the shelter of the trees. The wind had been wild and high and there had been a tumult in the branches over their heads like the tumult of the sea. It was winter's death agony and the boy had trembled as he lay listening to it, suddenly afraid of the world in which he found himself and the life that lay before him; hearing rumors of pain and grief in the drip of the rain from sodden trees and a prophesying of disaster in the clamor of the storm that had swept up so suddenly out of the darkness and filled the vault of the night with its power.... He had fallen asleep still trembling, and waked up in the pitch black of the hour before dawn to a stillness so deep and so perfect that even to breathe had seemed a desecration. It had seemed wrong to be alive in this depth of silence and darkness, and he had understood how at this hour more than at any other sick men yield themselves to death. ... And then, imperceptibly, it was death and winter that yielded, and life and the spring stood at the door and beckoned.

Outside in the chill mist he greeted again the things that belong to the morning; the strong crooks of the young bracken pushing up out of the wet earth, the new crinkled leaves that stained the mist over his head to a faint green, and the sudden uprush of joy in his own heart. He was poor and ragged and dirty and hungry, but what did that matter? He was in Shotover Forest, within a few miles of Oxford and the end of his pilgrimage, and in a short while he would see the city of his dreams, the city that was to change him from a disreputable young vagabond into the most renowned scholar of sixteenth-century England.... Or so he thought.... And the gift of faith was his in full measure, together with a good brain and a certain amount of cheek, so perhaps he was right.

The ghostly trees dropped raindrops on his head and the undergrowth drenched him to the skin as he pushed his way through to the bridle path that followed the crest of Shotover. He stumbled across it and came to a field that curved sharply over the brow of a hill. It was dotted over with low gorse bushes that he would have thought were crouching animals but for the faint scent that came from them. Here he felt himself to be high up on the roof of the world, with the quiet shapes of pines and beech trees looming up behind him and in front of him, circling round the hill on which he stood, a valley filled with mist. Here he stopped to wait for the sunrise. It was the first of May, and winter had died in the storm of the previous night, so he knew it would be a sunrise worth waiting for.

Suddenly, from high over his head, a lark, the plowman's clock, sang a quick stave of song, and from the unseen woods below, a robin called. The heaven had cried out for joy, and the earth had answered, and between the two the smell of the gorse rose up like ascending prayer and linked them together. Music and scent were alive once more in the world; only color tarried, waiting upon the sun.

It came slowly. The mist that had been as thick as sorrow became tenuous and frail. It had been gray like the rain but now it was opal-tinted. The green of the woods was in it, and the blue of the sky, and there was a hint of rose color that told of the fires of the earth, of the sun and the warmth of daily living.

The light grew yet stronger and showed Faithful that his valley was filled with trees and backed by low hills. He followed the curve of it with his eyes until they reached a certain spot to the right that the gypsies had told him of, where they stayed, his heart looking through them as though the eyes of a lover saw his mistress.

Gradually, with the same mysterious slowness with which night had changed to day, towers rose out of the mist, and he looked down from the heights of Shotover upon the city of Oxford. It could not be real, he thought. It was a fragile city spun out of dreams, so small that he could have held it on the palm of his hand and blown it away into silver mist. It was not real. He had dreamed of it for so long that now, when he looked down at the valley, the mist formed itself into towers and spires that would vanish under the sun the moment he shut his eyes. . . . He shut his eyes, opened them, and the towers were still there.

2.

Having proved the city's reality he suddenly became rather unpleasantly conscious of his own. He had felt, as he gazed on the beauty all round him, at one with it and so beautiful too, but now he remembered that no amount of spiritual union with beauty has the slightest effect upon one's own personal appearance. . . . More's the pity. . . . The moment when one remembers this is the death knell of any moment of exaltation. . . . He was still himself, Faithful Crocker. He wiped his nose on the back of his hand and had a good look at as much of himself as he was able to see, and the sight was not reassuring. His jerkin, made of coarse brown frieze, was dirty, and so torn that his elbows showed through the holes, and as for his shoes, he had walked them to pieces and they were kept in place on his swollen, bruised feet by strips of dirty rag. It was many weeks since he and a looking-glass had come face to face but it was too much to hope that there had been any change for the better between then and now, and it was with gloom that he recollected what he had last seen. . . . A boy of fourteen with a head far too large for the puny body it was set upon, a round face pitted with smallpox, a snub nose, a large mouth with a front tooth missing, and a shock of rough, dust-colored hair that stuck out in plumes over the large ears that did not lie flat against the head but projected at the side in a very distressing manner. Would Oxford, when this creature presented itself at the gates of the city, be impressed? . . . Faithful feared not.

Yet, though he did not know it, he was attractive. The Creator, when He thought good to take Faithful out of eternity and cast him upon the earth, had taken him out of the same box as the baby donkeys and the penguins, and his ugliness had an endearing quality that made it almost as valuable as beauty. . . . And he had a few good points. . . . His fine mind declared itself in a wide clear forehead that the smallpox had not touched, his gray eyes had that expression of peace that is noticeable in those who know their own minds, and the good humor of his grin was the most disarming thing in the world.

From gloomy consideration of his personal appearance Faithful let his thoughts slip back over his equally disreputable past. It held, he felt, only one qualification that fitted him to present himself at the city down below, and that was his passionate love of learning. He had pursued it from his cradle. He had been hitting his nurse over the head with a horn-book, so said his father, at an age when most infants were brandishing rattles, and he could lisp out sentences from Virgil when other children were still entangled in their A.B.C. When as a small boy he became a scholar at Saint Paul's, Westminster, where his father was a master, he was hailed as a prodigy, and his path seemed to stretch straight and easy before him, winding over hill and dale to Oxford, that goal of pilgrimage to which came rich men, poor men, saints and sinners to drink deep of the well of learning. . . . Or at least so thought Faithful, ignorant as yet how many other things could be drunk deep of within the walls of the city of dreams.

But poor Faithful had no luck, for his father, an improvident and tiresome person who had already done Faithful an injury by giving him for a mother a slut out of the streets whom he had not bothered to marry, now got himself dismissed for petty theft and then died, leaving Faithful entirely alone in the world and with no possessions at all except his clothes, a cat, his father's Virgil and a tattered copy of Foxe's "Book of Martyrs." Faithful's subsequent adventures would have filled an entire book. He, the cat, Virgil and the Martyrs went on the streets together and proceeded to pick a living as best they could. The cat who, like all cats, was a snob, soon decided to better herself and took service with an alderman, but Virgil and the Martyrs, hung round his neck in a bag, stuck to Faithful, and together they washed pots at taverns, swept chimneys, cleaned windows and carted garbage. At one time they fell in with a performing dog and ran a little theatrical performance of their own with him; Faithful standing on his head with Virgil balanced on his feet and the dog standing on his hind legs with the Martyrs balanced on his nose. Another time they, like Shakespeare in his bad days, were employed to hold the horses outside a genuine theater; but the poor dog got kicked and died of it and Faithful had not the heart to go on. Yet he did not become embittered by these experiences; on the contrary, they did him good. His great gift, that peacefulness that could create an oasis of calm about himself and other people wherever he might be, stood him in good stead even when stuck halfway up a chimney, and his amazing intellect fed itself on every experience that came his way. But nevertheless he was not contented. He still wanted above all things to be a scholar and go to Oxford, and standing on his head in the street did not seem likely to get him there.

Then quite suddenly he decided that he would walk to Oxford, risking starvation and death by the way; and here his luck came full circle back again for, with Virgil and the Martyrs still hanging round his neck, he was able to attach himself in the capacity of valet to the person of a famous bear who was traveling from inn yard to inn yard for the bear baiting. Unfortunately halfway to Oxford his path and that of the bear diverged and he had to go on by himself, begging his way and suffering horribly from the cold, until he fell in with some kind-hearted gypsies and tramped with them as far as Shotover. . . . And now here he was. . . . How he was to find a friend who would tell him how to become a scholar, or where he was to find the gold to buy his books and clothes, he did not know. He just hoped, with that confident hope of childhood that is as strong as faith, and which was still his despite his fourteen years, that the friend would meet him at the gate of the city, and that across his path would bend a rainbow at whose foot he might dig for his crock of gold.

3.

He got up and ran back to the gypsy encampment. The sun was up now, the gorse was golden and the pines and beeches were splendid against the sky. A bright note of scarlet shone out where a tall, cloaked gypsy woman moved out to meet him from the huddled shapes under the trees. She was a magnificent creature, with the gypsy's wild dark eyes and high cheekbones, who held a four-year-old little boy in the crook of her arm as though the weight were nothing to her; a child in strange contrast to his mother, for his hair was fair and his drowsy eyes a speedwell blue. Sara had been good to Faithful; he had a real affection for her and the child and hated to say good-by to them both.

But Sara cut short his stumbling words of sorrow and gratitude with a laugh, thrust her hand into the bodice of her dress and brought it out again with a silver piece lying on the palm.

"I can't take that," said Faithful firmly. . . . Sara told fortunes and many silver pieces came her way, but Faithful knew that she needed them for herself and the boy. "No," he repeated.

Sara's eyes flashed and she showed her teeth like an animal. She had a will of iron and if she wished to dispense charity she did so, quite regardless of the wishes of the recipient, whose acquiescence was forced with a blow if need be.

"Take it," she commanded. "There'll be no hedge to sleep under down there in the city, and no gypsy to give you food for love. . . . Take it, or I'll give you a clout on the head you'll not forget in a hurry."

Faithful took it and bowed low. She smiled at him, agreeable once more now that her will was obeyed, laid a dirty brown hand for a moment on his shoulder and then turned back to the encampment under the trees. But the child, kicking and squeaking, scrambled down out of her arms and ran after Faithful.

"Here, you can't come with me, Joseph," said Faithful.

He called the child Joseph because with his fair hair and blue eyes he seemed as much out of place among the gypsies as Joseph among the Egyptians.

"Let him be," said his mother. "When his belly aches he'll turn back to his breakfast."

So Faithful went on and Joseph trotted at his heels. He did not follow the bridle path to Oxford, he turned to his left and plunged straight down through the woods to the valley below; for he had all the time that there was and he thought he would enjoy himself.

And Shotover Forest on that first of May was enjoyable. Down in the valley the willows were a green mist with the birches on the higher slopes rising above them like silver spears. Further up still came the beeches, where the pale green flowers were hung out like tassels on the branches, and in the further distances the wooded heights were crimson-russet, purple in the shadows, with the wild cherry trees flinging showers of foam against them. As Faithful plunged downwards the grand distance was lost to him but under his feet was a carpet of primroses, ground ivy, violets and cowslips, with a woven shawl of dead bracken and brambles spread over it to protect it. At every step he took the scent of wet earth and flowers came puffing up into his face and went to his head to such an extent that he shouted for joy. Rabbits were scuttling everywhere, the birds were singing uproariously and a cuckoo was tirelessly repeating himself. "Cuckoo! Cuckoo!" Sara had told Faithful that the souls of the gypsies, who have no abiding place in life or death, go into the bodies of the vagabond cuckoos, and he could well believe it. The cuckoo may be an evil rascal, thought Faithful, and his voice an ugly one, yet no one like him can express so well the joy of the earth in its resurrection. It was no wonder that the enemy fled when English soldiers charged them yelling, "Cuckoo!" It was a victorious cry.

"Cuckoo!" called Faithful.

"Cuckoo!" called little Joseph.

"Cuckoo!" called the cuckoo, and they all three, homeless vagabonds as they were, forgot their parlous state as they shouted one against the other because the winter was dead and the spring had broken through.

Faithful was nearly at the bottom of the hill when he discovered that Joseph had left him. Looking back he saw the little boy, clad in brown rags the color of winter bracken, scrambling up the hillside making for Sara and breakfast. His love for Faithful had weighted one side of the scales and his empty belly the other, and the latter had won, as his mother had foretold.

Faithful felt a sudden pang. The old life of vagabondage had been hard but it had had the ease of familiarity. When Joseph should be out of sight it would have deserted him and before him there would be the birth pangs of a new life. He watched the little brown figure with the golden head until the trees seemed to bend about it, gather it in and hide it, and then he turned resolutely away, dashed through the undergrowth and landed with a run and a leap upon the path that wound through the valley.

4.

And at once he saw the figures of the new life coming to meet him. He stood on a rough path running through the valley towards Oxford and down it came trooping a gay crowd of young men and girls and little children, carrying green branches and bunches of flowers. They were singing and laughing and waving the branches over their heads and Faithful gazed at them with his mouth open, for it really did seem as though they were coming out to welcome him. . . . Then, with a rueful grin at his own stupidity, he saw that he was wrong, for they swerved aside to their left and disappeared in a grove of chestnut trees.

His moment of astonishment passed and a burning interest took its place. He padded on down the path until he could see where it was that they were going.

Under the chestnut trees was a chapel, a small gray place that seemed very old, and near it were some buildings that might once upon a time have been those of a monastery. The whole place looked delicious on this May morning, for herb gardens and flower gardens spread their colors and scents round the buildings and on the tall chestnut trees the white flowers were in bloom, each candle cluster standing erect upon his own platform of downward drooping green leaves.

Faithful hid himself behind a wild rose bush and gaped at the flowery procession that came singing down the path from Oxford and filed singing into the chapel. He couldn't imagine what it was they thought they were doing but whatever it was they were doing it beautifully, and in their very best clothes. The girls were garlanded with flowers and wore farthingales and kirtles of scarlet and green and blue, so that they looked like flowers themselves, and the little scampering children carrying great

bunches of kingcups and bluebells were gaudy and gay as humming-
birds. There were some soberly dressed figures in the crowd, College
Fellows who wore the long gown and the square tufted cap of a Master
of Arts, and a horde of scholars discreetly garbed in russet and dark
blue and dark green; but even these had flowers stuck behind their ears
and flourished green branches, and were singing fit to burst themselves.

As they were bound for a chapel, and presumably a religious service
of some kind, Faithful thought they ought to have been singing psalms,
but they were not, they were singing the old songs that for centuries
had been sung in welcome to the summer and farewell to the hate-
ful, cold dark winter that oppressed the land like a curse for so many
dreary weeks.

> *Summer is a coming in,*
> *Loud sing cuckoo!*
> *Groweth seed and bloweth med,*
> *And springeth the wood anew—*
> > *Sing cuckoo!*

The girls and the young men laughed and jostled each other merrily,
and the children shouted and capered, while up in Shotover Forest the
real cuckoo called joyously back to them.

> *Cuckoo, cuckoo, well singest thou, cuckoo:*
> *Nor cease thou never now;*
> *Sing cuckoo, now, sing cuckoo,*
> *Sing cuckoo, sing cuckoo, now!*

Everyone who could squeeze himself inside the chapel by dint
of kicking and shoving and hitting his neighbors over the head with
branches of greenery had now kicked and shoved and hit and got
there, leaving a large crowd of the less muscular seething about outside
the door.

Faithful suddenly felt that he must join them, disreputable though
he was. He polished up his face on his sleeve, stuck a bunch of primroses

in his doublet and tacked himself on to the merry crowd. Wriggling and pushing, and kicking very politely, he got to the open chapel door and looked in. It was lovely inside. Tall candles blazed on the altar in front of the east window, flanked by pots of flowers, and between them stood a big golden bowl. The packed congregation had flung down their flowers to strew the aisle like a carpet under their feet and the scent of bruised primroses, cowslips, violets, lady-smocks and kingcups filled the chapel like incense.

"I will lift up mine eyes unto the hills, from whence cometh my help." Pagan songs were now left behind outside in the sunshine and the whole congregation sang the psalm as one man, making such a row that Faithful marveled that the chapel roof was not lifted off by it. As they sang some of the congregation looked at the chapel windows, glanced out through the clear glass panes, and then looked away again. Faithful looked too and then shut his eyes with a gasp of horror, for crowded up against the panes were the ravaged faces of lepers, looking in. . . . So this must be the chapel of a leper hospital outside the city gates. . . . The contrast was terrible: the flowers and the lights and the beautiful girls and young men in their fine clothes, and outside those stricken outcasts.

Faithful's throat grew dry and hard and he stopped singing. The fear he had felt in the night returned, accompanied by a sick rage. Life was a fair-faced cheat, a beautiful slut who tempted a man outside the city gates to tread a flowery path under a clear sky, and changed overnight into a devil who betrayed her lover to the shapes of darkness and terror that she set about his path to mock him as he stumbled to his death. "Outside the city gates," tolled a voice in his mind, and his eyes were dragged back unwillingly to the figures at the window. . . . Why do we live, oh God, why do we live, when the end is death?

"God's blessing, my friends, upon you all, and upon this fair spring-time, and upon our beloved city of Oxford."

The deep but amazingly clear voice rang out through the packed chapel and reached effortlessly to the crowd outside. In a few moments it had banished Faithful's misery so that he was once more aware of the sunshine, the young men and girls in their bright clothes, the little children and the flowers; and the figure of a man in a long black gown who had stepped out from the congregation and now stood before the altar to speak to them.

Those who were in the chapel had sat down so that Faithful, standing up and leaning against the door-post, had an uninterrupted view of the speaker.

At this first sight he reminded Faithful of one of those tall thin trees that grow upon hilltops and are twisted to fantastic shapes by the storms that blow upon them. He could not be called ugly, though he was certainly misshapen, as the trees are misshapen, because his figure, like theirs, had been formed by endurance and the sight of it was as invigorating as a trumpet call. Faithful thought he had never seen anyone whose past life was written upon him so clearly. . . . The man was like a map. . . . You could tell the way he had come simply by looking at him. Faithful could have taken his oath that this was a priest and scholar who had suffered persecution for his faith in the reign of the late unlamented Queen Mary; for his body had the angularity of obstinacy, the gauntness of starvation and the bowed shoulders of indefatigable scholarship. His face, seamed by his sorrows, had a keen look, as though the mind behind it were sharp in dealing with muddles and shams, but his blue eyes were gentle and dreamy. He was an elderly man and time had robbed him of all his hair except a gray circular fringe like a tonsured monk's. He was clean shaven and but for his white ruff he looked a monk whose background should have been a crucifix upon the wall of a cell. He had the overwhelming attraction of anything that stands upon a mountain top and Faithful found himself staring at him as though this was the first man he had ever seen.

As the man spoke his glance swept over his congregation, pausing perceptibly at each window where the lepers were gathered. They could not hear what he said but his look, and a movement of his hands, gathered them in and placed them where they longed to be, once more among the living. To Faithful there seemed something of prophecy in the gesture and his sense of proportion was given back to him. The lepers too had once known love and the sun's light and nothing could take that prophetic knowledge from them. . . . There is life and there is death, and then there is life again.

"Most of you know why you are here," continued the speaker, "but some of you younger ones, perhaps, do not, so be patient with me while I tell you a story. For more than two centuries has this leper hospital of Saint Bartholomew stood without the East Gate of the city of Oxford, and in the old time that is past forty days' indulgence or pardon of sins was granted by the bishop to all who would say their prayers at the chapel of Saint Bartholomew upon the Saint's day, and give of their charity to the lepers. But in the times of trouble and persecution through which we and our city have so lately passed few men had money or thought to spare for the poor lepers and they, whose sufferings were already so great, suffered even more by reason of the hardness of the times. . . . But now, my friends, that gracious turning of the wheel of time that brings back joy and prosperity again and again to men who had thought them lost forever, has in these later days set our feet upon a fair path and blessed our city with peace; and it has seemed right to us of the University that in our happiness we should not forget the afflicted, and we have brought to life once more this old festival of Saint Bartholomew.

"But other times, my friends, bring other thoughts, and we do not now think that pardon for sin can be bought with gold but only with sorrow; yet we do think with our forefathers that the glorious resurrection of spring is one that can be echoed in the hearts of men, and that the song of praise that we sing for joy of it should be a song of charity. . . . Therefore have we elected to celebrate this festival upon the first of May, the feast day of the spring, and among the flowers upon the altar have we placed a golden bowl for alms. . . . My friends, if you love the spring, if you look beyond the changes and chances of this life to a resurrection of immortality, remember those upon whom the burden of mortality now weighs most heavily. Lay your silver pieces with joy in this golden bowl and your sins with sorrow at the feet of God."

He turned to put his own silver piece in the bowl, then stood beside the altar while the congregation came pressing up to follow his example;

the Fellows and scholars first, then the townspeople and the little children. When the Fellows had gone back to their seats they began to sing an anthem of five parts, and their music accompanied the soft swish of silk dresses and the patter of children's feet as the congregation moved backwards and forwards over the strewn flowers, leaving their silver pieces in the golden bowl and their sins at the feet of God.

And now it was time for those outside to go up to the altar and a hot wave of dismay engulfed Faithful. He had his silver piece all right, the one that the gypsy had given him for food and lodging, but he realized with horror that he was the only person in this crowd who was not well dressed and well-to-do.... The only one except those lepers outside.... He looked down at the dirty rags that kept his shoes on and he wished he was dead. Everyone was staring at him, he felt, and wondering when he had last washed himself.... Come to think of it he couldn't remember himself when he had last washed; not for months any way.... He wished the ground would open and swallow him.

But it refused to oblige and he made his way up the aisle stumbling over the flowers, his face dyed scarlet with shame and his shoes going flip-flap like the webbed feet of an ungainly duck. Everyone stared, and some people tittered, and it seemed to him that the few feet of open space about him widened into so many miles so that he became a little insect crawling by himself in the center of a great plain; an object of derision to all the world.

And then something made him lift up his eyes and he found that the tall man beside the altar was looking at him with a queer concentration, as though Faithful had some special significance for him; there was amusement in his look, compassion, admiration and encouragement. Faithful suddenly ceased to be either ashamed or frightened. He fixed his eyes upon the man's face and flapped on towards him with no more effort than is felt by the needle moving towards the magnet. When he reached the altar, and stretched up to put his silver piece in the golden bowl, the eyes of the two again met and the man bent forward to speak to him. "Wait for me outside, my son," he whispered. Then Faithful suddenly knew who this man was.... The friend who would meet him at the gate of the city. . . . Feeling as brave as a lion he nodded, bent his knee before the altar, then turned and flapped back over the lady-smocks and kingcups to his place beside the door.

The service came to an end with another psalm and the blessing and Faithful rose to his feet so as to be waiting for that man when he left the chapel. . . . But he had reckoned without the May-Day exuberance of the rest of the congregation. . . . Forced, in the very middle of a noisy celebration of the pagan feast of Flora, to sit still for a solid half hour and have their sympathies and their consciences unpleasantly stirred and probed, they suffered, upon release, from a violent reaction. They poured out of the chapel door and hurled themselves upon the crowd outside, shouting and singing. The thought of their magnificent charity inflated them, causing them to shout the louder, and the desire to escape even from the memory of those lepers at the window lent wings to their flying feet. Faithful was caught up and carried along like a leaf upon the surface of the river. He was quite accustomed to kicking and scratching his way out of crowds but today, what with an empty stomach, bruised feet and disturbed emotions, he seemed to have no strength left in him. A jolly apprentice seized hold of one of his arms, a shouting scholar seized the other, a buxom girl dealt him a slap on the back that nearly winded him and his feeble struggles and protestations were drowned in the general jubilation. It seemed to him that a great wave washed over him, drowning him in a sea of color and song. . . . He sank down and down, like a drowning man.

5.

Meanwhile Gervas Leigh, priest and returned emigré, Canon of Christ Church and one of the most noted scholars of his time, stood in the sunshine outside the chapel door and looked anxiously round him. He was surrounded by the Fellows of New College, they who had revived this particular May-Day celebration to help the hospital of Saint Bartholomew, and they inquired politely if he had lost his hat. . . . It was usual for Gervas Leigh to lose everything not actually attached to his person by a string, the habit of dissociation from material things being the first to be acquired by men of saintly character.

"A boy," he muttered distractedly. "I have lost a boy."

The Fellows of New College shrugged their shoulders and looked about them. A few of them, remembering the succulent breakfast of beer and beef awaiting them at New College, regretted that they had invited Gervas Leigh to preside at their service this morning. His fine voice and presence were undoubtedly an asset at any religious ceremony, but the time wasted in getting him together and starting him off home afterwards weighed very heavily upon the debit side. What kind of a boy, they asked politely. There had been so many boys present here this morning, a good hundred or more. Was it one of his own boys?

No, it was not, said Canon Leigh, peering short-sightedly behind a rosebush, it was just some strange boy he had taken a fancy to and wanted to see more of: a ragged boy, a tinker's boy, perhaps, with a pock-marked face and hair like thatch.

Oh, *that* boy, said the Fellows disgustedly; for they had remarked Faithful's unwashed presence among them and regretted it; undoubtedly he had now returned whence he came and in any case, surely, all of them being busy men with academic duties awaiting them, the finger of duty now indicated a speedy return to Oxford and breakfast rather than a useless poking about here in search of an elusive vagabond who was probably no better than he should be.

But Canon Leigh was not to be turned aside from the search. "I told him to wait for me," he said, and insisted upon walking all round the chapel, looking behind every tree and even inquiring at the hospital in case Faithful had hidden himself there. The Fellows, feeling it would be impolite to leave a senior member of the University to pursue a vagabond hunt alone, trailed gloomily in the rear, poking half-heartedly at bushes and peering round corners in a growing depression of spirit. . . . They considered that Gervas Leigh made an absurd fuss about trifles. . . . He had the emigré's outlook, that of a man who has suffered great extremes in his life: persecution and peace, exile and security, destitution and comfort; and whose battered nerves will not again allow him to take the cheerful comfortable view of those who have suffered the extremes of discomfort only in imagination. . . . Yet in spite of themselves the man's quiet despair affected them, and when he at last gave up the search and led the way towards Oxford and belated nourishment they followed him with a funereal gait and mien most inappropriate to May-Day. . . . That was the worst of Gervas Leigh; such was his intensity of feeling that he dragged everyone else down into the whirlpool of his own emotion. They might like it, or they might not like it, but they were in it up to the neck. It was the secret of his power over men, perhaps, but to those of independent spirit and the opposite way of thinking it was intensely annoying. . . . The Fellows were intensely annoyed and talked little.

Canon Leigh, overwhelmed by his sense of loss, did not talk at all. That boy had appeared to him in the chapel in a way that he would never forget. He had been standing up to speak to his congregation and had suddenly been visited by one of those moments of acute misery and terror that leap like thieves out of the night upon men of his temperament. He had looked from the prosperous happy folk within the chapel to the outcast lepers beyond the windows, and had found himself once again confronting the awful fact of human suffering and had, as always, gone down before it. After a moment of prostration he had mentally picked himself up again, forced himself to face the terror of the unexplainable, subdue it and pass on, but the misery of his impotence had remained with him. . . . For it seemed to him that suffering built up a barrier between the happy and the unhappy, like the stone wall of the chapel that separated the sick from the whole. The happy might busy themselves with their golden bowls and silver pieces, they might look through the window in pity and fear and congratulate themselves upon their charity, but only one man in a thousand knew how to knock down the wall and of his own will unite himself to those outside; and in spite of a lifetime of struggle Gervas Leigh did not consider himself yet of their number. . . . His warm tidy gown had seemed to hang on him like fire, so burning with shame had been his well fed body, and when he began to speak he had seemed to be listening to his own voice as though it belonged to someone else, noting its cultivation and detesting it. To his fancy the bright crowd filling the chapel had undergone a change and become as they would be when their hours of suffering were upon them; the hues of old age and death had seemed to creep over them, dimming their colors, twisting their figures and tarnishing their beauty. . . . And there was nothing he could do to prevent it. . . . He could do nothing but stand up there in his fine gown and talk in his cultivated voice. His misery had nearly overwhelmed him, while inwardly he prayed that there might be something, something he could do besides talk.

It had been eased by a sudden realization of response in the crowd before him. He had established contact with someone there. Like all actors and preachers, he knew these moments. Something said, or something only thought, has got there; perhaps it has pierced the consciousness of the audience as a whole, perhaps the heart of one person only. . . . This time Gervas Leigh had known it was one person only. . . . The crowd in front of him had seemed to melt away leaving one figure as the personification of suffering, that of an ugly ragged boy whose face had reflected the misery of his own mind. In a flash he had banished it, forcing his voice to ring out cheerily, mentally reaffirming his own faith in the resurrection of all strength and beauty, even making a movement of his hands as though to show the whole to the sick as a symbol of it; and saw as he did so how the boy's face cleared and brightened. . . . Sinner that he was that he had allowed his defeatism to last long enough to cloud the outlook of another. . . . In making amends to this boy he would find the answer to his prayer.

But the boy had disappeared and with him seemed to have gone his chance of lessening by so little the sum of the world's suffering. As he turned towards Oxford, walking with the limp that had kept his body lagging irritatingly behind his impetuous spirit ever since he had been put to the torture in the days of the late Queen, the sun seemed suddenly dim to him and the new yellow flowers in the meadows sank out of sight.

6.

But to Faithful, far on ahead of him in the jostling crowd, they had suddenly blazed out in all their glory.

After an interval of being dragged along by the crowd in a state of semi-consciousness his powers were momentarily restored to him; he kicked himself free of the boys who held him and pushed his way to the edge of the crowd so that he could see the way that they were going, and so excited was he that for the moment he forgot that he had lost his friend of the chapel.

They were walking through the fields towards the city. The Oxford that he had seen from the heights of Shotover was now standing in front of him, no longer dwarfed by distance to a miniature city that would sit on the palm of his hand but towering up before his eyes in full-size reality. Towers and spires, many of them still white from the masons' hands, piled themselves against the blue sky and the golden clouds of early morning in a sort of arrogant loveliness, as though they thought themselves the equals in beauty of the gold and the blue that they blotted out with their whiteness. The old bastioned walls still swept round the city to protect it, looking at first sight one with the earth, rough and gray like her natural rock and stained with the brown and green of her fields and meadows; while the towers and spires were of the sky, formed of her vapors and blown into airy shapes by the winds of heaven. The river curved about walls and towers as though in added protection, and the water meadows, spangled with lady-smocks, buttercups and king-cups, swept right up to the city like the green tide of the sea.

Close to the bridge that spanned the river, outside the city wall, a tall tower soared up from the block of College buildings beneath it. It stood head and shoulders above the other towers, incomparable in beauty. Exquisitely slender yet very strong, its simple base set firmly upon the earth and its ornamented belfry fretting the sky like wing tips, it stood beside the East Gate like an archangel set to guard the city. . . . For the rest of his life Faithful felt that while Magdalen tower still stood no harm could come to Oxford.

The May-Day holiday was being celebrated inside the city as well as beyond the walls and as Faithful passed under East Gate all the bells were pealing. I come in a happy hour, he thought, and though he knew the bells were not really for him he grinned in delight.

Inside the city there was pandemonium, for the morris dancers were in possession of the High Street. They had come down to East Gate to hear the singers on top of Magdalen tower welcome May-Day and now they were preparing to dance round the town. It seemed to Faithful that all the citizens who had not gone out to Saint Bartholomew's must have assembled in the High Street, and now that the Saint Bartholomew's crowd was added to the High Street crowd there seemed very little space in which to breathe. He was dimly aware of a street that went winding up into the heart of the town; a gracious street with a leisurely slope and gentle curves; a street that was not itself in a hurry whatever anyone else might be. In honor of the day the kennel in the middle had for once in a way been swept clean of refuse, and the rain in the night had made the cobbles clean and wholesome. On each side of the street were gabled, curly-roofed houses, timbered with oak to which exposure to weather had given a pleasant gray tint, the top stories projecting over the lower and leaning outwards in a very friendly sort of way. Today each of them had a branch of may hung out over the front door and out of each window peeped the laughing faces of the little children and the old grandmothers who had not dared to trust themselves in the crowd below.

In the center of the crowd were the morris dancers in their spring green, with bells tied round their arms and fastened to their garters and shoes, and colored handkerchiefs in their hands. They were attended by their drummers, their pipers and the immortal heroes and heroines of May-Day: Robin Hood, Little John, Friar Tuck, Maid Marian, the Queen of the May, the Fool, the Hobby Horse and the Dragon. They had just finished a dance and were drinking ale and stuffing themselves with cakes and apples that the laughing townspeople threw to them. A cake intended for the Dragon flew into the air over Faithful's head and he leaped and caught it, stuffing it into his mouth with the greed of an urchin who had not eaten for nearly eighteen hours. The Dragon, flinging back his painted head, rose upon his hind legs and fell upon Faithful with a roar of fury. They rolled over and over on the cobbles, punching each other, while the crowd swayed and shouted above them.

Suddenly Faithful found himself on his feet again and staggering up the High Street clinging to the Dragon's tail. He had had his head severely bumped and at first could see little but stars, but he realized that he and the Dragon were at the tail end of the procession and that in front of them the morris dancers were dancing their way uphill into the city. He could see their green threading its way through the holiday doublets and farthingales of scarlet and russet and rose color, purple and azure and gold, while the bells pealed, the pipers piped, the drummers thundered on their drums and a hundred gay handkerchiefs fluttered in the blue air.

I have come in a happy hour, thought Faithful again, and it seemed to him that the bells were echoing his thought. "A happy hour," they pealed. "A happy hour. . . . Come in. . . . Come in. . . . Stay long."

CHAPTER II

A STIRRING HOUSEWIFE

With merry lark this maiden rose,
And straight about the house she goes,
With swapping besom in her hand;
And at her girdle in a band
A jolly bunch of keys she wore;
Her petticoat fine laced before,
Her tail tucked up in trimmest guise,
A napkin hanging o'er her eyes,
To keep off dust and dross of walls,
That often from the windows falls.

She won the love of all the house,
And pranked it like a pretty mouse,
And sure at every word she spake,
A goodly curtsy could she make;
A stirring housewife everywhere,
That bent both back and bones to bear.

THOMAS CHURCHYARD.

1.

FAITHFUL was still in the chapel of Saint Bartholomew when a little girl and a dog, fast asleep in a big bed at Christ Church, opened their eyes to the new day. Pippit, the Italian greyhound, woke first. He knew quite well that the dawn had come. The great four-poster where he slept with two other little dogs and three little girls was heavily curtained, and inside it was almost as dark as night, but Pippit knew all the same. He could feel the dawn as an itch in the soles of his paws and a twitch in the tip of his tail. His slim body was so tightly wedged between the plump persons of Meg and Joan that he could not move, but he turned his head sideways on the pillow and licked Joan's chin very gently.

Joan sighed, wriggled, awoke and sat up very cautiously, so as not to wake the others, for she and her twin sister were the youngest girls of the family and as such were spanked if they made a nuisance of themselves. . . . Little children knew their place in the sixteenth century and kept it lest worse befall.

"Quiet, Pippit!" she whispered, and gathered him into her arms, holding him tightly squeezed against her plump chest. Pippit, his eyes bulging from his breathless state, did not make a sound, for he too would be thrashed if he made a nuisance of himself.

Out in the garden a robin called, one clear note like a fairy trumpet, and Joan and Pippit thrilled together. They were of an age, Joan being in her sixth year and Pippit in his second, to feel that a new day was a thing of mysterious wonder. It stretched before them like a fairyland, full of hot scents and colors and unimaginable glories as exciting as a voyage to the Spanish Main or a journey to the city of London. And this particular dawn felt unusually adventurous. The world outside the darkened bed seemed to Joan to be surging up against the curtains with a quickened life; as though she were a little fish in a shell and the tide was coming in to pick her up and carry her to new and wonderful places.

At thought of this new day she dared to give a pull to the curtain beside her and a shaft of light pierced through the chink and lay across the darkness of the bed like a golden sword. It must be a magic sword, Joan thought, because it was too lovely to be of the earth. She touched it with the tip of her finger but she couldn't feel anything, and Pippit, smelling it, found to his astonishment that it had no scent. . . . And was annoyed because for some unexplainable reason he had expected it to smell like rabbits. . . . But if it had neither substance nor scent it had a soft light like a lantern's that showed Joan that the others had safely weathered the dangers of the night and were still there.

They were carefully arranged like sardines in a tin. Joan and Meg lay at one end of the bed with Pippit between them. At the other end of the bed lay Grace, aged thirteen, with Posy and Spot, two rotund and spotted mongrel dogs, one on each side of her. They all slept excellently, the dogs having been trained to lie perfectly still under the bedclothes with their heads on the pillows, and during the long cold winter nights the nearness of the six little bodies to each other kept them as warm as toast.

Meg and Joan were as round and rosy and solid as apples, with soft, straight, honey-colored hair and eyes like speedwells, but Grace, though she was as round and compact and blue eyed as her sisters, had dark hair that curled softly round her rosy face and long dark eyelashes that were lying now on her cheeks like delicate feathery fans. . . . Joan, peering at her, thought that Grace looked very pretty when she was asleep, and decided that she liked her best like that; for Grace when awake was a person of forceful character with strong ideas on the bringing up of younger sisters. . . . But nevertheless she was glad Grace was still alive, and she hoped that her elder sister Joyeuce, and her little brother Diccon, who slept in a further four-poster with the domestic cat, were still alive too.

These children were motherless, for Mistress Leigh had died four years ago soon after the birth of her eighth child and fourth son, young Diccon, and Joyeuce her eldest daughter had been left at the age of twelve to bring up three sisters and four brothers as best she could. . . . And poor Joyeuce was not very practical. . . . Yet so hard had she struggled that at her present age of sixteen she was considered one of the best housewives in sixteenth-century Oxford, a time and a place where housewives were incomparable, and the younger children were as well behaved as was possible under the circumstances.

These circumstances included a father, Gervas Leigh, Canon of Christ Church, whose learning and piety were very great but whose arm lacked strength when it applied the rod to his offspring; and a terrifying old great-aunt, Dame Susan Cholmeley, who lived with them for no adequate reason that Joyeuce had ever been able to discover and whose tyrannous temper and insatiable curiosity, alternating with fits of indulgence, did nothing to help Joyeuce in the bringing up of her brothers and sisters. . . . She missed her mother more than anyone could possibly understand.

Blackbird and thrush and tomtit and jenny the wren answered the robin, wishing him good day and joining him in praising the God Who made them, and at each of the four corners of the bed, where the curtains did not quite meet, there was now an upright golden spear of light. Meg, awaking, distinctly saw the four tall angels who stood against the carved bedposts holding the spears; she saw their huge wings, reaching to the ceiling, and their steady eyes and smiling lips; and then she was silly enough to rub her fists in her eyes and wake right up and there was nothing there but the inside of the bed and her sisters and the dogs. . . . Dull, of course, but possessed of a sweet familiarity. . . . Before she had time to remember that she must not make a noise she had punched them all with ecstatic squeaks of pleasure and turned the inside of the bed into a confusion of legs and tails and yelps and squeals. Joyeuce was rudely awakened and the day began, as so often in the Leigh family, with trouble.

"Be quiet, children!" cried Joyeuce, bounding from her smaller bed and running barefoot to the bigger one. "Be quiet, you'll wake Diccon!"

It was too late, for a loud and sustained roar announced the return of Diccon to life and power and thought, while a tapping on the wall of the adjoining room showed that Great-Aunt was disturbed and mentioning the fact with the aid of her stick. . . . And when Great-Aunt was disturbed in the early morning the rest of the day was a nightmare for Joyeuce. . . . She pulled back the curtains, dragged the twins summarily from their warm nests, turned back their little embroidered night rails and smacked them hard.

They made no sound, and the merry placidity of their round faces remained unaltered, for they were chastised so often that their behinds had become quite hardened; moreover they had been told so frequently that smacking was the road to heaven that they believed it, and they were very anxious to get to heaven, which was from all accounts a more comfortable place to spend eternity in than hell.

"Now you're awake you can all get up," said Joyeuce. "It's broad daylight, and broad daylight on a May morning is time to be up and doing."

"Why, it's the first of May!" cried Joan.

"And Father hasn't taken us to Saint Bartholomew's with him," said Meg.

This was a grievance with them. Other children were permitted to go with their flowers to Saint Bartholomew's, or alternatively to watch the coming of the dawn at Magdalen tower, but they, because of their father's ridiculous fear of draughts and diseases for them, had to remain in bed snoring through the glorious hours of May morning like so many insentient pigs.

"Nasty selfish cruel man," said Joan cheerfully.

"He's an ogre," said Meg. "An ogre who ill-treats little children."

If it was not the fashion of the time for children to express their candid opinion of their parents to their face a good deal of satisfaction could be obtained from doing it privately.

"You dare speak like that about Father, you naughty little girls!" said Grace, bounding indignantly from bed. "You wait till I catch you!"

The twins doubled and dodged over the herb strewn floor, shrieking with mirth, but being careful not to let Grace catch them, for she could smack even harder than Joyeuce. Their room was big enough to allow of escape for it stretched through the whole width of the house, with one window looking on the garden and the other on the College quadrangle. Tapestries made long ago by Canon Leigh's grandmother and great-aunts, mother, aunts and sisters, covered the walls. They had been designed to elevate the mind as well as delight the eye and showed Adam in the Garden of Eden praying to God in the cool of the evening, Ruth in the arms of Naomi and baby Moses in the bull-rushes. The flowers of England, spring and summer and autumn blossoms all mixed up together, filled the Garden of Eden, Ruth and Naomi were journeying to the land of Judah in farthingales that must have measured yards round, and the wooden cradle in which Moses lay was richly carved in the Elizabethan manner. The smoke of winter fires and the hot suns of many summers had dimmed the original bright hues so that now they were soft as the colors on a pigeon's breast. The beds, and the chests where the children kept their clothes, were as gloriously carved as Moses' cradle, and the bed curtains were of olive green embroidered with forget-me-nots and sops-in-wine. There was no other furniture, and no pictures and no ornaments to distract the mind from the beauty of those beds and chests and the glory of that tapestry.

The domestic staff of the Leigh household consisted of only two, Dorothy Goatley and Diggory Colt, and neither Dorothy nor Diggory could spare time to go dashing about the place with jugs and basins for people to wash themselves in, after the modern habit, so the children washed, if they washed at all, at the well in the middle of the kitchen floor.

The twins scampered back to bed, picked lavender and rosemary from between their toes, pulled the curtains a little way and proceeded to dress themselves. There was a great lack of passages in the house, one bedroom opening out of another, which meant a distressing lack of privacy in one's bedroom, so the great four-poster was dressing-room as well as bed and the more private part of one's toilet was performed behind its drawn curtains. The girls' room could only be reached through Great Aunt's and she had a very trying habit of walking suddenly in and commenting unfavorably upon their persons and garments, so that they were careful to put on their petticoats, stitchets, and gray worsted stockings clocked in scarlet well out of sight within their beds. When these garments were in position they emerged and helped each other into the simple dark blue homespun gowns that they wore in the mornings, with lawn ruffs and caps and aprons edged with lace, and their hornbooks hanging from their waists. Joyeuce and Grace made all their everyday clothes. They spun the wool, dyed it and wove it into cloth, and made the lace that edged the ruffs and caps.

Joyeuce dressed herself before she dressed Diccon. She would have been beautiful had she not been the eldest of eight. She had a tall upright figure and lovely hands and feet. Her hair, demurely parted under her cap, was straight and honey-colored like the twins', but her blue eyes were so dark that they looked almost purple and she had Grace's dark brows and lashes, a contrast that made her small pale pointed face curiously arresting. But being the eldest of eight had a little marred Joyeuce's looks. A permanent worried frown wrinkled her forehead, her lips were set in too hard a line, and the figure that should have had the grace of girl-hood was always stiffly braced to meet the action that was demanded of Joyeuce from the time she woke up in the morning until the time when merciful sleep lifted her burdens off her, and set her free to run and sing and dance in a dream world where there was no washing day, and no Great-Aunt, and where she found her mother again.

Diccon would never find living a burden. If he derived from the Leighs at all he derived from the happy side of the family, the side of the mother who had died smiling, murmuring to her stricken husband that to die giving birth to a baby was the very nicest way for a woman to die. "A new life for an old," she had said. "A good exchange."

But if Diccon had Mistress Leigh's optimism he was like no one but himself in looks. His head was thickly covered with tight dark curls with a hint of red in them, and his eyes were bright green. His brown little face was covered with freckles that Joyeuce strove valiantly to eradicate by bathing his face with dew, but it was no use, the more she dewed him the more he seemed to freckle, until now at the age of four there was scarcely room to put a pin's head between one freckle and another.

There was a distressing amount of the old Adam in Diccon and what he would be like in another two years his family trembled to think. Joy-euce, who loved him passionately even while she deplored his wicked ways, knelt down to pray for him whenever she could spare a moment from her baking and washing and spinning and weaving, and Canon Leigh occasionally spent whole nights wrestling in prayer, laying before the Almighty the evil propensities of his youngest son.

So naughty was Diccon that the frightful idea had been expressed by Great-Aunt that he was in reality no child of theirs but a changeling. Mistress Leigh had died leaving her son shouting the place down in fu-rious hunger, and so outraged had been his yells that a foster mother had been imported with more haste than discernment. She had been a gypsy woman, a magnificent black-eyed creature who had walked into the house with head held high, her gay, ragged clothes sweeping round her like the silks of a queen and her own child held negligently in the fold of her cloak. She had remained for four days, crooning strange songs to the two little babies who lay in utter content, one on each arm, and had then suddenly departed, taking with her one of the babies and all of the spoons. Another foster mother had been imported, a widowed girl whose own baby had died, the same Dorothy who was with them still. But from the start she had had grave misgivings about Diccon.... He took his food, she said, with a greed and determination shocking in a Christian baby.

Diccon had not cried at all at his baptism, so that the devil was obviously still very much in him, and when the water had touched his forehead he had kicked in a very worldly sort of way.... It was on the evening after his baptism, when he was making up for his previous silence by a display of frightfulness hitherto unexperienced in the Leigh family, that Great-Aunt had hazarded the suggestion that he was no child of theirs.

"Had he been the gypsy's child he would have had black eyes like hers," poor Joyeuce had said as she tramped up and down the parlor with the shouting infant.

"Who knows whether the child she brought with her was her own child?" Great-Aunt had retorted. "We don't," she had continued ominously, "know what it was."

And indeed as Diccon increased in size and wickedness he developed a good many fairy attributes. There were his dancing green eyes, for instance, and his ears that were undoubtedly pointed at the tips, the way he could fall and roll in all directions and never hurt himself, his mischievous tricks and the frightful noise he could make, a noise out of all proportion to the size of his body; and then, in contrast to all this, the sweet loving little way in which he would suddenly come running to you and climb on your lap and lie with his curly head snuggled against you, your hand rubbing his cheek. He would lie like this for five minutes, cooing like any turtle-dove, and then suddenly turn his head and bite the caressing hand hard. His baby teeth were white and pearly, and daintily pointed like his ears, but of an inconceivable sharpness.... And upon his back was a triangle of three small moles; the mark, so said Great-Aunt, that the fairies set upon their own.

But Canon Leigh and Joyeuce wouldn't have it that Diccon was a changeling. He had, they thought, absorbed a certain wildness with the milk of his first foster mother, but he was their own dear child and by prayer and the help of God this should be cast out.

The roar with which Diccon had greeted the dawn had been short-lived. He always bellowed at any moment of transition, such as that from night to day or eating to not eating, but he never bellowed for long. The noise he made was merely the fanfare of trumpets that announces to adoring subjects that royalty is now doing something different to what it was doing a short while before.

Having announced that he was awake he shut his red mouth abruptly and scurried on all fours to the bottom of the bed, where he sat with his back to the room, industriously picking a crimson embroidered carnation out of the curtain with his sharp little nails. He had been working at that carnation for a week and had nearly finished it. When his activities were discovered he would be smacked, but he had no objection to being smacked. If he had any nerves at all they were made of steel and never incommoded him.

By his side sat Tinker the cat, watching gravely, with his tail twitching slowly from side to side. Tinker was black, with eyes as green as Diccon's own, and he was Diccon's inseparable companion. They did everything together and seemed to have a great affection for each other, though their sufferings at each other's hands were shameful. Diccon would drag Tinker round the garden by his tail, remove from him by force those just perquisites, his mice, bury him in the earth when playing at executing traitors at Tyburn and put him down the well when playing at Joseph and his brethren. A hundred times had Tinker been rescued at the point of death, yet his devotion to Diccon never wavered. . . . Though he retaliated. . . . Diccon's face and hands were a mass of scratches and on one occasion the child had nearly died of blood poisoning, Tinker having bitten him immediately after refreshing himself at the Deanery garbage heap.

There was something ominous, Great-Aunt said, in this friend-ship of the child and the cat. . . . For do not witches consort with black cats? . . . There was no denying that Tinker had introduced himself into the Leigh household on the very same day that the gypsy woman had arrived, strolling in from the quadrangle dripping wet with a tin can tied to his tail.

"It is time to get dressed, Diccon," said Joyeuce.

Diccon gave her one of his lovely, rippling smiles, leaped from the bed and dragged his night-rail over his head.

"No, no, Diccon!" cried Joyeuce in horror, seizing his little bare body and lifting him back on to the bed. "You must be dressed behind the curtain, like a modest child."

Diccon was lacking in modesty, and one of the most frightful of his escapades had taken place on a hot afternoon last August, when he had called at the Deanery with nothing on. For this his father had beaten him, for the first time, with the rod that he kept for use upon the older boys. Asked for an explanation of his behavior he had said, through sobs, for the rod had really hurt, that he had felt hot and he liked the Dean. Asked not to do it again he had not committed himself.

Diccon looked fascinating when he was dressed. He wore doublet and trunk and hose of russet, with a little pleated ruff at the neck. . . . It had been the pricking of his ruff round his neck that had led to the regrettable incident of that hot August.

As soon as he and the little girls were dressed Joyeuce knocked at Great-Aunt's door for permission for the children to walk through her room on their way to wash their hands and faces at the well, which was given by Great-Aunt's usual remark of, "Tilly-vally, tilly-vally, why did God make children! Hurry up, then, malapert poppets!"

Joyeuce lingered behind to straighten the untidy beds. This done she drew back the curtain that covered the window looking on the quadrangle. She always waited until the children had gone before she pulled back this curtain, for it would have been a thing not easily forgiven by their father if a passing scholar should have seen a twin in her petticoat. . . . And she had another reason for waiting. She had grown from a child to a girl in this house, she had loved and laughed and suffered grief and pain in it, and somehow the view of Christ Church and Oxford seen from its windows for so many years as the setting of her home had become extraordinarily valuable to her. She liked to be alone when she drew back the curtain, like a connoisseur before a picture or a worshiper before a shrine.

2.

She pulled it aside and opened the diamond-paned lattice window, leaning out. She got up so early that to her the dawn was a well known friend, not a casual acquaintance seen so seldom that its appearance is greeted with astonishment. She knew all the dawns: the golden dawns of fair weather, the gray dawns of rain and the flame and indigo dawns of storm. She watched them morning by morning as their banners unfurled and streamed across the sky, and she loved them, even though the moment of unfurling was to her a moment of dread as well as of joy. . . . For each day one marches out to fight behind those banners, and the stout and lusty like the fighting but the timid, as they buckle on their armor, cannot help a beating of the heart. . . . Today was a fine weather dawn and on the banner of it was embroidered a golden-hearted flower whose blue petals crisped into saffron at the edges.

The rough grass of the quadrangle was still misted and the buttercups and daisies in it were tightly shut up. Presently they would open their eyes and look at the sun and then the quadrangle would look like Grace's Sunday kirtle, green silk scattered over with yellow and silver dots.

The north side of the quadrangle had not yet been built and Joyeuce looked from her window across the grass to a thicket of hawthorn trees that were a froth of silvery blossom. Beside them, to the right, were Peckwater Inn and Canterbury College, and beyond them were the roofs of the city and towers and spires rising out of the morning mist in marvelous beauty. To her right, as she leaned out of the window, Joyeuce could see the tower of the Cathedral surmounted by its thirteenth-century spire, and to her left she looked on the Fair Gate. It still lacked its bell tower, and Great Tom, the bell that was destined one day to hang there, now tolled out the hour from the Cathedral, but if it boasted no tower the Fair Gate was yet very fair, with the arms of Henry

Tudor and Cardinal Wolsey "most curiously set over the middle of the
Gate, and my lord grace's arms set out with gold and color."

The whole view was gloriously fair and Joyeuce almost worshiped it.

She was a romantic to whom as yet the details of practical living
brought no joy.... She missed her mother.... She did her duty as housewife with thoroughness, a sense of duty having been whipped into her
from babyhood up, but she did not think that doing one's duty was very
enjoyable. The life she wanted seemed always to elude her, to be around
her and in front of her and above her but never quite within her reach.
She did not quite know what it was that she wanted, she only knew that
it was not what she had. The view that she saw from her window every
morning was to her the symbol of this life. She stood in her house, surrounded by a hundred irksome problems and duties, and she looked
out at a loveliness that she could see but could not grasp.... Yet if she
left the house and went outside, treading the green grass with her feet
and touching the silvery hawthorn with her hands, her worries would
go with her, making the grass wet and cold and setting thorns among
the flowers; the ideal world that had seemed to be there outside would,
like a mirage, recede yet a little further.... Would life always be like that,
she wondered. Did the things that men longed for and fought for always
disappoint them as soon as they had grasped them in their hands? Did
one go on and on like that, chasing a will-o'-the-wisp until you and he
went down together into the darkness of death? Perhaps, she thought,
once you were through that darkness he suffered a change. Perhaps he
stood still, then, and let you catch him, and the grip of his arms would
satisfy at last.

But Joyeuce could not feel certain that that would happen, and anyhow it seemed a very long while to wait. She wanted something nice
now. She wanted the beauty of earth that was outside her window to
become to her something more than a painted picture, she wanted it not
to recede like a mirage but to take some actual form that would come
in to her and bring her comfort and reassurance.... Like her mother
had done.

"Good morning, Mistress Joyeuce."

Leaning with her elbows on the sill, her eyes on the white hawthorn and white towers against the sky, her ears filled with the song of the birds and her thoughts wandering, Joyeuce had forgotten time and place. At the moment her feet were not on the earth and the figure who stood outside in the quadrangle seemed not of the earth either. She did not know if it was a man or a woman. It was just a figure that gathered up into itself all the elusive beauty of that outside world and brought it close to her. It was not receding, it was coming nearer, standing right under her window so that she could almost have touched it; touched the beauty of earth, the gold and blue and green and silver.

Then her wandering thoughts suddenly recollected themselves and their duties. They came hurrying back, very shamefaced, and folding their wings curled themselves up into the tight, hard ball that is the grimly recollected mind of a housewife in the early morning. . . . There was a tiny click in her head, as the component parts fitted together, and Joyeuce started and looked down into the upturned impudent face of what was after all only one of the scholars.

He was a stranger to her and it was clearly her duty to blush with maidenly modesty and withdraw from the window with grace and dignity; but somehow she did not. Her thoughts might have returned to their duties but they were not yet exercising as much control over her actions as could be wished. She stayed where she was, staring down at the face below her with a concentration that bordered upon the bold, and instantly every detail of it seemed to be graved almost painfully into her memory. In one moment she knew his face almost as well as she knew Diccon's, that she had been learning hour by hour and day by day all through his short little life. And there was a certain likeness between the two, a likeness that bespoke them both the sons of Belial. These eyes, though they were as dark as sloes, had the same dancing points of light in them and when their owner laughed they were transformed, as Diccon's were, from round twinkling orbs to narrow wicked slits. His eyelashes were as long as a girl's and his eyebrows had that faint upward kink at the outer edges that, together with the suspicion of a point to the ears, is one of the sure marks of mischief. The fine texture of his sunburnt skin was girlish too but the lips were full and strong and the chin obstinate and deeply cleft. . . . Altogether a face so full of contradictions that nothing at all could be foretold about the future of its owner. . . . Joyeuce's truant eyes, all unbidden by her will, took as serious note of these things as though his face were the page of a book that she must at all cost get by heart.

With a sigh she stirred and got up, aware at last of the clamoring, outraged commands of her thoughts; she blushed a little, smoothing her snowy apron, and the practical world once more flowed maddeningly around her. Holding herself now as stiffly as a poker she had another good look at the young man before her; but this time her eyelashes were lowered and she peeped through them with the cold aloofness of a superior tabby kitten.

Morning prayers were at five o'clock in the Cathedral and this young man was the first out. . . . There was something about the jaunty way he wore his gown, the twinkle in his eye and the crisp curl in his hair that suggested that he was always the first out. . . . His clothes were simple, for it had been ordained that every Christ Church scholar should "go in fit and decent apparel," and might not on any account burst upon the scene clothed in "white or pricked doublets, galligaskins or cut hose, welted or laced gowns, upon the several pains next before rehearsed." So Master Nicolas de Worde was clothed in a plain dark blue doublet, with a simple ruff, and no part of his person was pricked, cut, welted or laced; but the fineness of the dark blue cloth and the snowy whiteness of his ruff, together with a certain arrogance in his bearing, showed him to be a young man of means and breeding. He was also a gentleman of some age, Joyeuce thought, eighteen or so. Scholars could present themselves at Christ Church at any age, the youngest recorded age of any gentleman arriving to devote himself to learning at that institution being twelve years old, so eighteen was to Joyeuce very much years of discretion, and she answered his greeting with the respectfulness due to age and learning.

"Good morning sir," she said, and curtseyed.

Nicolas regarded her with interest and amusement. When he had first seen her she had been apparently kneeling on the floor, with her elbows propped on the window sill and her chin resting in her hands. She had been illumined by one of her rare moments of beauty; her pale little face softened by her dreams and her bearing relaxed into grace. She had looked frail and sad, too, and Nicolas, who always enjoyed the best of health and spirits himself, was always attracted by frailty and sadness; succouring the afflicted increased his own sense of strength and well-being and that was nice for him. He had noticed Joyeuce before but never to such advantage. He would like to see her close to, he had thought, for he was a connoisseur of pretty ladies, and as he always did what he liked unless forcibly prevented he had immediately crossed the quadrangle and planted himself beneath her window. And to his delight she had returned his scrutiny with interest. She had opened her eyes wide and gazed at him as though he were the personification of all beauty and all joy. . . . Nicolas had a good opinion of himself and he was overjoyed to find her in such evident agreement with him. . . . She had beautiful blue eyes, almost as dark as violets, set strikingly in that ivory face beneath dark eyebrows like delicate feathers, and smooth honey-colored hair. . . . A nice girl. . . . And when she suddenly changed from a melting and rather forward goddess into a stiff, demure maiden he discovered that she was one of the few women who can blush becomingly. . . . Your rosy maidens, Nicolas was apt to say when expatiating on the beauties of the sex, are all very well on the whole but they show to disadvantage in moments of embarrassment, while your pale maidens, though they may be less striking in the ordinary way, put on an added beauty with added heat. . . . For himself he liked pale maidens.

"You have not gone maying, mistress?" he asked.

Joyeuce shook her head a little sadly. . . . She had always longed to go maying.

"Nor I," said Nicolas arrogantly. "I hate the vulgar crowd at Saint Bartholomew's. . . . Besides, I overslept."

Joyeuce, not noticing that the grapes were sour, immediately saw that it had been quite wrong of her to want to go maying. She blushed again, and changed the subject.

"Who are you, sir?" she asked humbly. "I have not seen you before."

A ludicrous expression of astonishment spread over Nicolas's face, for he was accustomed to be known and admired and took recognition of his merits and admiration of his person as his due.

"I've been here for years," he said indignantly, "and I've walked past your window a thousand times if once, and I sat opposite you last week in the Cathedral."

"I never noticed you," said Joyeuce.

"You can't be observant," he said, slightly nettled.

"I was saying my prayers," explained Joyeuce.

Nicolas considered this a joke, and laughed.

Joyeuce drew herself up yet more stiffly, her eyes flashing, for she had been well brought up and knew what should be laughed at and what should not. "And so," she said, "should you have been."

"But we say so many in this place," he complained bitterly. "Every morning at five o'clock do we pray, wet or fine, warm or cold, dark or light. Jupiter, the horror that are College prayers at five o'clock on a January morning!"

"How did you know my name?" asked Joyeuce.

"No one can walk past this house and not know your name. It is bellowed by every inmate of your household from dawn till night. 'Joyeuce, the cat is in the cream! Joyeuce, where are my shoes? Joyeuce, the children are making too much noise! Joyeuce, I have bumped my head! Joyeuce, the dogs are out in the quadrangle again! Joyeuce, the twins are lost!' When I saw you in the Cathedral, surrounded by the children, praying so earnestly for the cat, dogs, shoes, twins and bumped heads I knew that you were Joyeuce.... A most inappropriate name."

"Why?" demanded Joyeuce.

"Can so burdened a lady be joyous?" He came a little nearer, his head tilted back and his hands creeping wickedly up the wall as though he would pull her down out of her window, compassion and mischievous invitation comically mingled on his face. "Do you ever do joyous things, Mistress Joyeuce? Dance to the music of the virginal? Go hawking? Run through the kingcups in the meadows with your shoes and stockings off?"

"No!" whispered Joyeuce in horror. "Of course not!"

"By cock and pie it is a disgrace!" he announced. "This evening at seven o'clock you will meet me at the Fair Gate and we will go—I do not know where we will go—but it will be somewhere lovely. Do you hear me, Mistress Joyeuce?" He laughed, keeping his eyes fixed on hers so that she could not look away, drinking in the flattery of the palpitating longing and dismay that robbed her of breath so that she could not answer.

"Joyeuce!"

The exclamation, deep-toned, astonished, outraged, yet with a hint of amusement behind the outrage, came from Canon Leigh, brought to a standstill on his way home from Saint Bartholomew's by the shocking sight of his eldest daughter leaning from her bedroom window and talking to that malapert scoundrel Nicolas de Worde, a creature unworthy of the name of scholar, the horror of his Greek being equaled by nothing except the outrage of his Latin.

Joyeuce jumped back as though detected in a burglary but Nicolas remained unflurried. He bowed with exaggerated gallantry first to Joyeuce and then to her father, smiled bewitchingly at them both and strolled off to his rooms beside the Fair Gate, disappearing with a whisk of the tail end of his gown that reminded Canon Leigh of a cock robin; never a humble bird. He watched that flourishing tail vanish from sight with a cold eye, and then turned back to his daughter.

"I shall see you," he said, "later," and disappeared through the front door below.

Joyeuce stood back from the window with her hands pressed against her hot cheeks. She cast an anguished glance at the sky and saw that the golden clouds had all disappeared, swept away by the wind that had sprung up and was rustling the hawthorn across the way. Only one cloud sailed across the sky from west to east, from the Fair Gate to the Cathedral, a galleon of unsullied white in the warm blue of full day. . . . She must have been dreaming and gossiping for half an hour, with the children up to goodness alone knew what down below; and she had not even said her prayers. She knelt down beside her great bed and covered her shamed face with her hands. In thirty short minutes she had committed the three sins of day-dreaming, laziness and impropriety, and she was almost too ashamed to pray. It was so much worse, she thought, to sin in the morning than to sin in the afternoon, for a fall once taken it is hard to recover foothold and now she would spend the whole day being disagreeable to everybody. "Ne nos inducas in tentationem," she prayed, Nicolas's unforgettable face mocking her within the darkness of her closed eyes, "sed libera nos a malo."

Canon Leigh, an economical man, had taught his children to pray in Latin so that two birds might be killed with one stone, the soul and the Latin being strengthened together.

She got up, shook dried herbs out of her dark blue skirt, straightened her apron and cap and stood for a moment, braced, before facing Great-Aunt. Then, her courage screwed to sticking point, she knocked at the door.

Great-Aunt admitted her, as always when displeased, by a short, peremptory bark.

Great-Aunt's room was smaller than the girls' though it suited her better owing to its extremely central position in the house, enabling her to keep her finger on the pulse of the household's life. One window looked out on the garden and the other looked down into the big combined hall and dining-room of the house, a glorious stone-floored, oak-paneled place that stretched right up to the raftered roof. Great-Aunt was therefore very happily placed. Her outside window enabled her to see all that went on in the garden and her inside window commanded not only the hall but the great oak staircase, the front door, the dining table and the doors into kitchen, study and parlor. Nothing, therefore, could happen in the house that Great-Aunt did not know about, and nothing did. Her felicity was further increased by the fact that her room was over the kitchen and she could hear everything that Dorothy Goatley was up to down below. It was unfortunate that the yew hedge hid the stables and the loft where Diggory Colt slept from her view, and still more unfortunate that Dorothy's bedroom was downstairs on the other side of the house, but to counterbalance these drawbacks, the girls' room was reached through hers and they could not even fetch a clean kerchief without her knowing it. . . . And one cannot have everything, as she was constantly remarking to Joyeuce, and for those blessings which are ours we should be thankful to a beneficent Creator.

Joyeuce entered and stood waiting for Great-Aunt to pop out from behind her bed curtains and express herself as to the row Diccon had made in the early morning. It was part of Great-Aunt's technique always to leave a few moments' awed silence between the entry of her audience and the delivery of her own remarks, tension being thus introduced and the point of her discourse much strengthened.

Joyeuce could never get over the fear that the furnishings of Great-Aunt's room had implanted in her when she was still a child. The enormous bed, curtained in purple velvet and reached by a flight of steps, was like a catafalque, and the tapestries of Great-Aunt's choice, representing the Day of Judgment and Salome presenting King Herod with John the Baptist's head on a charger, covered the walls with purple clouds, green lightnings and crimson drops of gore. Great-Aunt disliked the modern fashion of herb-strewn floors and the black, polished boards gleamed somberly like the inky water of a bottomless tarn; one of those tarns where murdered bodies sink down and down and are never found.

When Canon Leigh and his young wife had first come to live at Christ Church, happy beyond words at the prospect of a beautiful home of their own, Great-Aunt, then resident at Stratford and intensely bored by the life of a dignified, childless widow of ample means, had written suggesting that she should live with them. They had hastily written back pointing out all the disadvantages to Great-Aunt herself of her proposed change of residence; for she was exceedingly well off, enjoyed excellent health and had no claim whatsoever upon their charity; but before the letter had time to get there Great-Aunt herself, a woman the reverse of dilatory, had arrived at Oxford. Going out for a stroll one afternoon they had beheld her ambling up to the Fair Gate on her white mule, sitting sideways with her feet on a board, four packhorses behind her carrying her tapestries, bedding and other personal luggage. At the age of seventy-nine she had ridden all the way from Stratford, putting up at the inns along the way, and had derived great enjoyment from the adventure. It was impossible to disappoint so gallant an old lady; moreover Canon Leigh after a night of wrestling in prayer felt the visitation to be the will of God; so Great-Aunt was unpacked and arranged at Christ Church. With the Dean's permission, withheld at first but granted after a stormy personal interview with Great-Aunt herself, a window was knocked in her bedroom wall so that the few years that remained to her—she numbered them at two or three—might be enlivened and sanctified by the spectacle of innocent children and learned divines partaking of nourishment in the hall below. Mistress Leigh herself had failed to see any indication of the divine Purpose in Great-Aunt's arrival—the old lady was Canon Leigh's aunt, not hers—but she had submitted, as was her wifely duty, and had hung up the Salome tapestry with her own hands. . . . After all, she had reflected, the old dame could not live for ever. . . . But the old dame had outlived Mistress Leigh herself, had indeed contributed to her death by worrying her frantic during her months of pregnancy, and now at the age of eighty-five, after six years' residence at Christ Church, was enjoying better health than ever.

And yet, though she was really rather a nasty old lady, it was impossible not to feel for Great-Aunt the admiration that abounding vitality in the very old always calls out in the young and the middle-aged. Great-Aunt had lived for eighty-five years in a very terrible world. Her Catholic brother had been hanged, drawn and quartered at Tyburn by the command of Henry Tudor, her Protestant husband had been burned at the stake by Henry's daughter Mary and her four children had died in one of the terrible visitations of the plague. That she had weathered it all and now in her old age faced life with undiminished zest implied a courage of no mean order. . . . Though it must be owned that Great-Aunt had had very little sympathy with her heroic brother and husband. If her relations liked to be martyred for their religious convictions the more fools they, she said; as for herself she had always trimmed her sails to whatever winds might blow and here she still was, hale and hearty in her old age.

Great Aunt's head, encircled in fold after fold of nightcap, popped out from between the purple curtains and Joyeuce jumped as at the eruption of a jack-in-the-box.

Dame Susan Cholmeley had once been beautiful. Her dark eyes under black, bushy brows still had the depth of velvety color and the bright sparkle that had enslaved the lovers whose number increased by ten every time she told the story of her early triumphs to the children, and her wrinkled cheeks were still rosy. Her most alarming feature was her large, hooked nose, that nearly met her chin and gave a witch-like look to her face. She had lost all her teeth and it was the difficulty of mastication and conversation under the circumstances, and not ill health, that led her to spend most of her time in her own room. She was still capable, had she wished it, of riding her mule from Stratford to Oxford and enjoying it.

"*I* heard you, Joyeuce Margery Leigh," remarked Great-Aunt. "And a more disgraceful exhibition of impropriety I never overheard in all my life. . . . And let me tell you, child, I've overheard a good deal in my day."

Joyeuce smiled in spite of herself. Great-Aunt had a naïve way of exposing her own weaknesses that was very endearing, and it was a relief that Joyeuce's greater sin had driven Diccon's early-morning yells out of her mind, for if there was one thing that Joyeuce could not endure it was criticism of Diccon.

"Had I the strength I used to have," said Great-Aunt, "I should take a slipper to you. . . . And who was the young man?" she continued eagerly in almost the same breath.

"Master Nicolas de Worde," said Joyeuce, standing meekly beside Great-Aunt, her hands folded on her apron and her eyes cast down. "He said good morning to me."

"It takes a long time to say good morning nowadays," commented Great-Aunt drily. "And is it your intention to meet him at the Fair Gate this evening?"

Joyeuce looked up sharply, the crimson blood running up into her cheeks. Though Great-Aunt's hearing was preternaturally sharp it was quite impossible that she could have heard Nicolas's request, made out in the quadrangle. It was just another instance of what the children called "Great-Aunt's second sight." The old lady had in reality no more second sight than a rabbit, but after eighty-five years of life in this world she knew the unvarying reactions of human nature to the circumstances that beset it. "Meet me at the gate" was the first coherent remark made by all lovers; though no doubt, poor creatures, they thought their idea original. They all ran to gates: city gates, palace gates, garden gates; for gates are symbolic of the entry from one state of being to another and even to stand at them, looking out, gives you a sense of freedom. . . . Great-Aunt had presented herself at a good many gates in her day and had indeed perfected herself in the technique: the man must be kept waiting at the gate that his ardor be inflamed, but not too long, lest it should cool; the weather, too, must be taken into consideration, and the kind of gate; for tall gates are made to be peeped through coquettishly, short gates to be leaned upon in intimate conversation, flat-topped gates to be sat upon while sunsets are admired, while the gate that has an easy latch is made to be escaped through to quiet places of woods and streams where time does not pass and prying eyes do not tarnish. . . . Great-Aunt, always deeply interested in the affairs of the heart, forgot her annoyance in curiosity and decided that the time had come to give Joyeuce a little elementary instruction in these things, and opened her mouth to begin; only to discover to her rage that the malapert girl had left the room.

For the instinct of escape had already seized Joyeuce and suddenly turning on her heel she had done what she had never presumed to do before: left Great-Aunt without Great-Aunt's permission so to do. As she stood outside in the passage that divided the old lady's room from the rooms where Canon Leigh and the boys slept, closing the door softly behind her, Great-Aunt's indignant shouts were battering at her ears, but she went resolutely on down the passage and down the glorious great carved staircase to the hall below where her father was waiting for her; had been waiting for her, sternly and patiently, his sense of humor well battened under, all the time she said her prayers and interviewed Great-Aunt.

Canon Leigh found the bringing up of his motherless children an arduous business, for the time given to a parent in which to do it seemed so short. Fourteen being a marriageable age the children must by then be

ready to shoulder the pains and burdens of adult life with strong characters and tested courage. The period of training was therefore short and
intensive and the worst crime a parent could commit was that of spar-
ing the rod and spoiling the child. But poor Canon Leigh, desperately
endeavoring to combine the tenderness of a mother with the sternness
of a father, found himself as he grew older attaching more and more importance to the value of gentleness and less and less to that of discipline.
. . . He could no longer bring himself to beat his daughters, and did not
beat his sons with any real concentration or enthusiasm. . . . He loathed
beating them. . . . This weakness in him was a sin, and he knew it and
confessed it during the long hours when he prayed for them, but it was
a sin that even with the help of God he could not conquer. He tried to
make up for it by lashing them with his tongue instead, but the tongues
of learned and holy men are always singularly wanting in lash and at the
end of a long scolding his children were sometimes unaware that there
had been one. . . . All except Joyeuce, as sensitive as her father and with
the same capacity for suffering as his. She always knew when he was
trying to scold and gave him all the help she could.

That there must be one now she knew and she went steadily across the
hall to the great fireplace before which he stood, and knelt for his blessing.

He gave it, his hand on her head, and there was then an anxious
pause.

"Yes, Father," she encouraged gently, getting up and standing before
him with bent head. He still said nothing and peeping at him out of the
corner of her eye she saw him scratching his bald head in perplexity. . . .
She must tell him what to say, as usual.

"I must not talk to young men out of the window," she said. "It was
indiscreet and a bad example for the younger girls."

"Thank you, Joyeuce," he said with eager gratitude.

"I entirely forgot myself," said Joyeuce, looking him straight in the
eyes. "I have never done it before and I will never do it again; or anything
else of an indiscreet nature."

"You are my very good daughter, Joyeuce," he told her, and kissed
her three times, on each of her eyelids, that were always a little shadowed

with purple because she had too much to do, and on her pointed chin. "I have not hurt you?" he asked anxiously. "I have not said too much?"

"Not a word too much, Father," she comforted him, and she went to fetch the children and Dorothy and Diggory from the kitchen for prayers.

The kitchen led directly from the hall and looked out on the garden. A huge open fireplace with spits for roasting the meat occupied almost the whole of the wall to the right as one entered, while against the left wall stood an open cupboard holding tankards and pewter pots, with a door beside it leading to the still room, a stone-floored fragrant place where the preserves were kept, and the store of herbs and the presses for the linen. Leading out of the still-room were Dorothy Goatley's tiny slip of a bedroom, and the pastry and the bolting house, where the bread was baked and the flour sifted. From the latter, stone steps led down to the huge dark cellars so thoughtfully provided by Cardinal Wolsey for the beer, the Xeres sack, the skins of Greek wine and the casks of burgundy, to which he had himself been so attached. . . . Only judging others by himself he expected them to have such a lot of it, for the cellars stretched the length of the house and went down into the bowels of the earth. . . . There was never anything in the Leigh cellars but a very modest supply of the inevitable beer.

The kitchen, like the hall, was stone-floored, with a large well in the center. During the day this was kept carefully covered, and the kitchen table was placed in position over it, but in the early morning both cover and table were removed so that the day's supply of water could be drawn up and the children's faces washed.

They were kneeling round the well now having their ablutions superintended by Dorothy Goatley, and watching in a fascinated silence while Diggory Colt let down bucket after bucket into the cool depths of the well and brought them up again filled to the brim with cold, sparkling water. The river ran so near them that there was never any lack of water in the well, and during the rainy winter months there was a further supply of water in the cellars, where it stood two feet deep and gave Canon Leigh the rheumatics.

Dorothy was a delightful round, rosy, blue-eyed person in the middle twenties. Figure she had none, her person being shaped like a loaf of bread: a smaller bulge above being set upon a larger bulge below, with a region of great tightness between the two. She was always clothed in a gray homespun dress covered by a large white apron, and her hair, if she had any, was completely hidden beneath her white cap. Her life had one great love, for her foster-child, Diccon, and one great hatred, for Great-Aunt; the rest of the world she regarded with tolerant amusement.

Diggory was an old man, though neither he nor anyone else had the slightest idea how old he was. He looked like a withered apple and might have been any age. He had been groom at Mistress Leigh's old home, had taught her to ride and had never left her, sharing her fortune or misfortune with complete indifference. When she died he made no comment at all but set himself to serve her husband and children with the same morose devotion with which he had served her. He seldom spoke but should there be any little difference with any of the tradesmen he could hit hard. The children and horses and dogs loved him and it seemed he had but to touch the earth with his horny fingers for flowers to grow.

The little group of children and animals at the well was now augmented by Will and Thomas, aged nine and eight. Giles, the eldest son, was now fifteen and a man full-grown. He was a scholar of Christ Church, and a brilliant one too, and had his own rooms in College, strolling home now and then to shed the light of his countenance upon his family when he felt it would do them good.

Will and Thomas were very alike and almost as inseparable as the twins. They were cheerful, untidy children with matted shocks of the Leigh honey-colored hair, wide, inquiring gray eyes and large mouths that required a lot of filling. They were thoroughly naughty in a healthy way but they had none of Diccon's deliberate wickedness. As far as Canon Leigh could see they had no intelligence at all, and neither had the twins. The brains of the family were in the brilliant Giles, Joyeuce and Grace. It was impossible as yet to form any judgment as to Diccon's mental equipment. Cunning he had in plenty, and concentration and immense strength of will, but with what ends in view he would choose to exert these gifts no one dared prophesy.

"Father is here and it is time for prayers," said Joyeuce.

Grace, Will, Thomas and the twins hastily jumped up and rubbed their faces dry but Diccon, lying flat on his stomach peering into the depths of the well, had to be lifted up, yelling loudly, and forcibly placed upon his feet.... Another of the unfortunate traits in Diccon's character was that he would never be devout unless forced to it.

Joyeuce led the procession from the kitchen back to the hall, the children following her in order of age and Dorothy and Diggory and the animals bringing up the rear.

The children knelt in a row before their father to receive his morning blessing, each little head being bent in turn as his hand was laid upon it; with the exception of Diccon's, and Diccon never lowered his head unless it was to bite. He had, on one terrible occasion, bitten his father when his father blessed him, but the punishment meted out to him later by his outraged brothers and sisters had been so severe that he had decided against repeating his performance.

There was a window on one side of the front door and passers-by in the quadrangle who happened to look in at a quarter to six in the morning always saw a sight they did not forget; they were moved to edification or to mirth according to their several convictions and temperaments but were all alike impressed by the beauty of the picture.

In front of the fireplace, where nearly all the year round a log fire burned, for the room faced north and was cold, Canon Leigh would be standing, looking like a monk with his bald head and long black belted gown. In front of him in a long row stood his children in gradually decreasing order of age and height, and behind them stood Dorothy and old Diggory. Tinker the cat would be clasped in Diccon's arms, and the three dogs, Posy and Spot and Pippit, would be sitting very reverently upon their haunches beside Diggory.... Canon Leigh loved animals as dearly as his children did and saw no incongruity in the attendance of these quadrupeds at family prayers.... The flickering light of the flaming logs would gleam on the dark wood of the paneled walls and the

glorious carved staircase, on the long oak dining table where in summer
a beau-pot of flowers always stood, on the fair heads of the elder children
and the ruddy darkness of Diccon's mop of curls, on the rich ebony of
Tinker's fur and the soft, mousy velvet of Pippit's coat. . . . And last but
not least the macabre apparition of an old woman in a frilled nightcap
looking out of an overhead window, a sinister, black-browed witch of
an old woman who laughed a silent, toothless laugh when her mocking
bright eyes fell on the group below.

"Funes ceciderunt mihi in praedaris," Canon Leigh would say in
his deep, amazingly beautiful voice, and the children and servants, who
knew the verses by heart, would reply, "Haereditas mihi praedara est
mihi." They would recite turn and turn about until they got to the end,
Diggory's deep bass growl mingling with the children's piping trebles,
and then they would kneel, holding up their clasped hands, and say the
Lord's Prayer; the dogs lying flat with their noses between their paws
and Diccon forced to his knees by Dorothy's vigorous hand dealing him
two blows, one behind each little knee. . . . This was the best method yet
discovered of making Diccon pray. . . . Though when he had been forced
into the correct posture for devotion, and knelt with his green eyes fixed
on the ceiling—he always refused to shut them—and his plump hands
piously clasping Tinker to his breast, who knew whether the thoughts
in his mind were those his well-wishers would have chosen? . . . It was
feared not.

On most mornings the Lord's Prayer was followed by breakfast but
every now and then Canon Leigh, who did not seem to feel the pangs of
hunger like other people, and was really more suited by temperament to
be one of those Indian mystics who sit out a lifetime praying on the top
of a tower with their legs round their necks, than the father of a family,
would suddenly be lifted up on the wings of prayer and go on soaring
higher and higher, oblivious of the hungry, earth-bound bodies of his
wretched family.

He did this today. He began praying for the suffering, the homeless,
the destitute and the sick, above all for the hungry children who had not
where to lay their heads. He went on and on. His family were only too

pleased to pray for hungry children, provided they were given their own breakfast first, but while they were still themselves among the afflicted they found it difficult. Dorothy, who had left the milk on the hob, cast agonized glances at Diggory, the younger children stirred restlessly and Great-Aunt began to beat an impatient tattoo upon her windowpane. But Canon Leigh, passing on from the general to the particular, began to pray for a certain destitute boy whom he had that morning encountered. . . . That he might be found. . . . Comforted. . . . Fed.

Great-Aunt could stand it no longer. She flung open her window and leaned out. "Gervas," she shouted, "hold your tongue!"

Canon Leigh started and looked up; taken by surprise, bewildered and uncertain of himself, he got to his feet without knowing what he was doing, while Dorothy fled to the kitchen and the children ran to seat themselves round the table before he could change his mind and begin again.

Seated in his big carved chair at the head of the table Canon Leigh again looked up at his aunt and marveled at the power she had over them all. She was a wicked destructive old lady who had worried his wife into her grave, ruined his home, and now, so it seemed to him, spent her time seizing hold of all the fair flowers of piety and love that might blossom in his house and pulling them up by the roots. . . . And yet, with her burning vitality, her iron will, her good humor when she got her own way, and bearing still in face and figure the remnants of great beauty, she was attractive, and he could not but smile at her as she nodded and waved from her window.

She was in fine fettle now that Dorothy had brought her a good brimming tankard of ale and a plate of cold roast beef minced up very finely, and looked down benignly upon the children and their father below, with their mugs of milk and manchets of coarse bread. A wishy-washy diet, she considered, and responsible for their wishy-washy characters. She had the lowest opinion of all of them, except Diccon, and interfered with good-humored contempt in their talk of the boy whom Canon Leigh had so unfortunately lost. . . . The children were sorry about the poor boy now that they had had something to eat.

"I wish you hadn't lost him, Father," mourned Joyeuce.

"Perhaps we'll find him again," said Grace hopefully.

"Heaven forbid," said Great-Aunt, and chewed a spoonful of minced beef with enjoyment.

"Dame," said Canon Leigh gravely, "I desire that you will not turn aside the thoughts of my children from the love of charity."

"Bugs," said Great-Aunt. "That's what charity is: the bringing in of bugs to the house," and she took a draught of ale.

"You will be so good," said her nephew sternly, "as to shut your window."

"Tilly-vally! Tilly-vally!" exclaimed Great-Aunt, but having had enough of them she banged the window shut and gave her whole attention to her food.

Canon Leigh, though he had apparently won a victory that should have compensated him for his previous defeat, felt no sense of satisfaction in it. . . . He knew that Great-Aunt's rare retirements from the field of battle were the result not of defeat but of boredom. . . . He drooped in his chair, worrying about that boy; wishing for the hundredth time that there were still monasteries in England, and that they opened their doors to married men.

The twins, observing his depression of spirits, slid solidly to the floor, trundled across to him and climbed each upon a knee. "Never mind, Father," they cooed, "*we'll* find that little boy," and laying their fat cheeks against his they squeaked engagingly.

They had a habit of squeaking, like mice, that was peculiar to themselves and was used with much effect to express affection, surprise, condolence, happiness, or any other emotion which might seem called for at the moment; though it was the happiness squeak that was used most often and was the most attractive, in spite of a tendency to end in hiccups. For it was the happiness of the twins that made them so adorable. They were as happy as the first buttercup lifting its face to the sun, or as a blackbird singing at sunset, or as the streams when they "make sweet music with the enameled stones." They would always be happy, their father thought, being of that radiant company whose business in life it seems to be simply to be joyous, their joy a vindication of the eternal rightness of the foundations of this life. . . . With a twin in each arm he suddenly ceased to feel the attraction of the cloister.

But time was going on. There was a constant patter of feet on the path under the window, and a succession of flying figures crossing the quadrangle, for work began at six and scholars were hurrying to their lectures. Great Tom boomed out the hour from the Cathedral tower and Canon Leigh set the twins hastily upon the floor and hurried into the study to fetch the hooks he needed for his six o'clock lecture.

Sighing, and wiping their mouths with the backs of their hands, Will and Thomas slid to the floor and got their school books from the chest under the window, just as Dorothy entered from the kitchen with their dinners in little leather bags. They attended the grammar school at Queen's College, where they went every morning at six o'clock, returning at five-thirty in the evening. Of this eleven hours' working day two hours, eleven to one, were free for eating the dinners of cold meat and bread that they brought with them, and for shooting at the butts, but the rest of the time was devoted to grammar, logic, rhetoric, arithmetic, music, geometry and astronomy.

> 'Tis Grammar teaches how to speak,
> And Logic sifts the false from true,
> By Rhetoric we learn to deck
> Each word with its own proper hue.
> Arithmetic of number treats,
> And Music rules the Church's praise;
> Geometry the round earth metes,
> Astronomy the starry ways.

They had holidays, of course, eighteen days at Christmas, twelve at Easter and nine at Whitsuntide, but it was extraordinary how quickly they seemed to pass. . . . They envied the twins, who stayed at home and were taught by Great-Aunt.

Not that the twins envied themselves. Joyeuce and Grace had long ago learnt all of the little that Great-Aunt knew and Grace now helped

Joyeuce in the work of the house, so the twins and Diccon received Great-Aunt's instructions in solitary glory, and it was awful.

As they stood at the front door, seeing the men of the family off to work, their hearts sank down and down. . . . Oh, if only they were grown up, or men, or dead, or anything so that they need not receive instructions from Dame Susan Cholmeley. . . . But it would be best of all to be grown up.

CHAPTER III

THE MADONNA

See, where she sits upon the grassy green,
 (O seemly sight)
 Yclad in scarlet like a maiden Queen,
 And ermines white.
 Upon her head a cremosin coronet,
 With damask roses and daffodillies set:
 Bay-leaves between,
 And primroses green
Embellish the sweet violet.

I saw Phoebus thrust out his golden head,
 Upon her to gaze:
 But when he saw how broad her beams did spread,
 It did him amaze.
 He blushed to see another sun below,
 Ne durst again his fiery face outshow:
 Let him, if he dare
 His brightness compare
With hers, to have the overthrow.

Bring hither the pink and purple columbine,
 With gillyflowers;
 Bring coronations, and sops in wine,
 Worn of paramours.
 Strew me the ground with daffodowndillies,
 And cowslips, and kingcups, and loved lilies:
 The pretty paunce,
 And the chevisaunce,
Shall match with the fair flower delice.

EDMUND SPENSER.

1.

GREAT-AUNT delivered her instructions from half-past six till half-past eight in the parlor, a little room reached by a door under the staircase, and here the three children sat on low stools waiting for her.

The parlor was a lovely room, paneled in oak and with a beautiful modeled plaster ceiling. Over the fireplace was a carved overmantel where the arms of Cardinal Wolsey and Henry the Eighth were set in a frame of leaves and Tudor roses, wonderfully rich and luxuriant. In the winter they burned sea coal in the fireplace, and a great luxury Joyeuce and her father felt it to be. In London sea coal must not be burnt while Parliament was sitting, lest the health of members be affected, but Oxford laid no such restrictions upon its use. In spring and autumn they burned the wood that had been torn from the trees in the Christ Church meadows by winter gales, and the twins liked that best, for the flames from the wood seemed to them prettier than the flames from the coal because they were of different colors, as though each different tree had a different flame flower: some yellow, some orange, some blue and some red. In the evenings, when it was growing dark, the reflected flames leaped and danced on the dark paneled walls so that you thought that that wood too was on fire with flowers.

There was very little furniture in the room; a few stools and chairs, the chest where the children kept their needlework and lesson books and the clavicytherium that Joyeuce, the musician of the family, played to their father in the evenings. It was like a spinet set up on end and if its compass was no larger than that of the human voice the harp music that came from it was very sweet.

The parlor's one window looked out on the street that ran past the Fair Gate, leading from the center of the town to the South Gate of the city. Its real name was South Gate Street but it was always called Fish Street after a certain Master Fish, a mayor of corpulent and happy memory. It was not always a pleasure to have this window open because the housewives of Fish Street flung all their slops cheerfully out of the window to drain down through the cobbles to the kennel; but today, after the downpour in the night, the smells were nicely damped down and Fish Street quite at its best, with little blue pools between the cobbles that reflected the blue sky above, and the wet roofs of Saint Aldate's church and the Christ Church almshouses shining brightly across the way.

This outside world was so tempting that the children left their stools and ran to the window to look out. . . . From the town came distant and thrilling sounds of pipes, drums and jingling bells. . . . Joan, who had felt when she woke up that this was going to be a particularly adventurous day, jigged up and down on her toes and squeaked excitedly. "It's the morris dancers," she said, and then, a little mournfully, "everyone has a holiday on May-Day but us."

"We do not join in these vulgar holidays because we are Well Born," said Meg, passing on an explanation of their hard lot already given her by Great-Aunt; but she sighed as she gave it, for the advantages of Blue Blood seemed at the moment few.

Diccon, hanging out of the window with his short legs well off the floor, was taking no notice of their conversation. "I can spit further than you can," he announced, and gave a demonstration.

"You can't!" cried Meg indignantly, and showed him at once that he was mistaken.

Joan did not waste her breath on words but used it all to reach further than either of the others; and at this unfortunate moment Great-Aunt entered.

When dressed for the day she was an awe-inspiring sight in any mood; but when in the grip of righteous indignation, she struck terror to the hearts of the boldest. She stood in the center of the room leaning upon her ivory-topped stick, arrayed in her black satin farthingale over a green kirtle embroidered with purple daisies. She wore a wig of jet black curly hair and over it a veil of lawn edged with lace. She had jewels in her ears and on her fingers. She looked magnificent, if a trifle barbaric, with her dark eyes sparkling with rage and her mouth set so strong-mindedly that her nose and her chin almost met.

The twins seized Diccon's legs and pulled him to the ground, whirled him about to make his bow and sank themselves into agitated and rather wobbly little curtseys. . . . . But it was too late. . . . Great-Aunt had seen.

"Children," she said in a terrible voice, "hold out your hands."

They held out their hands and she produced from the black satin folds of her farthingale a very potent little cane that had been presented to her by her husband upon the occasion of the birth of their first child, and had been used by her with great effect ever since. It was unbelievable that an old lady of eighty-five could have such strength in her arm. When she had done with them the three little palms were on fire and tears were trickling down the twins' cheeks. . . . They never cried when Joyeuce spanked them, but then Great-Aunt could hit harder than Joyeuce and there was something in the way she did it that hurt their feelings. . . . Joyeuce spanked them because she loved them but Great-Aunt caned because caning in itself gave her pleasure.

"Weak little poppets," she snorted, regarding the tears with disfavor. "Look at your brother. He does not cry though he's still but a babe."

Diccon grinned wickedly at her, his green eyes narrowed to slits, and thrusting out his bright pink tongue—his tongue was of an unusually vivid pink—he licked his smarting palm. He was not afraid of Great-Aunt but when with her he usually behaved himself, for in Great-Aunt he had met his match. It cannot be said that they loved each other, for neither of them had much power of affection, but they saw each in the other qualities that they themselves possessed, and being both of them chock-full of conceit they were naturally full of mutual admiration.

Great-Aunt had no use for sensitiveness in any form. That idiotic shrinking from giving pain that characterized both Joyeuce and her father, together with their imbecile reserve and morbidity of conscience, aroused in her nothing but contempt. She cared as little what she did to other people as she cared what they did to her, and as for reserve, if you did not say straight out what you wanted, how could you expect to get it? This attitude towards life was also Diccon's and their aim being the same they got on uncommonly well.

"Put your tongue in, Diccon!" thundered Great-Aunt. "And collect your thoughts for the morning's instruction. Sit down, little girls, and take up your hornbooks."

Great-Aunt seated herself majestically upon a big carved chair, with the children's lesson books ready to her hand on a stool by her side. She fancied herself as an instructress and example to the young and was not now recognizable as the same old lady who had made such unfortunate remarks at breakfast.

The children seated themselves upon their stools and took up the hornbooks that were attached to their waists by cords and accompanied them through their day. The hornbook was intended for purposes of edification and that it was also used for purposes of battledore and shuttlecock was unfortunate, but inevitable owing to its shape. A sheet of vellum, covered by a thin sheet of horn to protect the vellum from the soiling of grubby little hands, was fastened to a piece of wood with a handle, very much the shape of a square hand mirror. On the vellum were inscribed the essentials of education. First in importance came the cross, followed by the rhyme,

Christ's cross be my speed
In all virtue to proceed.

Then came the alphabet and then, reading and writing being now presumably mastered, a dedication of learning. "In the name of the Father, and of the Son and the Holy Ghost." Then came the Lord's Prayer and finally, but only if there was room, the numerals, for the genius who designed the hornbook was probably a monk in one of the monastery schools who thought moneymaking arithmetic less important than prayer and dedication. The children, too, quite understood the relative importance of these things. Christ's cross, they knew, came first, and they called the hornbook their criss-cross, after it, and the alphabet the criss-cross row.

When they had repeated the prayers on the hornbook Great-Aunt set them to do a little juggling with the numerals.

"If I had five apples," she said, "and you took away two, what then?"

"You would cane us," said Diccon, and licked his palm again.

"Insolent varlet!" cried Great-Aunt, and felt for her cane; but Diccon grinned at her and she thought better of it.

"Three apples, Great-Aunt," squeaked Meg, the more intellectual of the twins, and the arithmetic lesson pursued its way in comparative calm.

When it was over Great-Aunt took from the table beside her a battered little brown book on deportment for the young. Every day she and the children went solemnly through this book, Great-Aunt reading out the precepts and the children repeating them after her. There were a great many precepts, dealing with every department of manners, though special attention was paid by the author to table manners.

1. Bite not thy bread, but break it, but not with slovenly fingers, nor with the same wherewith thou takest up thy meat.
2. Dip not thy meat in the sauce.
3. Take not salt with a greasy knife.
4. Cough not, nor blow thy nose at table if it may be avoided; but if there be necessity, do it aside, and without much noise.
5. Spit not in the room, but in a corner, and rub it out with thy foot, or, rather, go out and do it abroad.
6. Stuff not thy mouth so as to fill thy cheeks; be content with smaller mouthfuls.
7. Blow not thy meat, but with patience wait till it be cool.
8. Sup not broth at the table but eat it with a spoon.

The author also laid stress on the necessity for courtesy. "If thy superior be relating a story," said one wise precept, "say not, I have heard it before, but attend as if it were to thee altogether new. Seem not to question the truth of it. If he tell it not right, snigger not, nor endeavor to help out or add to his relation."

There was yet another that might have been laid to heart with advantage by Nicolas de Worde. "Be not hasty to run out of Church when the worship is ended, as if thou wert weary of being there."

It took them nearly an hour to get through the book from cover to cover, and sitting bolt upright on their stools their backs ached dreadfully, but at the least suspicion of a sigh or a yawn, or the tiniest relaxation of the vertical backbone, Great-Aunt's hand felt for the cane, so there was nothing for it but endurance.

But at half-past seven the agony was over. Diccon was allowed to go scuttling back to the kitchen and his cat while the little girls took up their samplers. This, of course, was a fresh agony, but not so bad as the first because the twins were naturally domesticated and took readily to their needles.

The samplers were very beautiful, worked in minute cross-stitch upon fine linen. Round the edges the twins were working a border of forget-me-nots, honeysuckle and sundry sorts of spots from a wonderful new book that had just come out with the imposing title, "Here followeth certain patterns of cutworks; newly invented and never published before. Also sundry sorts of spots, as flowers, birds, and fishes, etc., and will fitly serve to be wrought, some with gold, some with silk, and some with crewel in colors. And never but once published before. Printed by Richard Shorleyker."

When they got tired of this they cheered themselves up by re-threading their needles and doing a little work upon some breathless remarks they were embroidering in the center of the sampler.

In life there is no sure stay
For flesh as flower doth fade away
This carcass made of slime and clay
Must taste of death there is no way
While we have time then let us pray
To God for grace both night and day

While the twins worked Great-Aunt read aloud to them from a book called "De Civilitate Morum Puerilium: a little book of Good Manners for Children: into the English Tongue by R. Whytyngton. 1540." It was a book written by Erasmus and it had a picture on the title page of good,

well-behaved little children which the twins were allowed to look at at
the end of the lesson.

It is doubtful if they derived as much benefit from this book as could
have been wished because reading aloud was not one of Great-Aunt's
gifts. She took her breaths at the command of nature instead of at the
command of Erasmus, who had thoughtfully placed commas where
breaths should be taken but was not attended to by Great-Aunt; also her
lack of teeth made articulation a little difficult. However they all three
liked to feel that they were studying Erasmus, who was after all a noted
scholar and who deserved to be patronized by them because he had had
the good taste to like Oxford and its people. "The air," he had said, "is
soft and delicious. The men are sensible and intelligent." The girls, he
had gone on to say, were divinely pretty, and the kiss of greeting which
they bestowed upon all and sundry was most delightful to receive. . . .
Certainly a man to be taken notice of.

But at half-past eight Great-Aunt had had enough of him. She shut
"De Civilitate Morum Puerilium" with a bang, sighed to the twins to
put away their work and leave the room, leaned back in her chair, folded
her hands in her lap and closed her eyes. . . . She would slumber now,
dreaming of the glories that were past, until it was time to go to her room
for ten o'clock dinner.

2.

The twins scuttled joyously from the room, for now they might go
and play in the garden. This was to them the loveliest hour of the day
because it was the only time when, except for the darling dogs, they were
alone together. Diccon and his wretched cat, whom they and the dogs
hated, were shut up in the kitchen with Dorothy, and Joyeuce and Grace
were doing the housework.

There was a cupboard under the stairs, beside the door into the
parlor, that was the children's own special cupboard, and from this they
took their leggings and their little dark blue cloaks lined with scarlet,
with the hoods that came right over their heads and protected their

snowy caps. They sat on the floor and pulled on their leggings, giggling and squeaking happily, while the dogs sat and watched and thumped their tails on the floor.

Also in the cupboard were the children's toys, their dolls and pop-guns and battledores and shuttlecocks, and Diccon's white woolly lamb with tin legs, bought for the most part at the annual St. Giles' Fair that was the greatest excitement of their lives.

Meg's favorite doll was called Bloody Mary. The family had implored Meg to think of a nicer name, but Meg wouldn't. She thought Bloody Mary sounded well, and she had a sensitive ear for sound. Bloody Mary wore a black velvet farthingale over a kirtle of purple satin, with a plain ruff and coif. Her hair had come off and her composition face was very pale because she had once been left out in the rain, so that her likeness to the late Queen was really very remarkable.

Joan's favorite doll, Queen Elizabeth, was quite different. Her hair was rich and red and her cheeks were painted a bright scarlet. Her red velvet farthingale was trimmed with gold braid and her green satin kirtle had orange flowers embroidered on it; her ruff was splendid and her coif spangled. The bodies of these ladies were not jointed, like the superior bodies of their twentieth century descendants, so that they could not take up any position but that of the horizontal or the vertical, but on the other hand they had a stiff dignity, a blandness of expression, a fixity of regard and a magnificence of attire which if copied by their successors would most certainly prolong their lives. . . . For these dolls were not dolls with whom liberties could be taken.

Meg and Joan, now fully attired in cloaks and leggings, lifted their darlings—usually referred to as Bloody and Bess—tenderly from the cupboard, laid them in the crooks of their left arms and trotted through the kitchen to the garden, the dogs following. Dorothy was momentarily out of the kitchen and Diccon in her absence had betaken himself and the cat to the cupboard where the raisins were kept. He popped out his head and made a rude noise as the little girls passed, but they took no notice.

It was lovely in the garden. The house was on the south side of the great quadrangle of Christ Church, and the garden lay between the back

of the house and the Christ Church meadows. It was small but packed
as full of flowers as Joyeuce could get it and as gay and neat as a patch-
work quilt. Paved paths led between beds edged with rosemary, lavender, marjoram and thyme, their centers filled with the blue and golden
flowers of spring: cowslips, primroses, daffodils and forget-me-nots.
When the summer came they would be filled with rich warm flowers,
roses and pinks and pansies and sops-in-wine. There were fruit trees in
the garden, apples and cherries, and on the west side a yew hedge with
a clipped peacock at each end hid the stables and outhouses, built out
at an angle from the house. Beyond the garden the trees in the meadows
were wearing the fresh green of spring, a garment as mistily mysterious
as the rain-drenched grass below and the blue sky above.

It still felt cold and fresh after the rain in the night but the bright
sun poured down a wealth of light and filled each wet flower cup with
a twinkling golden coin. The twins ran all round, visiting their friends
and touching them very gently with the outstretched tips of their right
forefingers; very gentle forefingers that hardly disturbed a drop of rain
when they touched. The late daffodils were bowing and curtseying to
the west wind and Joan thought they looked like beautiful ladies dancing
the pavane. Their farthingales, she pointed out to Meg, were a lovely pale
yellow, pale as the first clouds of the morning, but the kirtles underneath
them were much richer in color, like the kingcups beside the river or
the buttercups in the quadrangle. The twins had once been taken to
see some beautiful ladies and gentlemen dancing the pavane in Christ
Church hall and they had never forgotten it. One day, they told each
other, they too would be grown up and dance in Christ Church hall,
and the candle flames that would be burning in their hundreds to light
the dance would not be so yellow as the dresses they would wear. . . . It
must be a wonderful thing to be grown up. . . . Like being born again.

The apple trees were a mass of exultant pink and white blossom and
when Meg and Joan ran up to them they threw out breaths of delicious
warm scent that made the twins wrinkle their noses in delight. These
apple trees seemed a miracle to the little girls. Only a little while ago they
had seemed old, almost dead things, just gnarled black wood drenched

by the winter storms and twisted into ugly fantastic shapes like the poor old beggars one sometimes saw in the streets. And then quite suddenly they had been plastered all over with comic fat buds that entirely altered their expressions, as though the surly old trees were trying to smile. The cold spring winds had shaken the buds and the rain had streamed over them, but nothing daunted they had slowly opened and green leaves had appeared, as though tightly shut hands unclosed and were held up to the sun, palms upward and fingers crooked in supplication, begging for warmth. The tip of each green leaf had been faintly tinged with red, as though the warmth had already been given and the fingers glowed. And now the warmth had spread and deepened until the ugly old men, the beggars, had become rich and radiant as young gods. . . . It was very odd, the twins thought, very odd indeed, and they wondered if they would be as changed when they grew up and wore those yellow dresses and danced in Christ Church hall.

They turned their backs on the fruit trees for a moment to survey the center of the garden, where the soft, silver gray of the herbs edged the blue forget-me-nots like mist upon water, and then ran eagerly to the yew hedge that hid the stables, for in the depth of the yew hedge there was a bird's nest. It was a wonderful nest, its rough outside made of twisted twigs from the meadows and straws from the stable yard and its inside a perfect smooth bowl of grass and moss. There were five eggs in it, blue-green in color with little specks of brown upon them. The twins did not stay long by the nest, lest they should annoy the parents, and they were careful not to touch, they just peeped hastily to see that all was well and then ran away. They had personally entrusted the nest to the care of Romulus and Remus, the two yew peacocks, and these birds had up to date justified the confidence reposed in them.

An archway had been cut in the center of the yew hedge and this led through to the stables. A visit to the stables was the last item in the program of early morning inspection but it took a very long time owing to the enchantment of the stables. One went under the archway into the yard, where tufts of bright green grass grew between the cobbles and where the garbage heap led its interesting life. This latter exercised a deep fascination not only over the dogs but over the twins too, for the things that could be found in it varied day by day and were always of an attractive nature, including as they did dead rats and mice in various interesting stages of decay, bones, old shoes, old pots and pans and scraps of wool and silk left over from the weaving. The twins played all sorts of fascinating games with the things they found in the garbage heap, and the dogs were safe here from interruption by Tinker the cat, for Tinker was nothing if not a snob and despising the Leigh garbage heap invariably betook himself to the superior one at the Deanery.

To the south of the yard was the outhouse where the harness and gardening tools and oddments were kept, with the room where Diggory slept above it. His window looked straight out on to the garbage heap but Diggory, as completely inured to smells as other Elizabethans, suffered no inconvenience. To the west was the stable proper, with the loft above it, and to the north a cobbled lane led between the stables and the house to Fish Street.

There were three inmates of the stables: Great-Aunt's old white mule Susan who had brought her from Stratford, Canon Leigh's black horse Prince and the children's pony Dapple. Diggory was busy grooming Dapple and Prince and Susan, and leaving the dogs to dig happily in the garbage heap the twins ran to the stable to help him.

Diggory never minded being helped by the twins. He suffered them in silence until they got in the way and then picked them up very gently, put them outside and shut the door; and they never seemed to resent this dismissal, or to question it. The relations existing between Diggory and the children were rather puzzling to Canon Leigh. They talked to him by the hour together quite undeterred by the fact that he never made any answer except an occasional grunt. And what did they talk to him about? And how is it possible to talk for two hours at a stretch to a person who never answers? Or was there a world of meaning in each of Diggory's grunts that the children and the animals alone were able to interpret? Canon Leigh could only suppose that those very near to the earth, the peasants whose life is regulated by her seasons, the animals who make their homes among the roots of her trees, and the children to whom her flowers and grasses are still enchanted forests, are bound together in a closer understanding than can be comprehended by those others whom education and the customs of so-called civilization have carried far away from the source of their being.

The twins, having kissed Dapple, Prince and Susan on their gentle noses, spent half an hour helping Diggory and talking to him so incessantly that not a pin point could have been inserted between one sentence and another. At the end of that time he silently picked them up and put them outside the door.

"Diggory," they called from outside, "could we go up into the loft?"

For answer Diggory silently picked them up again, one under each arm, and placed them one in Dapple's manger and one in Prince's. From here they were able to scramble up by hoisting themselves through the rafters over their heads, left open so that fodder could be lowered down from the loft to the mangers below.

Scrambling and kicking, and pushed by Diggory from behind, they emerged from the mangers and arrived on all fours on the floor of the loft. Picking themselves up, and removing streamers of hay from their own persons and those of Bloody and Bess, they surveyed the loft and found it as attractive as ever, with its one cobwebby window looking on Fish Street and its fascinating smell of well-kept horses, hay and sunshine. . . . That sunshine has a scent, and that it lives in hay long after it is cut and dried and brown as autumn leaves, all the Leigh children firmly maintained. It is not a scent that can be defined but when you smell it you think instantly of gorse and the song of the lark. . . . There was real as well as preserved sunshine in the loft, that fell through the cracks in the roof in long rays in which the motes of dust hopped and skipped with a gaiety that warmed the very cockles of the heart. Sparrows built under the eaves of the loft and their chatter filled it all day long. The generous load of hay that had been brought from the Christ Church meadows last summer had dwindled during the winter, so that most of the floor space was left free and made a fine dancing floor.

Meg and Joan danced here daily. Laying aside their cloaks and Bloody and Bess they picked up their skirts on either side and curtseyed gravely to each other, pointing their booted feet with as much delicacy as was possible under the circumstances. They went carefully and seriously through the steps of the stately pavane that they had picked up from watching Great-Aunt teach them to Joyeuce and Grace. Their chubby faces were composed in earnest gravity and their eyes had a faraway look. Between the fingers and thumbs that held their rough homespun skirts they could feel the softness of yellow satin, the chattering sparrows were the players of lute and viol and virginal and the slanting rays of light that touched their fair hair to gold fell from the hundreds of candles burning round Christ Church hall.

It was while they were dancing that they heard again that exciting sound of pipes and drums and ringing bells. At first it was only a faraway sound, at one with the music of their imagination, but gradually it grew louder and their pattering feet began to keep time with it, and then it became a regular uproar, drowning the chatter of the sparrows and the hissing sound that Diggory was making down below.

"The morris dancers!" shrieked Meg.

"Coming down Fish Street!" yelled Joan.

They dashed to the window, pushed it open and leaned out. Down from the town that glorious crowd came dancing, a stream of color that washed up against the walls on either side as though it would lift up the houses and carry them with it. The merrymakers were more uproarious than ever now, for they had been on the go for some hours, imbibing cakes and ale all the time, and their enjoyment was absolutely irresistible. The twins leaned further and further out of their window, squeaking excitedly, watching the figures of fairy tale and legend passing by under their very noses. . . . The Men in Green, Robin Hood, Friar Tuck, Little John, Maid Marian, the Queen of the May, the Fool, the Hobby Horse, the Dragon, and that hero of the best fairy tales, the Younger Son. . . . It was this last character who attracted the twins most of all because though they had heard about him so often, following his career over and over again as they sat by the fire on winter evenings listening to Joyeuce's bedtime stories, they had never actually seen him before, and now they found that he looked exactly as he ought to look:

ragged and dirty but jolly and laughing, and such a gentleman that, after a bath, he would have been a fit mate for any princess.... The twins knew he was a prince in disguise because of a certain royalty in his bearing; he moved as a man moves whose reason controls his body and whose immortal spirit has climbed up far enough to sit enthroned as king of his reason.... Where was he going, they wondered. To London to be Lord Mayor? Out of South Gate and up into Bagley Forest to kill giants? Or far away into the blue distance to look for a crock of gold buried at the foot of the rainbow?

Wherever it was it seemed to the twins that it must be the most exciting place in the world. Why shouldn't they go there too? Why must they, because they were Well Born, be shut out from all the fun in life? Why could not they too join that glorious dancing colored crowd and go with it over the edge of the world into fairyland? They never had any need to speak their thoughts to each other, for their spiritual nearness was so great that they were practically one child; what one thought the other thought, and what one did the other did, and so instantaneously that there was hardly time for others to notice the quick leaping of thought from mind to mind, or to see more than a tiny chink of daylight between the ballooning skirts as one bustling little body followed the other into action. So now it was as one child that they took a firmer hold on Bloody and Bess, leaned out of the window and yelled to the people below, "Lift us down! Lift us down!"

Some obliging apprentices did so, one boy standing on the back of another and handing the twins down to a third, who placed the fat little creatures firmly upon the cobbles and pulled down their petticoats with great kindness and condescension.

"Thank you, sirs," panted the twins. "Thank you very much, sirs," and were instantly absorbed into the crowd like drops of water into the ocean.

Faithful, clinging to the tail of the Dragon and reeling over the cobbles drunk with color and noise and excitement, was astonished when he looked down and saw two fat little girls with voluminous dark blue skirts, white aprons and caps, dolls clutched in their free hands

and round pansy faces turned up to him in unconcealed adoration. . . .
Faithful, adored by two females for the first time in his life, turned a
bright pink.

"Where are we going?" asked Meg. "To London Town?"

"I don't think so," gasped Faithful in some confusion. "I've just come
from there."

"Let's look for a crock of gold at the foot of the rainbow," panted
Joan.

"Would you like a crock of gold?" inquired Meg, looking up into
Faithful's face as she pattered along beside him.

"More than anything else in the world," he gasped.

"We'll find it then," announced Joan, and the pace at which they
were going having now robbed all three of breath the thing seemed
settled.

At the South Gate of the city the cavalcade was brought to a full stop
for further uproarious refreshment. Cakes were again thrown out of the
windows and tankards of ale carried out of the houses from beneath the
branches of may above the doorways. No one seemed to question the
presence of the two fat little girls and their dolls among the May-Day
crowd. They were quite in place among those fairy-tale people. They
were sat up astride the Dragon's tail and given cakes to eat, and even
sips out of Robin Hood's tankard of ale. . . . Sips that went to their heads
at once, so that they rolled about on top of the Dragon, squeaking with
ecstasy, laughing so much that their eyes disappeared into rolls of fat,
and kicking their short legs among their voluminous petticoats in a way
that would have turned Joyeuce pale with horror had she seen.

Then suddenly they had turned round and were off again, drums
thundering, bells ringing, handkerchiefs fluttering and feet pattering,
streaming back up Fish Street like spring let loose.

As they went a shower passed over them, but the two little girls,
clinging to the Younger Son while he in turn clung to the Dragon's tail,
did not care in the least; for it did not seem like real rain; it was like
the rain that falls in fairy tales, lovely crystal drops that only refreshed
without soiling the flower-like figures it touched, and quite cleared away

the fumes of ale from little girls' brains. It swung away on the wings of
the west wind and the sun came out again, lighting every dancing figure
to a dazzling blaze of color, washing the wet cobbles with silver and
turning every thread of raindrops on windowsill and gable to a string
of diamonds.

"The rainbow!" squeaked Meg.

It shone ahead of them, one end of it planted firmly in the heart of
the town and the other disappearing into the sailing mass of cloud that
had given them their shower.

"Come on!" squeaked Joan, pulling at Faithful's jerkin and bouncing
uphill at a great pace. "Come on! Come on!"

Faithful came on, by now so bewildered by fatigue and noise that he
hardly knew where he was or what he was doing; indeed grown man of
fourteen though he was he almost believed himself to have fallen head
over heels out of the world of reality into that fairy world whose figures
surrounded him. . . . The little girls one on each side of him believed
themselves to be in it, and perhaps their faith was contagious.

The rain was falling again, though the sun still shone. The Fair Gate
of Christ Church floated by in a golden mist and he found they had
reached the heart of the town again, a place where four ways met, and
had swerved to the right, back once more into the High Street. Looking
up through the rain and the sun he saw the sign of the Mitre Inn swinging
over his head, with above it the beautiful outline of a gabled roof, and,
springing straight up from the roof into the sky, the dazzling curve of the
rainbow. He let go of the Dragon's tail and stood stock-still, gazing at it.
He could not help himself. It was the loveliest rainbow he had ever seen.

The wide-open inn door, yawning like the black mouth of a cavern
beneath the swinging sign, was absorbing the fairy-tale figures. One by
one they danced in and were lost in the darkness: the morris dancers,
the drummers, the pipers, Robin Hood, Little John, Friar Tuck, Maid
Marian, the Queen of the May, the Hobby Horse and the Dragon; they
were gone and only the rainbow remained, springing from the roof of
the inn, glowing more and more brightly as though it had absorbed into
itself the vanished colors of fairyland.

Faithful might have come to himself at this point, he had indeed already raised his ragged sleeve to wipe the sweat off his forehead and the dreams out of his eyes, but the twins had not returned to normal and had no intention of doing so for a long while yet. "Come on!" they cried, pulling at him. "The rainbow went right down through the roof. The crock's inside! Come on!"

They dragged him over the threshold into the cool, ale-scented darkness of the stone-flagged hall beyond. To their right a door shut off a tumult of sound that was the merrymakers sitting down to a dinner of roast beef to which the ceaseless absorption of cakes and ale through-out the morning had been a mere preliminary. But the twins knew better than to go in there. The crock of gold, they knew, was always buried deep down, and deep down being associated in their minds with darkness they made instantly for the place where the shadows were deepest. . . . Under the old oak stairs that led up to the gallery above.

There was a door there, and they opened it. Spiral stone steps twisted downwards into the depths of the earth, lit by a light that came from somewhere down below, and a strong smell of spirits made them pause and wriggle their noses like inquiring rabbits. "It's only the cellar," said Faithful, and was for going back.

But the twins knew that cellars are the most romantic places in the world. Wonderful things are found in cellars: skeletons, barrels full of rubies and pearls, and crocks of gold. They pattered fearlessly down the steps, clasping their dolls to them, Faithful following be-hind, holding firmly to their skirts lest they should fall and hurt their button noses.

The stairs led them to a narrow passage, dank and musty, lined on each side with bins for the wines. A guttering candle, evidently left there by Mine Host of the Mitre when he fetched the ale for the merrymakers above, stood on the floor and flung their shadows eerily over the damp walls patched with mildew. The little girls blanched at the sight of those leaping shadows, but they did not turn back. In all the best fairy tales the reward is to the courageous, and little girls with fair hair are always supernaturally protected.

The passage turned a sharp corner and led them into pitch darkness. A long way in front of them was a thin line of light, that might have been coming from a door left ajar, or that might again have been a spear held by an archangel, such as Meg had seen when she woke up that morning. They did not know how far away it was, it might have been miles, but they went on towards it, feeling their way cautiously, Meg going first with Bloody outstretched in front of her like a drawn sword.

They reached it, and it was a door. They pushed it open and went in, and were instantly confronted by a blaze of light, all the colors of the rainbow springing upwards in a slender pillar of glory from clustering tongues of flame that burned about its foot like golden flowers, "The foot of the rainbow!" cried the twins, "the foot of the rainbow!" and running forward they fell on their knees before the golden flowers, pointing at them with their fat forefingers, laughing and chattering and exclaiming with that lovely note of sheer delight in their voices that is in the cooing of happy doves and the crowing of young cockerels in the first light of dawn. . . . The fairy tale had come true.

3.

But Faithful, who saw the scene before him as it actually was, stood on the threshold rooted to the spot by a mixture of awe and fear and wonder. He stood in a little vaulted chamber that had once been part of the wine cellar but was now a chapel. In front of him, in an alcove hollowed out of the rough stone wall, stood a richly ornamented altar, hung with fine tapestries and carrying a carved crucifix and some richly gilded figures, and to one side of it, standing well forward in the chapel and challenging attention even before the altar, was that pillar of color before which the twins were kneeling. It was a statue of the Madonna, and perhaps one of the loveliest ever made. Her robes of blue and scarlet hung in lovely folds from shoulder to foot and her face was serene and smiling beneath a jeweled crown that was as bright and golden as the sun itself. She held her babe in a crook of her arm, a lovely golden-haired babe dressed in a little green shift, who laughed and held up two fingers in blessing. A great bunch of spring flowers had been laid on the pedestal at her feet, because May was her own month, and she was the real Queen of the May, and below them burned clusters of candles, their lovely light illumining the rough walls of the chapel and the figures of the saints that stood there in little niches. The smell of incense hung about the place, conquering the smell of must and damp, and a faint blue haze of it clung overhead, almost hiding the shadowy spaces of the vaulted roof and the long silver chain with a small lamp at its end that hung from it, motionless before the altar. . . . . Popery. . . . Nourished upon Foxe's "Book of Martyrs" as he had been Faithful was as bigoted a Protestant as ever stepped. He sank upon a wooden bench near the door with his legs giving way beneath him and the hair of his head rising straight up in horror like the bristles of a disapproving porcupine.

He knew that such places existed, of course. Popery was not stamped out because Queen Mary was dead and Queen Elizabeth sat upon the throne of England; though it was driven underground it lived on; and in these early years of the Queen's reign, before the menace of Spain had turned her tolerance to bitterness, it was still possible for men and women to attend mass without peril, though in secret. The Roman Catholics of Oxford would have been astonished had they known how many of their fellow citizens knew about that chapel beneath the Mitre Inn; knew about it and said nothing.

But to Faithful, with his imagination luridly lit by the flames of Smithfield, it was as though he had fallen straight into the bottomless pit, and when a huge black shadow in a dark corner on the other side of the door uncoiled itself and shot up towards the roof he could have screamed aloud.

But it was not the devil, it was merely a tall young man who had been kneeling in the corner saying his prayers, and who now got up and came and stood beside Faithful, looking down at him in comical bewilderment. "How did you get here?" he whispered. "Did I forget to lock the upstairs door?"

"Yes, good sir," breathed Faithful. . . . As well to be polite, he thought. Otherwise he might be taken off to an adjoining cellar, tied up to a stake and made an end of.

"My absent-mindedness," said the young man, "will be my undo-ing," and he rubbed his chin ruefully.

Reassured by his kindly tone Faithful ventured to take a good look at him. He was dressed as the preacher at the other Chapel of Saint Bartholomew had been dressed, in a white ruff and a long gown, and his fine ascetic face, too, reminded Faithful of that other man, his friend. They were of the same type, he felt. This man was now young and straight and comely but if he too were to suffer persecution he too might become as misshapen as a storm-twisted tree; and yet keep the attraction of anything that stands upon a mountain top. It was odd, thought Faithful, that two such similar men should think so differently about religion; should be ready, as he had no doubt from the look of them that they were, to die for their divergent beliefs. Man was very odd, he thought. But then life was very odd, and became odder and odder the more you thought about it. . . . And it seemed very odd to him that a man who by his dress was evidently a college don should be saying his prayers in a Popish chapel. These things, thought Faithful, ought not so to be. As a prospective and most Protestant scholar he shook his big head in considerable concern, and blushed for the stranger.

But the stranger failed to be shamed by the blush, for he did not see it. He was looking at the two little girls where they still knelt at the feet of the Madonna, holding their dolls in the crooks of their arms as she was holding her baby in the crook of hers, squeaking happily as their fat fingers pointed out to each other all the glories of her lovely clothes and golden crown. "That is a lovely sight," said the stranger.

Faithful thought it was a dreadful sight. There were those two dear little girls, whom he had no doubt were as earnest, orthodox Protes-tants as he was himself, kneeling before a Popish image in the attitude of worship. No doubt, poor little dears, once they had realized that the Madonna was not the foot of the rainbow they thought she was some sort of big doll. . . . But even so he could not forgive himself for having unwittingly conducted two innocent females into this sink of iniquity. . . . The only one of the group by the Madonna whom he could bear to contemplate was the white-faced doll with the black velvet farthingale, the one who had been introduced to him as Bloody Mary. She looked at home. She, he remembered, had gone first down the passage.

"Meg, Joan," said the stranger softly.

They scrambled up from their knees, saw his face smiling kindly at them in the candle-light and flung themselves upon him. "Master Campion!" they cried. "Master Campion!" and pulling him down upon the wooden bench they cuddled up to him, one on each side, with squeaks of pleasure. For beneath all the excitement of their great adventure they had been feeling secretly a little frightened. To find Master Edmund Campion of Saint John's, their father's friend, with them in this strange lost place in the depths of the earth was like seeing the lights of home as one trudged through the rain and the wind on a dark night. Their secret fear, that having once fallen into fairyland they would not be able to scramble out of it again, was stilled. . . . Master Campion would get them out.

"But how did you get here?" he asked in bewilderment.

Meg and Joan burst simultaneously into a long confused narrative about stables and dragons and rainbows and crocks of gold of which Master Campion found himself unable to make head or tail. Faithful, from the other side of Meg, was obliged to chime in and give a lucid account of their adventures from the moment when the littler girls had descended from the stable window until the moment when they had blundered down the dark passage into the chapel in search of the rainbow. He grew pink with shame as he told it. It seemed ridiculous that he, a grown man, should have taken part in so ridiculous a performance. "I hardly knew what I did," he murmured. "I was so confused."

"And footsore and weary?" questioned Master Campion kindly. "And homeless and forespent?"

Faithful hung his head and Master Campion, noting the pallor that had followed the boy's flush, and the dark pits into which his eyes had sunk, lifted Meg on to his knee that he might be nearer to him. "And so it was for you that these children wanted the crock of gold?" he asked. "How would you use the gold if they found it for you?"

"To buy books," whispered Faithful. "I have tramped to Oxford to be a scholar." He spoke hoarsely, and twisted his hands together, for of all the things that had been hard to endure in his life of vagabondage the hardest had been the fact that because he was a vagabond he was never believed. Specious rogues were so numerous that an honest poor man had never a chance of winning faith.

But Master Campion, who himself set great store by books, and who knew the authentic note of yearning when he heard it in another man's voice, believed him. He put Meg down, got up and crossed the chapel floor to the statue of the Madonna. Faithful watched him as he stood there with head bent, and heard the words that he whispered. "Sancta Maria, Mater Dei, ora pro nobis peccatoribus." Then, with a pounding heart, he saw him take something from his wallet and slip it beneath the flowers piled at the Madonna's feet. Then he came back and sat down again at the boy's side.

"Once upon a time," he told Faithful, "there was a poor boy who tramped to Oxford as you have done and became, as you will do, a famous scholar. We call him Saint Edmund. It is a story that every scholar in Oxford knows by heart, for he was the father of us all. I will only tell you this about him, that he loved Mary the Mother of God with a love that was the inspiration of his life, and at her feet he found salvation." He paused, flashed a smile at Faithful and went on again, his eyes on the Madonna. "With her golden crown she has always reminded me of the fair sun, a glory shining forth from Paradise to which we poor shadows are forever flying. But now I shall think of her smiling face as the rainbow, a laughter in the sky that heartens us between storm and storm."

Ten minutes ago Master Campion's heretical remarks would have brought Faithful out in a cold perspiration of horror, but now, sitting there in the dark little chapel, he felt nothing but an overwhelming sense of peace. Wherever men had found God, he supposed, there was always peace, even though the men who searched and found were heretics who extremists thought should be sizzling at the stake. . . . But then he supposed that to Master Campion he himself was a heretic who should be sizzling at the stake. . . . It was all very odd.

"You little girls must be taken home," said Master Campion suddenly and firmly. "I have no doubt that by this time your frantic family has sent the Town Crier out after you."

Meg and Joan slid eagerly to the floor and shook out their skirts, nothing loth. They were tired of fairyland. They were hungry, and there was nothing to eat there.

"Have you forgotten the crock of gold?" asked Master Campion, smiling.

They had quite forgotten it. The astonishment of having the rainbow turn into a beautiful lady with a crown on and a baby in her arms had driven the thought of it out of their minds. But now they remembered it and scuttled eagerly back to the Madonna. "Might it be under the flowers at her feet?" suggested Master Campion. Cautiously, poking their fat hands through the tall pillars of the candles, they lifted the bluebells and kingcups that lay there, and in a moment a chorus of squeaks broke out that for sheer unselfish joy and praise had surely never been equaled even by the Alleluia Chorus of the angels in heaven, even though in musical value theirs was doubtless superior.

For a whole minute they stood there, holding the purse between them, squeaking, picking up the gold pieces and letting them fall back again with delicious chinks. Then they closed the purse and ran to give it to that Younger Son who in the best fairy tales always gets the luck that he deserves.

To Faithful it was too much. In a chapel outside the city gates he had found a friend and in a chapel within the city he had found his crock of gold. In the first chapel he had given away a silver piece, all that he had, and in the second it had come back to him increased a hundredfold. It was too much. He put his ragged sleeve over his eyes and cried.

Master Campion got at the moment no more thanks than that, but he wanted none. Full of the palpitations and misgivings that assail all impulsive givers of indiscriminate charity the moment it is too late to undo what they have done, he busied himself in blowing out the candles burning at the feet of the Madonna, for except for the dim flame of the sanctuary lamp this secret place was always kept dark between the visits of the faithful. Would the boy know how to spend the money wisely? Well, it was too late to think of that now. Had he perhaps done more harm than good? Well, he should have thought of that before. He supposed that he must now see to it that the boy and his money came to no harm. And he was a busy man. He sighed. When would he learn that endless trouble always followed impulsive giving? Then he looked up at the face of the Madonna, smiling dimly in the light of the one remaining candle. You have done no harm, she said. Comforted, he took up the last candle and led the children towards the door.

Two last impressions remained with Faithful as he left that little chapel that he would never see again. One was of his friend's figure becoming once again, in the dimness, that wavering black shadow that he had been when he just saw him; and the other, as the light from the candle shone through the closing door upon the chapel wall, was the sudden shining out in the darkness of a garland of roses and lilies painted there. Someone had once told Faithful that a garland of roses and lilies is the emblem of martyrdom. We are all shadows, his friend had said, flying towards the sun, and those who get there, thought Faithful, pass through flame.

4.

They were out in the High Street and Master Campion, again rubbing his chin ruefully, was wondering aloud what to do with Faithful.

"He must come home with us!" cried the twins, clutching him. "We want him." He was the Younger Son, a fairy-tale figure, and after their journey into fairyland they were not going home without a memento of the visit. "We'll take him home to Father," they added.

Thankful though Master Campion, a busy man, would have been to shift the burden of Faithful on to the shoulders of a busier one, he felt that he must demur, and did so.

"But Father likes poor boys," said the twins, in the same tone of voice in which they would have declared that Father liked sugar plums.

"Father lost one at Saint Bartholomew's this morning. He'd like to have another."

Master Campion still demurred, but a glorious light broke upon Faithful. "Did your father really say that he had lost a boy at Saint Bartholomew's Chapel?" he asked the twins.

"Oh yes," they said. "We prayed about him for hours. Breakfast was very late."

"It was me," said Faithful to Edmund Campion.

In happiness they turned the corner into Fish Street and walked down the hill towards Christ Church. The sun was high in the heavens now and flooded the rain-washed world. Faithful held his head proudly, for now he was going to the house of his friend with money to pay his own way in the world. For the first time in his life he was a gentleman of means.

At the Fair Gate, when Master Campion parted from them, he said simply, "Thank you, good sir," and stood very upright before Campion with his clear eyes looking straight into his and the purse of gold held against his ragged breast with both hands. His attitude, his rags, and the queer look of peace which his face wore, touched the man strangely. He seemed the personification of the perfect pilgrim, unashamed of poverty, taking what wealth might come with gratitude, at peace whether the road were rough or smooth. He would not forget this boy. His image was stamped upon his mind. He paused a moment and then asked what for the sake of others he must ask, though his pride shrank from it. "Can you forget what you have seen?"

Faithful nodded gravely and then looked doubtfully at the two little girls, who were pulling at his jerkin in eagerness to get him home.

"Their narratives are seldom coherent," smiled Campion, "and it will have been to them such an adventure as happens only in dreams; when they wake up it will be hard to remember it."

He smiled and left them, and Faithful lingered a moment to watch his tall dark figure go up the street before he followed the little girls under the lovely gateway of the place that would seem to him forever after the center of the world.

5.

At dinner time it was discovered by their family that the twins had disappeared. They had been last heard of in the loft, from which apparently they had vanished into thin air. Canon Leigh, Joyeuce, Grace, Dorothy and Diggory, gathered together in the hall after a fruitless search in house and garden, faced each other in growing concern while the roast beef, left unregarded on the table, wrapped itself in a gray blanket of congealing fat, and Diccon, also unregarded, helped himself and Tinker to a whole meat pie each.

"Must we starve," demanded Great-Aunt from above, "because two naughty little poppets are momentarily mislaid?" And she thumped upon her windowsill with the handle of her knife. . . . And at the same moment there came a thumping on the old front door that sent the whole household as one man to lift the latch.

Outside upon the doorstep stood the twins and Faithful, in a great state of dirt and dishevelment; aprons awry, faces smeared, Bloody and Bess by no means as queenly as they had been; but beaming with the joy and pride of successful accomplishment.

A perfect tornado of reunion now broke out; the twins were hugged and kissed, Faithful, hanging back in shamefaced uncertainty, was pulled over the threshold by Canon Leigh as though he were the returned prodigal son and had the door slammed behind him by Grace as though she meant him to stay forever, the dogs barked, Diccon shouted, everyone talked at once and Great Tom boomed forth eleven o'clock from the Cathedral tower.

"And now," ejaculated Great-Aunt icily into a sudden moment of silence, "may I request that I be served with my dinner?"

AGES PAST

As if, when after Phoebus is descended,
And leaves a light much like the past day's dawning,
And, every toil and labour wholly ended,
Each living creature draweth to his resting,
We should begin by such a parting light
To write the story of all ages past.
And end the same before th'approaching night.

WALTER RALEIGH.

1.

ALL day under the hot sun the citizens had celebrated May-Day with enthusiasm, clamor and heat, yet when evening came down through the woods of Shotover, passed under the East Gate and stole into the city, a hush fell; they were all tired; they trailed thankfully back to their houses, kindled log fires against the coming of night, loosened their doublets and waistbands and put their feet up on the hob.

Under the Fair Gate of Christ Church Heatherthwayte the porter also loosened his doublet, stretched his legs and yawned, while at his feet his dog Satan, a black and woolly person with plumed heraldic legs, lay down to snatch a little slumber. They had had an exhausting day. Keeping the scholars in and the merrymakers out had taxed their powers to the uttermost and they felt themselves entitled to a little slumber.

Heatherthwayte, his hands folded on his stomach, snored. His snore was one of the well-known noises of Christ Church, and only a little less impressive than his laugh, a loud, deep roar that reverberated under the

Fair Gate like thunder. When Heatherthwayte was amused the whole College knew it. He had a figure like Falstaff's through which his laugh rumbled and rolled for a long time before it emerged through his gigantic mouth. His large, bushy red beard, when laughed into, seemed to act like a megaphone and increased the noise tenfold.

It was not often that Heatherthwayte slept, for he and Satan found their life an interesting one. Life flowed round them in full tide, all the many streams in their splendid variety running together into one rich flood of community life. Heatherthwayte, though one of the streams himself, was yet always conscious of a certain detachment. He watched and he listened. He scanned the faces that went in and out and heard the talk that flowed past him; they were his books and his lectures and he learned them well. These scholars might study their Latin and Greek, their Law, their Medicine and their Astronomy, but Heatherthwayte in his study of human nature thought he had the advantage of them. For amusement, for edification and for an Awful Warning, said Heatherthwayte, and Satan entirely agreed with him, give them Men as a branch of learning any day.

Satan did not spend quite so much time in study as Heatherthwayte did for he had a good deal of work to do. He was a very important member of the community whose duty it was to keep the quadrangle clear of sheep and cattle and hogs; no easy task in high summer when these poor animals, driven into the city from the country for slaughter, and feeling hot and thirsty and afraid, saw through the Fair Gate the grass of the quadrangle waving high and tall and set with moon-daisies and golden lady's-slippers.

Then he had to keep his eye upon human beings as well as animals. He knew quite well who had the right to canter his horse across the quadrangle and tie it to the iron ring in the east wall, and those who had not the right and yet presumed through ignorance or criminal cheek found themselves attacked under the Fair Gate by a satanic animal of great power and size, and the din of clattering hoofs and wild barking that echoed through the precincts was shattering if you were not used to it. Satan knew, too, that the laundresses might fetch the scholars' dirty linen between eight and ten on Monday morning and return it between two and four on Saturday afternoon, but they might not come at any time but they might not venture inside the Fair Gate. The College servitors brought the linen to the Gate and received it again, and Satan kept a careful eye upon proceedings. The apple-women, too, might come no further than the Fair Gate, and Satan bit their ankles if they tried to. . . . So what with one thing and another he got quite tired sometimes, and was glad when the western sky was a sheet of gold behind Saint Aldate's and in the quadrangle the shadows spread deep pools of quietness.

"Heatherthwayte! Heatherthwayte!"

The porter and his dog both opened a reluctant eye, then sat up in brisk attention. Joyeuce, her afternoon farthingale of peacock blue held well up on each side so that she looked like a winged creature, and her slender feet in their little red shoes poised tiptoe on the cobbles as though she had alighted on them for a moment only, was standing breathlessly before them. A little bunch of violets stuck in the bodice of her dress, that lay so flat over her still childish figure, rose and fell agitatedly and she was so pale that her face looked like ivory against the black velvet coif that curved about it. Heatherthwayte and Satan, expecting to hear some pitiful tale of death and disaster in the Leigh household, rose instantly to their feet, ready to fly off upon the instant to fetch the Physician, the Undertaker, the Constable of the Watch, or even the Vice Chancellor himself should the tragedy that had occurred prove too great for alleviation by the lesser brethren. . . . Heatherthwayte and Satan loved the Leigh children very dearly and there was absolutely nothing they were not prepared to do for them.

"There now, mistress! Tell Heatherthwayte!" implored that worthy, his tenderness reverberating upwards through his vocal cords and booming out through his great beard very comfortingly. Satan, producing a long pink loving tongue from behind the fierce barricade of his teeth, passed it consolingly over Joyeuce's hand and suggested with a circular motion of his tail that nothing was ever as bad as it seemed. . . . A little color crept into Joyeuce's face and she found her voice.

"At seven o'clock," she whispered, "if you see a—a—gentleman waiting about please will you tell him that I—I—must not come?" And at that, with a light patter of feet and a swish of silk, she took flight and vanished, leaving behind her a little breath of scent from the bunch of violets that had tumbled out of her dress as she ran.

Heatherthwayte lowered himself back on to his seat, flung back his head and laughed, showing all his strong white teeth and a cavernous expanse of throat, his merry little eyes disappearing among the rolls of fat into which his face folded itself in moments of mirth. . . . So she was growing up, was she? . . . He remembered the winter night six years ago when the Leighs had first come to Christ Church. It had been wild and wet and he had hurried out from under the Fair Gate with his lantern when he heard the clatter of their horses' hoofs. The little Joyeuce had been riding pillion behind her father and he had himself lifted her down. She had been so cold and stiff that when he tried to set her on the ground her legs had doubled up beneath her and he had picked her up, he remembered, and carried her into the house, and she had thanked him very prettily. A thin, white faced, good little waif she had been even then, though not quite so good and white faced as she had become after her mother died.

Heatherthwayte suddenly ceased laughing and shook his head gravely. . . . These good, motherless little maidens were no judge of men. . . . He, Heatherthwayte, who reverenced the memory of Mistress Leigh, must keep his weather eye open.

He began at once, rolling it this way and that as scholars and towns-people strolled by in the quadrangle or the street, and by the time seven o'clock boomed out from the Cathedral, and Nicolas appeared in a leaf-green doublet and a nut-brown cloak, he was in quite a perspiration of worry and fuss. . . . But it was relieved by the sight of Nicolas, for Heatherthwayte, possessed of some occult power by which he knew the ancestry, character and goings on of every man in College simply by sitting still on a bench under the Fair Gate, was particularly fond of Nicolas. It was true the young gentleman was over quick with a word or a blow, and had a much higher opinion of himself than there was really any need for, but he had a sense of humor and his generosity was un-bounded. Many an escapade of Nicolas's had Heatherthwayte hushed up and many a round gold piece had found its way from Nicholas's pocket to Heatherthwayte's ready palm, their affection for each growing with every secret shared and coin added to Heatherthwayte's bank balance under his flock mattress. . . . It was his intention to retire one day, a wealthy man waxed fat upon the evil deeds of Christ Church scholars.

"Ah!" he ejaculated sepulchrally, when after five minutes Nicolas was still there, stamping up and down and snorting, and he rolled one eye and closed the other. Satan, his head on one side, thumped his tail on the ground and made curious noises in his throat.

"He's talking," said Heatherthwayte.

"Who's talking?" snapped Nicolas.

"Satan," said Heatherthwayte. "He has a fellow feeling, as you might say. His own fancy, a water spaniel up High Street, is very fanciful in her ways at times."

Nicolas swore loudly, though swearing was forbidden by the College regulations, and stamped up and down with increasing warmth, for he was not accustomed to being kept waiting by ladies on whom he had cast a favorable eye. He frequently kept them waiting—it was good for them—but such were his attractions that the reverse was seldom the case.

"I was to tell you," said Heatherthwayte, "that Mistress Joyeuce Leigh is kept at home. . . . And those," he added, pointing a horny finger at the little bunch of violets on the cobbles, "are all the company of hers that she can give you."

"She left them for me?" asked Nicolas.

"She did," said Heatherthwayte, casting up his eyes to heaven and wiping a tear from his eye. "Kissed them and laid them there where they lie now, right in the middle of the Fair Gate where I've had all the trouble in the world to prevent the whole College trampling on 'em. . . . . But if you show yourself unworthy of them violets," continued Heatherthwayte with some heat, "it's me you'll have to reckon with, young man; me, Thomas Elias Heatherthwayte."

"Mind your own business," snapped Nicolas; but he picked up the violets and stuck them in his doublet.

"It'll be her father that's kept her," consoled Heatherthwayte, quite melted by this display of sensibility. "But if you was to turn to the left and stroll down Fish Street, sir, you could see her through the parlor window."

"I am not asking you for your advice, Heatherthwayte," said Nicolas with dignity, and with his head thrown back and his lips pursed in a whistle he sauntered out of the Fair Gate, turned to the right and strolled up towards the town. . . . However, in another ten minutes Heatherthwayte saw him strolling down again on the other side of the road. . . . Heatherthwayte chortled into his beard and pushed Satan slyly with his feet, Satan responding with a thud of his tail and a glint in his eye.

2.

Nicolas crossed the road diagonally and glanced with a great assumption of carelessness through the Leigh parlor window. The fire danced gaily and a little mouse sat washing itself in the middle of the floor; but there was no one else there. Infuriated, Nicolas strolled on under South Gate and down the street towards the river and Folly Bridge. He felt sore and angry and tantalized. . . . Under the Fair Gate nothing but a bunch of violets and in the parlor nothing but a mouse. . . . Man cannot live by bread alone and neither do flowers and a mouse give any permanent satisfaction. He was aware of wanting something that was not being given to him and he was not used to not having what he wanted. He felt hot inside and his throat tickled. He kicked savagely at the refuse in the street and splashed noisily through the puddles; until it struck him that he was behaving like a six-year-old and he was obliged to laugh at himself, his eyes narrowed as he looked up at the quietness of the evening sky.

The wind had dropped but the clouds were still moving slowly, drifted by the memory of it; their creamy whiteness a little flushed, as though the memory was a good one. The trees in the Christ Church meadows, nearer to the peace of the earth and more easily stilled, were motionless, spreading their green shelter over the early fritillaries. From where he stood, leaning over Folly Bridge, Nicolas could not see the fritillaries, but he knew where they grew, in faint drifts of color between the brazen kingcups, the curve of their bell heads the most delicate thing on earth. In the far distance were the lovely shapes of low hills, blue and intensely quiet, resting against the sky. Under his feet the water slipped, running very quietly because it had been a dry spring, passing from Godstow to Iffley, and on through the meadows to the towers and spires of the city of London. There were not many buildings beyond South Gate, only Saint Michael's at the South Gate and a few houses round it, and there was little to interrupt the view of Christ Church that showed the tower of the Cathedral rising superbly above the splendid stretch of the hall roof. . . . A bell was ringing in the town and in the trees by the river the blackbirds called, yet the bell and the bird song seemed more the voice of silence than of actual music. . . . A strange sound, harsh yet with a quality in its beating, rhythmical strength that made one's heart leap up in delight, made him look up. Six swans were flying one behind the other, necks stretched out and great wings rising and falling, white against the blue of the sky. They flew right over the roofs of the city, calm, determined and unhurried, and when the sound of their passing had died away the silence seemed absolute.

3.

The processional passing had been like the passing of humanity itself, Nicolas thought, and he began to think dreamily of all the men and women who in their journey from birth to death had passed through this city.

Nicolas, though he was generally too busy enjoying himself to pay much attention to it, had imagination, and on the rare occasions when he found himself with nothing better to do he would let it open its wings and carry him away. It was that rare brand of imaginative power that can leave self entirely out of the picture, so that Nicolas's dream figures did not crowd about him playing a petty drama of which he was himself the hero, and completely obstructing the view, but passed distantly by in pomp and beauty like clouds across the sky. Standing well back from them he could see them without their surface imperfections; grand figures who had each his appointed place in the pageant of history.

The road where Nicolas stood was the oldest road in Oxford and had been there before the city itself. It appeared out of the shadows of Bagley Forest, rolled across the meadows, humped itself to pass over the bridge and then disappeared under South Gate into the city; and down it came marching the figures that Nicolas dreamed of.

In the vanguard came the handful of wild men who had first looked with favor upon this bit of earth, the hunters who had noticed a patch of dry ground between the rivers and marked it down as a place of security where a home could be made. The rivers were the city wall, a protection against possible enemies; within it rose a village of rough huts and thin spirals of blue smoke found their way through the mist of the willow trees and rose up into the air to tell the world that Oxford was born. . . . Not that there was anyone likely to pay much attention; only the wolves and the boars, the wild birds and the fishes, and the blue hills that stood around the valley where the rivers ran.

The hunters thrived in their village. They took to themselves wives and their little children played among the willows, and picked armfuls of the water plants that grew everywhere like a thick carpet, and laughed to see the sunset and the sunrise reflected in the streams and pools that paved the valley. . . . Up in the blue hills the Roman legions passed and re-passed but if they saw the thin spirals of blue smoke they did not think them worthy of attention. . . . But if the legions neglected them the missionaries did not. Augustine the Roman had landed in England with the good news of Christianity and the knowledge of it came down the waterways to Oxford.

The hunters were secure enough now to think of other things besides their daily food. They built a fine house for their king Didanus and on the spot where later the Cathedral stood they built a nunnery for his daughter Frideswide. This very road where Nicolas stood ran by it from the ford below to the rising ground above where four ways met, and round this nucleus of a nunnery, a street and a little hill, grew first churches and houses within a city wall, then a Norman castle, then a great Augustinian Abbey outside the city, then the royal palaces of Beaumont and Woodstock.

Oxford was now a place of importance, favored by royalty, and magnificent figures passed by in her pageant: kings and princes, noblemen and men-at-arms, with colored cloaks over their armor, clattered through the narrow streets and rode in gallant companies in and out of the gates of the city; priests bowed before the altars in the churches, saying masses for the souls of the dead who had already passed by to the tolling of the bell, and candles burned before the shrines of the saints; the sound of chanting drifted out into the streets to mingle with the clattering of horses' hoofs upon the cobbles and the shrill cries of peddlers, tinkers, merchant apprentices, thieves and vagabonds.

Then came the great merchants, figures of importance who sunned themselves upon their doorsteps, hands folded over portly stomachs, or strolled with patronage over the cobbled streets, holding up their fine furred gowns out of the way of the mud and refuse that strewed them. They were now the princes of Oxford, they and the swarthy financiers who by day issued forth from the Jewish quarter in the heart of the city, one of the wealthiest Jewries in England, and strolled through the streets in their yellow gabardines, and at night sat in dark little rooms lit by rushlights and counted their gold with a kindling eye. Their magnificent Guilds were the glory of Oxford: the Weavers, the Shoemakers, the Glovers, the Barbers, the Tailors, the Goldsmiths, the Corporation of Cooks; they had their revels and their processions, when they paraded the city on horseback with drums beating and torches burning, and they had their special chapels in the different churches, where they burned candles and celebrated mass. The commerce of southern England mainly flowed through the Thames valley and people would stand on the bridge outside South Gate, where Nicolas stood now, and watch the great barges of the merchants passing up and down the river.

These merchants and financiers had it all their own way at first and perhaps they hardly noticed, as they picked their way up the winding High Street in their fine gowns, groups of badly dressed, hungry looking youths crowded together round some narrow entry listening to the words of an older man, lean and poor as themselves, who stood above them on the steps. They would scatter when the merchant barged carelessly in amongst them but they would come back again when he had passed, for the teacher on the steps had food for their minds if not for their bodies and what shall it profit a man if he gain the whole world and lose his own soul? A new Guild was struggling into being, a Guild of Learning that was to be the greatest of all the Guilds and crowd the others almost out of existence; the merchants and the Jews, cursing the ragged scholars who got in their way, did not as yet consider it worth their attention.

They knew, of course, that learning, hitherto confined to the cloister, where in their opinion it should have remained, was creeping out into the world. It was partly their own doing, for the flourishing state of trade had brought a tranquillity in which men's thoughts turned to the things of the mind, but it was also the doing of Henry Beauclerc the scholar king, who had built Beaumont Palace, and of his grandson Henry the Second, who took it into their heads to become the champions of literary culture. . . . Learning was becoming the fashion. . . . The merchants shook their heads in some disgust at the distressing and effeminate trend of the times, but did not yet realize the tremendous significance of this invasion of their commercial city by a handful of ragged scholars.

But when the handful turned into a horde who blocked up the narrow entries, fought at street corners, got drunk in the taverns and turned the whole place into a Tower of Babel by arguing all day and all night about the existence of God in half a dozen different languages, the merchants made a few disgusted inquiries and found that most of these rogues and vagabonds had come from the University of Paris. France had suddenly become tired of foreign students within her borders and had ejected the lot. In steadily increasing numbers bands of them had crossed the Channel, landed at Dover and marched northwards, billeting themselves upon monasteries and ecclesiastics and eating them out of house and home as they went. They might have settled down at Canterbury, Lambeth or Saint Albans, and the Oxford merchants heartily wished they had, but it was Oxford that drew them; Oxford with her wealthy Guilds, her Royal Palace, her Priory of Saint Frideswide, her churches and fine houses within the city wall, her river winding through the valley between green willows, and all protected from winter storms by a rampart of low hills and dense forests.

The majority of these scholars were English, for it was with the English and their treatment of Thomas à Becket that France was particularly enraged, but scholars from other European universities had come too; for the mediaeval scholars and masters had the migratory habits of birds and if insulted in one university bands of them would indignantly snatch up their books and decamp halfway across Europe to a second, upon which they would settle like locusts until the fancy took them to cross the sea and swoop down upon some protesting city where could be laid the foundations of yet a third.

The Guild of Learning grew with strength and determination into Oxford University. Pious founders established halls where the scholars could be housed and one by one these elbowed their way up between the houses and the church towers, even as more and more hungry looking scholars elbowed their way through the narrow streets. . . . And the merchants resented this invasion with a fury that lasted for centuries. . . . But neither their fury, nor that of the Jews, had any effect whatever. Upon this spot of earth between the waters men had fought first for security, then for wealth, and now for knowledge, and it was the seekers after knowledge who stood triumphant in final possession.

And now to the figures of Kings and Queens, Merchants and Financiers and triumphant Scholars, passing by in procession, were added the cowled figures of the Friars. Learning had found its way out from the cloister into the world and after it came the monks themselves. New orders were founded of brethren who should tramp the streets of the cities and give their lives to the service of the poor. In the overcrowded slums of Oxford, where filthy narrow lanes, heaped with rubbish, wound between hovels where the rush-strewn floors were never cleansed and leprosy and plague were familiar guests, went the barefoot followers of Dominic and Francis. Order after order founded its house at Oxford: the Grey Friars, the Black Friars, the Carmelites, the Brothers of the Sack and the Crossed Friars soon became as familiar figures in the Oxford streets as the scholars themselves. At first they were content to be unlearned men, vowed to poverty, but later, longing for converts among the scholars as well as among the poor, and finding the love of learning infectious, they too became members of its Guild. They laid aside their poverty to accept gifts of money and land that they might build schools and halls and libraries where friars from all over Europe might come and study. ... From where Nicolas stood he could see the little gatehouse built over the archway of South Gate that had been the study of Friar Bacon the Franciscan scientist, where, so Nicolas had been told, he had written his great books and raised the devil. ... The old religious orders followed the example of the friars, founding halls for their student monks, and the University suffered a monastic invasion.

At first it was pleased, but later, as more and more cowled figures jostled the secular scholars in the streets, grabbed the best seats at lectures, and argued, as only ecclesiastics can argue, about this and that and the other till everyone's head went round, it was as indignant as the merchants had been when the vagabonds from Paris descended upon them out of the blue. A state of war was declared between the secular and religious scholars and went cheerily raging on until, with another cycle completed, the times were ripe for yet another new birth.

It was called the New Learning and it arrived as unobtrusively as the University itself had done. Fifteenth-century Oxford scholars were shocked by the news that the Turks had taken Constantinople, the eastern home of learning and philosophy, and then they thought no more about it and went back to their squabbles and their Aristotle, their horses and dogs and dinner. But meanwhile a handful of scholars had again snatched up their books and migrated halfway across Europe; this time fugitives flying from Constantinople to Rome, bringing with them a few rescued manuscripts and the wisdom of Greece. Italy flung herself eagerly upon the New Learning, and while her scholars were learning Greek, and rescuing the thought of the ancient world from oblivion, Germany was inventing the art of printing that should diffuse it through the world.

And now renowned and learned men took their part in the pageant, the men who brought the New Learning to Oxford, almost contemporary figures who were not lost in the mists of past ages but walked in the sunlight, plain to see. Cardinal Wolsey and Thomas More were among them, with Erasmus the Dutchman and the humbler figure of Haddon Rood of Cologne who set up Oxford's first printing press.

In Oxford the Renaissance chiefly took the form of a religious revival; it meant the study of the New Testament in Greek, a getting back to the original truth of things that had been obscured by medieval accretions of ignorance and superstition; it meant, through the printing press, a New Testament in the hand of everyone who could learn to read. The good news of this new birth seemed to its messengers more glorious than any that had gone before, for how could there ever again be war or wickedness or degradation, these scholars asked each other, when it would soon be possible for every man, woman and child to read with their own eyes the record of the life of the Son of God? "I would have those words translated into all languages," wrote Erasmus, "so that not only Scots and Irishmen, but Turks and Saracens might read them. I long for the plowboy to sing them to himself as he follows the plow, the weaver to hum them to the tune of his shuttle, the traveler to beguile with them the dullness of his journey. Other studies we may regret having undertaken, but happy is the man upon whom death comes when he is engaged in these. These sacred words give you the very image of Christ speaking, healing, dying, rising again, and make Him so present that were He before your very eyes you would not more truly see Him."

And for a little while it seemed that the Golden Age was on the way, for all over the world Oxford was now famed for her beauty and her learning. The greatest scholars of Europe were amazed at her loveliness; the woods and streams and meadows outside her walls, the great churches with their wonderful stained glass and treasures of gold and silver, the abbeys with their hospitals and priceless libraries, and the beautiful Colleges that were still rising gloriously.

One of the fairest of these was Wolsey's Cardinal College at Oxford, which he built as a home of the New Learning. He built his quadrangle of stone from Headington that in its freshness gleamed gold in the sun and white in the moonlight, like the Acropolis at Athens, and he embellished it with every lovely art that man could devise. To the south was the great dining hall where a hundred and one men, Dean and scholar Canons, could feast royally in the intervals of applying themselves to learning, and to the east the priory of Saint Frideswide became the Cathedral church, where chaplains, lay clerks and choristers were to praise and worship God with fitting glory and honor.

In his imagination Nicolas saw the quadrangle of his College full of an army of ghosts, busy architects, masons, carpenters, artists, glaziers, scholars in their long gowns and round-faced cherubic choristers; and in and out among them, cheering, inspiring and commanding, moved the portly figure of the great Cardinal, clothed in scarlet and mounted on a palfrey.

But upon this busy and happy scene there entered an ominous figure; a vulgar bloated man with a paunch and swollen legs, the predatory monster into whom the charming young Henry Tudor had unaccountably developed. He entered magnificently, clothed in crimson and gold that accentuated the imperfections of his figure, with trumpets blowing and drums sounding, with a gorgeous retinue and the assumption of geniality and friendship; but his coming was as destructive to Oxford as an earthquake.

For the mania of the King's Grace for matrimony, and the consequent habit of marrying one wife while her predecessor was still alive, led to a quarrel with the Pope and the denial of his authority in England, while the failure of Cardinal Wolsey to secure a divorce for Henry brought about his own downfall and that of his College. The wealth of the monasteries, that formed so large a part of the treasure of Oxford, was at the mercy of the King's greed, he being now by his own appointment head of the Church, and those of her sons who dared stand firm for Pope and conscience were doomed.

Oxford endured loss upon loss: the death of Wolsey, who, when in his last days he bethought him of his not yet completed College, "could not sleep for the thought of it and could not write for weeping and sorrow"; the execution of Thomas More, once High Steward of Oxford and always her friend; the destruction of the religious houses; the looting of the churches and libraries; the impoverishment of the people and the destruction of laughter and the singing voice.

But the monster had a certain reputation as an enlightened patron of learning and having dissolved Cardinal College, sold its lands to hungry courtiers, stolen the Cathedral vestments and ornaments and swept away its greatest treasure, the Shrine of Saint Frideswide, he bethought himself of this reputation and set to work to build up another College on the foundations of the old. He united the episcopal see with the collegiate foundation and called it Christ Church. The foundation consisted of a Dean and eight Canons, including three Regius Professors, a hundred scholars, twenty-four servants and officers and twenty-four bedesmen. Life of a sort flowed into it again. Laughter rang out once more in the quadrangle and the sound of chanting drifted out from the Cathedral. . . . It was the germ of the College that Nicolas knew and loved.

But the Guild of Learning, that had lain sick unto death while libraries were sacked and churches despoiled, was given only a short breathing space of peace. Men were learning to adjust themselves, to rejoice that a foreign Pope could no longer command their allegiance, to become firmly set in new convictions that suited the temperament of an independent people, when Queen Mary the bigot, daughter of one Spaniard and destined wife of another, came to the throne set upon the reversal of all her father's actions, and the tide of persecution turned and flowed back again. For three and a half years it swept through Oxford in a horror of blood and fire. The English Bibles that Erasmus had hoped to see in the hands of every plowboy, weaver and traveler were burned in the market place, the martyrs were dragged through the streets to be burned at the stake outside North Gate and men's hearts failed them for fear. The choice of those who could not change their convictions to order was between exile and the stake and men who, like Gervas Leigh, were finally able to escape to loneliness and poverty abroad counted themselves the favored of fortune. England was no longer a country fit to live in. It had neither unity nor spirit. To all intents and purposes it was a province of Spain.

But every horror and stupidity has its ending and peace comes back. One dark morning in November the citizens of Oxford woke to hear the bells ringing. What was it? It was not May-Day for the damp fogs of winter were gathering thickly upon them, and it was not yet Christmas; and there seemed little in the life of this tormented city upon which it could congratulate itself. Then the word went round—the Queen was dead. From every tower in Oxford the bells rang out: the bells of Christ Church and Saint Mary the Virgin, the bells of Saint Martin's and Saint Michael's at the North Gate, of All Saints', Saint Aldate's and Saint Ebbe's; the foggy air seemed alive with their joy and clamor. People ran out into the streets, laughing and exclaiming. They told each other that the birds were singing as though it were spring. Surely, they said, this new age would be a time of resurrection from the horrors that were past. . . . One name was on all their lips. . . . Elizabeth. . . . The Queen was dead. . . . Long live the Queen. . . . The bells rang out afresh and the sun broke through the clouds.

To Nicolas this was contemporary history. Englishmen had turned in something like despair to a young woman for salvation and she had not disappointed them. The worst horrors of religious persecution were over and laughter and the singing voice were coming back.

It was yet another period of renewal for Oxford. The scholars who had gone into exile returned rejoicing and with quiet minds and hopeful hearts looked again for the Golden Age. To their eyes Oxford had clothed herself in a fresh beauty, though it seemed to them a frightened loveliness, as though in remembering past violence that men had committed against her she feared for yet worse at their hands in years to come.

But for the moment there seemed nothing but good. To Oxford's great profit the Queen's Grace was a lover of learning and was herself no mean scholar; and having found much delight in learning it was her pleasure that others should do the same. In past years Oxford scholars had seldom been drawn from the nobility but now, goaded to it by the Queen herself, young gentlemen of birth were presenting themselves at the University, to get a little something into their heads if possible and to enjoy themselves at all costs. The Queen's Grace was taking a particular interest in Christ Church, the College founded by her father. She had appointed Thomas Godwin, "a tall and comely person" much in favor with her, to be its Dean* and she assigned certain of the Christ Church studentships to boys educated at her own royal foundation of Saint Peter's Westminster. The vanguard of a long line of pilgrims from Westminster to Christ Church were in these later days traveling over hill and dale and knocking for admittance at the gates of the College. . . . They were the last figures in Nicolas's dream pageant and as they clattered by him it seemed to him that they picked him up and carried him with them under South Gate and up the street to Christ Church. It was a surprise to him to find himself standing quite alone outside the Fair Gate.

It was late; night had draped the sky in violet shadows and one star burned in the sky. The ghosts had vanished and the curfew that rang out now into the silence was a bell that tolled for their passing. Nicolas, as he turned in under the Gate, was not quite sure if he were the last mourner in a funeral procession or the first messenger who comes hard upon its heels with the tidings of a new birth. The violets that he still held crushed in his hand were the color of sorrow, but their scent was the scent of the spring.

---

*Note. The Queen continued to take an interest in the Deans of Christ Church, particularly if good looking, for "she loved good parts well, but better when in a goodly person." Thomas Godwin remained in favor until he insisted upon pleasing himself rather than the Queen's Grace in the matter of his second marriage, when Her Majesty became "alienated." With only one Dean, Richard Cox, it is recorded that she seriously fell out, and then only after she had made him a bishop and he had dared to differ from her in regard to her plans for his garden. "Proud Prelate," she wrote, "you know what you were before I made you; if you do not immediately comply with my request, by God, I will unfrock you. Elizabeth."

CHAPTER V

THE TEACHERS ON THE STEPS

Where man's mind hath a freed consideration,
Of goodness to receive lovely direction;
Where senses do behold th'order of heavenly host,
And wise thoughts do behold what the Creator is.
Contemplation here holdeth his only seat,
Bounded with no limits, borne with a wing of hope,
Climbs even unto the stars.

PHILIP SIDNEY.

1.

THE June sun, flinging a shower of gold in at the uncurtained window, rescued Faithful from an unpleasant dream in which he was still a chimney sweep and was stuck in a loathsome pitch black chimney, unable to get either up or down. He woke up still bowed down by that awful sense of oppression and filth, and it was with amazement that he found himself lying in a pool of golden light, and stretching his body found himself free and unfettered. . . . Then he remembered where he was. . . . In one of the scholars' rooms at Christ Church, a room that he shared with Giles Leigh.

The windows faced east and sitting up on his flock mattress, hugging his knees, he looked out across the quadrangle to the tower of Christ Church outlined sharply against the sheeted gold of the sunrise. He could tell by the feel of the cold air that it was very early yet and he need not get up for a little while. . . . He could sit and gloat.

He was a scholar of Christ Church. He had got what he wanted and he was so utterly and completely happy that he felt as though he had been born again. He realized that his experience was unique, that not many people got what they longed for, or if they did get it liked it when they had it. He was intensely grateful to whatever gods there were that he had been allowed this satisfaction. Perhaps, he thought, his present joys would not always satisfy; there would be fresh hungers, and he would set out on new journeys towards goals that he might never reach; but at least, he thought, the fact that he had once been satisfied made life worth while. Nothing in life, he thought, is so lovely as fresh beginnings, and nothing breeds more courage. He saw all the fresh beginnings in a man's life burning like prophetic torches along the way, beckoning him on, crying aloud the good news in the charactery of flame upon darkness, and the little figure of man passing from darkness into light and then into darkness again, until it disappeared at the end of the journey into a blaze of light to which those torches that had seemed so bright were as night's candles to the light of day.

The power of the sun increased, wrapping him round with its warmth, filling the room with beams of light that were like pointing fingers showing him all the furnishings of the room, severely practical furnishings that yet seemed fine to Faithful because they were bathed in the glamour of his new life.

There were the two narrow truckle beds in the further corners of the room, each with "bedding sufficient and meet for one man," with the chest between them where Giles and Faithful kept "the honest apparel and comely for a scholar" insisted upon by authority. The room had two windows and in each of them stood a combined bookshelf and desk. At them Faithful and Giles would work for hours on end, straining to catch the last hours of daylight. There were a couple of stools in the room and a second chest containing bows and arrows, lanterns, snuffers and bellows. . . . That was all. . . . And Faithful, whose business it was to do the housework, but who as a scholar of Christ Church was more interested in the things of the mind, thought it quite enough.

It had not been so difficult, after all, to give him his heart's desire. For a week after his arrival he and Canon Leigh spent every free moment locked in the latter's study hammering at the classics, very often late into the night, so that Joyeuce thought they would kill each other with overwork, and protested through the keyhole with loud protestations that were taken no notice of. Faithful had an amazing memory and Canon Leigh was astonished at all he had remembered from his early days at Westminster; it made a very considerable foundation stone on which to erect new knowledge. At the end of the week Faithful had an extra good wash, rubbed himself all over with civet so that he should smell nice, arrayed himself in the new clothes purchased out of his crock of gold and was hailed by Canon Leigh before the Dean to show what he could do. Standing in Dean Godwin's study, with his legs planted far apart and his hands behind his back, quite unabashed and unafraid, he had shown what he could do to some purpose. Set to dispute in Latin he went on so long that the panting Dean raised an imploring hand and begged him to stop. His Greek seemed to the Dean to be better than his own and what he didn't know about astronomy was not worth knowing. His arithmetic made one dizzy and his rhetoric was without blemish. . . . Only about music he knew nothing at all; his singing voice being like a donkey's and his ear, in spite of its physical size, being non-existent in the musical sense. . . . Nevertheless it was clear that the boy was a genius.

"Take him away, for the love of heaven," said the Dean to Canon Leigh, wiping his brow, "he makes me positively ill. Had it not been for his ignorance of music I should have died."

So that was the first difficulty surmounted.

Then came the question of ways and means, for though the crock of gold went far it did not go the whole way. This was got over by making Faithful Giles' servitor. It was usual for a well-to-do scholar, a nobleman or squire's son, to come up to the University accompanied by a poorer friend, the son of his village parson perhaps, who would act as his servitor and share his room, his food and his work, and so live almost free of charge. So Faithful became Giles' servitor: kept his room in order, ran his errands, delivered his clothes to the washer-woman at the Fair Gate, dusted his books, saw that his bows and arrows were in good condition and concocted frightful medicines for him when his food disagreed with him. All this Faithful, a born hero-worshiper, found very agreeable, and Giles, born to be worshiped, found it agreeable too.

At the moment there was nothing to be seen of Giles but a confused heap of arms and legs under the bedclothes and the back of his dark head on the pillow. Giles, who did everything with thoroughness, slept so deeply that he might have been dead, but Faithful, looking at him and thinking of him, saw in imagination his paragon parading the room in all his princely beauty and arrogance.

He was the most strictly beautiful of all the Leighs. He had Joyeuce's grace and height, his father's perfect features and Grace's dark hair and blue eyes. But in everything he progressed a little further in beauty than they did. He was taller than Joyeuce and far more graceful, being without that stiff bracing of the figure that marred Joyeuce's carriage, for, unlike her, he met the shocks and jars of life with a strong will rather than taut nerves. His features, though the same as his father's, were more sharply cut, flawless yet without a soft line anywhere, for hesitancy was unknown to him. He was acutely sensitive yet his sensitiveness was of a different kind from his father's and Joyeuce's, being entirely of the mind and not of the imagination. He could detect any smallest undercurrent of meaning in the printed argument or the spoken disputation but he had not the slightest idea when he was, or was not, trampling upon a person's feelings. His intellect had developed far in advance of the rest of him. It was like a flame in which every desire but the desire for learning was burned to ashes. A brilliant future was foretold for him. He worked in a way that caused the adoring Faithful to shake his huge head in considerable concern, for Faithful in his multifarious experiences had acquired a sense of proportion. Giles worked nearly all night sometimes. Anyone would have thought he had heard, from several centuries ahead, the advice given by Cyril Jackson, Dean of Christ Church: "Work very hard and unremittingly. Work like a tiger or like a dragon, if dragons work more and harder than tigers. Don't be afraid of killing yourself." . . . And Giles wasn't. . . . But yet with all this he was not so fine a scholar as Faithful for he lacked Faithful's humility. Erasmus's daily prayer, that God would give to him a sense of ignorance, would have seemed wisdom to Faithful but tomfoolery to the arrogant Giles.

A well aimed shoe hit Faithful on the head and sent him bounding from bed like a jack-in-the-box. He had been almost asleep again and Giles was the first to be out of bed and standing in the sunshine, his lean brown body perfect as that of a young god but his temper entirely human.

"You sleep like a pig, Faithful," he growled. "You ought to be up first. You're the servitor, aren't you? Anybody'd think I was, the way I have to waste my time hurling shoes at your head. Where are my clothes? Do we wash this morning?"

"There's no need," said Faithful. "We washed last Wednesday and we're still quite clean." He spoke with relief for when Giles took it into his head to want to wash Faithful had to go all the way downstairs to the well on the floor below and heave up a bucketful of ice-cold water with much labor and sloppiness. . . . And then Giles made such a mess all over the room that it took him twenty minutes to get it all mopped up.

"We don't wash, then," said Giles. "Good. Here, give me my clothes. There's the bell going for prayers."

They struggled rather feverishly into doublets, trunks, hose and ruffs while the unhurried bell tolled solemnly from the Cathedral. They were still smoothing their tousled hair with their fingers, and struggling into their gowns, as they raced down the wide oak staircase and through the doorway carved with the pomegranate of Catherine of Aragon, set there to commemorate the visit that she had paid to Oxford years ago, dashed across the quadrangle and through the cloisters to the Cathedral door.

Kneeling in the Cathedral, listening to the monotonous drone of the Latin prayers, Faithful found himself watching the sunshine streaming over the shrine of Saint Frideswide, that had been destroyed by Henry and restored again when Queen Mary came to the throne, and thinking not so much of the Saint as of Queen Catherine of Aragon, Mary's mother, whose pomegranate ornamented his own doorway.

She had come to Christ Church in 1518 when the court was at Abingdon, to worship at the shrine, and she had been personally conducted by Cardinal Wolsey who wanted to show her the site where he had planned to build his Cardinal College. Faithful pictured her riding up Fish Street with her courtiers clattering behind her and her trumpeters going before, and the proud Cardinal riding beside her dilating on the glories of his College that was to be. She would have listened politely and courteously, Faithful thought, reining in her horse when they came to the site marked out for the Fair Gate, and in her pretty low voice with its foreign inflection she would have said how clever it was of him to have planned it all out himself, and how wonderful the Cathedral looked against the blue sky, but did he really think he ought to pull down the nave to make room for his quadrangle? But at this my Lord Cardinal would have turned a little huffy and she would have hastily changed the subject to the glories of the proposed College kitchen. It was to be a marvelous kitchen, he had told her, and was to be begun before any of the other College buildings, my Lord Cardinal understanding almost as well as a woman the relative importance of the different departments of life. How many oxen had he told her would be roasted in it at once? No, not really! His huffiness would by now have been dispersed and chatting amicably of culinary affairs they would have walked their horses in and out between the hovels of the common people that now cluttered up the ground where the Cardinal proposed to build his College quadrangle. . . . These hovels, the Cardinal would have explained to the Queen's Grace, would of course be swept away. . . . Catherine would have wondered what would happen to the common people when their hovels were pulled down, but she was a little frightened of my Lord Cardinal and she wouldn't have liked to ask. She was glad, perhaps, to get off her horse and go into the cool Cathedral, for it had been hot and dusty riding from Abingdon, and she was not very strong, and the Cardinal had talked a lot. Kneeling before the shrine of the saint, with the tapers burning and the choir chanting and the incense rising into the musty-smelling air, she would have covered her face with her hands, so that the crowd kneeling round her should not see her tears, and prayed with the desperation that informed all her prayers; that God would not let her babies die one after the other in the way they did; that she might keep just one little living son, only one; that Henry might not leave off loving her because her sons died; that it might not be true, as Henry was beginning to fear, that God had cursed their marriage. Surely, surely it couldn't be true! Was their marriage a sin? She had not meant to sin. This saint, this Frideswide, had been a king's daughter who had refused to marry a king. He had courted her hotly, as Henry had courted Catherine, but she had run away and hidden in the woods until his ardor cooled, and then she had come back and lived in a nunnery upon this very spot. Ah, she had been a wise woman! It was not very happy to be married to a king. Holy Saint Frideswide, pray for me! Mother of God, pray for me! Deus, propitius esto mihi peccatori! Well, it would be over sometime. The misery of her life would be over sometime and she would die and be forgotten of men.

But Oxford, bewitched by Queen Catherine on that memorable visit, had never forgotten her. There had been furious indignation when Henry threatened to divorce her, the women of Oxford creating such a disturbance in the streets that thirty of them had had to be shut up in the town prison of Bocardo. . . . And Faithful, kneeling every morning before the shrine where she had knelt and running in and out under her pomegranate twenty times a day, remembered her always.

2.

The half hour after prayers was a busy one for servitors. Faithful fetched Giles's breakfast of bread and ale from the kitchen, delivered it to him where he stood sunning himself with other lords of creation in the quadrangle, and raced upstairs to "do" their room and eat his own breakfast of one stale crust at the same time. Material things seemed to him unimportant compared with the things of the mind and he spent as little time as possible over both these activities. With his crust held in his left hand he straightened the top covers of their beds with his right. . . . The underneath covers he left as they were, for as he frequently remarked to Giles, and Giles quite agreed with him, what was the use of tidying bedclothes that were thrashed into disorder again ten minutes after one had got into bed?.... This done he bolted the rest of his crust, removed the dust from the furniture with the bellows and refreshed the floor by sweeping the rubbish out of sight under the beds. As he worked he whistled happily, for this was the day when they went to the Schools for Thomas Bodley's lecture on Greek verse, and Thomas Bodley, Fellow of Merton, could lecture in a way that set your mind on fire to such an extent that the flame of it could burn up all boredom, dullness and inattention.

A shout from Giles in the quadrangle down below made him fling the bellows into a corner and fly down the stairs again. The scholars were breaking up into groups and dispersing to their various lectures and Nicolas de Worde, also bound for the Schools, was standing beside Giles.

"Where's Philip Sidney?" demanded Giles. "Mooning over his verses as usual. Go and fetch him, Faithful."

Faithful scurried off with the utmost cheerfulness, for of all Giles's friends he liked Master Philip Sidney the best. There was no one in the world like him, he thought, and there never would be.... He was unique.

Philip's rooms were in Broadgates Hall, a lodging-house for Christ Church scholars just across the way from the Fair Gate, and Faithful ran across to them so often with messages from Giles that he had come to know the cobbles and smells of Fish Street quite intimately; today he ran along with his nose nipped between finger and thumb, for it had not rained lately and Fish Street had a certain aroma.

He clattered up the dark stairs to Philip's room and stood in the shadows knocking at the door with a beating heart. It was odd, he thought, how the knowledge that he would see Philip again in a couple of minutes always set his heart thudding as at the approach of some danger.... For what danger can there be in loving a person? . . . The worst danger in the world, whispered the shadows, the danger of irreparable loss.... He knocked again, urgently, gripped by unreasonable panic, suddenly afraid of the darkness in which he stood and the silence beyond the door.

"Come in."

In a sort of fury of relief he pushed open the door and precipitated himself like a young tornado into the sun-filled room.

Master Philip Sidney, seated at his desk in the window, writing a love song with a large squeaking quill pen, looked over his shoulder, mildly surprised. "Is anything the matter?" he asked.

"I beg your pardon, I just thought perhaps you'd gone," said Faithful vaguely.

"Where to? Sit down a minute while I finish this. What rimes with case?"

"Grace," said Faithful, after long and painful thought.

"Thank you!" said the poet ardently, and dipping his pen in the ink was immediately lost again in the fairyland of creation.

Faithful sat on the extreme edge of the oak chest where Philip Sidney kept his worldly possessions and stared as unblinkingly as an owl at the object of his adoration. Some friendships develop gradually, putting out a leaf here or a shoot there, attaining their full strength only after years of growth, but others arrive with a crash and a bang, a fanfare of trumpets and a streaming of banners, and a day that dawned in the usual poverty closes in the possession of great riches. . . . It had been like that when Faithful first set eyes on Philip Sidney. . . . All the loveliness of his new life, the sun-drenched beauty of the town where he lived and the woods and streams that surrounded it, the warmth of his new relationships and the joy of his work, seemed to him to be summed up in the human being in front of him. He could not say thank-you to the woods and streams, he could not pay his debt to the sunshine, but personified in Philip he could serve them and do them reverence. This sense of symbolism was both the joy and the bane of human beauty, he had discovered. Those who are beautiful stand to their lovers for more than they are; and when their beauty has waned that which it stood for seems dead too, and the whole world darkened.

Philip was about Faithful's own age. He had a slender body with long, narrow hands and feet and a small head finely poised. His hair was fair and smooth and shining and his eyes hazel in a luminously pale oval-shaped face. His beauty and delicacy were those of a girl but there was nothing effeminate in the set of his lips or in his proudly braced shoulders. His dark green doublet was of the finest cloth and his ruff

and cuff of spotless lawn. He wore a tiny golden dagger and shoes of
Spanish leather, and his hose fitted without a wrinkle and were gartered
at the knee with scarlet. . . . Not that these outward symbols of haberdashery were needed to show that Philip was a person of importance;
his breeding was expressed in every one of his fine bones and in what
his friend Frank Greville called "his staidness of mind, his lovely and
familiar gravity."

"Listen to this," he adjured Faithful, swinging round and flourishing
his pen in the air. "It's a sonnet to the moon. Did you notice the moon
last night? She's the midsummer moon that brings back the fairies and
the ghosts of dead lovers. But she is sad because love is a cruel thing, and
when she wanes again she and her ghosts and her fairies will be forgotten."

Faithful, his mouth wide open owing to the greatness of his love
which made him feel as though his chest was full of wind, listened with
half his mind, while with the other half he was wishing that Philip would
not write about the midsummer moon that waxes and wanes like the
life of a man, but about the sun that is always constant in the heavens as
God Himself. He did not wish to be reminded again of that moment of
unreasonable panic on the stairs.

> With how sad steps, O Moon, thou climb'st the skies!
> How silently, and with how wan a face!
> What! May it be that even in heavenly place
> That busy archer his sharp arrows tries?
> Sure, if that long-with-love-acquainted eyes
> Can judge of love, thou feel'st a lover's case;
> I read it in thy looks; thy languished grace
> To me, that feel the like, thy state descries.
> Then, even of fellowship, O Moon, tell me,
> Is constant love deemed there but want of wit?
> Are beauties there as proud as here they be?
> Do they above love to be loved, and yet
> Those lovers scorn whom that love doth possess?
> Do they call virtue there ungratefulness?

"It's wonderful," breathed Faithful. . . . It was a marvel to him that Philip, who to his certain knowledge had no lady love and who at this stage of his career had a profound contempt for the opposite sex, could be so eloquent on the subject of love. He was not aware that experience is unnecessary to your true poet, who can feel any and every emotion simply by sighing, sticking his tongue out at the side of his mouth and dipping his pen in the ink.

Philip performed these rites and turned back to re-read his poem. It was good, he thought. It was good enough to be kept and added to the book of poems that he would publish when he was a man. But was he really a great poet? He found it difficult to be sure. While he was actually writing a poem he knew for certain that it was the most marvelous thing ever written, but when he had finished it he found himself assailed by heavy doubts.

"Master Bodley's lecture?" suggested Faithful tentatively.

Philip jumped up, swearing softly. . . . He had learned a lot of new oaths since he came up to Christ Church and they were a great pleasure to him. . . . Then he put his manuscript down his back—he always kept his literary works there so that he could go on with them in odd moments—stowed away his writing materials in the leather wallet at his waist, smilingly handed Faithful his books to carry and preceded him courteously through the door.

3.

Giles was prancing impatiently up and down when Philip and Faithful joined him and Nicolas.

"We shall be late," he moaned.

"All the better," said Nicolas. He had been up at Christ Church for years, always putting off the accumulation of a little learning to a later and more convenient date, and was by now sick of lectures; even Thomas Bodley's.

They set off at a good pace, Philip, Nicolas and Giles going on ahead and Faithful trundling after, burdened with the books of all three of them. Yet wherever he went in this city, no matter how burdened, every step of the way was a delight to him. The miracle of the spring was now passed and the hawthorn that Joyeuce had looked out upon from her window was tarnished, dropping little white moons of blossom on Faithful's thatch of hair as he passed beneath it; the June sun had burned up the fresh scents of April and the song of the birds had lost its ecstatic note of surprise and was taking the return of warmth and beauty entirely for granted. Yet Faithful thought this full summer season had something precious that the spring had lacked, a richness and pride in the warmth of the sun and the deep color of the flaunting summer flowers that promised a continuance of good things. In the keen joy of the spring there was a sadness, because it went so fast, but the beauty of the summer stole away slowly, no pace perceived; one could cheat oneself into a certainty of possession and know content.

They hurried along between the old buildings of Peckwater Inn and Canterbury College and then turning to their left ran breathlessly up Shidyard Street into the High Street.

In spite of their hurry Faithful lingered a moment to look up the street to his left to the Tower of All Saints' church behind the pig market, and then in front of him at Saint Mary's, the University church. High above his head the glorious spire crowned the tower below it like a king seated upon his throne, while round about the throne the life-size figures of kings and queens and saints stood like courtiers. Of all these figures the one that Faithful loved best was Edmund Rich, the saint of whom Master Campion had told him, the father of all Oxford scholars and the first M.A. of whom Oxford has any record.

He had been born at Abingdon, in those very early days of the University when lecture rooms were street corners and narrow alleys, and the scholars merely a handful of ragged scarecrows whom the wealthy merchants elbowed out of their way as they trod the streets of the city. Yet their fame had already spread beyond the city wall and reached Edmund at Abingdon. He loved two things with a burning love: learning and holiness, and it seemed to him that he would surely find them both in that city where the spires of great churches rose to heaven and bells rang all day long to call men to worship God, and where men were not afraid of starvation for their bodies if only they could find food for their minds. So he said good-by to his outraged family and with his bundle on his back, and his staff in his hand, he set out to tramp through the dark and terrible forest of Bagley to Oxford. It was a wonder he was not killed by the wild boars and the vagabonds in the forest, but he survived, for round his neck, as protection, his mother had hung a gold ring with engraved upon it "that sweet Ave with which the angel at the Annunciation had hailed the Virgin." And so at last, footsore and weary and dreadfully hungry, he crossed the river and reached the South Gate of the city.

He attached himself to a band of scholars who had built themselves a rough school, with clay walls and thatched roof, in the churchyard of Saint Mary's, and with them he studied and worshiped.

He was very devout, and the glorious music of the mass, as it echoed through Saint Mary's church, thrilled his very soul. Yet he was not without his carnal temptations, and one of them was games. He had a strong, straight body, and he could run hard and aim straight and jump like a frog. . . . He adored jumping like a frog. . . . One day in the very middle of the sermon his legs ached and his back itched him and the Devil tempted him to go and jump like a frog outside, and yielding to the temptation he got up and slipped surreptitiously out of his place. But at the north door a divine apparition suddenly appeared and told him what it thought of him, and he was so ashamed that he went back and heard out the sermon to the end. And from that moment his devotion grew more fervent.

One evening he was kneeling in the church, praying by himself. It was growing dark, so that the distant places of the church were filled with purple shadows and the roof over his head was dim as the sky at midnight. The air was heavy and sweet with incense and he felt a little drowsy. Then something made him look up and his eyes were drawn to the one bright spot in the church, the place where light was burning before the statue of the Virgin. The candle flames shone on her rainbow-colored robe and her golden crown and the child held in the crook of her arm, and as Edmund looked at her she smiled at him. Slowly he got up from his knees and crept like a little mouse through the shadows to her feet. There he knelt down and said an Ave, and then he took from his neck the ring that his mother had given him and stretching up he slipped it on her finger. He was hers now, her liegeman, and he would serve her with a chaste body and a pure mind until he died.

The years went on and Edmund became a Master of Arts. He was tremendously learned and scholars flocked to his lectures, but he never flagged in his devotion to the Virgin. He built her a chapel in the parish where he lived and he attended mass there every morning before his day's work began. He cared nothing at all for the carnal pleasures of this world—he never played leapfrog now—but only for holiness and learning. "So study," he said to his pupils, "as if you were to live forever; so live as if you were to die tomorrow." If a rich pupil insisted upon bringing him the fees that were paid to popular masters—unpopular masters, it seems, were not paid anything, and how they lived is a mystery—he was so indignant that he flung the money down on the windowsill, where it stayed till it was stolen by an unpopular master. . . . How Edmund himself lived, under the circumstances, is a mystery too.

But as in his boyhood the Devil had tempted him with games so now he tempted him with mathematics. Edmund's mind, strong and vigorous as his body had been, delighted in the jumps and twists and turns of mathematics, and it spent far too much time leaping about in this fascinating science. One day, when he was in the very middle of a lecture on mathematics, the ghost of his dead mother appeared. "My son," she said severely, "what art thou studying? What are these strange diagrams over which thou porest so intently?" Then she seized his right hand and in the palm drew three circles, within which she wrote the names of the Father, the Son and the Holy Ghost. "Be these thy diagrams henceforth, my son," she said. With that she vanished away and Edmund came to himself again; to the great relief of his pupils, who thought he had gone mad when they saw him standing there with his mouth wide open and the palm of his hand stretched out to nothing at all.

But for the rest of his life Edmund's eager mind leaped about in theology only, and with such success that in due course they made him an Archbishop.

One day His Grace was preaching to a crowd of the devout in the churchyard of All Saints' and a terrible storm came on. Over most of the city a sky like ink hung above the roofs and it rained cats and dogs; but over All Saints' churchyard was a round patch of sky the color of bluebells, and the devout who sat at the feet of the Archbishop were as dry as a bone and as warm as toast.... After that they made the Archbishop a Saint for who but the holiest of the holy are able to oblige like this in the matter of weather?

After his death Saint Edmund, as dead Saints should, went on being obliging. He took under his protection a certain well at Cowley Ford and if ill people crept through the evening shadows to the well, as he had once crept to the feet of the Virgin, and kneeling down said their prayers to her devoutly, as he had once said his, they were healed of their wounds and sickness.... And that Oxford might never forget him his statue looked down upon it from the tower of Saint Mary's.

4.

Leaving it the boys turned to their left under the west window of Saint Mary's and hurried up School Street into the quiet square beyond where Saint Mary's churchyard dreamed under the sun. Crossing it they plunged under a gateway into the quadrangle of the Schools, ran past the empty University Library whose priceless collection of books had been destroyed and scattered during the Reformation, and disappeared into their lecture room like unpunctual rabbits leaping into their burrows.

In it was a seething horde of scholars trying to find places on the few benches that were quite inadequate to their number or weight. Failure to find a seat meant sitting on the floor for two hours, or longer should Thomas Bodley get carried away by his own eloquence, which was unfortunately frequently the case. The battle was to the strong and those who, like Nicolas, could dislodge a whole benchful of smaller and weaker scholars with a sweep of the arm, were to be congratulated.... Although the last in it was only a matter of minutes before he and Giles and Philip were occupying the best seats, with Faithful sitting on the floor at their feet in a square inch of space, trampled upon and hemmed in on all sides by the perspiring bodies of a hundred pilgrims to the well of learning.

There was a sudden lull in the uproar and Faithful, peering up through a forest of waving arms and legs, beheld Master Thomas Bodley pushing his way through the crowd towards his desk on the raised platform at the end of the room. As he passed the noise ebbed away, like a subsiding storm in the branches of the trees, and when he mounted the steps to the platform and looked down upon his pupils there was a dead silence.

For Master Thomas Bodley was a personality, and such was his devotion to Oxford and to learning that it seemed that in him the spirit of Edmund Rich lived again. He was a young man, one of a group of young and brilliant men who were the most worthy descendants of those first teachers whose platforms had been a flight of broken steps leading up to the door of a hovel. Few men in Oxford were more beloved than Thomas Bodley, unless perhaps it was Faithful's friend of the crock of gold, Edmund Campion of Saint John's, and few could equal him in his power of capturing his pupils by the spell of his own attraction. And that done, holding in his hands their attentions like so many gossamer threads that passed from them to him and kept them tethered, it was an easy thing so to stir their imagination that learning seemed delightful to them and with one consent they handed him up their minds to be filled.

Thomas Bodley was tall and upright, his height increased by the long M.A. gown that he wore, with a look of directness about him that was prophetic of the straight clean road he would drive for himself through life. People talked a lot about Bodley and his probable future. A brilliant career seemed certain, with high position in court and government, and in the course of time he was caught in the political spider's web, dragged into it almost without his knowledge by the will of those in high places, and for some years he was a diplomatist, and a brilliant one. But the web could not hold him for long. He was haunted, as he made his brilliant way through the world, by the thought of that desolate library close to the room where he had lectured at Oxford, despoiled of its priceless treasures, its stalls and shelves sold for timber, created to be a place where scholars might study far removed "from the noise of the world" and now empty and dusty and haunted by the ghosts of those dead books. It seemed always crying out to him, asking him to help it.

So he came back to Oxford to fill it up again. It was an odd thing to do but that, he knew, was his vocation. "Whereupon," he said, "examining exactly for the rest of my life what course I might take, and having sought, as I thought, all the ways to the wood, to select the most proper, I concluded at the last to set up my staff at the library door at Oxford."

He offered to restore the library at his own expense, and the University gratefully accepted the offer. Faced by such a staggering financial proposition, some men might have been nonplused but not Thomas Bodley; he married a rich widow. His "purse ability" was now great and he repaired the room and endowed the library. Everyone loved Thomas Bodley and all his friends gave him books for it. He was a Devonshire man and west countrymen particularly put themselves out to steal books for him. When the English fleet, under Essex, captured the Portuguese town of Faro, Walter Raleigh, a captain in the squadron, saw to it that the fine collection of books they stole from a bishop and brought home as a souvenir was given to Thomas.

Generations later the empty room that Thomas Bodley filled was famous all over the world, and his name remembered with honor. . . . But no one ever gave a thought to Mistress Bodley.

But at the moment Thomas Bodley was filling not empty bookshelves but empty minds. The newly discovered plays of Euripides had been published in Venice at the beginning of the century and the wonder of it was still alive. A lecture on Greek verse made the heart beat and the pulses throb with a sense of voyage and discovery. These boys who sat at the feet of Bodley were one in spirit with the boys who had sailed with Cabot to America and who were sailing at this moment under the flag of the Merchant Adventurers, carrying the trade of England out to the New World. It was a great moment to be alive, thought Faithful, this moment when the mists of man's ignorance were lifting and worlds beyond worlds were opening out before his excited eyes, and of the two great adventures

that offered themselves, Commerce and Learning, who could say which
was the most wonderful? Commerce meant romance, danger, and a glory
of dreams, and in those islands beyond the sea, those fairylands of coral
and palm trees and screeching birds with plumy feathers all colors of the
rainbow, men could have their fill of fighting and color and the heat of
the sun; and come back with pockets full of gold, mouths full of strange
oaths, and tales to tell in the tavern that would keep the company hanging
breathless on their words from curfew to cockcrow.

Yet that adventure did not seem so wonderful to Faithful as this
other adventure of learning that carried them to other islands, less gaudy
but to his eyes more beautiful, where the rosy flowers of the asphodel
echoed the color of dawn-flushed, snow-covered mountain peaks, and
pale marble pillars stood in their loveliness beside the wine-dark sea.

> *Oh, the wind and the oar,*
> *When the great sail swells before,*
> *With sheets astrain, like a horse on the rein;*
> *And on, through the race and the roar,*
> *She feels for the farther shore. . . .*

Surely, thought Faithful, that ship of Euripides is the ship of the imagination, that can sail farther and faster than any ship built by man.

> *Ten score and ten there be*
> *Rowers that row for thee,*
> *And a wild hill air as though Pan were there*
> *Shall sound on the Argive Sea,*
> *Piping to set thee free.*

The voice of Thomas Bodley, repeating the poem, seemed to Faithful to
die away into the lapping of waves against the side of a ship. While he
traveled in the ship of imagination the whole of the universe was his, the
whole of time, past, present and to come. Those others, those Merchant
Adventurers, were at the mercy of wind and tide, but he was set free by a

wild tune piped from beyond death to sail over the horizon of the world into eternity. He was bound with no limits, borne with a wing of hope; he would climb even unto the stars.

5.

The lecture was over, Master Bodley was descending the steps, and Faithful was being trodden on. He was in the body once more and yelping with the pain of many feet upon his person. Giles rescued him with kindly patronage, shook him and dusted him down.

"The minute Bodley shuts his mouth you must leap to your feet," Giles explained. "Otherwise you'll be trampled to death. Catch hold of my books and come along. We're going up to Bocardo to cheer up Walter Raleigh. Sidney's just heard he's in prison for debt again."

"There's no time," grumbled Faithful. "We've a Latin lecture at Christ Church before dinner." He grudged every moment stolen from the pursuit of learning to which his soul was vowed like the soul of Edmund Rich before him. And he did not even know Philip's friend Walter Raleigh, an Oriel man of extravagant habits who probably deserved to be in prison, where, thought Faithful, he should be left uncomforted by the virtuous, quietly stewing in his own juice till better thoughts should dawn. "I tell you we've no time," he growled.

"Shut your mouth," said Giles, not unkindly. "There's time if we run. Come *on*, I tell you, come *on*."

Sighing, Faithful came on. He was only a servitor and he must do what he was told. Puffing and blowing he fought his way out of the seething horde of scholars that still filled the lecture room, back through the sunny quadrangle of the Schools and out into the High Street, where they turned to their right and raced uphill towards Carfax.

It was market day and the town was getting busy. In the pig market outside All Saints' Church the pigs were already arriving and the four scholars charged through them, hitting out at the fat squeaking sides with their books and shouting out like English soldiers charging the enemy, "Cuckoo! Cuckoo! Hey! Hey! Cuckoo!" The pigs were quickly

routed, skipping to right and left with all the nimbleness of which their
bulk and inadequate legs were capable, and pursued by the curses of
their drovers the four charged up past the Mitre Inn and round the corner into Cornmarket.

They did not linger here, for once you had left Carfax behind you,
with its fine Church of Saint Martin to the left and the Tavern with the
painted room to the right, Cornmarket became distinctly smelly; for
not to mention the kennel running down its center there was a tannery
in it, with the cordwainers, the workers in leather, conveniently near.
They were, on the whole, good scholars, and they left the Lane of the
Seven Deadly Sins, away on their left, severely alone, and ran on to the
Cornmarket proper, at the North Gate of the city, where the country
people sold their corn and hay on market days.

North Gate was a lively and attractive spot, in spite of the uncomfortable memories connected with the Bocardo lock-up built over the top
of it. The houses drew close together here, each story jutting out a little
further than the one below it, and up above them soared the eleventh
century tower of Saint Michael's Church, with its battlements cutting neat
squares out of the blue sky and the cock on its weathervane arrogant beneath the sun; and gazing down rather contemptuously upon its lesser
brethren who scuttled about over the cobbles below, hunting in the crannies for the grains of corn that the corn factors had let fall. There were always quantities of quadrupeds and birds about in Cornmarket; dogs, cats,
cocks and hens. And, when night came down and the streets of the city
were black and deserted, and the tower of Saint Michael's was just a black
shape that blotted out the stars, rats in their hundreds emerged from the
cellars and yards of the old houses and danced up and down Cornmarket,
from Carfax to North Gate and back again, frisking their tails in the light of
the moon and gorging themselves fit to burst on the refuse in the kennel.

As it was market day the four boys had to fight hard to get through
the crowd to North Gate. The stalls of the corn factors, placed down
the center of the street, divided it into two narrow lanes and up and
down them seethed a yelling, swearing, sweating, gesticulating crowd.
Countrywomen in their wide hats, with voluminous colored petticoats

beneath their great white aprons, baskets on their arms and dead fowls dangling from their wrists, bargained at the tops of their voices with the factors behind the stalls. Dirty, ragged little urchins charged everywhere, kicking up the rubbish in the kennel, banging into the stalls, falling over the squawking poultry and throwing stones at the yapping, snarling dogs. Sometimes a more respectable figure would pass: the physician in his long furred gown, making way for himself with vigorous blows of his long staff, apprentices dashing to and from the cordwainers, and now and then a horseman would ride under North Gate and plunge through the crowd, slashing his whip at the dogs as they scuffled and barked at his horse's hoofs.

The boys were experienced in getting through a Cornmarket crowd. Nicolas went first, kicking and elbowing his way, and Philip, a person not much use at either battering or being battered, for he was delicate and blows always seemed to hurt him more than they hurt other people, came behind clinging round Giles's waist. Faithful brought up the rear, with the books. Black looks, curses, mutterings and a kick or two came their way, and a rotten egg caught Nicolas neatly between the shoulders, for hatred between Town and Gown was still a real thing. The merchants and apprentices and ragtag and bobtail of the town had not forgotten that Oxford was once a great commercial city where Merchandise had reigned supreme. . . . And now it was almost wholly given over to these insolent young cockerels of scholars, with their malapert manners, boastful speech, and heads so swollen with divers useless Tongues and Arts and Philosophies that pity it was to behold the ruin of English manhood brought about by this same lamentable learning.

"Damn your eyes for a saucy, froward villain," shouted an enraged factor as Nicolas, staggering from a well-aimed kick that had followed the rotten egg, barged into his stall.

"Damn yours, you insolent thief!" replied Nicolas hotly, and swung round with his fist raised.

"Oh, come on, do!" implored Giles impatiently. He was a pacifist, not from conscientious reasons nor from cowardice, but because he considered war a shocking waste of a man's time.

"Thief? Who said thief?" roared the factor, a deeply religious and most respectable man. "Am I to be called thief by down-at-heel, out-at-elbow, rascally scholars who take the bread out of honest men's mouths and turn this god-fearing town into a sink of wickedness with their evil ways? No!" bellowed the factor, "I'll see 'em damned first!" and he got in a fine blow, straight from the shoulder. . . . An angry, muttering crowd came milling round Nicolas and things looked ugly.

"Get back, you dirty, scandalous, bullying vagabonds!" shouted Faithful, dashing to the rescue. "It's you, not us, who make this town a stinking dog-hole," he added pleasantly, butting in amongst them. "You'll be put in the stocks for this and serve you right, you scaly, blear-eyed devils."

Faithful had a command of language, picked up in the less desirable streets of London, that always stood him in good stead. Shouted in his pleasant voice and issuing from his wide, good-humored mouth, it never failed to make things pleasant all round. The crowd, shouting with good humored laughter, fell back, and Nicolas was delivered with nothing worse than a black eye and a bleeding nose and a shocking abrasion on the temper.

"Beasts!" muttered Nicolas. "Vermin!" and turning his head he squinted with his one remaining eye at the mess of egg down his back.

"Come, on!" urged his friends, "if we start again we shall be here all day," and they propelled him vigorously towards North Gate.

It was a tunnel not wider than twelve feet at the two ends and some seventy feet long, and over it was the famous lock-up, Bocardo, where the drunk and disorderly, and those unable to pay their bills, were incarcerated for their good. The four halted beneath the small barred window over the tunnel and called in the honeyed tones of deep sympathy, "Raleigh? Raleigh? Cuckoo! Cuckoo!"

Instantly a face appeared at the window, the face of a gentleman in his middle 'teens with curly dark hair, bright blue eyes, a boldly hooked nose, a laughing, generously curving mouth and a resolute chin. It was a proud, arresting, challenging face and Faithful stared at it in fascination, his eyes popping in his head and his mouth ajar. . . . Wherever he went in this wonderful city he was continually confronted by towers and spires, gardens and books and bells, men and women and children who made his eyes pop and his mouth fall open.

"Good morning, gentlemen," said Raleigh airily. "Fine day."

Neither his voice nor his manner invited commiseration and his friends knew better than to offer it. "Just exactly how much do you owe this time?" asked Philip, coming briefly to the point.

"I've no head for figures," said Raleigh arrogantly, and glared at them through the bars like a caged wild beast.

"Don't be an ass," Nicolas adjured him. "Throw the bag down."

Raleigh flushed crimson and exhorted them angrily to mind their own business. It was the correct thing, of course, for prisoners in Bocardo to let down a bag out of the window that their friends might relieve their wants, but to a gentleman of Raleigh's independent temper it was galling to the pride.

"Fool!" said Giles kindly. "Do you want to spend the whole summer term shut up there? You can pay us back later. Chuck out the bag."

Raleigh continued to glare, struggling with himself, his anger directed not at his friends but at fate that had given to his superb ambition the totally inadequate support of a frail and slender fortune. He ground his teeth, maddened afresh by the permanent incompatibility of his income and his expenditure. Heaven knew he did his best to make the one support the other, for he did not exactly enjoy spending a large proportion of his days inside Bocardo, but there was a fine careless grandeur in his mode of living that was natural to him and refused to be curtailed. He was of the stuff of which poets and heroes are made, a stuff not easily fitted into the restricted mold of sobriety and solvency but created to spread itself abroad in beauty like a banner on the wind, possessed of a grandeur that is perhaps more appreciated by later centuries than by the contemporary one that foots the bill. . . . Though Raleigh himself did things in such style, with such a fine courtesy and so grand an air, that his friends were generally happy to give what assistance they could when his elegant garments and entertainments worked out at more than he had expected.

"Come on," said Philip. "Out with the bag. We want you out of Bocardo for our own sakes, you know."

It was charmingly spoken, as only Philip could speak, and a flashing smile lit up the face at the window. He seized the leather bag on a string that lay beside him on the sill and shot it out of the window with such violence that it hit Faithful on the head and made him leap like an antelope.

"Got anything worth giving?" inquired Giles of the others, fumbling in his wallet.

Nicolas and Philip, the financiers of the party, nodded, and Philip produced one golden angel and Nicolas three. . . . The others whistled when they saw Nicolas's three, for three angels was a fabulous sum. . . . But then Nicolas's fine generosity to his friends always excited deep admiration in the breasts of everyone except his father.

Giles fished up a few groats, which was all he had, and Faithful hung his head and went scarlet to the roots of his hair, because he hadn't got anything at all; and as he had taken a passionate liking to the handsome face behind the bars the impotence of his poverty was doubly hard to bear; on an impulse he took from his wallet the little bag of herbs that Joyeuce had given him to sniff as a protection against the plague, one of his most precious possessions, and put it in the bag with the coins. The moment he had done it he wished he hadn't, of course, for only the greatest of the saints do not regret their good deeds as soon as done, but it was too late to change his mind for Walter Raleigh, purple in the face with mingled shame, rage and gratitude, was winding up the string and pulling the bag up to the window again.

"Is it enough?" asked the anxious donors, as he counted it out on the windowsill.

"No," groaned the prisoner, then, remembering his manners and flashing his smile superbly upon the group below, "but you have my eternal gratitude, gentlemen. You have shortened my incarceration by one tenth."

"I expect it won't be long," consoled Nicolas. "They'll take up a collection at Oriel, like they did before."

"They might," growled the prisoner, "but they're a stingy lot at Oriel these days. Getting me out of Bocardo is an activity that palls, they told me last time. And after drinking all my Canary wine at a sitting, too! The mean curs!" And he shook the bars angrily.

"Could I lend you anything to make the time pass?" asked Philip pitifully. "Books, or a lute?"

Suddenly all the rage died out of Raleigh's face and a light broke over it, making it beautiful as a woman's. "I have my charts," he said softly.

Philip smiled with the tolerance of one artist towards the lunacy of another. "Sea charts of the land beyond the sunset?" he asked.

Raleigh nodded, looking out unseeingly over their heads. "I've made two more," he murmured.

"He's been taken with one of his crazy fits," said Nicolas. "We might as well go home. . . . Good-by," he added at the top of his voice. "Oriel being so stingy I suppose it will be weeks before we see you again?"

Raleigh awoke from his dream, recollected himself, and glared. "Don't you be too sure," he said truculently. "You may find yourselves in here with me before you know where you are."

"*We're* never drunk or disorderly," boasted Giles. "Nor in debt."

"I shouldn't wonder," continued Raleigh, "if you were all in here by night. I thought this morning that you would be, for I had an Omen."

"What Omen?" they asked.

"Four bugs in my bed," said Raleigh, and disappeared from view.

Laughing, they fought their way back through the Cornmarket crowd.

"Why does he make charts of the land beyond the sunset?" panted the puzzled Faithful.

"He's going to fit out a fleet of great ships and win an Empire for England in the west," explained Philip.

"Surely that will cost a lot of money," said Faithful, and he shook his head doubtfully, for he had formed a poor opinion of Master Raleigh's financial capabilities.

"He's going to manufacture the money," said Nicolas. "He's hard at work discovering a great Cordial or Elixir that will turn base metal into gold."

"But is there such a thing?" asked the literal Faithful.

"Of course there isn't!" said Giles scornfully. "Raleigh's mad. His bonnet buzzes so loud with bees that you can't hear yourself think when you're with him."

Faithful's thoughts whirled excitedly as they ran on. . . . Charts of the land beyond the sunset. . . . He wished he could see them. Virtuous though he was he almost wished that he might be drunk and disorderly by night so as to be shut up in Bocardo and see those charts. For a full moment the Adventure of Commerce loomed larger in his mind than the Adventure of Learning. Under such a captain as Raleigh he could imagine himself setting sail for the sunset and finding in such an adventure satisfaction for the deepest longings of his soul. It needed a glimpse of Saint Mary's Church, as they ran across Carfax, with the statue of Edmund Rich looking down upon the hurrying figures of the scholars who were his children, to restore his mind to its proper allegiance. The Adventure of learning also had its captains. . . . The Teachers on the steps. . . . He seemed to see them linked in an unbroken chain that stretched from that now almost legendary figure down to the present day, to Edmund Campion and Thomas Bodley, and on again to a future so remote that he could not even picture it. . . . One day, he thought, he would be one of them.

CHAPTER VI

RIOT IN THE TOWN

Sing we and chant it,
While love doth grant it.
Not long youth lasteth,
And old age hasteth.
Now is best leisure
To take our pleasure.

All things invite us
Now to delight us.
Hence, care, be packing,
No mirth be lacking.
Let spare no treasure
To live in pleasure.

ANONYMOUS.

1.

I T was nearly suppertime and Faithful raised his heavy head from the bony knuckles on which it was propped and sighed a little. He and Giles had been working in their room for five solid hours and he wondered if perhaps they might rest a little now. A huge beefy dinner in hall at eleven o'clock, followed by archery practice, was not to his mind the best preparation for hard work. Starving vagabond that he had been he was not used to heavy meals, nor to violent exercise immediately on top of them, and they made him feel rather peculiar. He pressed his hot palms against his temples, that ached, and then upon his stomach, that ached too, rubbed his knuckles in his eyes to clear away an unwanted film of sleep, and looked at Giles, clearing his throat tentatively.

But Giles read on and on, blind and deaf to everything but the printed words before his eyes and the explanation of their meaning spoken in his ears. For when he worked there was always present with Giles that inspiration that is like the actual corporeal presence of a real person. The voice in his ears seemed to him not his own voice but someone else's, and when he wrote he could have sworn that a figure stood behind him, dictating. It was not so with Faithful. He was always conscious of the thing that he wrote as a lump of stone that must be hewn into shape by his own labors and no one else's. . . . Yet when they had finished working it was generally Giles, and not Faithful, who was the more tired of the two.

But today Faithful seemed unable to work properly. It was very hot and a bee kept buzzing in and out and disturbing him, and he could not fix his mind properly upon Aristotle because not only were his head and stomach aching but he was thinking all the time of Raleigh and the land beyond the sunset. . . . God give me singleness of mind, he whispered, God give me singleness of mind. . . . He shut his eyes and tried to concentrate, and instantly his big head fell forward like an overweighted peony.

"What in the world are you doing?" demanded Giles irritably.

"I think I was falling asleep," said Faithful.

"What do you want to go to sleep for?" demanded Giles indignantly. "You sleep like a hog for eight hours every night and keep me awake with your damned snoring. You'll never be an M.A. if you don't get your teeth into Aristotle."

Faithful gritted his teeth, Aristotle being presumably between them, and re-propped his top-heavy headpiece on his bony knuckles.

Giles was not unkind to Faithful, indeed he was very fond of him, but his very admiration for his brains made him stand no nonsense. Faithful should be turned into a first-rate scholar or he, Giles, would perish in the attempt. He must learn to work whether he was well or ill, tired or fresh, happy or unhappy, full of the roast beef of old England or not full of the roast beef of old England; until his mind had learned to function regardless of the state of his body he would not be worthy of the name of scholar.

Great Tom boomed out five o'clock and there was a stampede of feet, and a joyous shouting and yelling, in the quadrangle outside.

"Curse!" said Giles. "Can it be suppertime already?" and he smacked his big book shut. His face was flushed and the hollows at his temples looked deeper than usual. Faithful looked at him anxiously. Sometimes he thought that Giles's capacity for doing more work in one hour than most people did in three was not very good for him. . . . Yet there was no one on this earth who could stop Giles doing what he wanted to do.

They tidied themselves and ran down the stairs to join the yelling mob in the quadrangle that was surging towards the hall and food. The age of the scholars being anything from twelve upwards, and there being no rule as to keeping off the grass, the evening's progress towards the hall was not the decorous proceeding that it became several centuries later. Nor was the hall sacred to food alone, as later. It was the common room as well, and the noise that went on in it could be heard a mile off.

Rough stone stairs open to the sky led up to the hall. It was paved with yellow and green tiles and the sun shone through rich stained glass windows. The great fireplace was in the middle of the hall, with a louvre above to carry off the smoke. Even in summer a small fire of logs burned in it, and the wainscoting on the walls reflected the leaping flames of the logs and was patterned by the sun with the green and blue and rose-color of the stained glass windows, but far up above their heads the splendid roof of Irish oak was dim and shadowy. Faithful always caught his breath when he entered the hall because it was so beautiful. He had not yet got used to its beauty, and he hoped he never would.

Most of the scholars ate their supper in the lower part of the hall, at long oak tables set out with wooden trenchers and cups of horn, but the Dean, the Canons and the College dons sat at the high table on the dais, under the portraits of Henry Tudor and Cardinal Wolsey, and they ate from silver plates and drank out of tall, slender opal Venice glasses. Scholars who were the sons of noblemen dined with the Canons, and a great nuisance they were to the Canons, for they were most of them of a tender age, twelve or thereabouts, and their table manners left much to be desired. It was true they were waited on, as the Canons also were, by their own servants, who tucked their napkins in at their necks, picked up the pieces of bread they hurled on the floor, thumped them on the back when they choked over capon bones and saw to it that they did not drink more than was good for them; but even then they were a nuisance, and made intellectual conversation among the Canons totally impossible. ... It was only by the skin of his teeth that Philip had avoided being one of them. Had the Earl of Leicester, Chancellor of the University, been his father instead of mercifully only his uncle he would have. Philip, a humble person, daily gave thanks for his escape.

Pandemonium was reigning in the hall when Giles and Faithful entered. Leap frog was being played round and round the tables and a brisk game of club kayles was going on in the open space by the fire. Faithful joined in at once but Giles, bored and aloof, perched on the edge of a table and took his Greek Testament out of his wallet. ... The amount of Greek that he mastered while waiting for and eating his meals was incredible. . . . . Faithful was popular. Not only had he the kind of back view that simply cries out to be kicked but, what was more, he did not in the least mind having it kicked. It was fun, too, to jeer at him for his huge head and flapping ears, and the good-humored grin and well-aimed blow with which he received all mocking references to his person, and hid the hurt they did him, were very endearing. Giles, strangely enough, was popular too. There was a fire and a force in him that commanded respect and "youth with comeliness plucked all gaze his way."

Suddenly the hubbub stilled a little, though it did not cease, for there had entered upon them with arrogant step and princely stride the scholars over twenty years of age. These gentlemen were in a peculiarly happy position, for Wolsey's statutes had laid down that no scholar over the age of twenty was to be flogged, though under that age the great Cardinal considered corporal punishment highly beneficial. It was this happy immunity from violence that caused persons of over twenty to look so pleased with themselves. They could now swear as much as they liked and get nothing worse than a fine of twelve pence per cuss overheard by authority, which to a man of means, as many of them were, was a mere flea bite.

Glances of envy and hatred followed the progress of these gentlemen up the hall. Nicolas especially, playing club kayles by the fire, glowered like the devil himself. For Nicolas still had two more years to run before he reached the haven of twenty years and it was more than probable that he would have to go down from Christ Church without ever winning immunity from flogging. That very afternoon, upon returning from archery practice, he had been soundly flogged by the Senior Censor for having shot an Alderman. It was the Alderman's own fault. He had himself placed his person—of the usual Aldermanic shape, several yards round—between Nicolas's flying arrow and its mark at exactly the wrong moment. It was true that Nicolas had forgotten the rule of calling out "Fast!" before he shot, but that had been a mere oversight, in no way intentional. And anyhow the Alderman's figure was so enwrapped with layers of fat that the arrow had been unable to penetrate to any vital part, so Nicolas could see no necessity for the Senior Censor to make such a song and dance about it. . . . He was so stiff that he doubted if he would even be able to sit down to imbibe nourishment.

Then came a long, shrill blast on a trumpet, blown by a servitor posted at the hall door, everyone scurried to his seat and dead silence fell as the Dean, the Canons, the senior College dons—the Treasurer, the two Censors and the Readers in Natural and Moral Philosophy, Dialectic, Rhetoric and Mathematics—together with the noblemen and their servants entered the hall in procession.

Dean Thomas Godwin entered first. He was a breathtaking figure, tall and of an amazing dignity and comeliness. It was no wonder that the Queen's Grace, always peculiarly susceptible to male charm, went all of a dither as soon as she set eyes on him. His black gown, made of the finest cloth and most delicately perfumed, swept the ground as he moved and his ruff was snowy as blackthorn blossom. He had magnificent dark eyes with delicately penciled brows and a fine, gracefully pointed silky beard. The eight Canons and the College dons who followed him, like stately magpies in their black and white, might have been fine looking men, but one did not notice them beside Dean Godwin.

After them came the little noblemen in all their glory. The rules about modest garb that prevented other scholars from making much of a splash in the haberdashery line were found to be difficult of application to those of noble birth—their august fathers were apt to cut up rough at any curtailment of the wardrobe—so these small people were a sight to behold. They wore velvet trunks, with silken hose gartered at the knee with scarlet. Their little shoes were of softest leather worked in gold thread, with pompons on them, and trod the tiled floor in fine disdain. Their doublets were of all colors of the rainbow, encrusted with jewels, and one or two of them, and those the youngest, wore pearl drops in their ears. . . . Yet their passing lit no envy in the breasts of poorer scholars. . . . For these imps were future courtiers of Gloriana, destined for her service, and Gloriana ruled supreme over the breast of nearly everything in trunk and hose from north to south, from east to west, of the pleasant land of England.

The tail of the procession was made up of the servants of the great ones who had just passed by. In winter they would have carried the lighted lanterns that lit their masters across the dark quadrangle, but now, in summer, they carried only bowls of rose water, and folded napkins laid across their arms.

Dean Godwin mounted the dais, the Canons, dons and noblemen took their places, their servants behind them, grace was sung, and the pantlers, who had toiled up the stone steps from the kitchen below, entered one behind the other with the great dishes upon their shoulders.

At the tables in the lower part of the hall they had the usual beer and beef, bread and oatmeal, enlivened with fresh garden peas and a little fruit, but at the high table they had as well capons, pies, marchpanes and jellies. Their drinks were more varied, too, for as well as beer they drank burgundy and malmsey wine. The scholars below envied them their burgundy but not their malmsey. Years later one of them was to complain that the College malmsey "still tastes of the Duke."

The four friends sat together, or rather three of them sat, for Nicolas, unable as yet to bend the figure, stood, and held forth upon his woes at the top of his voice between each bite. Faithful and Philip, their mouths full, made sympathetic noises, and Giles, his book propped open in front of him, read, taking no notice of any of them, masticating his food meanwhile with the unconscious thoroughness of a cow chewing the cud.

A babel of voices rose and fell, swelled and roared, the sound bearing up to the ceiling and rolling in waves from side to side of the wainscoted walls. Jaws champed and heads were tipped well back that knives might shovel peas into capacious mouths without spilling half of them under the tables. Bones, when finished with, were thrown on the floor or hurled at the head of a dear friend. The pantlers, swearing and perspiring, rushed hither and thither, refilling the horn cups, bringing in fresh supplies of beef and dodging the crusts of bread thrown at them by wellwishers. The fumes of hot humanity and meat and drink mingled with the wood smoke and hung over the scene in a dense cloud through which the rich colors of the stained glass windows, the silver on the high table and the jewels of the noblemen, winked and gleamed like the lights of a harbor seen through a mist at sea. The noise, the smoke and the smell rose to a final crescendo of volume, aroma and density and then, suddenly, it was over, and the trumpet was announcing the departure of the Dean, Canons, dons and noblemen from the hall.

They departed as they had come, magnificently, the Dean holding a scented handkerchief to his nose with one hand and with the other lifting the skirts of his fine gown well above the bone-strewn floor.

It was now considered right that there should be a brief half hour of rest and recreation before the scholars returned to their work, and the din that broke out was unequaled by anything that had gone before. The interrupted games of leap frog became more and more violent, the pantlers meanwhile clearing the tables at peril of their lives, while by the fire the game of club kayles waxed very hot.

It was only ninepins, the pins being aimed at with a stick, but an elaborate system of betting had been evolved in connection with it so that a good deal of heat was likely to be engendered, the tall pointed pins, shaped like fir cones, coming in very handy as missiles. In the rhyme of the period young men were implored to "Eschew always evil company, kayles, carding and haserdy." But at Christ Church, if they had heard the rhyme, they had failed to lay it to heart.

2.

Afterwards, no one was quite sure how the great fight started. The scholars said it started on the dais, where the servants of the Canons were quarreling with the servants of the noblemen over what was left of the food, which was their perquisite. The servants, on the other hand, said it was nothing on earth to do with them; they quarreled about the food every evening, and nothing came of it; no, it was the fault of the young gentlemen playing club kayles by the fire.

And certain it was that Nicolas, already in a bad temper from one reason and another, had hit Toby Stapleton over the head with the kayles stick. He had reason to, for Toby had cheated, and had moreover a wart on the end of his nose that always annoyed Nicolas, but his action was unwise because Toby hailed from Westminster while Nicolas himself hailed from Ipswich.

The famous school at Ipswich had been founded by Cardinal Wolsey and naturally its boys came up to Christ Church in large numbers, and between them and the Westminster scholars there was naturally a loathing too deep for words. Westminster had to be careful what it said to Ipswich, and vice versa, for the slightest word, or a blow given with the best of intentions, was liable to be misconstrued and act like a torch set to a haystack.

The thing was in full swing before anyone knew it had started. Shouting and yelling the mob surged backwards and forwards, kicking, scuffling, hitting and swearing. The servants' quarrel on the dais somehow got tacked on to the scholars' quarrel down below and the minor quarrel, being conducted by grown men and strong, succeeded in pushing the whole horde of them out of the hall door and on to the staircase. Here the pantlers and cooks came dashing up from the kitchen below to join in, and the whole mass surged down the stairs and across the quadrangle to the Fair Gate. Heatherthwayte, of course, should have shut the great gates and stopped them, but he was having forty winks at the moment and by the time he had got his mouth shut and his eyes open and staggered towards the gates it was too late; he and Satan were picked up like a couple of straws by the advancing tide and carried out into Fish Street.

And out in Fish Street the row took an entirely new turn. Within half an hour of its occurrence Nicolas's little upset with the Alderman had been the talk of the town. The story grew with the telling as it was handed from corn factor to merchant's wife, from merchant's wife to servant girl, and servant girl to apprentice. Within an hour of the accident, what time Alderman Burridge was seated comfortably at home with a tankard of ale at his elbow, he was reported to be dying in agonies, and half an hour later he was dead. The Alderman was popular and the rage and fury of the town was unbounded. By six o'clock quite a nasty little crowd had collected at Carfax and a few bold spirits had marched down towards Christ Church and were considering the advisability of demanding that Nicolas be delivered up to justice. A few bargees, strolling up from the river to get a drink in the town, encountered these gentlemen and heard the latest version of Alderman Burridge's murder, so that by the time Westminster and Ipswich, locked in combat, reeled out of the Fair Gate they found the Town ready for them.

Word of the grand fight going on in Fish Street between Town and Gown, over Alderman Burridge's murder, flew round Oxford. Reinforcements to both sides flocked out of every College, house and inn in the town and rushed to the scene of action. In no time at all there was one dense crowd of fighting humanity right up Fish Street, across Carfax and down Cornmarket; seething backwards and forwards like a turbulent sea, shouting, yelling, kicking and swearing. The Proctors, with the Constable of the watch and his minions, were powerless. They danced up and down on the edge of the hurly-burly, shouting and threatening, but no one noticed them, let alone attended to them. The excitement rose to fever pitch and, quite suddenly, a flight of arrows appeared, shot by unseen bowmen inside the Swyndlestock, a tavern at the southwest corner of Carfax. It was not known for certain who shot them, whether

Town or Gown, though it was thought Town because of the raucous cries of "Who shot the Alderman?" that accompanied them, but a wild yell of fury rose up and rent the very heavens, for this was not playing fair; fists, nails, sticks, dead cats, rotten eggs and other missiles of a like character might be used in a Town and Gown riot, but not arrows. . . . Things began to look uncommonly ugly.

It was now that Dean Godwin showed the stuff of which he was made. Mounted on his black horse, still attired in his black gown and white ruff, and with his riding whip in his hand, he issued out of the Fair Gate. Forcing his terrified horse through the crowd, and slashing with his whip to right and left, he gained the summit of Carfax. As he sat there, reining in his horse but still using his whip, a little oasis of calm formed about him, the crowd falling momentarily back. . . . For Dean Godwin in a rage was an awesome sight and his whip, with the full force of his arm behind it, could sting. . . . But there was no possibility of making himself heard beyond the little circle immediately round him that contained, he saw to his astonishment, Philip Sidney the Poet and Faithful Crocker the Scholar, torn and disheveled and bloodstained and shouting as loudly as any there. . . . Really, thought the Dean in a moment of depression, if our scholars and poets can be corrupted into yelling hooligans in the space of a mere half hour the hope for civilization is small. . . . Stretching out his riding whip he hooked them towards him and looked upon them with disfavor.

"What are *you* doing here?" he demanded of Faithful.

Faithful removed a broken tooth from his mouth, spat out some blood, and shook his huge head in complete ignorance. . . . He didn't know why he was here; he only knew that he was enjoying himself hugely.

"And you, Philip Sidney," said the Dean sternly, "you can, I hope, at least tell me the cause of this disgraceful riot in which you, a man of birth and breeding, are behaving like one of the lower animals."

Philip had no idea what they were fighting about but, wiping blood from his nose, he had the grace to look ashamed of himself. He hadn't really wanted to come, for he imagined that he loathed riots; he had come because he hadn't been able to help himself. But now that he was actually in it he found to his surprise that even to the poets of this world physical combat has its joys.

"If you two are here to show the stuff of which you are made," said the Dean with sarcasm, "you will kindly show it by fighting your way to Saint Martin's and ringing the bell to get me a hearing."

The culprits bowed and accepted the task. Faithful with all his experience of London streets knew well how to get through crowds. Covering his eyes with his arm and lowering his head he butted his way through, kicking and pummeling when necessary, Philip joyously following. The crowd opposed them for all it was worth but they fought their way on, fighting now with an added joy because it was a Holy War, the cause of law and order for which they kicked draping a veil of seemliness over their primitive methods of attack.

But it was a relief, all the same, to reach the great gray rock of Saint Martin's, and they clung to it for a moment, panting, before they opened the door and went inside, stumbled up the dark spiral staircase to the cobwebbed belfry and fell upon the bellrope.

In another moment a tocsin was booming out over the clamorous city, as it had done in moments of stress since Oxford was first a town; when the Northmen had come up the river in their terrible longboats to pillage and burn, during the days of the civil war when the city stood for Queen Matilda and the army of Stephen was sighted coming up out of the mist, or again during the great riot of Saint Scholastica's Day, when Town and Gown fought each other for three days and nights and sixty scholars were killed. These memories and many others were present in the corporate memory of the crowd as the bell of Saint Martin's tolled out; a strange hush fell, full of only half-understood little undercurrents of fear, and the oasis of calm that had already gathered about Dean Godwin grew and spread, like oil poured on a turbulent sea, so that in a little while he found himself speaking into a dead silence.

It puzzled him. The sea of faces raised to his wore the stamp of fear; the crowd seemed turning to him as though he were there to save them from some awful danger; the stillness was deep with the pain of the silent poor who must suffer for the sins of the mighty. . . . For a moment he himself did not quite know where in time he was. He felt uncertain of his own personality, knowing only that he had sat his horse at the center of a Carfax crowd a hundred times before. The scene about him seemed to flicker and change, the buildings blocked against the sky took now one shape, now another, a hundred different crowds seemed to surge against him, one melting into mist as another was superimposed upon it, and he himself was by turn Soldier, Priest and King. Only the earth beneath his horses feet, the little hill of Quadrefurcus that had always been here, remained firm and unchanging and brought him back to reality. . . . The bell ceased tolling and he remembered that this occasion was quite a trivial one; he look a grip of himself and of the crowd.

What was the matter this time, he demanded. Why was this peaceful, God-fearing city turned into a bedlam? This was the sixteenth century, he shouted at them. This was the Present Day, not the Dark Ages. Anyone would think, from the fuss they were making, that the Danes were upon them again, or an invading army clamoring at West Gate. What was the matter with them?

The bell had stopped ringing and the spell was broken. The fear had gone and the silence had gone. The crowd was itself again and eager to give information.

"Alderman Burridge is murdered!" yelled a dozen voices.

"Murdered?" said the Dean. "I think not." he pointed with his whip to the Constable of the watch, propped panting against the wall of Saint Martin's. "Constable, go instantly to the house of Alderman Burridge and bring us word of his true state."

Nothing loth the Constable made off, for Alderman Burridge lived only just round the corner by Great Baily, and the Dean meanwhile harangued the crowd, his fine, sonorous voice rolling over them in a perfect tornado of chastisement. He had the gift of the gab, had the Dean, and he had not half finished what he wanted to say by the time the Constable came hurrying back.

"Well?" demanded the Dean. "Stand up here on my stirrup."

"Alderman Burridge," roared the Constable, mounting beside the Dean, "is very little injured, praise be to Almighty God, and has, so says his worship, enjoyed this evening's entertainment mightily."

A little gust of laughter blew up at the center of Carfax, gathered and spread, running through the crowd like fire, and soon the whole of it was rocking in a great gale of laughter. Those on the outskirts, who had not been able to hear what went on in the center, had not an idea what they were laughing at, any more than a great many of them knew what they had been fighting for, but hands on hips they roared with the rest.

Faithful and Philip, kneeling on the dirty belfry floor, peered through the narrow slits of windows at the scene around and below them.

It was a marvelous sight.

Sunset lay over the city. The sky above was a heavenly blue, unutterably peaceful and of a depth that seemed to reach to eternity, but to the west, behind the gray mass of the Castle, it was a molten streaming gold, as though a great furnace blazed beyond the rim of the world. The towers and spires of the city, quietly watchful, rose dazzlingly fair against the blue sky, and caught the reflection of that streaming gold on their comely crests, but down below them the huddled roofs of the city were bathed in tawny shadows. Beyond the town the meadows and the winding streams and the willow trees had drawn damp blue mists over their beauty, but beyond them the hills, like the towers, had light on their crests. And right at the heart of that beauty, a strange center for such peace, was the laughing, jostling, rowdy crowd, the city folk in their jerkins, caps and doublets of red and yellow and green, bright splashes of color among the sober-hued scholars. Their laughing faces, upturned to the stately figure on the black horse, caught the last of the sun and seemed alight with it, burning with an everlasting vitality. . . . No, there is no death, thought Philip, only a perpetual readjustment of the garment of life. . . . And how lovely, and how endlessly various, is this garment. The beauty of what he saw now caught at his breath and quick, broken little phrases of description came winging their way like butterflies into his opened mind. Swinging away from the window he put an arm over his eyes, trying to close his mind's door, to shut it fast on those phrases. They must lie there, dormant as an artist's tubes of colors, till he had time to take them out and fasten them together into a poem. . . . But would they stay there? . . . The loveliest phrases are winged, and when the poet opens the door of the place where he put them he finds that the tiresome creatures have flown away.

"Here!" shouted Faithful from his window. "They're taking Nicolas and Giles to Bocardo!"

It was too true. Dean Godwin, before running his horse and riding back to Christ Church, had indicated with his whip those who, in his opinion, had been ringleaders in the riot, and Nicolas and Giles were among them. Faithful and Philip could see them, Giles white with fury and Nicolas crimson with it, standing below the tower in the firm grasp of the Constable of the Watch.

Faithful and Philip were good friends and it was the work but of a moment to race down the steps of the tower and assault the Constable in the back. It did no good, however, for a couple of apprentices, self-appointed assistants of the Constable, seized them and cuffed them and in a moment all four were being marched down Cornmarket. It was a humiliating progress, for groups of uproarious townsfolk, reeling off to their houses and taverns with arms linked, mocked and jeered.

Giles was in a cold fury. . . . Here he was, wasting his time again. . . . It had not been his fault that he had joined in the riot, he had been lifted off his feet and planted down in the middle of it without being able to help himself, but it had been his fault that he had got himself arrested. In spite of himself he had got carried away by the excitement of the thing. He had had no weapon but his Greek Testament but he flattered himself that with that he had knocked out as many of the enemy teeth as other scholars had done with clubs and sticks.

"You'll have plenty of time to work in Bocardo," replied Nicolas sullenly, to Giles's complaints of his lot.

"No good without my books, you owl," snapped Giles. "Even my Testament's gone now. Some brute tore it out of my hand."

"You did a lot with it first," comforted Faithful.

"Never mind," said Philip sweetly from the rear. "Walter Raleigh will he so pleased to see us."

3.

But Raleigh had not spent an unhappy evening. At first, when the sounds of battle reached his ears, he had looked out of the window, clutching the bars and bitterly cursing his fate. . . . It was always the same. . . . Whenever there was something really exciting going on in the city, something, moreover, that could be enjoyed without any financial outlay, he was always locked up in Bocardo, and when University life pursued the even tenor of its way, and there was nothing cheap to do but work, he was free as air. He continued cursing, with vigor and an extraordinary flow of language, for several minutes, and then turned abruptly back to the stool and the rough table where he had been working. Well, let the solvent enjoy themselves without him. Insolvent though he might be he had that to think of which was worth all the street fights in the world.

Raleigh, like Faithful, went through life with his library attached to his person, but his gods were not Virgil and the Martyrs but Baldassare Castiglione and his half-brother Humphrey Gilbert. Castiglione's *Cortegiano* was always in his hand and Humphrey's collection of sea-charts buttoned up inside his doublet. He read the first to fit himself for the adventure to which the second called him.

In the *Cortegiano* Castiglione portrayed the perfect gentleman; well-born, well-dressed, free and forceful in speech, learned, accomplished, magnificent and charming, courageous in battle, a leader and captain of men. Raleigh studied this portrait, modeling himself upon it line for line, preparing himself for the day when his speech must light men's imaginations and his courage fire theirs, when his wisdom and knowledge must seem to them trustworthy and his personality one to be followed to the death.

His dream, to win for England an Empire beyond the sea, never seemed to him a dream too great to realize. He had a colossal pride. What he wanted to do he believed he ultimately could do. He was descended from the Plantagenets, he had the blood of kings in his veins, he had beauty and courage and vision, he had only to command men and surely they would follow. And his dream had been bred in him, it was bone of his bone and flesh of his flesh. It had been his in childhood when the chief excitement in his west country home, built among the moors above the river Dart, was the return of sailors from the sea. Many a bronzed mariner found his way to the manor house and sat before the fire with the Raleigh and Gilbert boys, telling mythical tales of the mystic west that set their minds on fire. Those were the days when Humphrey Gilbert, with little Walter to help, began to draw his sea-charts, half in joke and half in earnest. Some of them lay on the table before Raleigh now, inscribed with names that set his blood tingling. . . . America. Cathay. The Indies. . . . Strange fantastic coastlines had Humphrey given to these countries, and strange sea monsters had he drawn swimming the seas; and fine ships with bellying sails, not so big as the sea monsters but bigger than America, made their way unerringly to the place where they would be. There was an element of fun in these maps but there was gravity too. In the corner of one of them Humphrey had written words that Raleigh knew by heart. "Give me leave always to live and die in this mind, that he is not worthy to live at all that for fear or danger of death shunneth his country's service and his own honor, seeing death is inevitable and the fame of virtue immortal. Wherefore in this behalf, mutare vel timer sperno."

Raleigh shut his eyes, that no material sight might creep between him and the stately passing of the pictures that his fancy painted. The riot in the town came to him only dimly, like the beating of waves on the shore or the sound of the wind on the moors at home. America, he whispered to himself, Cathay. The Indies. And then again, America. Only the fringe of it was known. Beyond that lay a great no-man's land that held one knew not what, a land where they might yet be a great nation of English-speaking men and women. He beat his fists upon the table. God in heaven, what a time to be alive! It was like living in a fairy tale. It was like living in a hall with a hundred doors; you might choose which one you opened but behind them all there was mystery. He wondered if there would ever come an age when all the world would be known. If so, he thanked God that he did not live in that age. He thanked God that he lived now, at this moment of time when chinks of mysterious light shone from beneath closed doors, now when it was still possible for a man to sail out into the blue and build a new Empire for his country. Would he do it while he lived, or would he do it after death? Though he never doubted ultimate victory he sometimes thought that his dream was too big to be realized in this life. He knew that he was sometimes now hated for his pride. Other men's hatred might yet be the rock that would wreck him. Yet, he thought, though he might not realize his dreams he might die for them, and it only needed a small acquaintance with history to tell him that it is the dreams that are died for that live. Blood had a mystic quality. The life of a man was in it. Poured upon the hard earth it brought new things to birth. What did he care if he died? "Death is inevitable but the fame of virtue immortal." One day not only England but that great nation beyond the sunset, so far removed from him that he could not even picture the cities they would build or the glorious shaping of their history, would hold his memory in perpetual honor. He knew that they would. Arrogantly he placed himself among the immortal gods, drinking his fill of fame. Words formed themselves in his mind.

> My soul will be a-dry before,
> But after it will thirst no more.

4.

Steps stumbling up the stone stairs disturbed him, and he raised his head angrily. Who was coming here to break in upon his dreams? Drunken brawlers from that riot in the town? He sprang up, meaning to push the table across the door, to keep them out at all costs. Then suddenly he changed his mind. Whoever they were he would try his power over them; see if he could fire them with his own enthusiasm; see if it were true that he was a born leader of men. There was an altercation going on on the stairs and he had a little time. With long cat-like leaps

he bounded about the room, tidying his possessions out of sight, bringing out his supply of candles, lighting them and wedging them firmly in
their own grease on table and windowsill, placing a loaf of moldy bread
and a jug of water on the table, and then, as the door burst open and four
battered, disreputable scholars were pushed in by the old jailer, standing
with one hand at his hip and the other sweeping an imaginary hat from
his head as he bowed and bowed again. "Good evening, gentlemen," he
cried, "good evening. . . . By cock and pie, it's the four bugs!"

He burst into a great roar of laughter and Nicolas, Giles, Philip and
Faithful, who a moment ago had been feeling sore, dispirited and weary,
suddenly felt as though they had been picked up by a great wind and
set down in the one place where they wanted to be. They roared too,
holding their sides, staggering as Raleigh hit them on the back, going
into gale upon gale of mirth as though they had just been told the most
exquisite joke in all the world. The old jailer, bringing in four more straw
pallets, four more stools, some cracked platters and a villainous looking bit of cold meat, laughed too, tears of mirth running out of his old
eyes and his toothless gums showing in a wide grin. . . . There was some
magic in this young cockerel with the bright blue eyes, he thought, as he
took his final departure, some strange unexplainable magic for which,
unlearned as he was, he could find no name.

"Sit down, gentlemen," said Raleigh, motioning them with an impe-
rial gesture to take their places round the festal board. "There is venison here, lark pie, marchpane, pasties, ale, wines of all sorts. Take your
choice. Make yourselves at home. All that I have is yours." Laughing,
they pulled their stools up to the table and fell upon the feast with the
appetite of hungry lions.

The other three had fallen before beneath the spell of Walter Raleigh, they knew of old how his superb gestures could create an illusion
of grandeur that dazzled the eyes for just as long as he chose that it
should, but Faithful was coming into close contact with Raleigh for the
first time and was utterly bewildered. . . . This room where they sat was
no longer a dirty little lock-up but a room in a palace, the cold meat and
bread that they ate off cracked platters was venison and pasties upon

golden dishes, the water was the nectar of the gods and the flickering tallow candles burned as though all the stars of heaven had come trooping in to light them. They forgot their aches and pains and bruises, they forgot the dreary uncomfortable imprisonment that stretched out before them, they forgot everything but the figure of Raleigh sitting at the head of the table, waving his knife in the air and telling them exciting tales in glorious language and a strong Devonshire accent.

In sober moments Raleigh's friends had no faith in his stories, but tonight he held them spellbound. "In America," he said, "vines laden with grapes cling to tall cedar trees, and sitting beneath them the natives drink the powdered bones of their chieftains in pineapple wine."

"Why?" asked Nicolas. . . . The customs of these people seemed to him odd.

"That they may have their courage in them, of course," cried Raleigh, bringing his knife-hilt down with a crash on the table. "Don't you know that we all of us feed on the courage of the dead? If there had been no valiant men in the past to show us the way to live would we be anything today but spineless idiots? If we *are* spineless idiots in this generation will the men of the future have any chance of winning an Empire for England? No!" he shouted, taking a long pull of water from the jug. "It is now or never, gentlemen, now or never."

"Tell us some more," said Philip with kindling eyes. "Is it very beautiful, that land?"

"There are great mountains there," said Raleigh, "crowned with snow, higher than you can conceive, and cataracts fall from them, every one as high as a church tower, thundering to the ground with the reverberation of a thousand great bells clanging together. The waters run in many channels through fair grassy plains, and there are paths there for the deer, paved with stones of gold and silver. The birds towards evening sing on every tree with a thousand several tunes, and cranes and herons of white, crimson and carnation perch beside the rivers. . . . Do you wonder, gentlemen, that I should wish to win this land of beauty for the Queen? I would give my life that she might have a better Indies than the King of Spain has any."

"I do not think," said Philip softly, "that any land could be fairer than this land. I would rather give my life to keep the beauty of this one unpolluted."

Faithful looked from Raleigh to Philip Sidney and marveled at them both. Utterly unlike as they were they had something in common, some powerful attraction that would surely bring men tumbling at their heels wherever they might lead. Faithful, belonging to an age that attributed the unexplainable to the stars, told himself that no clouds had veiled the sky when they were born. They had more star-shine in their souls than most men. It shone out of them like the light of another country, expressing itself quite differently in their two personalities but the same in essence. In Philip it was a luminous beauty of character, in Raleigh it was an arresting combination of recklessness and intellectual power. He had the scholar's mind and the adventurer's temperament and the two together were as startling as a thunderstorm. Philip's leadership through the darkness of life would be like a lighted lantern going on ahead, but Raleigh's would be like lightning, more exciting, and revealing more of the surrounding country, but not so steady.

"What a liar you are, Raleigh," said Giles with admiration. . . . They were beginning to sink down now from the high level of excitement to which Raleigh had whirled them, and criticism, albeit admiring, was creeping in.

Raleigh grinned. He knew himself to be a consummate liar, and knew too that his inspired inability to draw the line between solid fact and the creations of his own fantasy was one of his most valuable gifts as a propagandist. He laughed as he realized that though they might be critical now he had yet been able to sweep them off their feet. He knew, and none better, "how to tell the world."

"But what I tell you now," he said, once more pounding his knife-hilt on the table, "is true. I have at last discovered the Great Cordial and Elixir of Life."

"Moonshine!" said Giles.

"You'll blow the roof off Oriel with your abominable stinks," Philip cautioned him.

Faithful, his head still whirling, realized that the talk had turned to Raleigh's chemical experiments. "Will the Great Cordial really make money enough for all you want to do?" he asked breathlessly.

Raleigh turned his shining eyes upon him. "It turns base metals into gold," he said, "and taken internally as a medicine it prolongs the life for no one knows how long. Alchemists have been experimenting to find the formula for generations but it has been left to me, Walter Raleigh, to succeed."

"And you've actually used the Elixir?" whispered Faithful. "You've turned something into gold?"

"Not yet," said Raleigh, "but as soon as I've paid my debts and am out of here you shall all come to Oriel and see me do it. . . . And then you shall drink of it yourselves and live forever."

No one but Faithful seemed keen.

"The roof would come off," Philip objected again.

"If we drank your muck we certainly should live forever," said Giles grimly, jerking his thumb towards the dirty floor. "Down there."

Raleigh's own enthusiasm was quite unquenched by their lack of it. "Do you write verse?" he asked Faithful.

Faithful shook his large head sadly. Everyone up at the University seemed a poet. They all wrote verse, whether they could or not, and Faithful was ashamed to be among the few in this city of laughter who lacked the singing voice.

"That's a pity," said Raleigh, "because I have a verse reading in my rooms every Sunday afternoon and at the next one I shall, before reading my verses, make a demonstration with my Elixir. . . . Never mind," he said generously, "you shall come all the same, even if you don't write verse, and help me clear up the mess."

"There'll be one," said Nicolas gloomily. "Bones and blood and the ruins of Oriel."

But Raleigh was still undamped. He took some papers scratched over with strange diagrams out of his wallet, spread them on the table among the remains of the feast and the drippings from the candles, and began to explain and argue and persuade, his eyes blazing in the candlelight, his voice growing rich and soft as a cat's purr as he cajoled them, mocked at their unbelief, and once more laid siege to their imaginations.

"No more poverty," he cried excitedly. "My Elixir will make gold as common as the cobbles in the street. We shall pave this city of Oxford with gold, I tell you, like the streets of the New Jerusalem. Away with the children of poverty, sickness and thieving and envy and hate, down with them into hell! As well as building a new Empire beyond the sea we shall build a new world in England. It will be the Golden Age at last."

"I wonder how many times men have said that before?" commented the skeptical Giles. "It's all very well to lay the foundations of a new world, it's often been done, but as soon as the walls are built up a little way something pushes them over."

"Death," said Raleigh. "The death of the men of vision who were the builders. . . . But with my Elixir the life of the great will be prolonged indefinitely. Those whom the gods love will live, not die. The earth will be peopled by upright kings, poets, dreamers, who will see their life's work through to the end."

"The rogues and vagabonds might want to have their lives indefinitely prolonged too," suggested Faithful. Enthusiastic as he was he could foresee a lot of difficulties.

"Croakers!" said Raleigh scornfully. "Oh ye of little faith, finish up the food and let's have some singing. Eat, drink and be merry, for tomorrow, without my Elixir, the likes of you will die."

They finished the bread and water and began to sing, roaring out song after song, thumping the table with the handles of their knives, until the whole of Bocardo rang with their singing. Other prisoners in their cells heard and sang too, and the old deaf jailer, sitting on the stone steps outside enjoying a little meal of his own, stopped eating to cup his hand behind his ear to listen. . . . Times were changing, he thought, times were changing. These were good days. He could remember other days, and not so long ago either, when there had been no singing in Bocardo. Men had spent their last days on earth in Bocardo. Archbishop Cranmer had been led out to die at the stake from that very room where those boys were feasting. The Archbishop had eaten his last meal there and he, John Bretchegyrdle, had served it to him. . . . He hadn't fancied it. . . . Well, times were changing, he thanked God, and a new world being built by these youngsters. He wished good luck to their building; he, an old man, who would not live to see what they had built. . . . He removed his hand from his ear, for the singing had died away, nodded once or twice and was asleep.

5.

In the prisoners' room they had spread their pallets and all but Faithful had fallen asleep too. They were so drugged by weariness and Raleigh's dreams that they had forgotten their cuts and bruises, the discomfort of their beds and the hardness of their lot. All night they would sleep blissfully, without moving, undisturbed by each other's grunts and snores, presented by fickle sleep with that blessed gift of oblivion that in her favoritism she bestows only upon the healthy and happy who do not need it.

But it did not come all at once to Faithful. The other four were sleeping side by side on the further side of the table but Faithful, being only a servitor, had thought it right to lay his pallet at a respectable distance, under the window that looked on Cornmarket.

But he could not get comfortable on it. He began to feel very itchy. He scratched himself on his back and he scratched himself on his chest, and he scratched himself up and down his thighs, and then he realized with horror that there were other people besides himself on, and in, this straw pallet. . . . The last prisoner to lie on it must have left them behind as a donation to Bocardo.

Faithful had become fastidious since he came up to Oxford, and he didn't like it. He rolled hastily off the pallet, scurried to the table and climbed upon it. The creatures would find him in time, of course, for they were intelligent creatures; they would climb up the walls, stroll across the ceiling and drop upon him from above; but he had a little while before they thought of that.

He sat cross-legged on the table, his body cold and tired and itching but his mind burning with excitement. What a day he had had! A glorious day of eating, drinking, learning, dreaming and fighting. Picture after picture flashed across his mind: the tower of the Cathedral clear-cut against the sky in the morning light; a racing sea, frilled with white-capped waves, over which a ship carried him to the Isles of Greece; the laughing colored crowd at Carfax lit up by the sunset; the mystic land of the west where carnation colored birds perch beside the rivers; and last of all Raleigh's dream of a city paved with gold where there was no more sin.

And suddenly the midsummer moon of Sidney's poem had risen. She came out from behind a cloud, round and white as a moon-daisy, and Oxford was flooded with her light. Cornmarket was clear as daylight, and the tower of Saint Martin's with a white cloud floating from it like a banner, and the Fair Gate of Christ Church with the stars above it. The rats were illumined too; dancing about in Cornmarket in rich happiness; for this was their hour and no man defrauded them of it.

This was his hour, too, thought Faithful. Today he had been happy, and neither the past nor the future could take today away from him. Suddenly he was so overwhelmingly sleepy that all discomfort vanished. He curled himself up on the hard table and went to sleep, to dream that he was king of the world.

CHAPTER VII

MIDSUMMER EVE

Praised be Diana's fair and harmless light,
Praised be the dews, wherewith she moists the ground,
Praised be her beams, the glory of the night,
Praised be her power, by which all powers abound.

Praised be her nymphs, with whom she decks the woods,
Praised be her knights, in whom true honour lives,
Praised be that force, by which she moves the floods;
Let that Diana shine, which all these gives.

In heaven Queen she is among the spheres,
In earth she Mistress-like makes all things pure,
Eternity in her oft change she bears,
She beauty is, by her the fair endure.

Time wears her not, she doth his chariot guide,
Mortality below her orb is placed,
By her the virtue of the stars down slide,
In her is virtue's perfect image cast.

A knowledge pure it is her worth to know,
With Circes let them dwell that think not so.

WALTER RALEIGH.

1.

THE next day was the feast of Saint John the Baptist and the University authorities, very stately in cap and gown, progressed in a body to hear the University sermon preached from the open air pulpit in the quadrangle of Magdalen College. The pulpit was hung with green boughs and the ground was strewn with rushes, in memory of Saint John preaching in the wilderness, the sky was blue and the hearts of all sang for gladness because in honor of Saint John the morning was free from lectures. It was true the sermon lasted for over an hour, but the rushes were sweet and fragrant to sit upon, and if thoughts wandered they followed the birds through sunshine and blue air to the place where the dreams come true.

There was a spirit of leisure abroad in Oxford that day, a light-heartedness that belonged to Midsummer Eve. The color of the flowers in the gardens seemed richer than usual, and their scent sweeter. The day was made for love and laughter, for staring at the lilies and praising the deep vermilion of the rose, and everyone hastened to put it to its proper use.

Even the industrious and learned felt singularly disinclined for labor. After the early dinner in hall the Dean and Canon Leigh found themselves strolling backwards and forwards over the trampled flowers and grass of the quadrangle, enjoying the warmth and the soft south wind that brought with it the scent of the fields and hedgerows beyond South Gate, discussing with an air of great gravity trivial matters that would not have detained them in the quadrangle for a single moment had the wind been in the east.

A stone in the center of the quadrangle marked the site of an old preaching cross, where the friars had preached to the common folk whose hovels Cardinal Wolsey had pulled down, and here they paused a moment, their thoughts going backward over the history of their College and forward to its future.

"What we want here," said the Dean, his foot upon the stone, "is a pond."

"What for?" asked Canon Leigh.

"If our scholars, in their last night's stampede from the hall to the Fair Gate, could have encountered a pond midway," said the Dean, "Westminster could have ducked Ipswich in it and there would have been an end of the trouble."

"It would be a bother to dig it," mused Canon Leigh. "The ground is made up of old foundations here."

"I shall leave it to posterity," said Dean Godwin. "I have no doubt that posterity will see the need for a pond. There could be goldfish in it, to give an ostensible reason for its existence and disguise its real purpose."

"No lives lost last night, I hope?" said Canon Leigh.

"No, but some injuries and a good deal of damage done. That scoundrel Nicolas de Worde seems to have been at the bottom of it as usual. He's in Bocardo."

"And I'm afraid that Giles and Faithful, my adopted son, keep him company," said Canon Leigh with shame.

"They but followed in the wake," consoled the Dean. "One behind the other like a school of dolphins. It'll do none of them any harm to stay in Bocardo till tomorrow morning. . . . Ah, look there! There's a sight to console you for the sins of your sons!"

Canon Leigh looked and his face lit up with pride, for his four daughters, together with his son Diccon and his dogs Pippit, Posy and Spot, had issued out from their front door and were crossing the quadrangle with mincing steps. They were going shopping, apparently, for each girl carried a basket of plaited rushes in one hand and a nosegay of flowers to protect her nose from the smells of the town in the other. They had taken off their aprons and on their heads instead of their white caps they wore coifs of velvet to match their dark blue gowns. Diccon was attired today in fairy green, like a miniature Robin Hood, and on his head was a tiny cap with a long peacock's feather in it, a new acquisition that he was wearing for the first time. The dogs were attached to the persons of the twins and Grace with substantial chains, for dogs, with the exception of Satan, were not allowed in College, and if the Canons kept them they must keep them under severe control and not allow them loose in the quadrangle. . . . The Leigh dogs largely spent their day lying just inside the door, waiting for an unsuspecting visitor or tradesman to open it, when they would immediately bound out, pursued by the entire household with lamentable cries.

"How happy is the man who has his quiver full," quoted the Dean.

He made this remark to Canon Leigh rather frequently; and though on some days Canon Leigh whole-heartedly agreed with him there were other days when a few doubts made themselves felt. Today, however, his family looked so charming in the June sunshine that he bowed his head in delighted assent.

2.

There was the usual trouble at the Fair Gate between Satan and the Leigh dogs. Satan naturally thought that if it was a College rule that only the porter should keep a dog that rule should be kept. Exceptions to rules should not be allowed in well run institutions. He expressed himself upon this point very frequently, and had it not been for Heatherthwayte's firm grip upon his tail he would have wiped out the Leigh dogs long ago. The children loved Heatherthwayte dearly, and he them, but owing to the presence of the dogs they could do no more today than smile hurriedly as they dragged their yowling animals past the enraged Satan.

"Where to?" asked Grace, as Joyeuce paused, considering her shopping list with a wrinkled forehead.

"The apothecary's first," said Joyeuce. "I want some century and wormwood."

The children groaned. Joyeuce concocted a particularly nauseous medicine out of camomile, century and wormwood, and now and then administered it to her family to clear the blood.

"It's all right," comforted Joyeuce. "This time it's only for Father."

They cheered up and marched on towards Carfax, the little girls keeping their noses buried in their nosegays of roses and lavender and Joyeuce keeping a firm hold of Diccon lest he should escape and get up to some of his evil tricks.

At Carfax they turned to their right and went down High Street. It was an exciting place, full of strange smells. It contained, besides the pig market in front of All Saint's Church, the butchery and the poultry, and also really beautiful shops like the aurifabray, the mercery, the spicer's and the glover's. There were no multiple shops, where you could buy all sorts of different things under one roof, for Parliament had decreed that "artificers and handicraft people hold them everyone to his own mystery," and the Oxford Town Council enforced this law very vigorously.

The apothecary of Joyeuce's choice lived just by Saint Mary's Church, in a dark little shop that made one feel indisposed simply to smell it, and the children stayed outside when she went in, holding each other's hands as she bade them, for there were always lots of people hurrying by in High Street and small persons were liable to be knocked flying if they did not hold together and stand foursquare to the bustle.

But they all went inside at the spicer's because it smelled good. You could buy cinnamon at the spicer's, and nutmeg and ginger, and all the wonderful new spices that the Merchant Adventurers were bringing home from foreign parts, and that new-fangled thing, pepper, that made one sneeze and ruined one's inside but was very smart and fashionable. Joyeuce bought some saffron to color the warden's pies and also a very little pepper as a treat for her father, and before anyone could stop him Diccon had thrust his inquisitive nose inside the packet and was sneezing his green fairy cap off his curls and his head almost off his shoulders. Then he roared, of course, and the spicer's wife came hurrying out from the back premises with a prune in her fingers to comfort him. Prunes were a delicacy that Diccon had not tasted before. He abruptly stopped roaring, ate it, spit out the stone and asked for more. But he did not get it, for Joyeuce, ashamed of him, hastily bade the spicer and his kind lady good day and removed him.

Outside in the High Street he roared again and they had to stop at the aurifabray to distract his thoughts from his woes. Behind the small, iron-barred window one could glimpse wonderful things; cups and platters all made of gold, gold chains, billements, brooches to pin gentlemen's plumes into their caps, rings for the fingers and ears of fair ladies and little gold bells to be tied to the cradles of wealthy babies. Great-Aunt was the only member of the Leigh family who could afford to be jeweled so that the girls and Diccon gaped at these glories with round eyes of amazement.

"I wish I had a pearl billement," whispered Grace.

"I should like a diamond ring," said Meg.

"I should like a big gold chain like the Mayor," said Joan.

"'I shall have that ruby brooch," said Diccon, pointing a fat finger, "to pin my peacock's feather. . . . I shall have it now."

"You will not," said Joyeuce. "Your days of foppery are not yet set in. When you are big you shall have it."

"How big?" asked Diccon. "When I am twelve?"

"You shall have it," said Joyeuce, "when you are as tall as Giles and as good as Master Philip Sidney."

The corners of Diccon's mouth went down and his little feathered head drooped like the head of a wilting poppy. He was yet so near the ground that it seemed impossible he could ever be as near the sky as Giles. And as for being as good as Master Philip Sidney, well, he knew he could never be that. He knew that the sun would turn to marchpane and the moon fall out of the sky and bowl like a hoop down the High Street before Diccon Leigh would be as good as Philip Sidney. He felt utterly stricken, for he wanted that ruby more than anything else in life. Two great tears filled his green eyes to the brim and running away from the window he felt blindly for Joyeuce's hand. The pointed toes of his little green shoes caught in the cobbles as he walked, so that he stumbled, and the tears rolled down his face and dripped off the end of his chin; but he made no sound, not even the ghost of a whimper.

Joyeuce and the little girls felt that a blight was cast over their day. Diccon, as a general rule so noisy in his grief, was occasionally smitten with this sorrow too deep for words, and the silent reproach of his woe always made everyone feel most dreadfully uncomfortable. Why, his silence seemed to ask, was I born into this cruel world? Whose fault was it that earthly life was given to me? Why was I dragged from the realms of celestial glory, where the angels gave me the comets to play with, to this earth where I stretch out my empty hands in vain for my heart's desire?

The answer to these questions not being forthcoming they turned the corner into Cornmarket in a gloomy silence.

But once past the tannery and the cordwainer's they brightened. Excitement lit gleams in their eyes and deepened the color in their cheeks, for unknown to authority they were bound on an errand of mercy to the opposite sex; and if anything thrills a woman more than being a ministering angel to a man it is being it forbiddenly.

Not that Canon Leigh had actually forbidden them to carry comforts to the prisoners at Bocardo, but knowing that he invariably refused to interfere with the course of justice they knew that he would have if they had asked him; so they had not asked him.

Joyeuce quieted her slightly restive conscience by telling herself that her father was wrong in this. She was sure there was a place in the Bible where it told one to visit prisoners in their affliction. She couldn't put her finger on chapter or verse at the moment, but she was sure there was, and she peeped under the recent purchases in her basket to see if the little packages she had brought from home were still safely there.

But, alas, when they reached Bocardo there were no signs of life at the barred window over the gateway. The five stood in a row, gazing upwards, uncertain what to do. To shout was unladylike, and to throw up stones at the window was also unladylike, and the gaze of the town was upon them.

"They're sleeping off last night," said Grace.

"Still?" queried Joyeuce sadly. This disappointment, coming on top of Diccon's exhibition of grief, was too much for her never very volatile spirits. . . . She felt utterly miserable. . . . Like Diccon she felt that living was nothing but a stretching of empty hands to an aching void.

But as she fell into her slough of despond Diccon suddenly arose out of his and their spirits passed each other, ascending and descending, a voiceless message passing between them.

"Giles!" shouted Diccon at the top of his voice. "Giles! I have a feather in my cap!"

His voice was clear as a bell, and as penetrating. The window of Bocardo, half-closed against the noise and smells of Cornmarket, opened wide and Giles was seen behind the bars.

"See my feather!" called Diccon, holding up his new treasure. "Diccon has a feather in his cap!"

Giles smiled in kindly patronage and his eyes fastened greedily on the basket. "Have any of you girls had the intelligence to bring my books?" he demanded.

"No," they chorused weakly.

"Idiots!" said Giles, and gazed down upon them with the stare of a gorgon.

"We have warden's pies," said Joyeuce stoutly. "Cinnamon cakes and comfits, and some soap, and you ought to be grateful to us instead of lowering like a thunderstorm. . . . Is Master de Worde there?"

She felt Giles' scorn less than usual because it wasn't really he whom she had considered in the stocking of her basket.

The catalogue of viands must have penetrated beyond Giles, for he was suddenly seized from behind and forcibly removed, while the expectant faces of Nicolas, Faithful, Philip Sidney, and Master Walter Raleigh of Oriel fitted themselves into a sort of pattern at the window. Philip and Faithful looked much as usual, though pale after yesterday, but Nicolas was a pitiful sight, with swollen nose and blackened eyes. The beauty of the face that had looked up at Joyeuce from below her window had momentarily departed, but as she in her turn stood below and looked up there was a new quality in her riveted, compassionate gaze, something enveloping and protective, that his vanished comeliness had not called out. For a moment his pride recoiled from it and his face hardened; then the frightened child in him leaped up in sudden gladness and his eyes as they met hers accepted what she gave.

But Philip, Faithful and Walter Raleigh were not at the window to watch an exhibition of sentiment, however touching, and the leather bag shot out of the window and landed neatly at Joyeuce's feet. . . . She started, and remembered what she was there for.

The bag made three descents and ascents and the ministering angels below basked in yet broader and broader smiles from those above. When it went up for the last time it had in it, beside a final pie and cake of soap, the little nosegay of crimson roses that Joyeuce had been carrying.

"Wait!" cried Nicolas, as the four heads disappeared from view with cheeks that were already bulging.

Joyeuce waited for what seemed to her a very long time, the children pulling impatiently at her skirts, and then the nosegay, with one crimson rose missing and something else in its place, came out of the window like a bird and alighted straight in the cupped hands she held up for it. ... A moment ago she had felt the hands were empty, held out to a void, but now they were full to the brim. ... Her spirit was mounting up now, into the very skies, and with a sudden passionate movement she knelt down and flung her arms round Diccon, who had set it mounting with his cry of "Diccon has a feather in his cap!" A feather, had he, the little love? Why, he had a hundred feathers; he was winged with them. He was love himself, little Cupid.

But Diccon was not feeling affectionate at the moment and bending low his curly head he bit her hard.

"Why did Master de Worde throw back the flowers?" asked Meg, as they journeyed homewards. "I think," she added, shaking her fair head more in sorrow than in anger, "that it was very rude of Master de Worde."

Joan also shook her head, and squeaked reprehensively.

"He kept one rose," said Joyeuce, and smiled secretly, for in the place in the nosegay where the stalk of the rose had been Nicolas had pushed a tightly folded note.

3.

It was twenty minutes to seven when Joyeuce stood trembling in the porch of Saint Michael's at the North Gate. "Meet me in the porch of Saint Michael's at seven o'clock," Nicolas had written on a bit of paper pulled from a corner of one of Raleigh's charts, and here she was, twenty minutes too early because this was her first meeting with her first lover.

She was trembling because of the frightful state her conscience was in. She felt as though it were inside her, rushing round and round like a squirrel in a cage, and also outside her, surrounding her with a scorching ball of fire. She knew now what the damned feel like when they are plunged into the lake of torment, and her heart ached for them, because she felt most uncomfortable. She pressed the palms of her hands against her hot cheeks and she wasn't at all sure she wasn't going to be sick.

The Devil had made it all most easy for her, had almost, you might say, strewn her path with roses. For it was a Thursday and it was her custom on Thursday to have supper with an old friend of her mother's, a Mistress Flowerdew, who lived by the East Gate, and to spend the hours from supper till bed with her. Mistress Flowerdew's serving man always saw her home in safety, so her family never bothered about her on Thursday evenings. . . . It had been easy, fatally easy, to send a note by Wynkyn Heatherthwayte, Heatherthwayte's little son who, evidently at the special instigation of the Devil, was paying a visit to his father at the Fair Gate, to tell Mistress Flowerdew she could not come that night. . . . Then she had put on her very best clothes, a pale green farthingale and a cream colored kirtle embroidered with yellow poppies, with a lace coif on her head and a dark blue cloak lined with yellow over all, and walked quietly out of the house, across Carfax and down Cornmarket to North Gate.

She had not actually had to tell a single lie, and she had every intention of spending the most respectable evening, but she had staged a deliberate hoax and she knew she was a wicked sinner. It struck her, as she stood there trembling, that this terrible deception had grown out of the smaller one of carrying comforts to the prisoners in Bocardo unknown to her father. One thing leads to another, she thought, and we gather speed and impetus as we roll on down the downward path.

The strange thing was that while she wrote that note to Mistress Flowerdew, while she put on her pretty clothes, brushed out her fair hair and coiled it up to lie like a crown beneath her coif, she had not felt wicked at all, she had only felt gloriously happy. It was not until she stood waiting in the porch that her conscience had started kicking up such a fuss.

It was the inaction, she thought, that made her feel so bad, and to give herself something to do she went into the church. After the warmth and brightness of the June sun outside it seemed cold as the grave and as dimly lit as a cavern in the cliff. The noises of the street seemed to come from very far away, like the beat of waves on the sea shore, and there was in the church that mingled scent of must and damp and mice and candle grease that is by association such a very holy smell.

Joyeuce sat down on one of the seats and looked about her. It was very old, this Saint Michael's at the North Gate, and very dark, for the daylight filtered in through stained glass windows that were one of the glories of Oxford. There was one strange window that Joyeuce loved particularly: out of a golden pot sprang a lily plant with five stems bearing five lilies, and among the lilies hung Christ crucified. In another window Saint Michael himself, with magnificent green wings, was trampling strong-mindedly on the dragon, and in yet another were two small fair-haired seraphs, each with six wings, standing on wheels as in the vision of Isaiah. They wore skimpy little white nightgowns and were exactly like the twins.

It was the sight of these little seraphs that steadied Joyeuce. The turmoil of her feelings suddenly subsided and she found herself thinking coldly and quietly. Her mother had left the children, Grace, the twins and Diccon, in her care, and if she married Nicolas she would be deserting them. . . . Somehow it did not occur to her that he might not love her; she took for granted that what she gave to him he would be able to give to her; she did not know yet that out of the depth of her own nature she made demands upon others that could not be satisfied unless their depth equaled her own. . . . To be happy. To be satisfied. To be fulfilled. . . . She looked at her longing, seeing it opposed to her duty, and tried to see it steadily for what it was. Those two worlds, the actual and the ideal, were before her again. The children stood for one and Nicolas for the other. One was a known love that had not satisfied and the other an unknown love that seemed to promise fulfillment but that might, too, disappoint when she moved onward to it and the ideal became in its turn the actual. Yet every instinct in her drove her forward and she had to remind herself that instincts are animal things and not to be trusted. . . . Instinct is not intuition. . . . She had no right to push forward for her own sake; she could not go on to new things unless the path was clear before her, and it was not, it was blocked by the figures of the children.

Suddenly she saw them clearly in all their dearness: the people who had until now made up her whole world. Why should she desert them

for a stranger? Of what worth was her love for them if she could not
suffer for their sake? From the beginning of the world lovers had died
daily and no love had ever been true love till the stamp of death had been
set upon its beauty, as the cross was set upon those lilies in the window.
Emotion swept over her again, setting this time in the contrary direction, and jumping up she turned blindly towards the door. . . . She would
go home. . . . She would not wait for Nicolas. Never would she desert her
darling twins, and never would she marry and leave them and Diccon to
the tender mercies of Great-Aunt. This new and selfish love was not for
her. She would stamp on the devil like the green-winged Saint Michael
in the window. She would confess her hoax to her father and be forgiven.
She had made her decision and it was irrevocable. She would never turn
back from it. . . . Dry-eyed and composed she pushed open the heavy
door and walked straight into the arms of Nicolas.

4.

The Elizabethan kiss of greeting was a useful thing, for it could so
easily develop into something more and yet be still nominally the kiss
of greeting. Handled skillfully, as by Romeo when he gave to Juliet and
took back again the sin of his presumption, it could go on a long time,
and it went on a long time in the porch of Saint Michael at the North
Gate. With Nicolas's cheek against hers and his arms straining so tightly
round her that she could hardly breathe Joyeuce felt as though she were
drowning. Locked together the two of them seemed sinking down into
the depths of some strange changeless element that they had not known
before. They felt aeons and fathoms removed from time and place, living so intensely that they did not recognize as life this strange thing
into whose depths they had fallen. The struggle Joyeuce had just passed
through was as though it had never been, and as for her irrevocable decision she had forgotten that she had ever made it.

Nicolas, less deeply drowned than Joyeuce, recovered first. Coming to the surface again, trembling, astonished and rather alarmed, he
looked down and blinked at the girl in his arms as though she were some

strange sort of wild creature that had fallen there from the heavens quite unaccountably.

"Joyeuce?" he said, speaking her name in a bewilderment that seemed begging her to explain this peculiar thing that had happened to them both.

But Joyeuce, though his question made her move in his arms and raise her face to look at him, only shook her head, for she could explain no more than he could.

"I'm still rather dirty," said Nicolas suddenly. "I ought not to touch you. I forgot."

He took his arms away from her very gently and took her hand ceremoniously to lead her into the street. Out in the sunshine, and away from the centuries-old darkness of the church, the world returned to normal again. They were a young man and a girl walking down the main thoroughfare of a modern city with the eyes of the world upon them, not two lone souls lost in a primeval darkness. They peeped at each other under their eyelashes with interest, even with amusement, appraising each other's good points and congratulating themselves upon their taste.

There was no man in the world so gallant or so fine as Nicolas, Joyeuce thought. It was true that he was distinctly grubby, and his clothes were torn from last night's fight, but he wore his gallantry with so fine an air that these things were hardly noticeable, and her red rose was stuck in his doublet.

"I ought to be in Bocardo till tomorrow," he told her as they walked down Cornmarket, "but I bribed the old jailer to let me out tonight. I'd just one angel left in my pocket."

"And the others?" asked Joyeuce.

"They're still there. The old curmudgeon would only let one go. Had I had four angels he would have let four go, he said. The others were pleased for me to go because of my nose."

"Your nose?" queried Joyeuce.

"It needs attending to," said Nicholas, feeling the injured member cautiously. "I think I may have broken it."

Joyeuce did not know where he was taking her, and neither did she care. She had forgotten everything in the world but Nicolas and at that moment he could have done what he liked with her. She was in reality the stronger in character of the two of them, and their relationship when from below the window of Bocardo she had looked protectively up at him had been the true relationship, but now it was he who was outwardly all protection. She clung to his arm as they picked their way through the refuse of Cornmarket, for though she was tall he was yet taller and her head only reached his shoulder. The slight blow to his pride that she had dealt him by the first look was healed by her clinging hands. . . . He stuck out his chest, smiled benignly down upon her, and strutted, singing softly to himself,

> *Greensleeves was all my joy,*
> *Greensleeves was my delight;*
> *Greensleeves was my heart of gold,*
> *And who but Lady Greensleeves.*

"We're going to Tattleton's Tavern," he told her. "Tattleton's a friend of mine. He'll give me clean clothes to change into, and some money to go on with, and you shall sit in the painted room and play the clavicytherium while you are waiting for me, and then we'll have supper in the garden where the eglantine grows."

Joyeuce bowed her head in silent assent, for the modest program filled her with an excitement too deep for words.

Tattleton's was a most respectable Tavern and Master and Mistress Tattleton people of refinement. Between the Inns and the Taverns of Oxford there was a great gulf fixed. The Inn was for the common people and the Tavern for the quality. Travelers could find food and lodging for themselves and stabling for their horses at an Inn but at a Tavern accommodation was given only to those who were personal friends of the host and hostess. It was more of a club than an hotel; gentlemen sat there of an evening to drink wines of an exquisite bouquet and flavor and to discuss the gossip of the town with their friends.

Master Tattleton owned both the Tavern and the Crosse Inn next door, and made a good thing out of them. They were on the east side of Cornmarket and were both of them fine houses. Joyeuce and Nicolas passed the Crosse Inn first, with its great archway leading into the galleried inn yard, and its painted sign, the red cross of Saint George on a white ground, swaying gently in the wind. The pillory stood just outside the Crosse Inn, serving a double purpose, for anyone who misbehaved himself inside the Inn could easily be run outside and put in it, and also it was a source of entertainment for guests drinking their beer at the windows.

But the Tavern was even more beautiful. It was a timber-framed house with overhanging timber gables and beautiful tall stone and brick chimneys, and it had the dignity of its long history. It had originally been an almost ecclesiastical building, a lodging house for scholars who would one day be priests, and religious signs and symbols were still to be found carved or painted over its fireplaces and around its cornices. When its scholars deserted it it had become the Salutation Tavern, but this lovely name smacked too much of popery for Elizabethan taste and now it was just Tattleton's.

Both Master and Mistress Tattleton came running when Nicolas, with Joyeuce on his arm, stood in the beautiful paneled entrance hall and shouted. They were comely, roundabout people, enslaved to the undeserving Nicolas by the spell of his charms. He presented Joyeuce to them, she blushing a little under the amused scrutiny of their twinkling eyes, and made his requests known in a lordly manner. Then he was carried off by Master Tattleton to get washed and changed and have his nose ministered to, and Mistress Tattleton led Joyeuce upstairs. The business of the Tavern was conducted on the ground floor, the private rooms of the family were on the first floor and the guest rooms were on the second floor.

They toiled up and up the circular oak staircase that wound round a massive octagonal oak newel, Joyeuce panting a little as she followed behind Mistress Tattleton's broad back, holding up her beautiful farthingale on either side.

"Never mind, dearie," consoled Mistress Tattleton. "You'll think it well worth the trouble when you get there."

With a final pant they got there and Mistress Tattleton paused outside the door, her head on one side and a tear in her eye. She was a kindly soul, and a sentimental, and Joyeuce in her green gown had taken her fancy.

"There's not many I let use this room," she said portentously, "they might do it an injury; but so sweet and fair a lady should wait for her lover in a fair room."

Then she abruptly strained Joyeuce to her bosom, flung open the door, paused a moment to hear Joyeuce's cry of pleasure, and went off down the stairs, lowering her bulk cautiously from step to step and chuckling to herself in fat delight. . . . So fair a poppet. . . . So handsome a couple. . . . So merciful a thing that she had strawberries to give them for their supper. Young love should always be fed on strawberries. Eat strawberries while you can, Mistress Tattleton was wont to say, for when you are older they may not agree with you.

5.

Joyeuce let her cloak drop to the floor and stood in the center of the room, gazing delightedly. It was sparsely furnished with a carved settle, a clavicytherium and a couple of stools with bowls of flowers upon them, one on each side of the beautiful herringbone brick fireplace; but it did not need more, for too many things in it would only have detracted from the beauty of its painted walls. Tempera painting on plaster was coming into fashion as wall decoration, and in many houses taking the place of tapestry hangings. But this happened to be the first example of the new art that Joyeuce had seen.

The craftsman who had painted these walls was an artist, and he had enjoyed himself; indeed his enjoyment cried out to the beholder from each of the four walls. The background of the painting was a rich vermilion-orange ocher, from the pits worked at Headington, the very color of delight, and on it was traced a trellis-work pattern in old gold, outlined in black and white. Within each of the linked compartments were painted lively posies of English flowers; canterbury bells, wind-flowers, passion flowers, wild roses and bunches of white grapes. They were not gaudily colored, for bright colors would have clashed with that glorious background, but painted softly in brown-pink, purple, green and gray. Words ran round the top of the walls in a painted frieze, and Joyeuce spelled them out under her breath.

First of thy rising
And last of thy rest be thou
God's servant, for that hold is best.
In the morning early serve God devoutly.
Fear God above everything.
Love the brotherhood. Honor the king.

The windows of the room were fast shut against the noise of Corn-market, but in any case it was quiet now because people had gone to their suppers. The silence was complete and cool and fragrant, and Joyeuce sat down on the settle, with her hands folded on the yellow embroidered poppies in her lap, and seemed to herself to be listening to it. Moments of beautiful leisure like this did not come her way very often and she was utterly and completely happy, even though she felt rather bewildered as to who she was, for she did not seem to be the same tormented Joyeuce that she had been half an hour ago. She felt very old and wise, as though Nicolas's kiss had taken her right back to the beginning of the world and she had had to live through all the intervening centuries between then and now in a few minutes, and yet at the same time she felt gloriously young, as though she had begun life all over again as a little child. She felt, too, very strong and very secure, for this new beginning had brought with it a welling up of new life, and it was with an assurance and gaiety that were not usually hers that she nodded at the lovely painted flowers around her. They made a sort of protective arbor for her, she felt, and her sense of security deepened. If love for the one person in the world could be like this, a cool fragrant hiding place built round the well of life into which one could creep and be refreshed when the storms of this world became more than one could put up with, then she understood why it was a treasure of such price that men and women were willing to die for it. She herself, she thought, would be willing to die again and again if this glorious renewal might come to her after every death.

The sudden and rather boisterous entry of Nicolas, washed and brushed and clothed in the crimson doublet of Jo Tattleton, Mistress Tattleton's eldest, seemed almost to do violence to her arbor; until she remembered that it was he who had built it up around her. She got up and curtseyed to him, as though he were the king whom the verse upon the wall told her to honor, then swept before him out of the door and down the stairs with so superb a pride and dignity that for the moment the volatile Nicolas was deprived of the power of speech.

6.

A pathway, walled on both sides, led from the back of the Tavern to the small walled garden. It was a very private, very charming little place. Square flower beds, filled now with blue canterbury bells and bushes of eglantine, starred all over with small pink blossoms, lay very demurely in green grass. The high walls were covered with woodbine and yellow climbing roses and there was a little trelliswork arbor roofed and walled with a green vine.

"Look," said Joyeuce, "there is another arbor."

"Another?" asked Nicolas.

"It is like the one upstairs," said Joyeuce. "Trelliswork and a vine. It was this garden, Nicolas, that told the artist what to paint on the walls upstairs."

She paused, smiling, picturing that unknown artist, when imagination failed him for a moment, running down the stairs, his paint brush stuck behind his ear, to have another look at the garden. It must have been a long way up and down, each time inspiration slackened, but then judging by his spirited designs he was a young man who had determined that Tattleton's garden, made as it was for lovers, should flower even in midwinter.

Mistress Tattleton had set two stools very close together inside the arbor, with a table covered with a linen cloth before them, and she had excelled herself in the matter of food. By the mercy of Providence, it being Tattleton's birthday tomorrow, she had that very morning concocted and baked one of her famous lark pies for the good man, and she set it upon the table in the arbor. Tattleton, of course, would now have to go without, but lark pie never really agreed with him and she could knock him up a nice little rabbit pasty that would be all he needed at his age. The lark pie had quite a mountain of pastry on top of it and was ornamented with two little sugar cupids with wings made from the larks' feathers. . . . Mistress Tattleton was an artist, and no mistake. . . . Joyeuce and Nicolas, sitting very close together on the two stools, said so over and over again and Mistress Tattleton herself, standing with arms akimbo at the entrance to the arbor and looking down at her handiwork with tears in her eyes—the cupids had reference to the first meeting of herself and Tattleton thirty years ago, when they had both gone to see a hanging at the Castle mound, had sat next to each other on the raised seats before the gibbet and fallen in love at first sight—entirely agreed with them.

There were other things to eat besides the pie, for Mistress Tattleton had six sons, and they had all been in Bocardo at one time or another, so she knew with what kind of appetite the released prisoner is restored to his friends. There were bowls of strawberries floating in milk, there was a dish of cherries, there were manchets of bread and a dish of comfits and last but not least there was the canary wine, for which the Tavern was famous, in exquisite glasses.

Mistress Tattleton helped them to pie, lingered a moment to give herself the pleasure of watching Nicolas's strong white teeth bite deep into her pastry, and Joyeuce's pink tongue daintily exploring the head of a sugar cupid that seemed to her too pretty to eat, and then took herself off. . . . The pretty dears! . . . She applied the corner of her gown to her eye, shut the door of the walled pathway firmly and informed her household at the top of her voice that no one, not even my lord of Leicester himself, was to be let into the garden till she gave them leave.

Joyeuce always had a scruple about eating lark. The brutalities of the age that other people took entirely for granted, the cock fighting, the lark eating, the bear baitings, the beheadings and the hangings, made her miserable. To each generation its own horrors, to which the majority are blunted by custom, but Joyeuce was one of those who in any age are cruelly awake to cruelty. She was in the minority, of course, and she knew it, so she thought no worse of Nicolas that he ate her share of lark as well as his own. . . . And he gave her his sugar cupid, so it was quite fair. . . . She did not eat either of them; she had only gently licked one to please Mistress Tattleton; she wrapped them both in her kerchief and put them in her wallet to take back to the twins.

It is to Nicolas's credit that in spite of his hunger, which had been no more than blunted by the dainties brought to Bocardo, he was very attentive to Joyeuce. She was too happy and excited to eat very much but he carefully fished out the spiders that had dropped into her strawberries and milk—the only drawbacks to the beautiful arbor were the things that dropped from above—and he hung cherries over her ears under her fair hair, and he said the sweetest things to her between each mouthful.

Nicolas was used to making love to pretty ladies, he had a flair for it and believed in using one's gifts, but this evening he actually meant what he said. Joyeuce in her green gown, with the shadows of the vine leaves trembling over the embroidered yellow poppies on her kirtle, like frightened fingers that wooed with an airy touch but dared not lift or handle, was certainly a sight for sore eyes. Her hair was the color of the woodbine on the walls, and the cherries he had hung over her ears seemed to call out an unwonted red in her cheeks and lips. Other maidens who had given Nicolas the opportunity of using his gifts had been more beautiful, more witty, more aristocratic, but none of them had had such a demure dignity as Joyeuce, or had been such a touching mixture of childishness and maturity. This girl was a woman who had worked hard and suffered much, and borne on her shoulders responsibilities that would have crushed Nicolas to pulp had they been laid upon him, and yet at the same time she was a child who could be transported into the seventh heaven of delight by a sugar cupid or a red cherry or a

butterfly kiss upon her cheek. As Nicolas petted her she seemed to get
fatter and rosier under his very eyes. Had she never been petted before,
he wondered, that such a very little of it could cause such a flowering of
beauty in her? His power over her gave him a self-confidence that was
like balm to his new manhood, while at the same time her maturity gave
him a most unusual feeling of humility. . . . He did not know whether he
liked the effect she had on him or whether he didn't, but at any rate it
was something quite different. . . . His feeling for Joyeuce seemed, now
and for the rest of his life, to be a thing apart, something locked for safety
in a casket of cool green leaves.

Joyeuce had not known that one could be so aware of anyone as
she was aware of Nicolas. Her capacity for love was large and she had
known, of course, long ago, how almost painfully the personality of the
person loved can impinge upon one's own. In the time of grief after her
mother's death her father's misery, that gave no sign to the world at large
and was hidden, he thought, even from Joyeuce, had been like an actual
physical illness in her own body. It had seemed round her like a black
coat of mail, pressing in on her, choking her breathing and clutching at
her heart so that she thought it would stop. The personalities of the little
boys and of the twins seemed mingled with hers, and as for Diccon, it
was difficult to realize that he was not her very own child, bone of her
bone and flesh of her flesh. Had she carried his body within her own, as
she now seemed to herself to carry his wicked little spirit within hers,
he could not have been more completely a part of her.

But her awareness of Nicolas, a man who was almost a stranger to
her, was so acute that it frightened her. Her mingled love and ignorance
made of his personality a thing so mysterious and wonderful that it filled
her world. The very shadows lying across the grass seemed shadows of
it, and the flowers were paintings drawn from the pattern of Nicolas.

And if these could give her news of him, the actual physical presence
of Nicolas, eating lark pie beside her in the arbor, must surely be as the
written pages of a book that tell of the spirit of it. Hating her ignorance,
longing for knowledge of him, she looked almost hungrily at the hollow of his temple and the way the hair grew above it, the curve of his

cheekbone and the golden down upon it, at the cleft in his chin and the line of his jaw and the way his head was set upon his neck. Then a wave of hot shame swept over her and she dropped her eyes in confusion; only to see his hand resting upon the table beside her, and to notice the shape of the fingers and the hollow in the wrist where she would have felt the pulse beating if she had put her finger on it. . . . The pulse. . . . Terror engulfed her. That beating pulse was such a tiny thing, yet if it were to stop he would be dead. The careless flight of an arrow, a slip on the stairs, a flash of lightning out of the noonday or the thrust of an angry sword in a tavern at midnight; such small things as these could still the even smaller pulse and the kindly body would be there no longer to give tidings of the spirit to its lovers.

"Nicolas! Nicolas!" she cried in terror.

He flung both arms round her and demanded what the matter was.

"You wouldn't let any harm come to you, would you?" she whispered.

Nicolas roared with laughter, his head thrown back so that his throat showed like a strong pillar defying the fates. "Not yet," he said. "Not till we've had time to love each other. . . . I promise."

He took her out into the garden—the dimness of the arbor, he thought, must be conducive to melancholia—and she was soon a child again, poking her fingers into the canterbury bells, rubbing the sweet scented eglantine leaves between the palms of her hands, and laughing at the drunken bumble bees who reeled from woodbine trumpet to yellow rose and from there fell heavily to lie upside down and protesting on the purple pansies growing in the bed below.

7.

But she had been a child for only a little while when a pealing bell and the fading sky over her head warned her that time passes.

"I must go," she whispered, her head drooping. She was sad now, for to the happy the bell that marks the passing of the hours brings bad news. Nicolas was sad too as he led her into the house to say good-by to Mistress Tattleton, and out in the street again, going home, they could find nothing to say. He led her silently, holding her hand, and only her silken skirts whispered softly as they walked.

At the Fair Gate they stopped and tried to say good night, but they couldn't. Although the sun had set it had left its warmth behind with them. There was a flame burning in them both that made it impossible to part; they were fused by it, bound together as though it created a tiny world of warmth for the two of them outside of which it was impossible to live.

"Joyeuce," whispered Nicolas, "it is Midsummer Eve and the fairies will be dancing in the meadows."

Joyeuce nodded her head. It did not matter to her where they went as long as they were together, and where the fairies are dancing is the place for lovers on Midsummer Eve. . . . She believed in fairies.

They went on down Fish Street and turned into an alleyway beside the South Gate that led through into the Meadows. Joyeuce had never yet been there so late and she caught her breath, for they did not seem the same fields that she knew in the sunshine.

They had left the sun behind them and walked into the country of the moon. It hung in a deep green sky and low on the horizon Jupiter burned like a lamp. The trees, heavy with their June foliage, stood up motionless and almost black against that strange sky and below them the grass had changed its color, had become a cold blue-green under the light of the moon. The flowers were visible, the tall daisies in the grass and the wild roses on the bushes, but all color had been drained from them, even from the yellow eyes of the daisies that by day ogled the sun. They looked like fragile motionless butterflies, or pale ghosts of the moon and the stars above them.

They went slowly on under the trees, hand in hand, and even Nicolas did not feel himself, for the green light and the absolute stillness of this moon country were so strange. This was an old country, the country of legend, where the spirits of dead lovers hid beneath the trees and the ghosts of their songs sighed and whispered over the grass. When he had asked Joyeuce to come with him into the Meadows the hot magic of the sun had been racing in his veins and he had been ready for he knew not what midsummer madness; but now he felt differently.

Joyeuce's hand in his, that had before been warm with excitement, was now cool, and looking at her he saw that the moon had taken the red from her lips and the color from the poppies on her dress; she was all green and silver, like a naiad. She was innocent as the moon and he could not hurt her.

And Joyeuce, too, her feeling born of his, felt different. Her painful awareness of his physical presence, that had made her feel ashamed, was gone. In the dim shadowy figure strolling beside her she was only conscious of the spirit of the man, and rejoiced in the sense of peace that it brought her. When he stopped under a tree and slipped his arms round her she was not afraid. There was no passion in them and his face against hers was cool. Love the creator had them in its merciless grip but the vestal moon had made it urbane and pitiful and it chose that night to ignore their bodies and work upon their souls. Yet the virtue was not only in the moon; Nicolas could lay claim to a little. Part of him was at the mercy of the time and the place and the magic of the night but another part of him was conscious of desire, and refusal, and increase of strength following hard on the heels of it.

A familiar scent reached Joyeuce and she lifted her head and sniffed. Then she saw that a hundred white moons, larger than those that sprinkled the bushes and the grass, were hanging low over their heads.

"Nicolas!" she whispered, "we're standing under an elder tree! Just sniff!"

"What of it?" asked Nicolas, sniffing.

"If you stand under an elder tree on Midsummer Eve you see the King of the Elves," whispered Joyeuce.

Nicolas looked down into her face and laughed. Her eyes were round as a frightened child's and she was trembling. There was nothing of the woman in her at this moment, and as he kissed her on her pointed chin and her shadowed eyelids he smiled to think that the woman who could grapple so courageously with the sorrows and the labor of her life should be such a little girl that she could tremble like an aspen leaf at an old wives' tale.

"You babe!" he laughed, "you absurd, adorable babe!" And then he happened to glance ahead over her shoulder and his jaw dropped and his eyes grew even rounder than hers.

"What is it?" she whispered.

Nicolas was incapable of speech but keeping his arms tightly round her, lest she should scream with fright when she saw what he saw, he swung her round a little way.

Clinging together under the magic elder tree they stood and stared. Not far away from them a tiny green figure was treading out a circle on the grass. He was a figure not of this world; ethereal, airy, and ready at any moment to vanish into thin air. Whether he trod a circle that was already there, or whether he was deliberately tracing one out with his small feet, it was impossible to say, but he moved on and on, slowly but rhythmically, half-dancing and half-walking, and crooning a little song to himself, but so low that it reached them as only the ghost of a sound and not sound itself. His head was down, watching his moving feet, and they could not see his face, but Joyeuce could distinctly see his little white ears with their pointed tips. . . . He was dressed all in fairy green and from the cap upon his head there drooped a long peacock's feather.

The lovers under the elder tree were speechless, stupefied and trembling. They were mesmerized by that low crooning song and the ceaselessly moving figure. It was a long time before that peacock's feather forced itself upon Joyeuce's consciousness, and when it did she could scarcely believe the evidence of her own brain and eyes.

"Diccon!" she gasped stupidly. "Diccon!"

"Diccon?" queried Nicolas. "Diccon?" He stared again and then dropped his arms from Joyeuce and blushed rosily. . . . For full five minutes had he, Nicolas de Worde, an enlightened man of the world, thought that he beheld a fairy creature. . . . He would have liked to have spanked young Diccon, for he was much discomfited.

"The little devil!" he said in heartfelt tones.

But Joyeuce had flown over the grass and was kneeling in the center of the circle that Diccon trod, her arms stretched out.

"Diccon!" she cried. "Baby!"

But Diccon took no notice of her at all. He moved on and on, still crooning his song, and his green eyes shone like emeralds in the light of the moon. Now that she could hear it clearly it seemed to Joyeuce that his song reminded her of something, though she did not know what.

"Diccon!" she cried again. "Diccon!" and leaning forward she clasped him in her arms. For a moment she felt that she had clasped thin air, and had a moment of terror, but then as she pulled him closer, she felt the round stolidity of him, and the delicious warmth of his baby humanity.

"Sweetheart," she cried, "how did you get here, all by yourself?"

"I was lonely," said Diccon. "I was lonely in the big bed."

Joyeuce picked him up and clasped him to her in an agony of reproach. He had waked up in the dead of night, the poor lamb, stretched out his hand and found her not there. She would never forgive herself, and she kissed him with such passion that Nicolas was jealous and strode towards them over the grass.

"Don't waste your kisses on such a wicked little elf," he mocked, standing beside her where she knelt with Diccon in her arms. "Look what he's been writing," and he pointed to a ring of flowers that surrounded them, daisies, purple milkwort and yellow lady's-slipper forming a perfect circle on the grass.

Joyeuce gasped and stood up, still clutching Diccon to her. She knew, as Nicolas did, though she believed it and he did not, that when the fairies have a message for mortals they are said to write it upon the grass with flowers; if mortals cannot read it the more fools they.

"What is it?" she whispered. "Is it for us?"

"What is it, Diccon?" asked Nicolas, and look the little green creature out of her arms that they might not ache with his weight.

But if Diccon knew he wasn't going to say. He smiled a secret smile and lolled his leathered head against Nicolas's shoulder.

"News from a far country," said Nicolas dreamily. "But we cannot read it."

They were suddenly sad, conscious of the restrictions of their mortality. Such mysterious worlds within worlds surrounded them and they could know no more of them than a faint echo now and again, or a flickering outline, like the shadow on a curtain of a great host passing by. They felt strangers in this country of the moon and held tightly to each other, scared by the silence and the eerie green light.

"Now then, Mistress! Come now, Master! Can you not tell the time by the stars in the sky and the dew on the grass? No time to be out and about." A cheery voice came booming through the shadows and a swinging yellow lantern illumined a large red beard and a pair of striding legs behind which skulked a black plumy creature whose eyes were like lamps in the gloom. . . . Heatherthwayte was on their tracks. . . . Bewildered by the light of his lantern they stood blinking at him like owls, they inside and he outside the fairy ring.

Heatherthwayte, too, was bewildered. He had seen them come together to the Fair Gate, try to say good night, fail, and pass on down to the Meadows. When they had not come back he had worried about them, scratching his head and making unusual noises in his throat that Satan found perplexing. Finally he had got up, lit his lantern, whistled to Satan and stumped off down Fish Street to find them. . . . These motherless maidens needed an eye kept upon them and he, Heatherthwayte, would keep it.

But now that he had found them within their fairy ring he hardly knew them. Nicolas standing tall and straight in his scarlet doublet, holding a little green elf in his arms, was a figure of legend, and Joyeuce in her green gown was surely a naiad who had drifted up with the mist through the water meadows from the river beyond. Heatherthwayte stared at them in stupefaction and Satan, used to greeting them with boisterous barks, lowered his tail and was silent.

But the light of the lantern soon brought them all to themselves. It banished the moonlight and with it flowed in remembrance of time and place. Satan barked and Heatherthwayte, though too superstitious to step inside the fairy ring on Midsummer Eve, stretched out a hairy hand and clawed the three towards him.

"A nice to-do there'd be over this if I was not to 'ush it up," he scolded. "And the child, too, out in the dew and the moonlight. . . . Moonlight's

not 'olesome. . . . Come along, mistress. Come, master. A couple of children you are, and should be whipped according." He turned an outraged
back upon them and led the way homewards, Nicolas following. Joyeuce, running after them, and seeing the little green figure of the child
clinging to the striding figure of the man in his scarlet doublet—not
even the moonlight had been able to take the color out of that doublet—
had one last magic moment. They made her think of a holly bush, that
brings romance in midwinter, and the two together, she thought, would
be the joy and the warmth of her life until the end.

Joyeuce, when she returned from Mistress Flowerdew's, always
came in the back way, along the cobbled lane that led from Fish Street
to the stables, and from there to the garden, so Nicolas parted from her
and Diccon in the lane, with loving but rather hasty kisses, and then followed Heatherthwayte towards the Fair Gate, feeling in his wallet as he
went for the wherewithal to reward a man who had rescued two lovers
adrift on the perilous sea of fairyland and towed them back safe to the
shore. The last Joyeuce heard of him was his voice singing,

> Greensleeves, now farewell! adieu!
> God I pray to prosper thee;
> For I am still thy lover true.
> Come once again and love me.
> Greensleeves was all my joy,
> Greensleeves was my delight;
> Greensleeves was my heart of gold,
> And who but Lady Greensleeves.

8.

In their big bedroom Joyeuce undressed Diccon by moonlight.
When they had come in they had found the little girls and the dogs fast
asleep, and quite unaware that there had been any unusual goings on.
But not so Tinker. He knew all about it and was sitting very upright and

severe on the pillow, lashing his tail. He was wide awake and his eyes shone like fire and were fixed on Joyeuce in an unblinking stare all the time she was putting Diccon to bed. . . . She felt most uncomfortable. . . . No one in this world, she had discovered long ago, can make one feel more uncomfortable than an indignant cat.

Diccon offered no explanation of his strange behavior. She did not know why, when he had waked up lonely in the big bed, he had dressed himself up in his fairy green and gone out into the Meadows, nor why he had been treading out that fairy ring and crooning that strange song. He was too sleepy to be asked questions, his curly head swaying on his shoulders with its weight of dreams, and in any case she did not want to know. . . . It was altogether too queer.

It was not until she herself was in bed, and Diccon was lying fast asleep beside her with the now somnolent Tinker clasped in his arms, that she remembered why his crooning song was familiar to her. . . . His gypsy foster-mother had sung something like it to the two tiny babies who lay in her arms.

She sat bolt upright in terror.

She had forgotten to draw the curtains and by the light of the moon she bent over and examined the face of her best-beloved. . . . It seemed he was still her best-beloved, for in her fear for him she had for the moment forgotten Nicolas. . . . His green eyes were hidden by his shut lids but their look of mischief seemed to have been transferred to the long eyelashes that were almost aggressive in their curl. His freckles seemed to have cast a shadow over his face and robbed it of that look of pearly innocence that makes the faces of sleeping children, however erroneously, as those of the cherubs in heaven. His red mouth, relaxed in sleep, was like a poppy. . . . How red his mouth was, Joyeuce thought. None of the other children had lips as red as his. . . . How unlike he was to all the rest of them. . . . How utterly unlike . . . Was he, could he be, a changeling? If she had not seized hold of him, as he trod his fairy ring on Midsummer Eve, would he have vanished away altogether?

Joyeuce lay flat on her back, her hands at her sides, staring out at that strange green sky outside the window and shivering a little with love, and happiness, and an eerie fear. Now and then she shut her eyes and tried to sleep but always, when she did that, she saw, between sleeping and waking, Nicolas and Diccon, dressed in scarlet and green, moving together through the moonlit trees towards the gates of fairyland while she, Joyeuce Leigh the stay-at-home toiling mouse, ran after them, desperately trying to keep up with their striding figures and to keep in her sight the portals of those gates that led into the country for which she longed.

Yet when at last broken feverish dreams took the place of her wakefulness she knew she was beaten. A great wind was blowing against her, pushing her backwards, until at last she could not stand against it any longer and it forced her to her knees; and she found herself kneeling in the church of Saint Michael at the North Gate, vowing herself to renunciation.

Then she opened her eyes for the twentieth time to find that the green sky had faded and in its place had come another, equally strange, of silver mist shot through with gold.

The cuckoos were calling and it was Midsummer Day.

CHAPTER VIII

SUNDAY

Leave me, O Love, which reachest but to dust;
And thou, my mind, aspire to higher things;
Grow rich in that which never taketh rust;
Whatever jades but fading pleasure brings.
Draw in thy beams, and humble all thy might
To that sweet yoke where lasting freedoms be;
Which breaks the clouds and opens forth the light,
That doth both shine and give us sight to see.
O take fast hold; let that light be thy guide
In this small course which birth draws out to death,
And think how evil becometh him to slide,
Who seeketh heaven, and comes of heavenly breath.
Then farewell, world; thy uttermost I see;
Eternal Love, maintain thy life in me.

PHILIP SIDNEY.

1.

WILL and Thomas Leigh, waking up three days later in their big bed, realized with pleasure that it was Sunday. They were not pious children and their pleasure sprang solely from the fact that they would not have to go to school today. They would have to go to church, unfortunately, but church did not take so long as school and there was no necessity to listen to what was said.

Will woke first and pulling aside the crimson curtains of the bed he peeped out at the room. It was over the study and was reached through Canon Leigh's, so that no nocturnal adventures were possible without their father knowing of them. Its tapestries, representing David getting the better of Goliath and Absalom at his last gasp hanging from the oaktree, were not as beautiful as the tapestries in the girls' room but no doubt more suited to the boys in subject matter, portraying as they did the reward of courage and the frightful fate in store for those who do not behave nicely to their parents. The crimson curtains of the four-poster were not embroidered, but then it was no good wasting fine embroidery on Will and Thomas, for they did not care for such things.

Will looked anxiously at Absalom hanging from the oaktree. If Absalom's beautiful hair looked very bright and golden, and if his terrified, dying face had a pink tinge to it, Will knew that the sun was shining and hastened to get out of bed, but if Absalom's death agonies were shadowed Will knew it was raining and burrowed back under the blankets again until someone dragged him out. Today Absalom was brightly illumined and Will awoke Thomas by a blow on the chest and pulled back all the curtains.

Thomas shut his mouth—he had adenoids and slept with it ajar—opened his eyes and lay staring at the crimson canopy over his head until full consciousness returned to him.

"Sunday," he said. "We shall have to wash."

They washed really properly on Sundays, all over, with hot water, and then they put on their clean clothes. Their hair had its weekly brush, and their nails were cleaned, and when they were finished they really looked quite nice.

Before they had time to get out of bed Diggory entered upon them with a huge basin and a ewer of hot water. Diggory's Sunday morning was most exhausting. He got up in what was almost the middle of the night and cleaned the animals, then he cleaned himself and then he cleaned Will and Thomas.

"You needn't stop, Diggory," said Will, "we can wash ourselves."

This remark was made weekly, as a matter of form, but Diggory knew better than to permit any such thing. He set the basin upon the floor, poured water into it, and advanced upon the bed in a grim silence, hailing our first Will and then Thomas.

He watched them while they washed, his old face set like a mask, and he made no sound at all unless he saw them skimping the job, when he bellowed like a bull and his hairy hands shot out to box their ears. When the agony was over he departed as silently as he had come, taking the basin and ewer with him.

"That's over for another week," sighed Will in satisfaction, and with chattering teeth he got himself into his clean shirt and his Sunday doublet of peacock blue.... It was cold work stripping so early in the morning.... In winter the family ablutions took place before the kitchen fire on Saturday night, and that was really pleasanter.

When they were dressed Joyeuce came in, carrying a hairbrush and two little snowy ruffs. She had been up till midnight the night before, washing and ironing the ruffs for them all, and plaiting them with pokesticks.

Joyeuce had been very odd the last few days and her family had not known what to make of her. Sometimes she had seemed marvelously happy, singing at her work, or falling upon her brothers and sisters and kissing them at the most unexpected moments, but at other times she had moved about the house as though weighed down by some guilty secret, and would set to and polish and spin and wash up with a grim energy, as though reproaching herself for loss of time. She was in this latter mood now. She brushed the boys' hair until they yelled for mercy, and the Spanish Inquisition would have been a picnic compared to the way in which she cleaned their nails.

"Ow!" squeaked Thomas indignantly, as with his right arm pinioned beneath hers she worked at his nails with a sharp silver instrument of torture.

"Filthy little pig," said Joyeuce. "What do you do to get your hands like this?" With a sigh of despair she spread out his grubby little paw and looked at it. She had not made much impression upon his nails with her silver instrument, though she had made some, but upon the actual hand Diggory's soap and water had made no impression whatsoever. ... The dirt was engrained. ... "I wonder what Mother did for your hands?" she pondered, her forehead wrinkled in a worried frown. She tried hard never to fall below her mother's standard of cleanliness and housewifery, but there were times when no one seemed to remember what Mother had done.

"But we didn't go to school when Mother was alive," said Will, "and so we didn't get like this. Education," he explained, "is very soiling."

"Don't be unhappy, Joyeuce," said Will. "Lots of good people are dirty. They say Saint Frideswide only washed once a year and the Queen's Grace herself only has a bath once in three weeks." He flung his arms round her and kissed her, for he was a loving little boy and he did not like to see her looking worried, and he did not squeak at all while she did his other hand.

They all had an extra large breakfast on Sunday, and really they needed it after all the washing they had done, a very satisfying breakfast of meat and beer and bread, and when it was over, and Joyeuce and Dorothy had washed it up and made the beds, they got ready for church.

The Sunday morning church-going was the great event of their week and took a lot of preparing for. . . . Great-Aunt came with them. . . . It was practically the only time in the week when she went out and she insisted on riding her white mule Susan to the Cathedral door. There was no reason whatever why she should not have walked the short distance, but the getting her on her mule, and the getting her off again, made a lot of fuss and commotion, and she liked fuss and commotion. Canon Leigh did not assist in getting Great-Aunt off to church. . . . He said his duties called him elsewhere.

No one but Joyeuce herself knew how exhausted she was by the time she had got the family dressed and they were all waiting by the front door for Diggory to bring Susan round from the stables; yet she had the satisfaction of knowing that they looked magnificent. Great-Aunt wore black velvet, over a crimson kirtle, and an immense ruff. The veil she wore over her black wig was worked in gold thread, and she had rubies in her ears and on the bodice of her gown. Grace wore her green silk kirtle, scattered over with yellow and silver dots, with a farthingale of rose color, the twins were dressed in forget-me-not blue, Will and Thomas in peacock blue and Diccon in his faerie green. . . . While as for Joyeuce herself, she wore the clothes she had worn on that never to be forgotten evening at the Tavern that was only a few days ago but yet seemed parted from her by several years.

Diggory came in through the Fair Gate, leading Susan in her saddle and trappings of crimson velvet, and Will and Thomas held Susan while Diggory and Joyeuce lifted Great-Aunt up so that she sat sideways on her saddle, with her feet planted firmly on the board below and her fine skirts billowing out over Susan's white back. She looked magnificent when she was in place but the language she used while she was being got there was staggering. The great ladies of the day could swear like the proverbial trooper, the Queen's Grace herself not being behindhand in the art, but Great-Aunt, when she really got going, could put the lot of them completely in the shade.

Then they started, Diggory leading Susan, Joyeuce and Diccon walking hand in hand beside Great-Aunt, and the twins, Grace, Will and Thomas walking behind. They all carried large prayer books, and the girls had posies of flowers to match their frocks.

From the other houses round the quadrangle, where lived the seven other Canons, came more family groups, and from the scholars' rooms the scholars came running in their sober clothes and snowy Sunday ruffs, while under the Fair Gate flowed a steady stream of people in their bright Sunday best. The sun shone gloriously and the blue air seemed clamorous with sound, for all the bells of Oxford were ringing their people to church. The bells of Saint Mary the Virgin, the bells of Saint Martin's at Carfax, of Saint Michael's at the North Gate, of All Saints,' Saint Aldate's and Saint Ebbe's, and clearer and more lovely than them all the famous bells of Christ Church, that for years had rung the monks to prayer at Oseney Abbey and now pealed out from the Cathedral tower. They had their own names—Hautclere, Douce, Clement, Austin, Marie, Gabriel and John—and personalities that matched their names, and they ranked only second in importance in the world of bells to Great Tom himself.

There was no way into the Cathedral from the quadrangle and the stream of worshipers passed by the staircase up to the hall and into the fifteenth century cloisters of the original monastery, and from there up a flight of steps into the Cathedral. Susan was brought to a halt at the bottom of the steps with a great clattering of hoofs on the paving stones, and Great-Aunt was with difficulty got down. She entered the Cathedral leaning on Joyeuce's arm on one side and her stick on the other, with Diccon walking before her carrying her prayer book and nosegay and the other children following behind. She made a point of entering at the last possible moment, and would even wait in the cloisters till that moment arrived, and then she would sail up the central aisle very slowly, with the whole congregation looking at her. . . . She adored it, and so did Diccon. . . . Joyeuce, Grace, Will, Thomas and the twins suffered acute agonies, but that was nothing to Great-Aunt and Diccon. The congregation enjoyed it too, and felt their hearts lifted up to heaven by the spectacle of that cherubic little boy and that saintly old lady entering the mighty Cathedral to praise their God.

Joyeuce, from her position beside Great-Aunt and behind Diccon, could not see their faces, but if she had she would have been overwhelmed with astonishment. Diccon walked with his head a little lifted and his gaze fixed upon the east window behind the high altar. His green eyes had a rapt, faraway look, as though they beheld not the rich stained glass of the window but the angels of the little children whose eyes behold the Father in heaven, and his red poppy lips had a pathetic, wistful droop that was very affecting. Great-Aunt, on the contrary, kept her piercing dark eyes fixed upon the ground, but over her face had come a strangely noble expression, and the dignity of her carriage and the gracious whisper of her velvets and silks over the stone floor of the aisle spoke volumes to the congregation of the saintliness of her character. When they filed into their seats under the tower, and knelt down to pray, Great-Aunt kept her face uncovered that all might see her devoutly moving lips, but Diccon bowed his curly head low and clasped his fat hands upon his chest. . . . No need today to hit his knees behind to make him kneel down. . . . When they both sat back on their seats they had reason to congratulate themselves upon a really magnificent dramatic performance.

Will and Thomas knelt too, with their peacock blue caps held over the lower parts of their faces and their wide gray eyes peeping over the top to see if they could see any of their particular friends in the congregation; when they did see a friend they removed their caps from their mouths and grinned broadly; they were nice, sincere little boys and they did not pretend they were addressing their Maker when just at the moment they didn't happen to be.

It is pleasant to be able to record that Grace and the twins really prayed, their prayers developing much on the same lines. "Please God, make me a good girl. Please God, bless Father and Joyeuce and everyone I love. Please God, help me not to think about my clothes in the sermon."

As for Joyeuce, for the first time in her life she could not pray. The battle that had been fought and won in Saint Michael's at the North Gate had now to be fought all over again. Her duty was perfectly obvious; confession of her appalling behavior to her father, rejection of Nicolas, lifelong devotion to her father, Great-Aunt, Will, Thomas, the twins, Diccon, the dogs and Tinker; and she knew that she ought to be praying for strength to do her duty. . . . But she did not want to do her duty. . . . With the whole strength and passion of her being she wanted to be a selfish, wicked, intriguing, untruthful girl. She opened her lips to pray but her throat felt dry and her lips felt hot and nothing would come. "Deus, propitius esto mihi peccatori," she whispered at last, and sat back on her seat with her face white and strained and her mouth sullen and a little defiant. . . . She had heard people say that it was good to be young, but she thought that the comfortable middle-aged people who so often made that platitudinous remark must have forgotten their own youth with its tormenting loves and problems and bewilderments. She wished she was old. She wished that her decisions were behind her and her heart at rest and her feet set firmly upon some path from which there could be no turning back.

Yet for a few moments, as she looked about her, the beauty of the Cathedral lifted the pall from her spirit. The Saxon pillars of the choir, massive and of colossal strength and seemingly as old as time, gave one a glorious feeling of stability, and the perpendicular clerestory that rose above them, and carried the eye up to the fine and graceful pendant roof, seemed like the arches of the years that carry a man's soul from the heavy darkness of the physical earth to the airy regions of heaven.

This strange mixture of architecture, that spanned the centuries in one great curve, never failed to affect the mind strangely. One felt cowed by it, a little confused by this leap through time, yet comforted too by a sense of union. Ancient glass, that told the story of Saint Frideswide's life, filled the windows and the sun shone through it to pattern with all the colors of the rainbow pillars and arches and the tombs of the dead that paved the floor.

From where she sat Joyeuce could see the Lady Chapel, that in Christ Church was built to the north of the choir instead of behind the high altar, so as not to interfere with the city wall that protected the east end of the Cathedral. In it was the shrine of Saint Frideswide and looming above it was the watching tower where in old times a monk sat day and night to protect the relics of the saint. It was the same shrine where Catherine of Aragon had worshiped, and the floor of the Cathedral, from the west door to the shrine, was worn by the feet of the pilgrims who had come there to seek healing and comfort of the saint.

Only a few years ago, in the reign of Queen Mary, a Canon's wife had had her history curiously mixed up with the history of the shrine, and now, in the days of Queen Elizabeth, the present Canons' ladies could not look at that shrine without a shiver of horror. . . . And nor could Canon Leigh, who was always seen to avert his eyes from the Lady Chapel when he walked in procession to his stall in the choir. . . . The horrible but veracious history haunted them all.

2.

Only fifteen years before, in King Henry's reign, Peter Martyr Vermilius, a Florentine who had adopted the reformed religion and come to England at Cranmer's invitation, was made Regius Professor of Divinity and Canon of Christ Church, and took up his residence at his canonry house in the quadrangle with Catherine his German wife.

Poor Catherine had a bad time from the very start. There were a good many Catholic scholars up at Christ Church and Peter Martyr, the pervert, was naturally the object of their hatred and a grand excuse for making a row. They smashed the windows of his house on the north side of the Fair Gate, they sang rude songs under the window of his study by day so that he could not work, and imitated cats under his bedroom window by night so that he could not sleep. Peter Martyr was upset, naturally, but poor Catherine was even more so. She was a foreigner and she couldn't speak the language. Her servants bullied her and the tradespeople cheated her and the Dean's wife, Mistress Cox, the only other lady living at that time within the precincts of Christ Church, was not as kind as she might have been because she was not quite certain whether Catherine was really a lady. What with being so bullied by day, and so frightened by night with the row the scholars made, and getting no sleep and being so homesick, poor Catherine got ill and after only two years at Christ Church she died. Christ Church was sorry, then, and wished it hadn't done it. It was too late now to be nice to the living Catherine but they were as nice as they knew how to the dead one; they gave her a splendid funeral and buried her in the Cathedral near the shrine of Saint Frideswide, on the same spot where a few years earlier that other tragic Catherine had knelt and prayed. The bones of the saint were no longer there, having been cast out fourteen years earlier by the command of Henry Tudor, and somehow or other completely mislaid, but the desecrated shrine still seemed to the people of Christ Church the heart of their college, and to be laid near it was an honor for Catherine that they hoped was appreciated by her in whichever of the courts of heaven she might happen to be at the moment.

Then Henry died, and Edward died, and Mary came to the throne; everyone had to change his religion once more and everything was in a turmoil. Peter Martyr, who had already changed his religion once and did not feel equal, at his age, to doing it again, fled from the country, and Richard Cox's place as Dean was taken by Richard Marshall, a gentleman of drunken habits who didn't care how many times a day he changed his religious beliefs provided he could celebrate the change in good liquor.

To him came the commissioners from Mary, sent to Oxford to cast out from the city heretics dead and alive, to inquire if it were true, as the Queen's Grace had heard, that Catherine Martyr, who had been buried beside the shrine of Saint Frideswide, was a heretic? As poor Catherine had been unable to speak English no one knew what her opinions were, she might have been a Mohammedan for all anyone knew to the contrary, so it was thought best to run no risk of contaminating the shrine and Dean Marshall was commanded to cast her out.

He was a loathsome, brutal creature, but even he did not like the task he had been set. He spent the day shut up inside the Deanery with a few boon companions, drinking deep, and when the sun was setting, and a sky like a rose was spread out behind the Fair Gate, he and his companions and some workmen, with crowbars on their shoulders, reeled off to the Cathedral and locked themselves in. When they came out again, carrying poor Catherine, the shadows were falling and the bright sky veiled its face in honor. . . . Not knowing what to do with the body Dean Marshall put it at the bottom of the Deanery garbage heap and hoped for the best.

Then Mary died, Elizabeth came to the throne and everyone quickly changed their religion again; though it gave pleasure to all that Dean Marshall, having mixed himself up in some plot or other, was thrown into prison and died there in the misery he so richly deserved. The Queen's Grace was very busy during the early years of her reign in finding out all that Mary had done and immediately doing the opposite. . . . Mary had said Catherine was to be taken out so Elizabeth naturally said she was to be put in again. . . . Orders were sent to Christ Church for the honorable re-burial of Catherine Martyr.

George Carew, the new Dean, a man of very different character from his predecessor, summoned his Chapter—of whom Canon Leigh was now a member—to his aid and together they removed Catherine from the Deanery garbage heap and conveyed her reverently to the Cathedral. While they were looking about for an obscure corner where she could be safely put for the moment they stumbled over yet another collection of bones, wrapped up in a silk wrapping.

"What on earth?" asked the Dean.

"Could they be Saint Frideswide?" suggested one of the Canons tentatively. "She got mislaid, you know, after the desecration of her shrine."

"Is this Cathedral never spring cleaned?" snapped the new Dean irritably. He was a cultured, fastidious man, and his nerves were completely overturned by the events of the morning. He scarcely dared move a step to right or left lest he fall over yet another dead body.

The Canons gloomily shook their heads. During recent years, with Bishops and an Archbishop being burnt outside the city wall and all men walking in peril of their lives, such customs as spring cleaning had rather fallen into abeyance.

"What in the name of heaven," demanded poor Dean Carew of his Chapter, "am I to do with these ladies?"

A burly Canon raised his head. "Throw 'em in together, Master Dean," he suggested helpfully. "Have a grand combined funeral service for both good dames."

So it was decided, and the Dean and Chapter went thankfully home to dinner.

For a short time the bodies of Catherine and Frideswide lay side by side in the Cathedral, reverently and carefully guarded, and on January 11, 1562, before a large concourse of people, they were laid to rest in a common grave with much pomp and ceremony. It was a great occasion. Bells were rung, hymns were sung and a volume of Latin poems was written to celebrate the event.

But Canon Leigh, as three years later he walked up the Cathedral in procession for Sunday morning service, averted his eyes from the shrine with a shiver of horror; for never, as long as he lived, would he forget the morning when they had looked for Catherine in the Deanery garbage heap.

3.

The great days of Cathedral worship, those days when the music of the mass sounded like the angels singing and the incense drifted in a fragrant cloud through the pillared aisles, had gone forever, but in this service of the reformed religion there was both dignity and beauty. The choir sang the psalms of David with simplicity, as the birds sing, and the prayer that Cranmer had written, repeated by Canon Leigh in his deep and beautiful voice, had a haunting beauty that smote hard upon each heart. "O God, the protector of all that trust in thee, without whom nothing is strong, nothing is holy; increase and multiply upon us thy mercy; that, thou being our ruler and guide, we may so pass through things temporal, that we finally lose not the things eternal."

They applied it, as all men apply great literature, to their own personal needs. To Joyeuce it brought an overwhelming sensation of comfort. The awful complication of "things temporal," the children and the dogs and the housekeeping and Great-Aunt, and now this further confusion of fiery love that for days and nights had been threatening to overwhelm her, seemed to sort themselves and fall into place. Under the guidance of God, it seemed, one could thread one's way through them and somehow or other come out the other side.

She lifted her head and looked across to the place where Nicolas knelt. His eyes were shut and his white ruff, even though it was not in quite the right place for a halo, yet made his beautiful face look very saintly. Looking at him with yearning love she saw that his lips moved and her heart leaped up in joy to think that he too was praying that prayer for guidance.

"Nine from seven you can't," whispered Nicolas—he always did his accounts in church—"Nine from seventeen is eight. . . . Damn . . . . I've spent too much. What'll Father say?" His lids flew apart in consternation and he found Joyeuce looking at him, her deep blue eyes fixed upon his face with a penetrating look that seemed to pierce his soul. He gave her one of his flashing smiles and then hastily lowered his lids again to shut out her eyes. . . . . They were too possessive altogether and Nicolas had no intention, at present, of undertaking responsibilities that might prove in any way inconvenient. The shouldering of responsibility, like the accumulation of learning, he was putting off till a later and more convenient date.

And Philip Sidney, kneeling beside Nicolas with his fair head buried in his arms, was thinking, as he always thought on Sundays, of the little church of Whitford, Flintshire, of which he was lay rector. His father,

Lord President of Wales, had made him rector of Whitford when he was nine and a half. A gentleman of the name of Gruff John was his proctor, lived in the rectory and did all the work, but Philip had an annual income of sixty pounds a year from his benefice and always found that it came in very handy. . . . And Philip, a deeply religious boy, loved to think that he was lay rector of Whitford. . . . As he knelt there, with his face hidden in his folded arms, he was seeing the little gray church squatting in a fold of the Welsh hills. At this moment Gruff John, a gentleman with a tremendous bass voice, would be booming out Cranmer's prayer over the heads of his kneeling congregation, a handful of shepherds and farmers with their wives and families. Outside in the churchyard the bees would be buzzing over the wild flowers and from up in the hills the sound of sheep bells would come faintly down the wind. Philip, kneeling in Christ Church Cathedral, prayed for his parishioners, for the burly farmers and the grizzled shepherds and their comely wives and rosy children. He prayed for his church, too, that it might always be a house of prayer, and for Gruff John, and for the sheep up in the hills, and for himself, that God would make him worthy of his sixty pounds a year.

Canon Calfhill, he to whom posterity would owe it that the story of Catherine Martyr was put on record, preached a sermon that was listened to by a small proportion of the scholars with burning attention. Later in the day they were all of them required to give an account of the sermon to their tutors, a tiresome regulation that was enough to drive anyone distracted, but they had evolved an elaborate system by which only one scholar on each staircase listened while the rest of them just thought great thoughts. Then after dinner the one who had listened instructed the ones who hadn't as to what they should say to their tutors, and all was well. They took it in turns to listen, of course, starting at the beginning of the year with the scholars whose names began with A and working carefully through in alphabetical order.

It was Philip's turn today to listen for his staircase, but he didn't mind because he liked sermons and always listened in any case. The sermon was preached in Latin, of course, and as Canon Calfhill was a fine Latin scholar it was worth listening to. Not only could he preach magnificently in Latin but he could write fine Latin verse too, and his epigram on Frideswide and Catherine was much admired.

> *Ossa Frideswidæ* sacro decorata triumpho*
> *Altari festis mota diebus erant.*
> *E tumulo contra Katharinæ Martyris ossa*
> *Turpiter in fœdum jacta fuere locum.*
> *Nunc utriusque simul saxo sunt ossa sub uno,*
> *Par ambabus honos, et sine lite cubant.*
> *Vivite nobiscum concordes ergo papistæ*
> *Nunc coeunt pietas atque superstitio.*

Canon Calfhill only preached for one hour because his congregation was for the most part young and he always said it was best to preach only short sermons to the young, lest their spirits should suffer weariness and so be alienated from religion, and then they all sang a hymn and filed out joyously into the glorious sunshine. Hautclere, Douce, Clement, Austin, Marie, Gabriel and John rang out again over their heads, answered by all the bells of Oxford, and Great Tom boomed out the hour for dinner.

4.

The College authorities never understood why it was that after dinner the scholars sat out on their staircases in the utmost discomfort instead of comfortably in their rooms. And it always seemed to be one scholar only, they noticed, who was doing all the talking, while the rest, hands locked round their knees, were attentively silent.

**Note.* The bones of Frideswide adorned for holy triumph on festal days were moved to the altar. From the sepulchral mound, on the other hand, the bones of Catherine Martyr had been shamefully cast into a foul place. Now the bones of each are together under one stone, equal is the honor to both, and without strife they lie. Live therefore, followers of the Pope, with us in concord, now piety and superstition combine.

Philip had been very much moved by Canon Calfhill this morning and sitting at the top of his flight of stairs in Broadgates Hall, with various be-ruffed gentlemen sprawling below him all the way down the stairs to the open door leading to Fish Street, he waved his hands in the air and held forth at the top of his voice. The others listened hard, cuffing anyone who shuffled his feet or coughed too loudly, for their account of the morning's sermon was always much admired by their tutors on the days when Philip had been listening to it. . . . For Philip could set them on fire. . . . He was a sort of spiritual Midas. Everything he touched, whether it was a Latin sermon or a way of life, or a cause or a personality, seemed to shine with a new glory.

He finished his exposition, and a little sigh of admiration rose like incense from the crowded staircase. It always amazed him that he, shy as he was, should have this power over his fellows. It did not make him proud, it only increased his humility, just as his beautiful home and his fine possessions increased it. . . . For to be dowered with lovely things through no effort and no virtue of one's own is very humbling, he found; the fear of unworthiness and the fear of mishandling kept one perpetually crawling to the feet of God. . . . Later in his life he inscribed his shield with the words, "These things I hardly call our own."

A figure suddenly appeared at the open doorway at the foot of the stairs, blocking out the sun, and Philip gazed at it with dismay, for the figure was a magnificent one dressed in the Leicester colors, and held in its hand a letter tied in scarlet silk. . . . And if there was one thing Philip disliked more than another it was being interfered with by Uncle Leicester.

Like mist before the sun the other scholars melted away, for they knew their place when the colors of the Chancellor were flaunted in the streets of Oxford, and the magnificent serving man advanced up an empty staircase and bowed low before the slender boy who sat at the top.

Philip received the letter with a dignified inclination of his fair head and felt rather anxiously in his wallet for a tip. There was, as he had feared, nothing in it but a couple of groats. These, however, he presented with such an air that they might have been ten gold coins, and the servant received them as though they were twenty. . . . Servants adored Philip Sidney. Though he was too shy to say much to them he always seemed to notice that they were there, and to be glad that they were.

Left alone, Philip perused the missive from his august relation with a heavy sigh. It was as he had feared. Uncle Leicester was in Oxford on business, was staying at Queen's College—the food was very good at Queen's—and would be at the Fair Gate in an hour's time that he and Philip might spend a happy afternoon together.

Philip went to his room with leaden footsteps and proceeded to wash himself, and scent himself, and put on his best crimson doublet and his pantofflces, leather shoes with exaggeratedly pointed toes, a new fashion introduced from Venice. He felt a fool in his pantoffles, but Uncle Leicester had given them to him so he must wear them.

As he dressed he took himself severely to task for his dislike of Uncle Leicester, who was so fond of him and so tirelessly good to him. . . . If only the man would not interfere. . . . Philip found it difficult to forgive his uncle for the letter he had written to the Dean of Christ Church when Philip first came up to Oxford. "Our boy Philip being of a delicate constitution," the Chancellor had written to the Dean, "it is our wish that he should eat flesh in Lent." And the Dean had replied that the wish of the Chancellor being law the regulation as to scholars eating only fish in Lent should be set aside in Philip's case, and Philip should eat flesh. Could anything, Philip asked himself, have been more unkind? It was quite bad enough to have a delicate constitution without having the attention of the entire College drawn to it. . . . In Lent, when he had to sit in hall choking his way through a huge platter full of underdone beef oozing red blood round the edge of every slice, and all the other scholars sitting round, disentangling fish bones from their teeth and looking at him, he could have cried. Indeed sometimes at night he did; partly from vexation of spirit and partly because if Uncle Leicester had only known it his delicate constitution and such quantities of underdone beef did not really agree together very well. . . . But then he must remember, as his mother, Uncle Leicester's sister Mary, was always urging him to, that

poor Uncle Leicester had no children and loved Philip as his own son.
... But then, as Philip couldn't help pointing out to his mother, if Uncle
Leicester had no children it was entirely his own fault for making such
a mess of his matrimonial affairs.

For Philip's family had a skeleton in the cupboard—Aunt Amy.
Philip had loved Aunt Amy very dearly and even though she had now
been dead for five years he could not forget about her. She had been
so pretty and loving, and so sweet to him when he was a little boy, that
he had loved her the best of all his aunts. He would never forget her
sitting on the grass at Penshurst, dressed in a pink frock, and making
daisy chains for him when he was small. She had been happy in those
days, and had laughed when she twisted the daisy chains round her dark
head and his yellow one. When he had eaten too much beef he had a
horrible nightmare in which he saw his pretty Aunt Amy, still to his
imagination dressed in her pink frock, come hurtling down those awful
stairs at Cumnor Place and falling in a pitiful heap at the bottom, with
her neck broken. In his nightmare he stood there at the bottom of the
stairs watching it happen, but with his feet chained to the floor so that
he couldn't run forward and catch her in his arms before she struck the
ground. He always woke up from this dream sweating and screaming out
in terror, so that his friend Fulke Greville, who had the room next to his
at Broadgates Hall, would have to come running in and give him a drink
of water, and hit him on the back and tell him not to be an ass, and sit
on his bed and tell him nice tales about bear-baiting and cock-fighting
before he was sufficiently comforted to go to sleep again.

Uncle Leicester and Aunt Amy had been very happy when they first
married. It was only later, when the Queen's Grace, completely bowled
over by Uncle Leicester's magnificent looks, showered honor upon
honor on his head, that it swelled up, together with the heads of his relations, and poor Amy seemed to them not quite equal to her great position. It was the fault of the Queen's Grace, of course. She fell in love with
Leicester's "very goodly person," and it was whispered in the Court that
he could have married her had it not been for Amy. Horrible scandals
about Elizabeth and Leicester were whispered everywhere. They heard

them at Penshurst, Philip's home, and Aunt Amy, even though she was not allowed to come to Court, heard them too and was very unhappy.

Of course it was not true, as everyone said at the time, that Uncle Leicester had sent her to stay at Cumnor Place so that his friend Anthony Foster, who lived there, should throw her down those stairs. . . . It was a clear case of suicide. . . . Her maid had heard her praying to God "to deliver her from desperation" and she had sent all her servants to Abingdon Fair on the night she died. But still, it was all very horrible, and Uncle Leicester had not made things better by never going near her body when it lay in state in Gloucester Hall, and absenting himself from her burial in Saint Mary's Church. Doctor Babington, too, one of Uncle Leicester's chaplains, who had loved Amy and who had to preach her funeral sermon, made everything worse by getting upset and describing Amy as "pitifully murdered" when he had meant to say "accidentally slain."

But the frightful scandal that there was about her death killed Leicester's hopes of marriage with Elizabeth. She made him Earl of Leicester and one of the greatest noblemen in the land, and she gave him his beautiful home at Kenilworth, but she could not now marry him.

Trying not to mention the word Cumnor in conversation—it was a word that must never be spoken in Uncle Leicester's hearing—and trying not to think about pretty Aunt Amy whenever he was with his uncle made intercourse with that gentleman extremely difficult for Philip.

But it had to be accomplished and at the appointed time he was waiting under the Fair Gate. He had not to wait long, for constant attendance upon the Queen's Grace had at least taught Uncle Leicester the virtue of punctuality. With a commotion of horses' hoofs on the cobbles he came clattering down from Carfax, with a few mounted servants behind him and his trumpeter going before. His splendid figure looked its best on horseback and the sunshine gleamed on his jeweled doublet and the great ruby that fastened turquoise plumes in his velvet hat. His dark beard was trimmed to a most elegant point and his fine dark eyes, as they rested on Philip, were softened and kindly. The trumpet sounded, Satan barked like mad, a little crowd gathered and Philip ran forward to hold his uncle's stirrup as he dismounted.

Uncle Leicester, as he stood beside his horse with his hand on Philip's shoulder, gracefully acknowledging the bared heads of the bystanders and the bows of Heatherthwayte, looked very grave and very intellectual. He was a first-rate actor and when he was treading the streets of Oxford as its Chancellor you couldn't have told, from looking at him, that he wasn't really a very suitable person for the position. . . . Though it must be said to his credit that though the classics bored him stiff he was a quite passable mathematician.

"Well, Phil, how are you?" inquired the great man genially.

"Very well, thank you, Uncle," said Philip. "I hope you are quite well?"

"Quite well, thank you," said the Chancellor, and shifted his hand from his nephew's shoulder to his fair head.

Philip realized with horror that it was his duty to kneel down and be blessed. This was quite as it should be, of course, but Philip did think that Uncle Leicester might have refrained from staging a pious scene in front of all these people. It wasn't fair, either, because if Uncle Leicester believed in God at all, which Philip thought doubtful, he didn't allow his faith to inconvenience him in any way, so what right had he to make it inconvenience Philip?

But there was no help for it and Philip knelt, covering his face with his hands to hide his shame. Uncle Philip blessed him very loud, in the accents of a Chancellor, and the crowd, especially its female element, was much affected.

"Well, Phil, and what shall we do now?" inquired the Earl, as they shook off their admirers and strolled together under the Fair Gate.

Philip thought a walk round the Christ Church meadows would be nice. . . . The meadows have always been a blessing to scholars burdened with relations up for the day.

As they walked the trodden paths through the feathery June grass, soft and warm against their hands as the breasts of little birds, and under the trees that lifted their heavy heads only lazily to greet the south wind that was driving white clouds like sheep across the sky, they made rather heavy conversation to each other.

Philip answered the usual avuncular inquiries as to the progress of his studies and archery practice, the state of his friends' health and his own health, the Dean's health and his tutor's health, with his habitual sweet and staid courtesy, and Uncle Leicester was more enslaved than ever.

For the Earl did really love Philip. He had a certain capacity for love, as was shown by his short-lived love for Amy and his lifelong devotion to himself, and Philip caused him to exercise his capacity to the full. He could, and did, put himself out for Philip and, with the Earl, that was the supreme test.

"Have you done any hunting, Phil?" he asked. . . . He was always afraid that Philip's love of study might crowd more manly activities out of his life.

"Yes," said Philip, "last Wednesday I hunted out at C—; I mean I hunted last Wednesday."

He went scarlet and fell over the long toes of his pantoffles, but Uncle Leicester didn't seem to notice anything.

"Stags good?" he asked.

"Splendid," said Philip.

"Where did you kill?" asked Uncle Leicester.

They had killed in the great park at Cumnor and Philip, in misery, and again falling over his feet, changed the conversation by asking Uncle Leicester what he was doing in Oxford.

"Ah!" said the Earl. "What do you think? I am sounding the University as to the expediency of persuading the Queen's Grace to visit us next summer."

Gone was all Philip's staidness of demeanor. He crowed and leaped like a small boy, and even seized Uncle Leicester's sleeve and shook it slightly. "The Queen?" he cried. "Will the Queen really come to Oxford?"

"I have taken her to Cambridge," said Uncle Leicester, "and now it is high time she came to Oxford."

"You oughtn't to have let her go to Cambridge first, Uncle," said Philip reproachfully.

"Cambridge claims to be the older University," said the Earl.

"It's not now," said Philip eagerly. "Not now that we've discovered that King Alfred founded us."

"How did you make that out?" inquired the Earl with interest.

Philip waved an airy hand but disdained explanation. The magnificent edifice of historical research, built up by those imaginative historians on whose word Philip had it that King Alfred founded Oxford University, looked well but was difficult of explanation to the outsider.

"He did," said Philip briefly. "And you shouldn't have taken the Queen's Grace to Cambridge first. . . . Not when you're Chancellor of Oxford."

"You forget," said Uncle Leicester, "that I am also High Steward of Cambridge."

It was true. Uncle Leicester experienced no difficulty in combining these two honors, together with any benefits that accrued thereto.

"Will the Queen come to Christ Church?" asked Philip.

"If you wish it," said his infatuated Uncle. "We'll lodge her at Christ Church, shall we?"

"When?" gasped Philip.

"Next summer," said the Earl. "And you and your friends shall amuse her with a masque in the hall."

Philip was pink with emotion and his eyes shone like stars. For the first time he almost loved Uncle Leicester. It was something, after all, to have an uncle who could twist a queen round his little finger in this way.

A postern gate let them in through the city wall into Merton College, and they wandered through the old, irregular buildings that lacked the plan and pattern of the other Colleges because Merton was the mother of them all. Her buildings were no more than a few old houses, and the church of Saint John the Baptist, adapted to the use of that first little band of twenty scholars who in the thirteenth century came there to fulfill the intention of their founder, Walter de Merton, that they should fit themselves by study and prayer for life in the great world. Philip, by whom the great world must be entered in a short time now, remembered them as he passed under the embattled tower and the great gateway, and looked up at the carving above it that showed Christ, with the dove over his head, coming to Saint John the Baptist to be baptized. Philip knew what that carving meant in connection with Merton . . . . Christ, too, needed to be prepared.

5.

From Merton they walked to Oriel. At this point Philip usually took the visiting relative up Shidyard Street to High Street, and so to Saint Mary's, but Uncle Leicester knew Oxford as well as Philip did, and anyhow, with Aunt Amy buried in Saint Mary's, one couldn't very well go there. . . . He stood for a moment on one leg and wondered what on earth to do next with Uncle Leicester. . . . The question was decided by the sudden appearance of Giles and Faithful from the gateway of Canterbury Inn. Emerging at the double they all but ran into the Chancellor, retreating only just in time in a paroxysm of bows.

Philip presented them to his uncle as two of his best friends and the Chancellor regarded the younger of them with growing horror. Giles was passable as a friend for his nephew but this ugly, flap-eared, shabby boy, with the huge head and no breeding at all, was impossible, utterly impossible. Really Philip should be more careful where he bestowed his favor. He seemed to have no sense at all of what was due to his position. Uncle Leicester had had occasion to speak of this to him before, and it seemed he would have to do so again. . . . While chatting to the two boys with kindly condescension he fixed Faithful with a cold and fishy eye.

Faithful withdrew a little behind Giles and looked down at his feet. The thoughts that passed through the Chancellor's mind were quite clear to him and he was too ashamed to lift his eyes. As he stood there he could actually feel his head swelling out and his ears getting larger and his clothes shabbier. His shoes, he suddenly noticed, had two slits in the leather, and as he looked at them the slits widened to gaping, mocking mouths. . . . You are ugly, they said, you are hideously ugly. Your father was a thief and your mother was a slut out of the streets whom he did not bother to marry. You will never tell anyone that, but it is true. Why don't you go back to the gutter, where you belong? What are you doing, masquerading as a gentleman in the streets of Oxford?. . . If Faithful could have moved he would have run away, but his feet were so busy laughing at him that they would not take him.

"And where are you boys off to?" inquired the Chancellor genially.

"To a verse reading, sir," replied Giles, "in Walter Raleigh's room at Oriel."

"Is it permissible for an old fogey such as myself to come too?" inquired the Chancellor. In the full flush of his splendid prime as he was, thirty-three years old and looking less, it delighted him to refer to himself as an old fogey and to watch the vehement denials that sprang into the eyes of his companions. And he liked the companionship of the admiring young. Even though their admiration might he based upon ignorance it was consoling after the truthful comments of one's knowledgeable contemporaries.

Philip, Giles and Faithful looked at each other a little doubtfully.

"Evidently it is not permissible," said the Chancellor with some pique.

"I am sure Walter Raleigh would be honored, sir," Giles hastened to assure him. "Only before the verse reading starts he is to put the last touches to a chemical experiment."

"Indeed?" inquired the Chancellor with interest. "What chemical experiment? And is private experimenting with combustibles in one's rooms allowed by the University authorities?"

The three politely ignored the last question and concentrated upon the first. "Walter Raleigh thinks he has discovered the correct formula for a Great Cordial or Elixir," they explained. "Applied externally to base metals it will turn them into gold and applied internally to the human stomach it will prolong life."

"In other words," said the Chancellor, "your friend has discovered the secret of perpetual youth."

"Yes," they said.

"Say no more," laughed the Chancellor, "but lead on," and ignoring Faithful he put his hands upon the shoulders of the other two and swung them round towards the gate of Oriel. . . . Over their shoulders they exchanged anxious glances with Faithful trotting behind. . . . What, they wondered, would be the penalty for blowing up the Chancellor?

They entered under the archway and into the quadrangle of the College, founded by a Rector of Saint Mary's and built up round the lovely old house of La Oriole. Raleigh's room, where a choice gathering of the younger poets met every Sunday afternoon, was on the north side of the quadrangle, high up, and the little party mounted the narrow stairs in single file, tingling with mingled anxiety and expectation. . . . Perhaps, whispered Faithful to Giles, who was just in front of him, it would be all right after all. They were a little late and it might be that Raleigh and the poets were already blown to pieces. One must hope for the best.

But no sooner had he expressed his hope than a terrific report reverberated over their heads. Philip, who was leading, recoiled upon the Chancellor and the Chancellor upon Giles. "The Great Cordial!" ejaculated Faithful, as Giles in his turn recoiled upon him and the whole party of them slithered into a dusty heap upon the stairs, Faithful at the bottom.

The Chancellor, fearing loss of life, extricated himself at once from his undignified position and raced on up the stairs, two steps at a time, the others stumbling after.

Raleigh's room was filled with smoke and strewn with the bodies of prostrate poets. Through the haze the Chancellor could dimly see a table piled with phials and tubes, and a tall boy stirring some evil smelling concoction in a big bowl.

"It's all right," announced a cheerful voice. "I know what I did wrong."

"I very much doubt if it is all right," said the Chancellor sternly. "All these young gentlemen appear to be dead."

"Fright," said Raleigh laconically, bending over his bowl with nose held between finger and thumb. "They're all cowards and skunks. . . . And who are you, sir, anyhow?" He suddenly raised his head and saw who it was. "The Chancellor!" he gasped.

But he was at a loss for only a moment.

"The Chancellor," he roared at the prostrate poets, dealing out a few kicks to right and left to awake them into reverence. Then he dashed to the windows, opened them to let out the smoke, bowed to the Chancellor as though a visit from him were a thing of everyday occurrence, removed Fulke Greville, who was prostrate upon the best chair, from there to the floor with a sweep of his right arm, removed a whole windowful of poets who obscured the view with a gesture of his left arm, seated the Chancellor and raised the whole confused gathering to its feet in a corporate bow all in the twinkling of an eye.

A young man who will go far, thought the Chancellor, and could not find it in his heart to offer any further rebuke. Instead, with his scented handkerchief to his nose, he found himself offering his condolences.

But Raleigh, emptying the Great Cordial out of the window and summoning a few poets to help him stow the basins and phials under his bed, waved them airily aside. "A mere error of judgment," he said. "Next time I shall succeed." His voice was vibrant with determination and his eyes shone as he launched forth into a glowing description of the golden age that was coming.... When there would be no more poverty, no more sorrow, no more sin.

A shout from outside interrupted his eloquence and sent him bounding to a window. Below in the quadrangle stood the Provost and other dignitaries of the College, outraged and indignant at this wrecking of their Sunday siesta by the noises and smells of Hades. This was not the first time, they said, that Master Walter Raleigh had disturbed the peace of Oriel upon the Sabbath, although he had been informed again and again that diabolical experiments upon the holy day were not permitted within the precincts of the College. They would be obliged if he would descend and give some explanation of his conduct.

"Sirs," cried Raleigh, bowing very low, "I regret that I am unable to do so. I am about to entertain the Chancellor at a verse reading."

Such incredulous noises greeted this statement that Leicester was obliged to show himself at the other window. "I crave your indulgence for this young man," he said to the astonished Provost in arrogant yet honeyed tones. "Any unpleasant aroma that may have titillated your nostrils, or slight sound that may have assaulted the delicate tympanum of your ear, were unforeseen accidents in a humanitarian effort for the betterment of the human race that, I think, should be commended in a son of Oriel. Master Walter Raleigh and his friends, following in his footsteps of the great alchemists of all time, were searching for that Elixir that shall turn all hard metals, yea, even the hearts of reverend and learned men, to soft and merciful gold."

The Provost glanced from the splendid but most unacademic figure of the Chancellor in one window to the equally splendid figure of Walter Raleigh in the other. . . . Adventurers both. . . . He bowed coldly and withdrew with his following.

Leicester once more settled himself comfortably in his chair for an hour that promised to be fruitful of entertainment, and the poets, with a deep sigh of expectancy and a rustling of papers, settled all over the room like a flock of birds. It was a beautiful room, furnished by Raleigh regardless of his father's expense, and now that the smoke and the smell were cleared out of it, and the Sunday afternoon silence and sunshine came into their own, it made a fitting background for the poets who sat in elegant attitudes, on the floor and on the chairs, attentive, as were all men always, to Raleigh's slightest word or glance.

They were a likely looking lot of youngsters, the chancellor thought as he looked round the room, drinking in the adulation of their eyes and of their quick, panting breaths. The sun poured in, lighting on fair heads, dark heads, yellow heads and ginger heads, all of them sleek and shining after the Sunday brush. Their snowy ruffs made the perfect setting for young faces and the subdued colors of their best doublets, plum color, dark green, dark blue, violet and russet, seemed to accentuate the vividness of their eyes and hair. . . . How the young do shine, thought the Chancellor. . . . Surely this lot had already drunk of their Elixir, for their youth lay upon them like a bright polish, as triumphant as the sheen of the spring world in early morning. It looked inviolable, impossible to tarnish, shouting aloud to the world that life was good.

Dreams. . . . That polish was nothing but the reflection of them, a thing as easily destroyed as dew upon the grass or the sheen upon the petal of a flower. When the gleam of their dreaming was rubbed off them would they call their dreams traitors or friends? He looked at them all, and for the death of their dreams he could have flung himself down upon the floor and wept, taking the measure of an unmade grave. . . . And being an Elizabethan he wouldn't have been ashamed of doing it, either, but the room was crowded and there was no space; and Raleigh had got to his feet to start the verse reading with one of his own poems.

For a few moments, as he hunted through a little manuscript book to find the right page, there was a deep silence filled only by the buzzing of a bee and a little shuddering sigh from Philip. Exchanging glances with his nephew the Chancellor discovered that they were thinking the same thing; what would Raleigh do if he did not succeed in concocting his Elixir? What would happen to him if his search for the gold that should remake the world ended in disaster, and death came unawares upon a man who had expected to be always young? What alternative had he for his Great Cordial?

Raleigh found the place and began to read. He read quietly, his usual vehemence stilled, and in a way that made the poem bite deep into the memories of his hearers, so that when years later he died for his dreams upon the scaffold those who were still alive remembered his room at Oriel, and heard his voice reading as though the summer day were only yesterday.

> Give me my scallop-shell of quiet,
> My staff of faith to walk upon,
> My scrip of joy, immortal diet,
> My bottle of salvation,
> My gown of glory, hope's true gage,
> And thus I'll take my pilgrimage.
> Blood must be my body's balmer,
> No other balm will there be given,
> Whilst my soul like a quiet palmer
> Travels to the land of heaven,
> Over the silver mountains,
> Where spring the nectar fountains;
> And there I'll kiss
> The bowl of bliss,
> And drink mine everlasting fill
> On every milken hill.
> My soul will be a-dry before,
> But after it will thirst no more.

The Chancellor was astonished. So that was Raleigh's alternative: blood. He would start joyfully upon pilgrimage, gowned in glory, and if he could not realize his dreams he would die for them. And he seemed to have no horror of the blood. It was to be a balm, a thing that would shine upon his body as once his dreams had done. It would be like rain upon the dry earth. Fresh life would spring from it. It was the whole duty of man to work for the golden age, to set himself to build Jerusalem in his own place and his own time. He would never succeed but his failure would be the triumph of his life. The thing was incomprehensible but true. . . . The rest of the verse reading seemed to the Chancellor to go by in a dream.

6.

A poem can be like two hands that lift you up and put you down in a new place. You look back with astonishment and find that because you have read a few lines on a printed page, or listened for a couple of minutes to a voice speaking, you have arrived at somewhere quite different.

Raleigh's poem had done that for the Earl of Leicester and Cranmer's prayer had done it for Joyeuce.

All day she said it to herself. She thought it was one of the finest prayers that had ever been composed by man, and how it was that she had never properly noticed it before she could not conceive. In its quiet insistence on what was important it seemed to still all confusion. And at the same time it was a challenge. It did not ask for ease in trouble or escape from pain, it did not even seem to think these things particularly desirable. In those two words "pass through" its insistence was all the other way. It swung her right back to the mood that had been hers in Saint Michael's at the North Gate, before Nicolas had plunged her head over heels into fairyland and sent all her values flying to the winds. Its bracing effect was such that by suppertime Joyeuce had decided to turn her back on love and concentrate on duty. Her life had done nothing to develop her sense of humor and she took herself extremely seriously, so it did not strike her as comic that a prayer forged as a weapon by a man who had had to face complications

more awful than anything she could conceive of, followed by imprisonment and martyrdom, should be used by her in her own mimic warfare.
. . . Not that her own particular trials ever seemed to her small, it took all
her strength to carry them and so they seemed to her colossal.

When the curfew bell was ringing, about the hour of nine, she
presented herself before her father in his study, her hands clasped very
tightly before her, her head thrown back, her face very white and her
blue eyes clouded to gray. Canon Leigh's heart sank, for this attitude
of the tragic muse usually betokened some terrible domestic crisis; the
cat had fallen down the well, Diccon had called at the Deanery again
without his clothes or Great-Aunt was dead.

"What is it, Joyeuce?" he asked.

"I have been very wicked," she said.

Her father was so astonished that he dropped his pen and sent
the ink spurting all over his tomorrow's lecture. In all the years that he
had known her she had never been wicked. The baby Joyeuce had not
screamed when she teethed, only bubbled at the mouth and moaned a
little, and as a child she had never stolen the comfits or run away from
her lessons. As a girl she had shouldered her responsibilities without
wincing and never in all her life had he known her lose her temper or
seek a single thing for herself.

"What have you done, Joyeuce?" he asked in horror.

Joyeuce took a deep breath and told him. She told him nearly everything; her visit to Bocardo, her lies to Mistress Flowerdew, the meal at
the Tavern, the kisses that accompanied it and the magic, moonlit walk
in the Meadows. She left nothing out except her love for Nicolas and
that she would not tell, because it was easier to renounce it if she did
not give it greater substance by telling of it. Her recital went on and on
and seemed to her afflicted father to last well into the night. In an agony
his mind fixed itself upon the thought that Joyeuce and Nicolas had
been in the Meadows at night, on Midsummer Eve in the moonlight. . . .
His heart fainted within him. . . . What was Joyeuce trying to tell him?
Something she could not put into words? She was silent now and the
silence seemed to him full of horror.

"Is that all, Joyeuce?" he asked hoarsely.

"All?" inquired Joyeuce, almost outraged. Surely, she thought, she had told him enough to make his hair stand on end for the rest of his life, and he asked her if it were all!

The worst of her ordeal over her eyes had gone back to their normal blue and were fixed on him with a child's wonder. With a shock of relief so overwhelming that the room spun round him he realized that she did not know what on earth he was talking about. . . . His respect for Nicolas de Worde, that up till now had been small, owing to the horror of his Greek and the outrage of his Latin, suddenly went up by leaps and bounds. His relief and astonishment were so great that he did not know what to say. Scratching his head in bewilderment he looked appealingly at Joyeuce, but for once she did not seem to know what he ought to say either. The situation was beyond them both. She burst into tears and flung herself into his arms.

While he patted and soothed her he wondered if she was crying as a child cries, who will soon forget its grief, or as a woman cries who will remember it. Hoping it was the former he treated it as the former and comforted her as he had comforted her when she had broken her doll or fallen full length on the stony path. Never mind, he said, it was over now. She had been a good girl to tell him and he was proud of her for being so brave. She must go to bed now and it would be all right in the morning. He patted her till she had stopped crying, then kissed and blessed her tenderly and took her upstairs to bed.

But Joyeuce, though she was comforted, only slept brokenly. In her dreams she saw again the figures of Nicolas and Diccon, scarlet and green, moving through the moonlit trees to the gates of fairyland. "Take me too!" she cried, but they went on and disappeared inside and the gate shut. She stood looking at the fairy gates until the walls of the house of her everyday life towered up around her like precipices and she could not see them any more.

Meanwhile Canon Leigh in his study did not know what on earth he ought to do; and when he remembered that he had four daughters who each of them might have five love affairs, making twenty all told, before he got them safely steered into the harbor of matrimony—though even then there might be upsets in the harbor—he came out in a cold sweat. Joyeuce had not known what he was talking about. But surely at her age she ought to have known what he was talking about.

He spent a bad night and in the cold light of dawn sat down and penned a note to Mistress Flowerdew, asking that he might wait upon her and receive her inestimable advice upon a matter of overwhelming importance.

CHAPTER IX

SAINT GILES' FAIR

Tell me, my lamb of gold;
So mayst thou long abide
The day well fed, the night in faithful fold;

Canst thou, poor lamb, become another's lamb,
Or rather, till thou die,
Still for thy dam with baa-waymenting cry?

Earth, brook, flowers, pipe, lamb, dove
Say all, and I with them,
Absence is death, or worse, to them that love.

PHILIP SIDNEY.

1.

THE long summer holidays, arranged to suit the harvesting, were upon them. All the scholars must go home, rich and poor alike, to help gather in the corn and the wheat and the barley that were clothing England in a robe of green and gold and orange-tawny that bent before the wind under a sky of burning blue.

The day when the scholars departed was a great day. Traveling in companies as protection against rogues and vagabonds they passed out north, south, east and west through the gates of the city, singing and laughing and shouting out final insults at the townspeople who thronged the streets to see them go.

Some evil imps of the town had mounted the belfries and rang out peals of thanksgiving as the companies wended their way past the guardian towers.

At North Gate and South Gate too Saint Michael guards the way,
While o'er the East and o'er the West Saint Peter holds his sway.

Some of the scholars chanted the old rime and looked up at the towers as they passed beneath them; some of them glad to be going, some of them sorry, and some of the older ones heartbroken because their time at Oxford was over and they would never come back again except as the old fogeys of the past.

The rich scholars, the noblemen and squires' sons, rode on horseback with their mounted servants clattering behind them; they would put up at the fine houses of friends and relatives and they had their best clothes with them in saddle bags; their friends would give them fresh horses and they would be home in no time. But the poor scholars had to walk, sleeping under hedges if the weather was fine or at the rough inns if it was wet, and it would be a long time before they got to their journey's end, with their faces brown as berries and their shoes worn through.

Philip, who was going to London for part of his holidays to stay with Uncle Leicester, rode under the Fast Gate and up the bridle path through the woods to Shotover. He was one of a large and gay company, for a great many of them were going London way. He rode a white horse, and had blue plumes in his hat, but he was sad because every departure from Oxford brought nearer the final departure that he dreaded. On the top of Shotover he reined in his horse and looked down, as Faithful had looked down in the dawn of that spring morning of his arrival, at the towers of Oxford below him in a haze of heat.

"They are always in a mist," he said, "like dreams that go away."

His face looked like the face of a puppy whose dinner has been removed before it has had time to do more than taste it, and Fulke Greville, beside him on a black horse, hastened to apply bracing treatment.

"You are coming back, you ass."

"Some day," said Philip, "we shall never come back. . . . Except in dreams."

"If everyone who ever loved Oxford comes back to it in dreams," said Greville, "the streets must be blocked with ghosts. . . . It's a wonder we living people can get by."

They were silent, brooding, their reins lying loose and their horses nosing in the wild thyme for edible bits of grass, until a shout from the others warned them that they were left behind. They turned their horses and cantered away over the springy turf, shouting to their friends, depressing thoughts left behind with the ghosts in the city.

Raleigh and the west-countrymen rode under South Gate, across the river, up the hill and through the Forest of Bagley. They were the noisiest crowd of all, for they were many of them going back to live within sight and sound of the sea, and they were glad to be going. Thomas Bodley, who rode with them, did nothing to check the row they made, M.A. and Fellow of Merton though he was. . . . In fact he made as much row as any. . . . Raleigh roared out roystering songs in broad Devonshire and they all joined in the choruses in the most unseemly manner. All the way through the flat water meadows beyond the river they sang, and up the hill, and they only fell silent when the great Forest of Bagley gathered them into its darkness. It would have been sacrilege to make a noise just then, for there were singing birds to listen to, and rabbits to watch, and under their feet was spread a carpet of bilberry leaves and green ferns that made the floor of the forest like the strewed presence chamber of a king.

And Nicolas, who lived in Gloucestershire, rode out through North Gate, in a leaf-green doublet and a bad temper. . . . He did not want to go away because he was leaving Joyeuce behind.

He had seen her several times since that evening at the Tavern but she was always very difficult and troublesome. When he greeted her in the street or the quadrangle she swept him such swirling curtseys that the wind of them seemed to blow him miles away, and when he tried to talk to her she lowered her lids and turned demure. She wouldn't go to the Tavern with him again, or for walks round the Meadows, and on the few occasions when she looked at him her blue eyes had faded to the color of rain and were clouded with beseeching. He thought he knew what she wanted. She wanted to be proposed to, of course. She wanted a ring on her finger and pearl drops in her ears and himself in leading strings to be shown off to all her friends. . . . Well, he wasn't going to propose to her: at least, not yet. . . . He wasn't going to saddle himself with a wife before he had even tasted the joys of manhood and the sweets of freedom. Joyeuce must wait. Why must she be in such a hurry? Why could she not enjoy, as he did, the fun of a little clandestine love and laughter? Why could she not shelve, as he did, serious things to a more propitious moment?

He could not know that he was denying to Joyeuce the luxury of proud martyrdom. How could she refuse to marry him when he did not ask her to marry him? She had worked herself up to a high pitch of nobility, even thinking out the beautiful words in which her refusal would be couched, and now the nobility was going sour in her for lack of use. At night she wept angry tears into her pillow. She supposed it was all a mistake and he did not love her at all. She was getting old now, she was sixteen, and no one had wanted to marry her yet. Was she, perhaps, unlovable? This was a thought that dragged her pride down into the dust, for though it may be a painful thing to refuse a proposal it is yet elevating to the pride, while to have none to refuse is a humiliation that Joyeuce at her age found it almost impossible to put up with. She told herself that a really nice girl would have been glad that Nicolas was spared the pain of loving a woman who could not marry, but looking at herself squarely and honestly at one o'clock in the morning she found that she was not a really nice girl. . . . She was always horrified when she took out her true thoughts and looked at them. . . . Laid on top of them to hide them was a beautiful coverlet of the noble sentiments that guide a Christian life, underneath, not so beautiful but still quite pretty, were the thoughts that she ought to think and usually thought she was thinking, and underneath again were her real thoughts, ugly things so utterly at variance with the actions of her life that she seldom dared face them as they were. She supposed that in time, with prayer and fasting, the glorious color of the surface covering would penetrate right down through all the layers of thought until they were all transformed as though wine had been poured into water. But at one o'clock in the morning that lovely unity seemed a goal that she would never reach. She was a poor tormented child dragged in pieces; too unselfish to live for her own pleasure and too selfish to accept frustration thankfully.

But Nicolas couldn't possibly be expected to understand all this and as he rode out of North Gate he was merely sore and angry, answering his companions with disagreeable grunts, feeling not the warmth of the sun but the chill of Joyeuce's cold fingers when she bade him good-by, and seeing no smiling, flowery fields but only Joyeuce's eyes that were now the color of rain.... Tiresome girl.... Why had he been such a fool as to fall in love with so serious a maiden, he who liked laughter and the careless heart? He vowed he would forget her. Surely the pain of the heart was a thing that could he controlled by a little abstention from the sight of the beloved face, just as the pain of the stomach could be controlled by a little abstention from food.... At the thought of food he cheered up a bit.... The lovely little hamlet of Woodstock was coming into sight, with its beautiful cottages sprawling down the hill, and they were to stop at Woodstock and have a good dinner there.

2.

Oxford was strangely quiet.

A deep silence brooded over the empty sunlit quadrangles. The curfew rang out as usual but no figures come scurrying to get in before the College gates shut. There were no brawls in the streets, no merry shouts from the meadows, while from the window of Bocardo the leather bag dangled flabbily on the end of its string, swinging to and fro in the wind that blew from the south, bringing hot summer scents of harvest fields and hedgerows to mingle with the smells of the town.

There were those who liked this quiet; Giles, for instance, who could work on hour after hour without a single distraction; and the exhausted senior members of the University; and the townspeople who could feel for once in a way that their own town belonged to them; but it bored Diccon to distraction.

When late summer came outrage was added to boredom because
Saint Giles' Fair, one of the greatest events of the year to the children,
was encamped without the North Gate, and they were not allowed to
go because it was rumored that there were cases of smallpox among the
Fair people. It was particularly hard on Diccon because Dean Godwin
had given him a silver coin with which to purchase a hobby horse. He
roared and stormed and kicked the furniture, but his father remained
adamant. . . . He would not have his family laid low with the smallpox,
and if Diccon kicked the furniture again, he would thrash him. . . . So
Diccon, unable to get what he wanted by behaving like a demon, suddenly turned cherub, smirked and crooned and bided his time.

Everything comes to those who wait, especially to those who have
no scruples about taking any evil opportunities that may occur. On one
very warm day when Dorothy, mazed by heat and a large dinner, dozed
off in her chair and neglected to keep her eye on him, Diccon seized his
woolly lamb Baa and his silver coin, and crept noiseless as a mouse out
of the kitchen and across the hall, lifted the latch of the front door and
scurried down the steps into the quadrangle.

He ran like the wind across it but when he got to the Fair Gate he
dropped on hands and knees and advanced with caution; for he knew
that Satan would know he was being naughty and might protest with
loud barkings and bayings that would bring the whole College running
out to catch him.

Heatherthwayte, as was to be expected on such a hot day, was asleep
on his bench with his hands clasped over his stomach, his mouth ajar
and happy snorts escaping from his nostrils.

But Satan, as Diccon had feared, was awake. He was sitting up in the
center of the Fair Gate, facing the quadrangle, with his front legs very
stiff and straight. One of his ears was hanging negligently but the other
was cocked and pointing straight up to heaven like the finger of an ac-
cusing angel, and his eyes were bright and observant.

Diccon, looking like a little animal himself in his suit of russet
brown, crept to within a couple of feet of Satan and then sat back on his
heels and looked at him; and Satan looked at Diccon.

Satan waved his tail in a friendly way and opened his mouth to laugh, letting a foot of dribbling pink tongue hang out at the side of his mouth, as was his habit when amused.... But there was a warning gleam in his eye.... Stay where you are, he seemed to be saying to Diccon, and all will be well, but budge an inch and you'll catch it.

Diccon crept an inch to the right and Satan growled softly in his throat; he crept an inch to the left and Satan gave a muffled bark that caused Heatherthwayte to open one eye; but he did not see the small brown figure crouched on the cobbles and shut it again almost immediately.

Then Diccon tried guile. He crept quite close to Satan, stretched out a finger and scratched Satan's chest. Satan liked that, for he had been somewhat bitten of late and the scratching was soothing to his irritation. He closed his eyes and raised his head to signify that Diccon might scratch him under his chin as well.

Diccon scratched Satan for ten minutes; on his chest, his stomach, his chin and in the soft places behind his ears; and all the time he was quietly edging round Satan until he was sitting behind him and scratching his back.

Satan was now in a state of enjoyment that bordered on the ecstatic, and in the semi-conscious condition that accompanies ecstasy. It was not until the blissful scratching had ceased, and he looked round over his shoulder to inquire the reason, that he discovered that the wretched child had fled. Barking wildly he leaped to his feel and rushed out into Fish Street, to see a little brown creature scuttling like a rabbit up the hill and across Carfax. Satan halted uncertainly, one forepaw raised, but his first duty was to the College whose guardian he was and he padded back to the Fair Gate and then rudely awakened Heatherthwayte.

"Not so much as a cat stirring," growled Heatherthwayte, "and you must make a row fit to wake the dead, you black-faced piece of garbage, you."

Satan was apologetic. He stuck his tail between his legs and grinned sheepishly, showing the whites of his eyes. He had been beguiled by the delights of the flesh and he was ashamed of himself. When

Heatherthwayte dozed off again he was unable to follow suit. He sat up miserably on his haunches staring at the Cathedral tower.

3.

Diccon had never been out in the town by himself before and a wild happiness possessed him. He was barefooted and bareheaded but neither the sun scorching down on his dark curls nor the burning heat of the cobbles under his feet incommoded him in the least. He adored the sun, just as he adored wild winds and sheeting rain; his hot blood and tempestuous temper bespoke him their child. He was across Carfax, up Cornmarket and under North Gate in no time, running so fast that few people had time to notice him before he was gone.

In the open country outside North Gate, in a grassy space between Saint John's College and Saint Giles' church and under the patronage of those two saints, Saint Giles' Fair was encamped, and Diccon's heart beat high. He had been taken to the Fair a year ago and the memory of it had remained with him like the memory of some thrilling dream. Everything that he loved best had been at that Fair, color and noise and excitement, and at it had been purchased Baa, his beloved lamb, with his legs of tin and his fine woolly coat, the person that he cared for only second to Tinker in all the world.

Diccon plunged into the Fair as a fish into the sea. The roar and scent and color of it engulfed him like waves going over his head, but he was not in the least frightened. In five minutes he was completely lost, with no idea where home was, or how he was to get back there if he wanted to, but that did not worry him at all. He was always a person who lived for the moment only, and the more exciting the moment the better he was pleased.

And there was no denying that Saint Giles' Fair was exciting. It was like a miniature town, with hundreds of booths set out under the blazing sun and narrow grassy alleys winding between them like the lanes of a city. The booths had bright awnings over the top of them, colored orange and red and green, as protection from sun and rain, and under the awnings were spread unimaginable glories. There were flowers and fruit, pouncet boxes, hawk's bells, dog whistles, colored kerchiefs, trinkets, garters, shoes, aprons, and every possible luxury that could tempt the eyes of the grownups. There were things for the children too: popguns and hobby horses and drums and kites, and wonderful things to eat such as gilt gingerbread and peppermint drops at twenty a penny.

A seething mass of people surged up and down the lanes between the booths, country people and townspeople with a good sprinkling of thieves and vagabonds and gypsies, arguing and shouting and bargaining with the Fair people who stood behind the booths. They were all dressed in their gayest and gaudiest as though they like the earth itself felt that the blazing golden sun and the deep blue sky of late summer were a challenge.

"Who can shine as I do?" cried the sun, and the earth laughed as she reared up sunflowers and golden rod on tall, strong spears that seemed trying to reach the arrogant heavens.

"Who dare match my color?" asked the painted sky as morning, midday, evening and midnight wheeled by in a glory of saffron and azure, rosepink and poppy red, amethyst and ebony pricked and washed with silver.

"I do," cried the earth, and there were peonies and michaelmas daisies in the gardens, golden fruits upon the walls and dandelions like stars in the lush green grass.

And human beings were as arrogant as the earth, it seemed, for color was awash in the lanes of the Fair, flowing up and down like water that reflects the colors of the sky above it. Sky-blue farthingales flowed over sunflower kirtles and scarlet shawls were folded over gowns of emerald green. The heads of young girls were bound with colored kerchiefs, and nodded like poppy heads, and the nimble legs of the young men were cross-gartered in scarlet and purple.

Diccon with his dirty bare feet and his warm curls seemed so a part of the landscape that few people noticed him. He darted in and out of the crowd like a dragonfly, quick and eager and unafraid. When anyone hindered him he hit out at the impediment with Baa's sharp tin legs and way was instantly made for him with curses and fists raised for a blow;

but he was always gone before the blow could fall and hard words slid
off him like water off a duck's back. His green eyes were the brighter for
the color they feasted on and the mingled smell of flowers, fruit and
sweating humanity was a smell that seemed good to him. Now and then,
when he felt the need for refreshment, he helped himself to a bite of gingerbread or a peppermint drop and had vanished before anyone could
catch him. He had no qualms of conscience about these thefts. On this,
the first day of real freedom in his life, he was the master of the world;
its color was a carpet beneath his feet and its golden sunshine a canopy
over his head, and between the one and the other were piled riches that
were his for the taking. For the first time, with freedom swinging open
a door before his eyes, he was aware of life stretching out illimitably in
front of him like a shining road and of himself as a young knight riding
out towards it. He felt suddenly powerful and splendid and hit out with
Baa as though the sharp tin legs were his lance and his sword and his
pointed dagger. . . . The earth was his and the glory of it.

Now and again the lanes of the Fair converged, like those of a real
city, upon an open square, and here there would be a sideshow or an
entertainment. Diccon stared with all his eyes at a fire-eater who appeared to be chewing up glowing coals as though they were so much
gingerbread, at a performing dog who could walk round on his hind legs
balancing a tankard on his nose, at a cat with two heads and a calf with
a tail sticking out in the middle of its forehead.

But it was in the fortune-teller's tent that the adventure of the day
awaited him.

It was pitched in a little square at the very center of the Fair, at its
heart, just as what happened to Diccon in it seemed to him ever afterwards to lie at the heart of his life. It was a small place, made of some
tattered crimson material stretched over pieces of wood roughly nailed
together. Its back was set against the back of some booths and in front
of it was a clear open space.

In this space stood a man, a splendid vagabond of a man with savage
green eyes and a torn green doublet open at the neck to show his great
hairy chest. Diccon was fascinated by this man and squatting down at

the edge of the crowd he gazed and gazed. He was not used to men like this. His father, Dean Godwin and the other men who had come and gone about him since his babyhood had been soft voiced, slender and clean. There had been something withdrawn about them. When he had looked up at them from his position on the floor he had seen fold upon fold of black gown, surmounted by a sort of cartwheel of white ruff; and when from above the ruff a cultured voice had asked him how he did it had seemed to come from the sky itself. Even when they had picked him up he had been so anxious to get down again that he had not really taken them in. . . . And anyhow, though he had tolerated and at times liked them, he had felt that they did not really belong to his world.

But this man did. He was like an animal, and Diccon liked animals. He was not worn and slender like Canon Leigh but bulkily huge, stocky and strong. He had a big head, with shaggy red-tinged dark hair and a dark beard, and great broad shoulders. Through his torn doublet and hose his arms and legs showed like huge strong pillars, burned almost black by the sun. In a voice like a bull's he was inviting the crowd to come to the tent and have their fortunes told. Sara the gypsy was inside and Sara never failed to tell the truth. His patter was splendid. Words poured from him in a stream, spiced with oaths, and the fascination of them drew the people one by one towards the tent. They went in rather fearfully but they came out laughing, their faces rosy with the reflected glow from the glorious futures the gypsy had foretold.

Diccon felt that he must see this splendid man close to. He pushed and burrowed his way to the man's feet and then sat down cross-legged and gazed again. . . . This was a god among men. . . . His voice flowed over Diccon's head like thunder and his gesticulating hands were so strong that they could have picked him up and broken him in small pieces. He was a freckled man, too, freckled like Diccon, and Diccon's bump of conceit led him to think that freckled men were the finest there are. His eyes never left his idol; they were fixed on his face, drinking in every detail of his rugged splendor, and presently their scrutiny was like a magnet that drew attention to him; the man paused in his patter and looked down at the child sitting cross-legged on the ground at his feet, gazing at him.

"Here, you!" he shouted. "What do you want? You get out of here!"

He made a movement as though he would have struck Diccon, but there was no flinching in the indomitable little figure and the unblinking stare never wavered. The man dropped his raised fist and bent low, hands on knees, to stare at the child. As their eyes met Diccon's poppy-red mouth curved into a smile and his green eyes shone as though lights had been lit behind them. To the onlookers it seemed that a curious change came over the man. "Eh?" he said doubtfully. "Eh?" All the stuffing seemed knocked out of him and the dirty, horny finger he stretched out to the boy wavered about uncertainly before it found the place it wanted; the warm, three cornered little hollow under the chin of Diccon Leigh. Diccon made no attempt to bite the finger that lifted his chin, instead he continued to smile like a little cherub and all his dimples peeped. The man was bending so close to him that the smell of sweat and dirt and strong drink almost stifled him, but he did not care. Other people would have said that this was not a nice man; a dirty, evil vagabond, they would have said; but if this man was a dirty vagabond then dirty vagabonds were the sort of men whom Diccon liked.

"You saucy little cockerel, you," said the man. "What do you want? Eh?"

The tone of his voice had changed. The threat had gone out of it and if it were possible for the voice of a bull to hold a caressing quality that quality would have been present.

Diccon could not say what he wanted. He wanted to be with this man for always; he wanted to follow him to the world's end, to clean his shoes and fetch his beer and run his errands. But he could not say so, he could only continue to smile and dimple.

The crowd grew a little restive. The dark man's patter, his oaths and gesticulations, were amusing and part of the show. They had not come here to stand about and watch him make a fool of himself over a child. "Here!" they adjured him. "Get on with it!" and one of them bent down and tried to lift Diccon out of the way. . . . To be bitten for his pains.

"Now then, son," adjured the dark man. "None of that! What do you want? Eh?"

"I want," said Diccon in a loud voice, "to have my fortune told."

He did not really want anything of the sort but to have his fortune told would, he thought, keep him well within the vicinity of the dark man.

The crowd jeered. "Let him show his bit of silver," they advised the dark man. "Where's his bit of silver to cross the palm of the gypsy?"

The eyes of the dark man were like those of a sad dog, for he was sure that Diccon would have no silver, but with a crow of delight Diccon thrust a fat hand into his little wallet and held up the coin that Dean Godwin had given him.

With a triumphant gesture the dark man gathered him up in the crook of his arm, lifted the tent flap and pitched him in.

4.

At first Diccon thought he had been flung into the middle of a lighted lantern, or into the heart of a rose, because it was all red; then he realized that it was the sun, shining through the red drapery of the tent, that made it so warm and rosy.

Standing with his back to the opening, with one little arm laid across his forehead as though to help him see better, Diccon looked at Sara. There was nothing at all in the tent to distract the attention; nothing at all but Sara sitting on a low stool. Her voluminous, ragged skirts swept the grass round her like the skirts of a queen; they were russet color, that same color that flows over the hills when the bracken is dying. Round her shoulders was a shawl of a brilliant, almost savage, emerald green, and there were gold rings in her ears glinting through the thick dark hair. The rosy light of the tent poured over her, softening the lines of her face, hiding the dirt on her shawl and the rents in her skirt, and behind its veil she was beauty incarnate.

"What a very little gentleman," she mocked softly. "What a very little gentleman to want his fortune told! Have you a silver coin, little gentleman?"

Diccon did not answer but slowly crossed the grass until he stood in front of her, looking up into her face, his fat hands laid on her knees.

Her eyes were dark pools into which he could look down and down, and her mouth, so close to him, was full and red as though it were made for kisses. She was opulent and rich and soft. Diccon felt that wherever he might press his finger it would go in, as though she were a cushion stuffed with goose feathers. He put up his finger and pressed her cheek, to see, and he was quite right. He caressed her cheek and crowed with delight.

But at sound and touch of him all the softness seemed to go out of Sara. She seized him fiercely with hands that felt hard, and stared at him. She looked at his eyes and his hair and his pointed ears, and traced the curve of his wicked eyebrows with a finger that shook. Then she pulled him roughly to her and dragged his doublet away from his back so that she could look at it. . . . So fiercely did she pull that his doublet ripped and tore. . . . Diccon didn't know what he had on his back but whatever it was it had an extraordinary effect upon Sara, for she picked him up and hugged him as though the hugging of Diccon was what she was born for.

Had Joyeuce or Dorothy hugged Diccon as Sara was hugging him he would have kicked, yelled, struggled and bitten, but from Sara he liked it. He wriggled himself comfortable on her lap, giggling contentedly, and a strange happiness stole over him. Her lap seemed to be made to be his throne. The hollow of her shoulder exactly fitted his head and her body was warm and soft about him. When Joyeuce and Dorothy cuddled him, Diccon never found them wholly satisfactory. Dorothy, though well upholstered, was hard, and Joyeuce, though soft, was inadequate; she was quite flat in front and her lap was so flimsy that it was apt to let you through. But this woman was just right. He nestled and cooed and crept closer, wriggling his bare toes in ecstasy.

Time stopped for them both. Sara rocked herself backwards and forwards, crooning a little song, and Diccon's long lashes descended to his cheek.

They were disturbed by a discontented murmuring outside the tent and by the head of the dark man protruding through its flap. "Be quick and have done," he whispered angrily to Sara. "Send the child away. These outside will not wait here forever." Then he withdrew his head and they heard him swearing at the crowd to pacify it.

Diccon, indifferent though he had always been to the feelings of those about him, was yet acutely aware of every emotion that thrilled through Sara. He had felt her love and her joy and now he felt her terror. Their lovely unity was threatened. They had come together, fitting into each other as those fit who once were one body, and now the noisy world was surging up against their rosy shrine where were only the two of them in their unity; in another moment it would have broken in; the crude glare of full day would wash over the rosy light of babyhood, putting it out, and mother and son would be one no longer.

Sara leaped to her feet, panting. She dragged and pulled at the red curtains behind her until they tore and gave way, leaving a space through which she could creep, pulling Diccon after her. They crept under one of the booths behind the tent, crossed the grassy lane beyond before anyone had time to stop them, or even to notice them, and in a moment were running like the wind, Sara holding firmly to Diccon and Diccon to Baa.

It seemed to Diccon that strange sudden shapes came looming up against them, trying to stop them, people and dogs and booths and bales and boxes, but doubling and dodging with the skill that was native to them both they went on till presently the Fair was left behind them, meadow grass and flowers were under their feet and before their eyes was a smooth, slipping ribbon of shining river.

They dropped down behind a hawthorn bush to get their breath, though creatures of the wild as they were they were less blown than anyone else would have been, and they hugged each other again and laughed because they had outwitted the world that would have torn them away from each other.

"So they thought they could take you away from me, did they?" jeered Sara. "The fools and the thieves, that think to take a babe from his mother! Eh, but your skin is fair, little son, fair and smooth like milk, and the soles of your feet are soft as butter. You need the hot sun to burn you and the earth under your feet to make them hard like those of a man. Why did I leave you behind in that house instead of the other? I was a fool, a fool! I thought to make my son a gentleman and I lost the core out of my heart and the light out of my eyes!"

She spoke in a strange language that Diccon did not understand, a strange tempestuous language that was like the wind in the trees, but he saw that she reproached herself and he would not have it. He kissed away the angry rears on her cheek and pummeled her with his fists to bring her to her senses.

She came to then and saw that they were not safe yet. She swung Diccon on to her back, her green shawl bound round him to keep him steady, and tramped on, walking with a slow swinging stride that yet covered the ground amazingly quickly.

They crossed the river by a wooden bridge and turned to follow a path that wound along beside its further bank. Oxford was left behind them, a walled gray city set like an island in an emerald sea of green meadow, and Diccon looked over Sara's shoulder at a world he did not know. He was not in the least frightened. Though all that he knew was left behind him in that gray city he felt nothing but a huge content. The hot sun blazed down on his head and the folds of the green shawl inclosed him like a pea in a pod. His head felt top-heavy with heat and happiness so that he laid it against his mother's shoulder and went to sleep.

5.

When he woke up again he was lying on a heap of dried bracken in a little hut with Baa beside him. In the center of the hut a fire was burning under a black pot that swung over it from a tripod of sticks, the smoke coiling up to escape through a hole in the roof.... Some of it, that is, the rest of it spread through the hut in a blue haze like the mist of dreams that always seemed to hang over Diccon's eyes when he first woke up.

For an awful moment he thought he had dreamed it all; the Fair, the splendid dark man and the glorious woman who had been made to be his throne; then he rubbed his fist in his green eyes to clear the dreams and the smoke away and saw through the blue haze an open doorway that held as in a picture frame a patch of blue sky, a few tufts of waving trees, and Sara and an old crone sitting side by side on the grass making baskets out of plaited rushes. They were talking softly together in that strange language and the rippling sound of their voices, the wind in the trees and the whisper of the flames on the hearth were a lullaby that nearly sent Diccon to sleep again.

He was jerked wide awake by a rustling in the big heap of bracken beside him. . . . Something was there, hiding under the bracken. . . . He pushed it aside, hoping for a cat like Tinker, and found himself looking straight into the eyes of a little boy of his own age; a dirty little fair-haired boy clothed in brown rags, with skin burned by sun and wind as golden brown as an acorn. In a paroxysm of shyness the little boy fell flat on his stomach and pulled the bracken over his head, but through it his eyes shone like two bright stars. Diccon also fell flat on his stomach, his head close to the little boy's, and through the dry, sweet-smelling fronds the blue eyes and the green twinkled at each other. Then they began to laugh, wrinkling their noses and kicking their bare legs in the air. They laughed more and more, rolling over each other, pushing the bracken down each other's necks and kicking and squeaking like a couple of puppies. They had come together at last and they were ecstatically happy. They had been born in the same hour on the same night, when all the stars were dancing. Their eyes had opened to moonlight and candlelight, heaven and earth shining together in welcome, and the first breaths they took were fragrant breaths that came blowing over the flowery earth. They had drunk the same mother's milk from a gypsy's breast and listened to the same songs crooned in their ears. They were fortunate children, born at full moon in the spring and dowered by the fairies with the gift of laughter, but never so fortunate as at this moment when they found each other.

When they were out of breath they rolled back to the bracken and sat curled up together, taking stock of each other, poking each other in the ribs and rubbing their heads together, establishing friendship as animals do by the contact of their bodies. Words were entirely unnecessary. They were part of each other, as Sara and Diccon were part of each other. Finally, as a mark of his esteem and to forge fast the bond between them, Diccon presented his foster brother with Baa. It was the first time in his life that he had ever given away something of his own, for his sense of property was strong at this stage of his life and his acquisitiveness even stronger, and the tremendous renunciation made him feel quite queer, as though when he rooted Baa up out of his life a part of himself clung to the roots and was given with Baa to the other boy to become a part of him. . . . He had made a discovery. . . . Later in his life he was to be scolded for the recklessness of his giving and would reply laughing that he hated loneliness like the devil.

Sara came in to them and ladled some of the stew that simmered in the black pot into a wooden bowl. Then she too sat down on the bracken and fed them with a wooden spoon, while they cuddled up one on each side of her with their mouths open like those of expectant young birds.

It was a stew made of poached rabbit and stolen fowl, seasoned with onions and herbs and drowned in a sticky, mud-colored gravy. Diccon thought it was the most delicious food he had ever eaten and continued to gape for more long after the bowl was empty.

"Greedy rogues!" cried Sara, and lifted them both on her lap, one on each knee. . . . She did not love the blue eyed child who had been borne by another woman any the less because she had found the green eyed child who was her own. . . . The blue dreamy haze hung over the three of them, as the rosy glow in the tent had done when they were only two, shutting out the world's clamor, and in quietness and peace they loved each other.

They sat there for a long time and would have been content to sit there forever, but the evening light was suddenly darkened and looking up they saw the figure of the dark man standing in the doorway, blocking out the sky. He was a very different man from the kindly creature who had chucked Diccon under the chin and thrown him good-humoredly through the flap of the tent. He had been drinking heavily and he was in a rage as complete, as abandoned and as royal as were the rages to which Diccon occasionally treated the household at Christ Church. He lurched through the door, strode over the fire and loomed like a thundercloud over Sara and her boys. After a moment of ominous silence the storm burst in such a torrent of abuse that the hut seemed to rock with it. It poured forth in the Romany language and Diccon could make neither head nor tail of it, though he gathered that Sara had done what she ought not and guessed that they should not have run away from the Fair. . . . But she seemed not to care. . . . She sat with her head tilted proudly back against the wall of the hut and her arms spread out one on each side of her to protect the small boys from the blows that would presently fall.

The blue eyed child shrank against her in terror but Diccon was highly interested. He had hitherto had experience of no one's rages but his own, and of one's own rages it is impossible to take an objective view. He gazed in fascination at the dark man's scarlet face, where the veins stood out like rope, and at his eyes that were so hot that they seemed to have red flames burning in them, and at his beard that wagged up and down at every furious word he spoke. His anger seemed surging all about them like a great wind and his voice was like the roar of many waters. . . . Diccon thought it was grand and his whole being went out to the dark man in admiration.

But suddenly it was not so grand, for the dark man began to use his hands. He fell upon Sara first, shaking her and knocking her head back against the wall with a sickening thud. Then he turned towards Diccon, but Sara leaned over her son with a cry, protecting his body with her own. . . . Out of the tail of his eye Diccon saw the other little boy, who had had previous experience of this sort of thing, wriggle between the dark man's legs and make a dash for it. . . . Then Sara's protecting body blotted out his view of the door and he saw nothing but the folds of her green shawl.

But he seemed to be feeling in his own body the blows that were falling on hers and a red-hot rage seized him. He loved Sara, loved her with the first real love he had ever known, and he wouldn't have her beaten. Struggling, he got himself free of her, seized hold of the dark man's hand and bit it.

Then the dark man struck him. Diccon had never been struck. He had been whipped for his good, but that was a different thing from a blow given in anger. The world was suddenly a terrible cruel place and instead of his rage he was brimful of nothing but terror. He forgot Sara, forgot everything but his longing to escape from this place where they struck you. Sobbing and crying, with his arm pressed against the place on his head where the dark man had cruelly hit him, he dashed through the flames of the fire, through the blue haze of smoke that only a few minutes ago had seemed so lovely, out through the door into the open.

He ran on and on, sobbing as though his heart would break. He did not know where he was going but he knew what he wanted. . . . He wanted to get back to that world where voices were never raised in anger and where cruelty was a thing unknown. . . . He thought that if he went on running and running perhaps he would get there.

But gradually the wild world to which he belonged, and which had dealt so hardly with him, began to comfort him. The green grass stretched up to lay cool balm against his hot, scorched little legs, and beside him a blackbird flew, chucking in consternation. He began to be conscious of flowers in the grass lifting their faces in sorrow, and of scarlet hips and haws in the hedges that were lanterns to light his way. These things comforted him and he was sure he would soon be home.

So he was not surprised when he saw a stone building looming ahead of him. . . . That must be the Fair Gate. . . . Soon he would see Heatherthwayte, and the dear black face of Satan, and beyond them he would see his father in his long black gown and Joyeuce with her shining head.

But when he got there it was not the Fair Gate but a little gray church standing under the trees. For a moment he stopped, sick with disappointment, then his fear drove him to run round it, looking for some place where he could hide himself.

He found it in a porch all overgrown with honeysuckle, with a wooden bench running along one side of it. He climbed upon the bench, curled himself up in the corner and cried and cried.

THE HOLY WELL

But you, fair maids, at length this true shall find,
That his right badge is but worn in the heart;
Dumb swans, not chattering pies, do lovers prove;
They love indeed who quake to say they love.

PHILIP SIDNEY.

1.

TO Faithful the summer holidays brought a deeper intimacy with the Leighs. He lived with them and became one with them in a way he had not been before. He began to know them all much better; they ceased to be just "the Leighs" and became individual people all of whom meant something different to him and called out something different in him. We are never quite the same person with everyone, he found; the clash of personality upon personality strikes out a different flame in every case and those we love the best are those whose impact upon us creates most light and warmth. And it was Grace, Faithful discovered, who did this for him. When he was with her the world was a warm place and so light that he forgot, as we do at midday when the sun is shining, that he had come from the dark and was journeying towards the dark again.

In the mornings he worked with Giles, or was coached by Canon Leigh, but after the early dinner he was with Grace and she taught him the things that she knew; very important instruction but of a different type from that given by Canon Leigh and Giles.

For unlike Joyeuce Grace was a born housewife. She had no need to force unwilling feet into the path of duty for the things that she had to do were the things that she liked to do. Anything to do with the running of a house, even the unsavory business of candle making, was a joy to her, and she knew of no greater bliss than the preparing of the fruits of the earth for their reception by the stomach of man. Her creed was simple. God made man that he might eat, and made woman from the rib of a man that she might prepare that which he ate. To Grace the whole world was a great larder stored with animals, birds, fruits, vegetables and nuts that had been created for purposes of consumption only; and above it all God the great housekeeper sat in His heaven, brooding benignly through the centuries over spread tables whose multiplicity and variety it baffled the powers of man to count or describe.

The problems that tormented Joyeuce, such as the purpose for which man ate, and why it was necessary to despoil the beauty of the world that he might eat, and how one was to satisfy the hunger of the soul that inhabited the well-fed body, troubled Grace not at all. Had she thought about these things she would have said that man ate to eat, and that corn looked nicer made into bread than getting knocked about outside in the rain, and that personally the longings of her soul were satisfied when her cake rose nicely and the joint was done to a turn. . . . The fact of the matter was that Grace was a plump child and the spirit within her body was so well cushioned that the shocks and jars of life had not hitherto waked it up to ask how, why, wherefore?

Yet being human she had her troubles and the chief of these was the non-recognition of her talents by the household. She was far more capable than Joyeuce and yet Joyeuce insisted upon treating her as though she knew nothing. She was able to tell her family exactly what to do in every problem that beset them but yet they never asked her advice, and if she gave it unasked they laughed. She was thirteen, and grown up, yet they all insisted upon treating her as though she was still a baby. . . . All but Faithful.

His respect for her talents was balm to her. Unused as he was to the comfort and order of a well-run household the things that she did for the welfare of them all seemed to him amazing, and he set himself in great humility to learn what she could teach him, so that his clumsy fingers could help her in the thousand and one tasks that seemed to him likely to break the back of so little a lady. She joyfully taught him all she knew, provided it had nothing to do with the mysteries of cooking, that no man should be allowed to inquire into lest he discover that they are not so difficult after all, and woman fall in his estimation.

He learned, for instance, that quaking grass, gathered and brought into the house, keeps away mice; an interesting fact and of value to those to whom a cat in the house is anathema.

Put a Tumbling Jockey in
June in your house
And he'll rid you forever of
Every mouse.

Grace repeated the rime to him and showed him the spire of quaking grass she had put in every room, so as to take no chances even though they had got Tinker, and he promised that next year he would go out into the June fields and pick them for her.

He learned, too, how to make pomander balls, with cloves stuck into dried oranges, so as to keep the plague away, and how to make pot pourri, and how to pick the lavender and herbs and dry them, and put them into little bags to lay between the sheets, or herb pillows to put under your head at night to make you sleep.

Faithful thought he had never been so happy as he was on the days when they bent together over the lavender bushes, snipping off the sweet flower spikes and putting them to dry on the stone paths, with the sun warm on their backs and the bees lurching about from bush to hush. Grace, very bustling and important, with her pink skirts bunched up to be out of the way and her wide-brimmed garden hat tied with pink ribbons under her round chin, was an engaging sight as she picked lavender. The sun of that hot summer had tanned her usually white skin a warm brown and she had four freckles on the tip of her nose. Her eyes seemed to get bluer every day, he thought, as blue as periwinkles, and when she was hot her black hair clung all round her face in kiss-me-quick curls.

Yet on such days her beauty seemed to Faithful a barrier that kept him away from her, a barrier that he could not pass because of the shut-away feeling that his physical deformity gave him. Beautiful people, he felt, are one with the starlit nights and the June fields and the poetry of the world, but ugly people belong with the toads and the spiders and the east wind rain. Even in the past, when there had been no Grace, he had had this feeling of isolation but he had always tried hard to conquer it. When another boy jeered at him because of his ears he immediately established personal contact by two good blows on the ears of his tormentors, and when he met in another the beauty that he had not got he immediately, figuratively speaking, took off his hat to it, for he knew that worship breeds love and not jealousy. He did not know how he knew these things. He supposed that the harder one's life is the more desperate must be the struggle to find out how to be happy, and the more likely to be successful.

But on the same eventful day when Diccon went to the Fair he had the courage to break through this barrier between himself and Grace. They were going round the Christ Church Meadows together, picking meadowsweet to strew the floors. . . . Meadowsweet was Queen Elizabeth's favorite strewing herb and therefore much in fashion just at present. . . . As they walked, or rather trotted, for walking was too staid a word to describe the motion given to their bodies by the lightness of their hearts and the fewness of their years, Faithful pointed out to Grace all the pretty things that strewed the floor of the world about them. It grieved him that Grace's practical mind was apt to pass beauty by, seeing in ripe yellow plums hanging among sun-silvered leaves potential pots of jam rather than those apples of gold in pictures of silver that Solomon in his wisdom spoke of, and he was always trying to make her just stand and look without thinking immediately what she looked at could be made into.

"You are as bad as Philip Sidney," he said to her, "who must always make everything he looks at into poetry."

"Cooks also are artists," Grace told him solemnly.

But she tried very hard to do what he wanted her to do, just stand and wonder and worship even though the activity seemed unlikely to lead anywhere, and she was gradually beginning to enjoy things just for themselves.... And there were lots of things to enjoy today.... The kisses of the sun upon the water, each kiss being held as a speck of shining light within the curve of each ripple; the fine veinings on the underside of grass blades, that are intricate as a spider's web and delicate as gossamer; the amazing beauty of a wasp, once one can persuade oneself to look at it with an unprejudiced eye, with its delicate wings like silver and its striped golden body quivering below a waist whose slenderness the Queen's Grace herself, thin in the middle though she was, might have envied. His companionship was like a pointing finger. Look here, look there, he said, and Grace looked and found that the world was beautiful.

But suddenly Faithful fell silent and hung his head, for Grace in her rosy beauty was like a jewel that fitted sweetly into its setting of veined grass and running water, making the green and the silver sparkle more brightly, but he in his ugliness did violence to them both. His sudden sense of his own disharmony hurt him like a blow.

"What is it, Faithful?" asked Grace softly.

"I wish I was not so ugly," said Faithful in a choked voice.

Grace folded her hands upon her stomacher in the matronly way that sat so comically upon her and flounced round upon him in real anger. The pink ribbons under her chin quivered with indignation and her eyes shot sparks. "How dare you say you are ugly!" she stormed.

Faithful glanced up, astonished. He had not yet experienced the possessiveness of a woman, and her fury when a thing of her own is scorned. Grace, too, was surprised by her own rage. Her maternal instinct had erupted all in a moment like a volcano inside her and Grace the little girl had become Grace Catherine Leigh the woman. "You're *not* ugly," she said, and stamped her foot. "No! You look so clever, Faithful, and different from other people. Men like Giles and Nicolas de Worde, with mouths and ears all alike, are so dull.... I tell you what it is, Faithful," she summed up. "You're distinguished looking."

Every woman in love with an ugly man lays this phrase like balm to his smart, but Grace did not know that; she had thought of it all by herself and she was very proud when she saw his painful flush fade away and his mouth tilt up at the corners. But she was nothing if not practical and she hastened to act as well as to speak for his comfort.

"At Binsey," she said, "there is a holy well that cures boils and pock marks."

"Are you sure?" asked Faithful.

"Perfectly certain," said Grace strong-mindedly. "Dorothy Goatley had a boil on her chin and Diggory fetched her some of the holy water in a bottle and the minute she put it on her boil it burst."

"Do you think," asked Faithful in a low voice, "that it would take away my pock marks?"

"Yes," said Grace judicially, "I do. It's not that I don't like them, Faithful, and I'm sure that other people never notice them at all, but I think you yourself would be happier without them."

"I should," said Faithful fervently. "It would be nice," he added wistfully, "to look like Philip Sidney."

"Philip Sidney!" snorted Grace contemptuously. "I should *hate* it if you looked like him. Why, he's just like a girl."

"Could we go to Binsey?" asked Faithful. "I know the way."

"We'll go now," breathed Grace. Her eyes were sparkling with delight and each of her cheeks had a large dimple where the finger of delight had prodded her to make her laugh. She had never been to Binsey, for young females never went outside the city gates except with the very strongest male escort, and she was wildly excited. Faithful, who had tramped from London to Oxford and thought little of it, did not realize that perhaps he ought not to take Grace so far. They ran home, giggling with happiness. Faithful's ugliness, that a few moments ago had seemed to him a barrier that separated him from Grace, seemed now a link between them; a sort of secret that they shared together.

They dumped their armfuls of meadowsweet in the hall and shouted up the stairs to Joyeuce. "We're going for a walk, Joyeuce."

"Very well," said Joyeuce. "Don't go near the Fair, because of the smallpox, and don't go far."

They made no reply to this last injunction but scurried hastily away again lest any awkward questions should be asked. Under the Fair

Gate they found Heatherthwayte asleep and Satan awake, but looking very depressed.

"What's the matter, Satan?" they asked, stopping to rub him behind the ears.

Satan thumped his tail deprecatingly, and licked their hands in humble apology. With tail and tongue and pleading glances of his sad dark eyes he tried to tell them that their evil small brother had run away only a short while since, and they had better go after him; but they were stupid and did not understand.

They ran up Fish Street to Carfax, turned to the left and went down Great Bailey towards West Gate and the grim old castle that in itself formed part of the city wall. The oldest part of it was a mound that had been reared as a fortification against the Danes. . . . For those terrible Danes who crossed the North Sea every summer in their magnificent carved galleys had penetrated even as far as Oxford. "Good Lord, deliver us from the Danes," was once a frequent prayer in Oxford churches, and the ringing of the tocsin that called them to arms against the Dane was one of the most terrible sounds a citizen could hear. . . . Next in age was the tower of Saint George, built in the eleventh century, and then came the twelfth-century castle itself with its five splendid towers.

Under the castle tower was the castle mill, with the millpond below it. The mill had begun to work in the eleventh century and it went on doing its work, year in and year out, for eight hundred years. Kings and queens might come and go, civil war, riots, fire and pestilence might ravage the city, but the living must be fed though the dead lay in heaps in the streets and through it all the old water-wheel went round and the old mill went on turning corn into bread.

Once outside West Gate Grace and Faithful had green grass under their feet, trees and singing birds around them, and in front of them the ruins of Oseney Abbey. It was still lovely, though the roofs were gone and the walls were falling and only the birds sang in the great church as big as a cathedral where the monks used to chant mass.

Faithful, standing with Grace knee-deep in the sea of flowers and grass that rolled right up to the walls of the Abbey, stared in a sort of sorrowful anger at the wrecked loveliness. From what was left he could reconstruct what had been; the splendid cloister and the quadrangle as large as that at Christ Church, the magnificent church, the schools and libraries, the Abbot's lodgings and the water-side buildings with their high pitched roofs and oriel windows. "Someone ought to paint these ruins," he said sadly, "before they fall to pieces altogether and we forget what they were like."

A few years later someone did. In the south aisle of the cathedral there was put up a window designed by the Dutchman, Van Ling, and among the trees in the background was a picture of Oseney Abbey. So precious was this window to Christ Church, with its picture of the first home of the Christ Church bells, that during the Civil War they buried it, and triumphantly dug it up again at the Restoration.

2.

Faithful and Grace went on their way. It was a perfect summer's day and between banks of meadowsweet and willow herb and green rushes the river ran through fields of shimmering grass.

There is something about a river that draws one on and on. It slips along so gently that one feels one can outstrip it, and the song of the ripples in the rushes is the best marching song in the world.

Over their heads was the blue sky of late summer, mirrored in the rippling water, and across the river to their right the glorious stretch of Port Meadow, the "town" meadow that had been given to the city of Oxford to graze its cattle on for all time. It was so wide and so flat that it was like a green sea, and reflected the high white clouds that sailed above it in drifting pools of deeper green. Black-winged swallows dipped and rose and dipped again beside the river, and it seemed to Faithful that plumb upon the center of every reflected white cloud in the blue water there sat a fat white swan. "There is no place in the world so beautiful as this," he said to Grace, "no place in all the world."

Leaving the river behind them they turned to their left and went across the meadow that led to Binsey. When they got to the tiny village

they turned to their right and followed the rough stony path that led to
the church and the Holy Well. Hips and haws shone scarlet on either
side of the path and the trees arched over their heads as though candles
were lit and a roof provided to help their pilgrimage. They met no one
and Grace had a feeling that home was hundreds of miles away. She and
Faithful were going a long journey together and she was enjoying it so
much that she hoped she would never get to the end.

Faithful, too, felt superbly happy. A few months before, when he
first began to live the life of an Oxford scholar, he had thought he was
as happy as anyone could be, but now he was happier even than that.
He had known joy, both the joy that comes from delight in beauty and
the joy of a fine mind in achievement, and he had known the exquisite
relief and sense of well-being when hardship and suffering are over and
one has a bed to lie on and a well-filled stomach, but he had never before
known this depth of content that he felt as he ran down the lane with
Grace beside him in her pink frock and the candles of the hips and haws
burning on either side. . . . He could find no words for what he felt.

"I am happy too," said Grace, just as though he had spoken. "It is
like when Mother was alive."

"Was it nice when your mother was alive?" asked Faithful.

"It was nice," said Grace. "One could tell things to Mother."

So then Faithful knew the true definition of a really comfortable
love: a cozy state of telling things. Their love would have none of the ups
and downs, the ecstasies and torments that lay in wait for Joyeuce and
Nicolas. Faithful's life burned far more strongly in his mind than in his
body. Even when he became a man the desires of his body would never
loom large in his life, and he would never ask more of Grace than the
quiet affection and understanding that cannot burn out because they are
lit eternally one from the other and grow with the giving. This placidity
would never have contented Joyeuce, who beneath the apparent cold-
ness of her nervously braced demureness was a passionate person who
found her happiness in a reaching out to the things beyond practical
living; but to Grace who found her pleasure in the things that lie near at
hand it would bring content.

A feeling of awe crept over them as they came into the churchyard and stood together on the path that led to the old gray church. The days of pilgrimage to the Holy Well were now over and thick green moss had grown over the path that once had been kept bare and hard with the passing of feet. The grass had grown high, hiding the tombs of the dead, and the trees had grown thickly and darkly about the weather-stained walls and lichened roof of the church. Nature was taking back again the holy place that once had belonged to man. Bit by bit her sea was lapping up, covering man's brown paths and gray stones with a slowly encroaching tide of green. Faithful marveled at the inexorable patience of nature. Let man attack her, cutting down her trees to make room for the smoke-grimed walls of his houses, rooting up her flowers to make space for his teeming streets, putting her birds to flight and sending her furry creatures scurrying away into exile, and she patiently withdraws herself to the horizon, gathering her creatures to her, brooding and biding her time. But let man loosen his grip for a moment, let him leave his house or neglect the paving of his street, and she is back again with seeds blown in the wind and the germ of growth alive in the sun and the rain. Her touch is that of Midas and the mark of her possessive finger is seen in a yellow wall-flower upon the wall, and the print of her returning feet in dandelions among the cobbles. They are forerunners of the returning tide, those specks of gold, and if man does not fight her in a few centuries green waves of meadow and forest will have swept over his houses and streets and only a few hummocks in the grass will show where his city has been.

But in Binsey churchyard nature was not yet conquered or conqueror and the enchantment of all moments of transition added its magic to the enchantment that haunts a place of pilgrimage. On the path pilgrim feet had traced a pattern of penitence and the moss that had grown over it was the brighter for its cleansing. Prayers had been said by the graves and the tall grasses whispered them over again when the wind blew. Nuns had sung hymns of praise in the church and the blackbird who caroled every sunset upon the roof-tree would sing a stave and then stop, his head on one side as though listening to echoes from the past, then sing again, triumphant, as though he had heard aright. And year in, year out, the water of the Holy Well bubbled up cool and limpid from the dark places of the earth that never change.

It was in the churchyard at the west end of the church. Four stone walls had been built round it to protect it from those who might profane it and its steep wooden roof was turfed. Little trees had seeded themselves on the roof; elders and briars and even an oak tree; elves of trees because they had so little foothold but perfect in their degree.

"It is the holy water that makes them so perfect," said Grace, and then she told Faithful how long ago Saint Frideswide and her nuns had come to live at Binsey for a little while, taking refuge from their enemies. They had had the little church built for them, dedicating it to Saint Margaret of Antioch, and some dwelling houses whose ruins were still to be seen. The country people who loved them had tilled the fields for them to give them bread; blackberries and elderberries grew on the bushes for their dessert and at the prayer of the saint the water of the well had sprung from the earth that they might drink. After her death the water of the well worked miraculous cures upon the faithful, like the well at Cowley Ford, so that for Frideswide as well as Edmund death made no ending of their service to their fortunate people of Oxford.

Fortunate the people of Oxford still might be, but not so believing, and Frideswide who had been a living presence in the churchyard was now but a ghost in the trees. Few came to her for help now; only the simple-minded like Diggory Coir or children like Grace and Faithful. So rusty was the key in the door of the well-house that it took the two of them, hands twining together, to turn it and force the door.

Inside was a clammy darkness and steps that seemed to go down to the bowels of the earth. They went down hand in hand, feeling their way and slipping on the slimy steps, till they came to the water welling up under a low stone arch. They were both a little breathless when they reached the bottom; partly from awe, partly because the slimy steps and the spiders' webs that tickled their groping fingers made them giggle; Grace hiccuped, which she felt she should not do in so holy a place. Faithful knelt down and scooping the water up in his cupped hands he bathed his face three times. The water looked black as ink as it lay under the archway but as he lifted it up the light from the open door turned it to trickling silver, and when he splashed it against his face it was cold as ice. "Three times only?" he asked Grace, and Grace nodded. That was the mystic number; Father, Son and Spirit; father, mother and child; birth and life and death.

They climbed the steps again and came out into a glory of sunlight that shone full upon Faithful's wet face, so that Grace turning eagerly towards him saw it shining brilliantly like the face of an angel.

"Faithful!" she cried. "You look like Saint Stephen."

"But are the pock-marks gone?" he asked anxiously, for the Bible gives no information as to whether Saint Stephen was pock-marked or not.

"They're gone!" cried Grace. "I can't see them any more!" and she flung her arms round Faithful's neck and kissed him. A glorious feeling of liberation fell upon Faithful, with its accompanying sense of the in-rush of new life. His ugliness had been the rusty bars of a prison but now they had fallen, and the prisoner that came running out from behind them was his love for Grace.

"Will you marry me one day?" he asked her.

"Yes," she said.

Their wedding was as easily arranged as that of two birds. The caution and calculation that come with age did not worry them at all. There were no past disappointments to embitter their love, no sins to soil it. They clung together in the perfection of ecstasy, their wet cheeks pressed together and the holy water like diamond drops on their lips. The action and place were symbolic, for their first kiss in a graveyard was cool and fresh as the love that lasted them till death.

For ever after it was the firm conviction of Faithful and Grace that his pock-marks were not noticeable; other people did not share their conviction, but then other people were unbelievers.

3.

Grace withdrew herself from her lover's arms to shut and lock the door behind them. She was her usual self again, practical and informative.

"Once the streams ran all round Binsey," she said, "and made an island of it. Binsey means 'island of prayer' in Saxon."

"Then we had better pray," said Faithful, and led the way up the moss-grown path to the dark, musty little church. They knelt very upright on the hard stone floor, facing the altar and the stained glass figure of Saint Frideswide above it, their backs as straight as boards and their hands placed palms together under their chins. They knelt as still as two be-ruffed figures on a tomb, so still that a little mouse crept out and sniffed at the soles of their shoes to see what they were made of.

But it was only Faithful's outside that was pressed into this cold statuesque mold of godliness; inside he was a burning fire of devotion and love and gratitude. He had no need to pray in words. His whole consciousness, mental and physical, seemed gradually to be absorbed in a great act of praise that lifted him up as on wings so that he lost all sense both of the place where he was and of himself as a person. Something that came from outside, something divine, touched him, and at the touch everything about him and in him had clicked into harmony so that there were no parts but only a whole, no time but only eternity. He was never to know a moment quite like this again. The emotion of human love that had swept over him at the well, an emotion as rarefied in its purity as any human emotion could be, had left him so sensitively aware that he could feel what he would never feel again. . . . Only long for with a longing so acute that the rest of his life would be a pilgrimage.

But such moments were not for Grace, for she belonged to that noble army of Marthas who cook the dinners that the Marys gobble up to keep them going between their visions and their dreams. Grace was the best kind of Martha. She would never mind how long the dinner took to cook and would take it quite for granted if there was not much left for her by the time Mary's hunger was satisfied. Yet if Grace could not know ecstasy she could perform the duties of religion very credibly. She knelt now very correctly, finger tip to finger tip and eyes glued tight shut, and she repeated all the prayers she knew in an inward voice so perfect in grammar and pronunciation that there was no excuse for the deity not hearing. . . . But when she came to the end of them she was floored. . . . She didn't know any more and she couldn't pray extempore. The cold paving stones penetrated through her dress and made themselves known to her knees. She had a crick in her neck from kneeling so straight and a touch of indigestion inside. She opened one eye and looked at Faithful. He was in his Saint Stephen mood again; oblivious of her, oblivious of everything; his inward eye gazing upon the opened heavens. For how much longer was he going on praying? She shifted her weight from one aching knee to the other and experienced a slight sinking of the heart, for it might be that married life with Faithful would be a strain at times. Then a wave of shame went over her and her rapturous love bubbled up afresh in her heart, so that shutting her eyes she too saw visions; of a spotless larder full of jellies and preserves made by herself without any interference from Dorothy, a well-filled linen cupboard with lavender bags between each sheet made by herself without any criticism from Joyeuce, and, best of all, a neat row of compact little babies picked up by herself and Faithful from under the gooseberry bushes to which they had fallen straight from God.

So vivid was this last vision that she could actually hear the compact little babies disliking the gooseberry prickles and crying to be fetched out; and then she realized that somewhere quite near a child actually *was* crying. She opened her eyes and listened intently, all the mother in her wide awake. Then she prodded Faithful.

"What?" said Faithful, returning from heaven with difficulty and some slight irritation.

"Listen," said Grace.

Faithful got to his feet with a sigh and rubbed his knees. The persistent voice of the world, crying outside in its woe, was not for the first time disturbing a saint in his visions and dragging him out of the house of devotion into the world of action. They made their way out of the shadows of the church into the porch, full of the streaming sunset light, and there, curled up in the corner, was Diccon sobbing his heart out.

Grace had never had much affection for Diccon; privately she had always thought him rather a nasty little boy, quite unworthy of the devotion lavished upon him by Joyeuce and her father; but his woe was desperately genuine and gathering him up in her arms she kissed him and crooned over him as though he were all the compact little babies rolled into one.

It was impossible to make out what was the matter with him, where he had been or what he had done or how in the world he had got where he was. When they questioned him he only shook his curly head, sobbed heartbrokenly and demanded to be taken home.

They took him home, carrying him pickaback by turns, the journey turned into a painful pilgrimage by his bulk. He was a dead weight on their backs, his curly head lolling heavily as though the sorrow of the world bowed it down and his body shaken periodically with heartbreaking hiccups. The whole sky was a sheet of gold and under it the green earth lay in a strange stillness, the river like glass and the trees unstirring, as though the whole world listened to the echo of a footfall; the feet of the day that departed and the feet of the night that came. And through the green and the gold the three children moved silently, listening too. The day had brought them new terrors and joys; love and ecstasy, freedom, cruelty and pain. Much that had been theirs had gone from them forever; the old childish carelessness and ignorance and happy self-sufficiency; and moving towards them were new things, half-seen shapes drawing nearer with glowing eyes that promised rapture and mercilessly pacing feet that promised pain.

But from the shadowy terrors there was a shelter. Built upon the green floor of the world, piled against the golden curve of the sky, were the towers of a city. Bastioned walls were strong against earthly danger, steepled churches held the powers of evil at bay, and flower-filled gardens and green arbors were a refuge to a man from the sorrow of his own thoughts.

"There is Oxford!" cried Grace. "There is home at last!"

Faithful, whose turn it was to carry Diccon, lifted his bowed head and wiped the sweat from his forehead, and Diccon opened his tear-swollen lids and gazed and gazed.

CHAPTER XI

DARK DECEMBER

Even such is Time, which takes in trust
Our youth, our joys, and all we have,
And pays us but with age and dust;
Who in the dark and silent grave,
When we have wandered all our ways,
Shuts up the story of our days:
And from which earth, and grave, and dust,
The Lord shall raise me up, I trust.

WALTER RALEIGH.

1.

THE autumn and the returning scholars arrived at Oxford together. With the first gale of wind and rain from the southwest, a gale that tore the last petals from the drenched rose trees and sent the clouds hurrying like flocks of frightened sheep across the sky, there came a clamor at the gates, a joyous shouting and singing of songs, the clatter of horses' hoofs on cobbles and the pealing of the bells with which the city welcomed her children home.

For though Oxford had been very glad to see the scholars go she was even more glad to see them come back. The blessed peace of their absence had turned into boredom as the hot summer weeks went by. After the long years of their occupation the life of the city had come to center around them, and if they were absent too long the life seemed drained of its purpose. . . . To see the cavalcades coming winding in from north, south, east and west, filling the quiet streets with their clamor, was like seeing sap flow again through the branches of a dead tree.

With her children once more stowed safely within her walls, Philip
Sidney writing poetry at Broadgates Hall, Nicolas playing the viol in his
room by the Fair Gate and Walter Raleigh flashing like a meteor in and
out of the gates of Oriel, the city put on a fresh beauty. She had become
a little tired and dusty, drained of her strength and color by the hot weeks
of harvest time, but now, swept of her dust by the life-giving gales and
washed clean by the showers of silver rain that went by on the wind,
beauty bloomed again. There were new flowers in the gardens, crimson
dahlias and the white starry daisies of Saint Michael, and the lawns put
on a fresh bright green that was like an echo of the vanished spring. Every
gray wall wore a cloak of scarlet creeper and the elm trees in the Christ
Church Meadows stood like tall knights arrayed from head to foot in
golden armor. Sandwiched between days of rain there were sunshiny
days of loveliness when the silence was so deep that wanderers in fields
and gardens were almost startled to hear the tiny tap of a falling leaf or the
twitter of a robin in the bushes. . . . On these days one felt drenched in a
melancholy quietude that was almost as enjoyable as happiness.

Even Joyeuce, when on fine mornings she drew back the curtains
on a world whose fragile beauty made her think of a rainbow or a soap
bubble, felt a rare tranquillity. Fine autumn days bred philosophy in one,
she thought, for the earth itself in autumn was so philosophic; faced
with the storms of winter, that would root up its trees and stamp its flowers into the ground, it seemed to turn itself backward to remember past
glories with such a passion of delight that on day after day it was almost
young again, so young that on some mornings you would have said that
memory had merged into hope and next spring was here already.

That was what she would do, thought Joyeuce. . . . Remember. . . .
Behind her were the happy days of childhood when her mother had
been with her and living had been like wings that carried one from one
joy to another, not a pack upon the back that made the shoulders ache;
she would remember those days and grow the stronger for reliving their
joy and freedom. And she must remember that evening of ecstasy when
she had thought that Nicolas loved her and had felt herself to be born
again; till her dying day she must remember that because surely never

again would she reach such a peak of joy. She realized that one could not live always on such a peak; if one did nerves and body would break under the strain; but from every experience of bliss as it passed away one could keep back a modicum to add to interior treasure. Surely these moments were foretastes of something to come, some freedom of spirit so heavenly that it would be cheaply purchased by all the garnered wealth of a lifetime. . . . After one of these early morning meditations Joyeuce would be so sweet-tempered that the children would bask in her smiles like kittens in the sun. . . . But when the day was over and she was in bed at night, with a little wind whispering round the windows and darkness lying over the world like a pall, Joyeuce would forget to be a philosopher and her tears would soak right through the linen of the pillowcase and drench the goose-breast feathers underneath.

Grace did not need to bask in another's warmth for she had more than enough of her own. She was so happy that three inches were added to her waist measurement and two to her height, while her hair broke into such a paroxysm of curl that each separate hair seemed alive and dancing with a life of its own. After serious consultation she and Faithful had come to the conclusion that matrimony had better not be mentioned to the family just yet. They were quite old enough to be married, of course, thirteen and fourteen being well on in years of discretion, but though they realized their seniority they doubted if the family did. . . . There was still a regrettable tendency to treat them as children. . . . They feared an outburst of protest and thought it better to keep their secret a little longer; until Grace was taller still and Faithful had made the whole College see his brilliant future in as rosy colors as he did himself.

And it was such a nice secret to keep; Grace was inclined to think it was sweeter to keep it than to tell it. Solemn and gentle kisses given and received behind the apple trees in the garden, whispered conversations under the stairs, quick darting glances exchanged in a crowded room, that had the queer effect of making the crowd dissolve into thin air, so that they two were left quite alone in a world that had been made for them only. To tell about these things at this stage would have been to spoil them. They would have to tell about them in the end, of course, but by that time they

would be like children who are tired of playing at make-believe in secret
and want to be the real thing in the eyes of the whole world.

But in her own eyes Grace was a wife already and behaved with a
bustling importance that Joyeuce found quite insufferable. She took to
wearing two extra petticoats to further increase her bulk, and finding
some old keys at the bottom of a chest she hung them round her waist
instead of the infantile hornbook which she now contemptuously dis-
carded, and went jingling and rustling about the house with a dignity
that would have been overwhelming in a matron of sixty.

"What's the use of wearing keys that don't unlock anything?" asked
Joyeuce with some irritation.

"They are a symbol," Grace assured her solemnly. "They increase my
authority with the younger children."

"But you have no authority over the children," objected Joyeuce.
"It's *my* business to manage the children."

"You're not very good at it," said Grace. "It would be much better if
you left it to me."

As the days went by the phrase "leave it to me" was constantly upon
Grace's lips. Entering the kitchen suddenly she would find Joyeuce immersed in the hated business of candle making, with the rushes mislaid and the melted fat fast congealing again while she looked for them.
"What is the use of starting to melt the fat when you have not got the
rushes handy?" she would ask. "Don't fuss, Joyeuce. Leave it to me."

Or again, when Joyeuce in her spinning made knots in her yarn, she
would say benignly, "You don't keep the thread taut, dear. Better leave
it to me."

Even the twins, though they loved Joyeuce far more dearly than they
loved Grace, began to form the habit of running to Grace rather than to
Joyeuce when they had run a thorn into a finger or torn a frock.... Being
quite incommoded by the fear of hurting them Grace's probings of the
finger were far less painful than those of the sensitive Joyeuce; and her
darning in its beauty was like that of the archangels in heaven.

Joyeuce was frequently infuriated to the point of tears. Was she to be
humiliated and flouted at every turn, she who had so heroically sacrificed

her own personal happiness—or would have, had Nicolas given her the chance—for these ungrateful children? She had constantly to remind herself that the children did not know she had sacrificed herself—or would have sacrificed herself had Nicolas had the grace to propose to her—and so could hardly be expected to be grateful. . . . But yet it hurt that they were not. . . . In her heartache she turned to Diccon; he had always been her very own little baby, her little poppet to whom all through his short life she had been all the world.

But Diccon was not very responsive. He had been exceedingly peculiar ever since the day when he had been to Saint Giles' Fair. He was able to give no account of his adventures on that day; he had just got lost, he said; but that there had been adventures no one doubted, for Diccon was not the same little boy he had been before.

When he had first been restored to the bosom of his family he had made a most unusual demonstration of affection. He had embraced them all round and bitten nobody. Upon his father in particular he had lavished such a quantity of moist kisses and bear hugs that Canon Leigh had become quite embarrassed. He was not used to expressions of appreciation from his youngest son.

But after a few days these transports died down and he became curiously aloof, even pathetic and bewildered, as though he had mislaid something and could not find it. His family was inclined to think that he grieved for his lost lamb Baa, but he said no, it wasn't Baa who was lost; asked who it was he seemed unable to say. Joyeuce and Dorothy were constantly finding him hiding by himself behind the embroidered curtains of the big bed, or inside the cupboard where the raisins were kept, not eating the raisins or unpicking the embroidery but just hugging Tinker and doing nothing. . . . Tinker, too, seemed depressed. . . . His whiskers drooped and he let the mice accumulate about the place in a shocking manner.

Now and then Diccon would come to Joyeuce to be cuddled but when enthroned upon her lap he seemed to find it curiously unsatisfactory. He would pound her with his fists, as though trying to make her a different shape, and when her figure remained hopelessly virginal he would give her up in despair and try Dorothy. . . . But she did not give satisfaction either. . . . "Too 'ard," he would tell her, "too 'eavy," and sliding down he would seize Tinker by the tail and trot mournfully off to the dark place under the stairs, where they would hear him sobbing.

Yet it was quite impossible to offer comfort, for if anyone tried to remove them from their hiding place Diccon made rude noises in his throat and Tinker spat. There was nothing to be done except to mourn for the merry elf who had vanished in Saint Giles' Fair and to try to coax this new sad little boy into some likeness of him.

So it was no wonder that Joyeuce's mood was autumnal and her chief happiness a looking back. The present, tarnished by the unappreciativeness of her family, was not hospitable to happy thoughts, and to a future shorn of Nicolas it was better to pay no attention.

For to think of a time when there would be no Nicolas just across the way was to invite despair. She saw little of him now, but still, he was there. She often saw him jauntily crossing the quadrangle to the Cathedral, and sometimes at night, when the children were asleep, she would creep out of bed and peep through her curtains at the light in his window and picture him poring studiously over some great learned book, becoming with every moment wiser and wiser, far too wise for an ignorant girl like herself. . . . If Nicolas, noisily playing club kayles with some boon companions, could have seen her kneeling on the floor in her white frilly night rail, her pale gold hair silvered by the moonlight and all other expression burned out of her face by a white-hot flame of longing, he would have lingered in his room for only as long as it took to pitch the boon companions into one corner of the room and the club-kayles ninepins into the other. . . . In the twinkling of an eye he would have been under her window, his hands creeping up the wall again, his love for her as hot as it had been on that memorable midsummer eve.

2.

But he could not see and it was upon a very lonely Joyeuce that the blow fell in the dark days of December. It had rained all through

November, a steady drenching that seemed to go on day and night, that turned the lazy river into a turbulent flood and filled all the little streams in the valley to overflowing. The citizens of Oxford grew anxious, for the beautiful waterway that was their chief pride and glory could be at times their greatest enemy. . . . For after the river had been in flood, disease always fell upon the city. . . . When a pause came in the downpour, they would put their cloaks about them and steal out of the city gates and look apprehensively at the gray water pouring under the bridges, and at night they would lie awake listening to the patter of the rain on their windowpanes and the drip and gurgle of it in the gutters. And at last the dreaded moment came. During a black night of rain the river overflowed its banks and slid over the green meadows to join the streams beneath the willow trees. When dawn broke, a fine dawn of frail sunlight and blue mist, the towers and spires of the city were reflected in a silver sheet of water and the swans flew low to watch the lovely ghosts of themselves that fled beneath them over the flooded meadows. . . . A lovely sight, but most ominous. . . . In less than a week the low-lying houses had flood water in their kitchens and even the cloisters of Magdalen were swamped. And then, after a week of sunshine, the river drew back its waters, leaving behind a legacy of mud, damp and disease.

Diggory brought them the bad news when they were at breakfast. "The sweating sickness has broken out," he said, "down in the houses outside South Gate." He spoke nonchalantly but as he set down a jug of milk his hand shook so that it was spilled upon the table. Joyeuce, Grace and Canon Leigh went white as their ruffs, and Great-Aunt, munching minced beef at the open window above their heads, dropped her knife with a crash upon the floor. Only the children, who could not remember the last terrible outbreak of sickness, ate on in comparative unconcern, though the eyes of the twins were rounder than usual as they looked at each other, and they squeaked into their mugs of milk with a rather apprehensive note.

But Joyeuce remembered that last outbreak. She remembered how hundreds of people had sickened in one night, and how hundreds had died. She remembered the deserted streets and the silent houses where the curtains were all drawn as though the houses had shut their eyes for sorrow. She remembered the tolling of the bells, and the sickening sound of cart wheels clattering over the cobbles in the early morning, and the cry that accompanied it, "Bring out your dead."

For herself Joyeuce had no dread of death, for she was one of those anxious pilgrims who look towards it as to a resting place where there is no more need for endurance, but she had a morbid horror of it as of a robber who might take from her those whom she loved, leaving her alone in a world where no sun shone. . . . It had already taken her mother. . . . In an agony her thoughts flew to Diccon, and then to Nicolas. Diccon, busily shoving bread and milk into his red mouth, with the morning sun bringing out the ruddy lights in his dark curls, looked a far too brightly burning creature to be easily quenched, but she had not got Nicolas before her to console her with the sight of his lustiness, and she thought with foreboding of that evening in the Tavern garden when she had thought how easily the pulse of his life could be stopped, by a slip on the stairs, a flash of lightning, or the thrust of an angry sword. . . . But she had not thought of sickness.

For days she kept an anxious eye on Diccon, and peeped with a beating heart through the windows to catch a glimpse of Nicolas's figure hurrying, late as usual, to lectures or Chapel. She watched her father, too, and felt the forehead of Grace and the children fourteen times a day if once, and she concocted a huge brew of her famous century and wormwood medicine and forced it down the throats of her unwilling family at the rising and the setting of the sun. And she was rewarded, for they remained in the rudest health, and the sweating sickness, so Diggory told her, was not spreading. It would, the citizens thought, be only a slight visitation this time.

She was feeling almost lighthearted when she came in one evening from a shopping expedition, just at dusk, to stow away some velvet she had bought in the oak chest in the parlor where they kept their needlework. The children had gone out with Mistress Flowerdew, their mother's friend, and she would have a quiet time all to herself in which to sit and sew and dream before the fire.

She pushed open the door with a sigh of relief, already savoring her hour of peace. The log fire was flickering softly, its golden reflection bright on the paneled wood of the walls, but the corners of the room were full of shadows and the blue dusk that hung outside the window gave no light.

So she did not see the dark figure sitting in the big chair by the fire, and when a voice said softly, "Joyeuce," she started and her heart began thumping against her stitchets so that she put up her hand to still it.

"Nicolas?" she whispered.

"It's Giles," he said.

Joyeuce slipped off her cloak and came over to the fire, standing before it with slender hands outspread to the blaze, and looked down in astonishment at the comely figure of her eldest brother. . . . For he came to see them so seldom now. . . . They had been great friends, he and she, when they were younger, and in bad times she had leaned her whole weight upon him, but now they had grown apart. With the world at his feet, and his brilliant brain as a sword in his hand to subdue it, his home had faded into insignificance and Joyeuce's problems, that had once been his too, had been forgotten. Joyeuce had borne no malice. It was natural that at the outset a man's work should absorb him to the exclusion of all else, for without the strength of single-mindedness how can he find a footing in the battle of livelihood, and the battle is to the strong. Moreover she had discovered that in the long run we bear our own burdens. Others, as they pass us, can put a hand beneath them for a moment only, but they do not stop for long, and at the turn of the road the whole weight is back on our shoulders again. Giles had once helped to bear the weight of the family pack but it was her burden, not his, and she had not reproached him when he slithered thankfully from beneath its weight. . . . Though she had missed his help.

He watched the firelight painting mid-winter roses on the green dress she wore, and looked appreciatively at her tall slender figure, robbed of all angularity by the kindly dusk, at her pale pointed face under the honey-colored hair and the slim hands that looked almost transparent as she held them before the fire.

"You are so pretty, Joyeuce," he said softly. "You are so like Mother."

There was a hungry note in his voice that took her back instantly to the old days of their grief, and one hand went up to her throat as though it were choking her again.

"If only I could be," she cried, stricken by her own sense of inadequacy, and then, aware of some crying need in him, "Are you wanting Mother very badly, Giles?"

Giles did not answer, for the weakness of human longing was a thing he was too proud to own to, but he moved his hands a little restlessly on the arms of the big chair.

Joyeuce slipped down to sit on the floor at his feet, her arm across his knees. Words never came to her easily. It was only by movement and gesture that she could comfort. But she was half-afraid that Giles might repulse her, for he did not always like demonstrations of affection, and her arm on his knees trembled a little.

"Silly Puss!" said Giles, going back to the name he had called her by in their childhood, and he stroked her cheek softly with a clumsy forefinger. "Do you remember the day we dressed up as demons, with horns and tails, and frightened Dorothy into screaming hysterics?"

Joyeuce began to laugh and a lovely happiness seemed wrapping itself warmly about her. She forgot she was the overburdened mistress of a household and was suddenly a child. The lovely security of childhood was hers again, and the brave certainty of happiness that had been hers in the days before sorrow or pain had touched her. She talked and laughed and told old tales with a gaiety that surprised her even while she was possessed by it, and Giles with a word here and there, a touch on her cheek, and sudden flashes of memory that were almost inspiration, seemed leading her further and further back into the far country where they had once lived as children but had forgotten. "News of a far country," Nicolas had said, as they gazed at the fairy ring traced on the grass on Midsummer Eve, "and we cannot read it." But it seemed that Giles tonight could read it and without words could communicate what he had read to Joyeuce, for both of them, for half an hour, knew perfect happiness.

The banging of the front door seemed for a moment something that suddenly shut them out into darkness. Joyeuce started and scrambled to her feet again. The room was almost dark and Giles's face was blurred and dim. "Time to get supper," she said. "Come and help me, Giles."

Giles shifted in his chair and she held out her hands to help him to his feet. "Lazybones!" she laughed.

And then her laughter died, for Giles's arms lay heavy on hers and when she had pulled him to his feet, he swayed. "Are you all right, Giles?" she asked sharply.

"A headache," mumbled Giles. "It went while you were talking. It's back again now."

In a sudden panic she flung her arms tightly round him, hiding her face against his shoulder, trying to recapture for a moment the happiness that had passed. But the door opened and the light that her father carried seemed a message from the outer world that made her lift her head and open her eyes, turning towards him. She saw him raise his light high, looking at her with amused tenderness, and then his eyes shifted to Giles's face, bent above hers, and she saw him go white to the lips with terror just as Giles's figure sagged suddenly in her arms.

3.

Somehow they had not expected this, though, as Great-Aunt repeatedly remarked to all who would listen, from the days of Pharaoh onward it has always been the eldest son, the best-beloved, whom the plague strikes. But Giles had always seemed so princely, so arrogant, so vital, that it had been impossible to think that death could touch him. Only Faithful, shaking his great head, was not surprised. . . . He had always said that Giles worked much too hard.

The same evening that Giles had been taken ill Faithful came quietly in through the front door and announced that he had come to stop, and from that moment he and Grace took over the entire management of the distracted household. Grace cooked, washed, ironed and organized with the quiet efficiency of genius, and Faithful ran errands and minded the children with such utter self-effacement that it never even occurred to anybody, not even to himself, that he was heartbroken.

Joyeuce and Canon Leigh hardly ever left the boys' room, where Giles lay in the four-poster with the crimson curtains, Will and Thomas having been banished to their father's room. They and Dorothy fought on hour after hour for Giles's life, frenziedly carrying out the instructions of a physician who had been full of foreboding from the first. "No stamina," he kept complaining, "no stamina at all." How they hated that physician as he stood there in his fine furred gown, stroking his long smooth beard and sniffing at an orange stuck full of cloves that he might not catch the infection. What was the use of his being a physician if he could not heal Giles? They saw him go with hatred, and yet they counted the hours till he should come again, for surely, surely he must be able to do something? But he, it seemed, with all his knowledge and skill, was as powerless as they were, and hour after hour the agony of their helplessness bit more deeply. Of what use to love, demanded Joyeuce of her tortured self, when one can give to the beloved neither relief from pain nor salvation from death, when one can do nothing but add to the weight of his suffering by the sight of one's own. The awful loneliness of pain terrified her. Though she was as physically near to Giles as she had been in the little parlor yet spiritually she seemed a hundred miles away from him. Because he was sick and she was well there seemed a great gulf between them. They looked at each other helplessly across it, he crying out for help and she longing to give it, but they could not now reach each other.

Giles died on a night of glittering starlight, a strangely warm and balmy night for December, with a soft wind blowing from the southwest and a placid bright-faced moon hanging low over the Cathedral spire. Joyeuce and her father, one on each side of the unconscious Giles, needed no light except the moonlight and starlight that flooded in through the uncurtained window. There was no sound in the night but the voice of Great Tom as he tolled the hour—nine—ten—eleven.

Joyeuce sat in a high-backed chair, her hands folded in her lap, her eyes fixed on her father where he knelt praying on the further side of the bed. Earlier in the night she had been kneeling, too, until suddenly her knees had doubled up beneath her and her father had come round and lifted her into the chair. She leaned back in it now, her body too exhausted to move but her mind intensely and horribly active, and tried to keep her eyes fixed on her father's face, its stern peacefulness the only thing in the room that she could bear to look at. Sometimes, against her will, her eyes shifted a little to the left and she saw that horrible tapestry of Absalom in the oak tree and seemed to hear a voice crying out in her father's tones, "My son, my son! Would God I had died for thee, my son, my son!" And then she would know what he was feeling behind that mask of resignation and would grip her hands together that she too might not cry out. And sometimes she would look at Giles, lying with a set face that still seemed to hold something of the rebellion that had been his while he was still conscious. For Giles had not wanted to die. He had not been afraid but he had been furious. His hot, angry eyes, seeking for the rescue that no one brought him, would, Joyeuce thought, haunt her until she died. Remembering them, she could not now look at Giles for more than a moment; her glance always sped back to her father's face and clung there, her immature faith sheltering desperately beneath his that was so strong. Sometimes, feeling her eyes upon him, her father would look up and smile at her, and repeat words for her comfort, words that seemed to her to come from a long way off and to mean nothing at all, even though she tried obediently to listen to them. "In the sight of the unwise they seemed to die," he would say, "and their departure is taken for misery, and their going forth from us utter destruction: but they are in peace." And then, trying to comfort himself and Joyeuce because Giles was dying so young, with all his glorious promise unfulfilled in this world, he would murmur, "For honorable age is not that which standeth in length of time, not that is measured by number of years. But wisdom is the gray hair unto men, and an unspotted life is old age. He pleased God and was beloved of Him: so that living among sinners he was translated. Yea, speedily was he taken away, lest that wickedness should alter his understanding, or deceit beguile his soul. He being made perfect in a short time, fulfilled a long time. For his soul pleased the Lord, therefore hasted He to take him away from among the wicked."

But some while after eleven o'clock had struck, and the deadness of the night lay heavy upon them, Canon Leigh was silent again and his face dropped into his hands so that Joyeuce could no longer see it. . . . She was obliged to look again at Giles. . . . And at the first glance she nearly cried out with astonishment, for a change had taken place in him. The last shadow of rebellion had gone from his face and he looked like the little boy she had played with years ago. She stood up and bent over him, her lips parted in eagerness, and almost at the same moment his eyes opened and he looked at her, smiling. At once the barrier was down between them and they were as close together as they had been in the little parlor. News of a far country. With one brief smile Giles told more of it than a hundred books could have done. Then he sighed, turned over, and buried his cheek in his pillow like a child going to sleep.

Joyeuce knelt down and covered her face with her hands, but her heart within her was like a singing bird. She heard her father get up and heard his shuddering sigh as he bent over Giles. Then he too knelt down and began to pray aloud, brokenly, stately Latin prayers for the dead through which beat, like a pulse, the deep notes of the clock striking midnight. It was a bell that tolled for Giles's passing, she knew, and yet her heart was like a singing bird.

Ten minutes later, leaving her father alone with his dead son, she was running like a winged creature through the moonlit house, her skirts held up on either side and her feet seeming hardly to touch the floor as she went. She had news to tell, good news, and she did not stand upon the order of her going as she ran from group to group of the wakeful, heartbroken household. On the stairs she found Grace, Faithful and the little boys huddled together in a forlorn heap, the tears on their faces bright in the pallid moonlight. "Do not cry, little loves," she adjured them. "Heaven is beyond the stars." Then before they had time to do more than gaze stupidly at her transfigured face she was off again, flying down the stairs to the kitchen where Diggory sat on a wooden stool, staring stupidly into space, and Dorothy sat at the kitchen table with her head in her arms. They too gazed at her stupefied as she stood in a moonbeam like a visitant from another world, tiptoe for flight. "You must not grieve," she told them. "There is another country."

And then she was gone again, flying back up the stairs to Great-Aunt. For the first time in her life she was not afraid of her, even though it was black night in Great-Aunt's bedroom, with the thick curtains drawn to hide the stars and only one rushlight to relieve the gloom. She did not wait for Great-Aunt to pop out from behind the curtains, she pulled them back herself, and stood looking tenderly at the redoubtable old lady where she sat stiffly against her piled pillows, her face in its starched nightcap suddenly become pathetically and incredibly old. For Great-Aunt had suffered during Giles's illness. It had brought back to her the deaths of her own children in a way that had actually hurt her. Moreover it had put her in mind of her own approaching end, and tonight, as the great clock tolled the passing hours, she had sat behind her curtains in the grip of a fear she had never known before. Her eyes, usually so bright, were without light, her chin trembled and her claw-like hands clutched at the counterpane.

"The boy is dead?" she whispered, and then her jaw dropped as she stared at her transfigured great-niece. . . . She had never seen any human creature look so unearthly. . . . Joyeuce looked as though drenched with light. She reminded Great-Aunt of some lovely flower held up between the watcher and the sun, so that each delicate petal is tipped with flame and the secret of the sun itself seems caught at the heart of the flower. Great-Aunt felt a pang of desolation as she realized that something had been told to Joyeuce that would never be told to her. She had enjoyed life, she had enjoyed it far more than Joyeuce was ever likely to do, yet at this moment, if she could have gone back to the beginning again, she would have given all her pleasure in exchange for Joyeuce's sorrows if she could have had with them only a few of those rare moments of sure knowledge.

"Not dead," said Joyeuce, "only born again," and drawing the curtains she passed on into her own room, leaving Great-Aunt to wonder if she had really seen Joyeuce or if what she had seen had been a vision from beyond the stars.

The twins and Diccon were all fast asleep in the four-posters. Joy-euece bent over them, glad that they were asleep, glad that they were still in the country of childhood where sorrow is only a rumor outside the gate that they hear vaguely but do not understand. They would meet Giles in that country, perhaps, meet him with a freedom and ease that would never be hers until her life was over and her sorrows done.

She shivered a little as she went to the window to draw the curtains across the view of her city that she loved so greatly. Her joy was still with her but it had heard the first whisper of the returning tide of sorrow and had shrunk in a little upon itself. It was with the knowledge that soon she would be wanting comfort and reassurance again that she opened the window and leaned out, her eyes clinging to the familiar outlines of roofs and towers that would last out the span of her own life and so would never forsake her. A little rustle of movement by the Fair Gate made her look down and she saw three cloaked figures, with a dog at their feet, sitting at the foot of the stairs that led up to Nicolas's room. They got up when they saw her open the window and stood uncertainly, not knowing what to do. . . . Heatherthwayte, Nicolas and Philip Sidney waiting for news of Giles. . . . She stretched out her hand towards them in pity, for their dark wavering figures, shadowy and unsubstantial in the moonlight, looked like poor wraiths lost in a night of bewilderment. But only one of them had the courage to come to her, and it was not Nicolas, it was Philip Sidney.

He stood under the window looking up at her, his bright hair sil-vered by the moonlight and his beautiful face grave and sorrowful. "You need not tell me, mistress," he said gently. "I know by your face."

"But it is all true, what they say," she whispered shyly, "it is only in the sight of the unwise they seem to die."

He met her eyes with a brave certainty that was steadier though less joyous than hers. "Spiritus redeat ad Deum, qui dedit illum," he said. Then he bowed to her courteously and drew back.

Over his head her eyes sought for the tall thin shadow that was Nicolas. It was he who should have come to her, not Philip Sidney, who was almost a stranger to her. Why had he been afraid to come to her?

As she turned away from the window returning sorrow was not a far-off whisper but an ominous mutter. She climbed on to the bed and fell face downwards, lying rigid, waiting as a sufferer waits for the return of inevitable pain.

4.

It so submerged her during the next few days that it was hard even to remember her faith and joy of a few nights ago. The door had opened to let Giles go from one country to another and for just a moment the light from that other country had shone full upon her, but now the door was shut and she could not see even a crack of light beneath it. Yet it had been. What had happened had happened. The light had been hers and it had come from somewhere. It was a fact. If just now she was too exhausted and stricken to rejoice in it she yet possessed it; it was a possession forever.

On the afternoon of the day following Giles's funeral, without even stopping to get her cloak, she ran out through the garden gate into the Meadows. The house and everyone in it pressed upon her so that she felt at breaking point. Great-Aunt, fretful and complaining, the children with their ceaseless questions, Grace with her irritating efficiency and her father as still in his grief as a winter stream bound down by ice. . . . If only he would not be so still. . . . She saw in his stillness a reflection of her own. When they were together they could only sit silently, powerless to help each other.

But outside, under the winter trees, there was help. It had been raining all the morning, a misty rain that had hidden the earth like a shroud, but now it had thinned and vanished into a soft blue haze shot through with sunshine. The exquisite coloring of the winter trees was lit by the pale gleams; in the distance the network of bare twigs showed faint amethyst and rust color, near at hand they were filaments of black lace strung with diamond raindrops. There were threads of silver where the streams ran though the rain-misted grass and beside them the smooth willow shoots smoldered orange and deep crimson, lit to flame when the sun touched them. The whole world was full of the muted sound of water, the steady murmur of the swiftly-flowing river and the soft drip of the water-laden trees. It was still strangely warm for December. The air was soft and moist and caressing. Twice, flashing from the silvered twigs of a tree-top to the crimson of the willows below, Joyeuce saw the blue body of a kingfisher. She was used to these days of misted warmth and color, for they came often in the sheltered Thames valley, blooming among the harsh dark days of wind and rain like roses in midwinter, but never before, she thought, had there been a December day as lovely as this one. In spite of her misery she could not help but be a little comforted by the beauty of it, for it was a fragile and tender beauty that crept into her almost by stealth. She would have shut tired eyes against the blaze of summer, but these soft colors were kind to weariness. The triumphant shouting of the birds in springtime would have seemed to her a cruel mockery but the soft drip of the raindrops was a sound attuned to her sorrow and held a kind of peace.

She felt a sudden uprush of thankfulness for the comradeship of the earth. It seemed to her at that moment the only friend who never failed. Its beauty was ever renewed and its music unceasing. Death could not touch it or the years estrange. While she lived the earth was hers and the glory of it, and standing still on the path she held out her arms to the gold and blue of the sun-shot haze, to the slipping silver water and the crimson willow shoots that edged it, to the rain-drenched grass and the blue swerve of the kingfisher's flight. . . . But her arms were empty. . . . Her friend the earth could sing her lullabies and brighten her eyes with its beauty but it was at once too frail and too great for intimacy. She remembered how once as a little girl she had kissed a wild rose in a passion of affection, but its petals had fallen to the ground at the touch of her lips: and another time upon a journey she had seen in the distance a little blue hill small enough to be picked up and played with; yet when she came up to it, she found it as tall as a church tower. She felt again, as she had felt on May morning, that sense of beauty's continual withdrawal. It is a light flickering always at the end of the road, a distant trumpet call from a land that is hidden behind a hill. A cold shivering fit took her and hiding her face in her hands she began to cry for the first time since Giles had died.

Then through the sound of her own sobbing and the drip of the raindrops she heard a queerly reassuring sound, the sharp snapping of fallen twigs and the sound of footsteps on the sodden path. She stopped shivering and a lovely glow of warmth stole over her. She did not need to look up to know who it was. Once before, on May morning, she had longed for the beauty and mystery of earth that she worshiped to be gathered up into some human form that she could love, and she had looked down from her window into the face of Nicolas.

So certain was she that she did not even look up when he flung his arms impetuously round her, but leaning her face with her hands still covering it against his shoulder cried with the abandon of a child. It was heaven to be, for once in a way, so abandoned. It was heaven to feel his arms tremble with rage at the fates that had so hurt her. It was heaven to feel so protected and so cared for. Love had been sweet on Midsummer Eve, but now, coming so hard upon the heels of sorrow, it was an ecstasy almost too great to be borne.

"Do not cry, little love," Nicolas implored her, but she only cried the more, and picking her up he carried her over the wet grass to where a little bench stood beneath a sparkling hawthorn tree. Then wrapping his cloak about the two of them he sat beside her, holding her so close that she could feel his heart beating and the warmth of his body like fire running through her veins.

"I was walking by the river," he told her softly. "There was no one in the Meadows. The world seemed empty. Nothing to be seen but the bare branches, nothing to be heard but dropping water. I thought of you and of how when you are unhappy your eyes are the color of rain. Then I looked up and saw you standing far off under the trees dressed all in black. I thought that you looked so mysterious, like sorrow herself. And then you held out your arms and so I came to you."

For the first time Joyeuce opened her eyes and looked at him for a moment, and used as she was to the hues of mourning his brilliance dazzled her. He must have been to some party, for his doublet was as

blue as the kingfisher's wing and his cloak was lined with crimson. He
had a little jeweled dagger in his belt and his ruff was as white as snow.
She fingered his dagger with the delight of a child and rubbed her cheek
against his cloak. "You must always be beautiful and gay, Nicolas," she
told him, rejoicing in him. "It would be terrible if you were not to be gay."

"That's as life wills," said Nicolas soberly, and she looked up at him,
startled, for she had never heard his voice so empty of laughter. And
his face, too, was changed. It was older and graver. The eyes were more
somber, as though there was new knowledge behind them, and the lips
pressed against each other almost sternly.

"Has anything happened, Nicolas?" she asked.

"Giles has died," he said.

Joyeuce nodded, understandingly. It was the first time in his life
that death had dared to touch anyone he cared for. She knew what that
felt like. She knew what a glorious expectation of certain happiness one
builds upon the foundations of a happy childhood, and how the first
grief sends the whole fabric tumbling into ruins.

"And it might have been you," whispered Nicolas.

Again she understood. He had discovered, now, the fear at the heart
of love. He felt the torment that she had felt in the garden at the Tavern
when she thought what a little thing might snap the thread of his life.
She twisted her hands together, wondering how to comfort him, how
to tell him what she now knew.

"It's not as bad as you think, Nicolas," she whispered. "The deeper
you go into pain the more certain are you that all that happens to you
has an explanation and a purpose. You don't know what they are but
you know they are there. You don't suffer any the less because of the
certainty but you would rather suffer and have it than just enjoy yourself
and not have it." Her voice trailed away and she looked out sadly over
the landscape of sunlit fields and trees and water. What pitiful creatures
were human beings, able to speak only so falteringly of what they knew,
separated even from those they loved best by ignorances and insinceri-
ties and reserves so innumerable that there seemed no sweeping them
away. Only the earth, with its winds and waters and its field sown with

a thousand flowers, could tell aright of the mystery of which it was the garment. . . . But our ears are too dull to hear.

But Nicolas's arms, strong and compelling, were about her again. "You are going to marry me," he said. "You are going to marry me as soon as ever it can be arranged."

"Would you be mated to sorrow?" she asked him. "You said, when you saw me in the distance, that I looked like sorrow herself."

"Sorrow and joy go hand in hand," he said, "and I want them both. The night Giles died, when Philip Sidney and I were waiting outside in the quadrangle and you opened your window and leaned out, I did not go to you as he did because I felt afraid of sorrow. And then the moon shone full on your face and when I saw the joy of it, Joyeuce, I wanted your joy more than anything else upon earth. I think I changed in that moment. I am not now what I was."

"But it is you who know all about joy," she said. "You are always gay."

"I can be gay," said Nicolas. "I was born knowing how to suck the last drop of fun out of every experience that comes along, and be so busy over it that I have no time to think and worry and question like you do, but I don't know joy. That's something different, something deeper. That's the certainty you talked of. It is a mystery to me, and I want it. In you I shall have it."

"Don't talk like that!" cried Joyeuce in a panic. "I am only an ordinary human girl. There is no mystery in me."

"If you did not seem mysterious to me I should not love you," said Nicolas wisely. "You seem to stand to me for all I long for. I do not quite know what I long for, but whatever it is I seem to have it when I have you."

"I feel like that too," said Joyeuce softly, and then, after a moment's silence, she cried out in dismay, "Nicolas, Nicolas, what will happen if we get to know each other so well that there is no more mystery? Will the end of mystery be the end of love?"

"Why should there be an end of mystery?" asked Nicolas. "Isn't a woman always a mysterious creature to a man, and a man to a woman? When you are an old woman I shall look into your eyes and find my joy there; and as for you, Joyeuce, I think you are so faithful that you will forgive me my sins again and again and find some beauty in me up till the end."

It was that word "faithful" that recalled Joyeuce to herself. He was saying that she was faithful. But she was not. The care of the children was a trust, and she was being faithless to it. In this time of grief, when her family surely needed her more than ever before, she was planning marriage with Nicolas. Still sheltered beneath Nicolas's cloak she pressed her hands together in an agony. Had the fight to be fought all over again? Here, close to Nicolas, she felt warm and safe and happy, but separated from him the cold of the gathering dusk would be all round her, and a loneliness unspeakable. . . . It seemed like the choice between life and death. . . . Yet in these last months her spirit had become so attuned to sacrifice that now she acted almost automatically, slipping from beneath Nicolas's cloak and sliding to the far end of the seat, both her small hands held out to warn him off.

"I can't, Nicolas," she gasped.

"Can't what?" asked Nicolas.

"Marry you."

"Why ever not?" he demanded indignantly.

She explained. With her eyes shut so that she could not see his face, so that she could not even see the fair world that would remind her of him, she told him the whole tale; her promise to her dying mother, her father's dependence on her, the children's dependence on her, the house and the servants and the animals that would all become disintegrated if her watchful eye were not upon them; when she had finished the sun had gone and a cold mist was rising from the river. She covered her face with her hands and waited for Nicolas's comment. When it came it was brief.

"Tomfoolery," said Nicolas.

She dropped her hands and opened her eyes in indignant astonishment. Nicolas, though his mouth was very tender, was looking very mocking. His face was almost the face of the old Nicolas. The upward tilt at the corners of his eyebrows was very pronounced and he was smiling so much that his eyes had disappeared into wicked slits.

"Do you know, Joyeuce," he asked, "what are the chief failings of the saints?"

She shook her head hopelessly and he leant forward and took her cold hands in his, rubbing them gently. "An exaggerated sense of their own importance," he said, "combined with a quite stupid love of martyrdom for its own sake. Couldn't Grace step into your shoes? Are you the only woman in the world who can spank a horde of children? If you think you are, you stand convicted of pride, Joyeuce, and pride is one of the seven deadly sins. And why squander your strength in suffering when there is no need for it? That's waste; another sin. Joyeuce, sweetheart, it seems you are a very wicked woman."

Suddenly the mockery went out of his voice and his smile died, for he saw she was not paying the slightest attention to what he said. Her chin was tilted at an obstinate angle and her eyes, feverishly bright, seemed to be looking right through him to something beyond. With a chill of dismay he remembered the stories he had been told of Canon Leigh's obstinate sufferings for his faith, and remembered that Joyeuce was his daughter. . . . Fanatics, both of them. . . . Impotent anger seized him and he gripped her hands so tightly that she gave a little gasp of pain.

"And what about me?" he demanded indignantly. "No man ever loved a girl as I love you. I want you and I must have you."

Awareness of him was once more in her eyes. . . . She even smiled a little, because in his impetuous anger he was now absolutely the old Nicolas. . . . But there was no relenting in that obstinate chin.

"I must do my duty, Nicolas," she said quietly. "You will forget me. There are other pretty girls."

But at this Nicolas boiled over into such a rage as she had never yet beheld in anyone, not even in Diccon. His face was turkey-red, his dark eyes shot fire at her and he spluttered so that she could scarcely hear what he said. "You dare say that to me!" was the burden of his remarks. "You know as well as I do that I shall never forget you!"

She bowed her head at the truth of this and whispered, "I'm sorry." No, he would not forget her. Between the new grave Nicolas who had held her in his arms a little while ago and the Joyeuce he had seen standing at the window on the night of Giles's death there was now an unbreakable link. Whatever was eternal in them was united. . . . But there were other bonds beside those of marriage. . . . "We can be friends, Nicolas," she pleaded.

"Friends!" snorted Nicolas. What did she think he was made of? Flesh and blood or milk and dough? He was a man, with a man's hot desire that had already been curbed for her sake, and she expected him to behave like a painted Saint Nicolas in a stained-glass window. Giles's death and his love for her had stirred unknown depths in him and just at the moment of discovery, when he had felt the spirit in him that he did not know he had, touched to awareness by something beyond that he had not known existed, she dealt him this blow. She seemed to be denying him not only herself but what she stood for. He felt as though he were being thrust back from new knowledge to the old ignorance, that would now be robbed of the old enjoyment because he had progressed beyond it. He had not known it was possible to suffer so deeply. His anger fell from him and he sat as though stunned, only vaguely conscious that Joyeuce was getting up and mechanically shaking out her black skirts.

"Come, Nicolas," she whispered. "It is going to rain again."

He got up, shivering a little, and looked about him. Every shred of color had gone from the world. The kingfisher had gone home and the willows were hidden in the swathes of gray mist that came rolling up from the river. Without a word he took her hand ceremoniously and led her under the gray ghostly trees towards the gray walls that were her home. At the garden door they stopped and Joyeuce tried to withdraw her hand. "Good-by, Nicolas," she whispered, and then stopped with a gasp as his arms went round her with such strength and passion that she could hardly get breath enough to protest. "Nicolas! Nicolas!" she moaned.

But he had no mercy on her. He held her so tightly that she felt as though he were trying to crush her heart into his body and his into hers. "My true love hath my heart and I have his," she thought, the words of Philip Sidney's new song that everyone was singing stumbling unbidden into her bewildered mind. "I'm not going to let you go, do you hear?" whispered Nicolas fiercely. "I'll find some way to get you, Joyeuce. We'll be together yet." Then he kissed her, hard and passionately, as she did not know one could be kissed. She cried out, feeling her denial of him a sword piercing her, and the gray mist about her seemed to turn into darkness. She was falling down and down into it, as once before she had fallen in the porch of Saint Michael's at the North Gate, only this time the darkness seemed like the darkness of death.

Then she found herself alone in the garden, stumbling towards the house. Nicolas had pushed her in, she supposed, and shut the door and gone away. She reached the house and groped her way through the dark hall towards the stairs. She was so exhausted that she could hardly get up them and dragged herself from step to step like a wounded bird, her wet black skirts clinging forlornly round her ankles. How grave and wise Nicolas had been, how wonderful and yet how childish and passionate and angry. How strange that love, that she had always thought of as so sweet and tender, could tear and bruise like this. Her renunciation was still a sword stuck in her heart, that she thought would stay there till she died. Surely she *had* died, outside the garden gate, when Nicolas kissed her and she still clung fast to her resolution, had died and come back to earth again a poor bedraggled ghost.

But yet, ghost or not, bewildered and miserable and bruised as she might be, the words that were singing themselves over and over in her mind were words of triumph.

My true love hath my heart and I have his,
By just exchange one for another given;
I hold his dear, and mine he cannot miss,
There never was a better bargain driven.
My true love hath my heart and I have his.

His heart in me keeps him and me in one,
My heart in him his thoughts and senses guides;
He loves my heart, for once it was his own,
I cherish his, because in me it bides.
My true love hath my heart and I have his.

CHAPTER XII

CHRISTMAS EVE

Come to your heaven, you heavenly choirs!
Earth hath the heaven of your desires;
Remove your dwelling to your God,
A stall is now his best abode;
Sith men their homage do deny,
Come, angels, all their fault supply.

His chilling cold doth heat require,
Come, seraphins, in lieu of fire;
His little ark no cover hath,
Let cherubs' wings his body swathe;
Come, Raphael, this Babe must eat,
Provide our little Toby meat.

Let Gabriel be now his groom,
That first took up his earthly room;
Let Michael stand in his defense,
Whom love hath linked to feeble sense;
Let graces rock when he doth cry,
And angels sing his lullaby.

ROBERT SOUTHWELL.

1.

NOT every scholar could go home for Christmas. Rich men who could afford horses, or who had hospitable friends near at hand, could leave Oxford, but for poor men who lived a long way off the journey over roads knee-deep in mire would have been interminable; they would no sooner have got there than they would have had to come back again. And Nicolas, this year, was one of the unhappy ones, for his family went down with the smallpox and he was forbidden to go near them lest the beauty of the son and heir should be tarnished by the pockmarks. . . . He was perfectly miserable. . . . Giles was dead, Faithful was absorbed by the Leighs, and all his other friends, including Philip Sidney, were of the fortunate band who could go home. He had no one to shoot with, no one to gamble with and no one even to curse with, and not being one of those who find pleasure in solitude he wished he were dead.

And he did not know what to do about Joyeuce. It was no use appealing to her again, he felt, for though good as the angels in heaven, she was at the same time obstinate as the devil himself. She might be stretched upon the rack, as her father had been before her, but she would not change her convictions. Sometimes he thought that he would go straight to Canon Leigh and demand the hand of his daughter in marriage, but then he bethought him of the horror of his Greek and the outrage of his Latin and he suffered from qualms. He was no favorite with Canon Leigh, that he knew well, and he feared that he might be shown the door. Wisdom was required, he felt, and tact and inspiration, and just at the moment he could lay his hands upon none of them. The star that guided his destiny seemed at the moment to have turned its face away from him. He must wait with what patience he could until its gracious beams once more lit his path.

As the month drew on the thought of the stars was in everyone's minds, for Christmas was coming in, in the traditional way, with frost and snow upon the ground and such a blaze of constellations in the night sky that it seemed the heavens were hanging low over the earth in most unusual friendliness.

And certainly the city of Oxford was good to look at, at this time. By day, under a brilliant blue sky, the gabled roofs and tall chimneys, the towers and spires, took on an added brightness from the tracery of sparkling frost that clung to them; and down below them the narrow streets were bright with the bunchy little figures of snowballing children, happy girls and beaming mothers going shopping with baskets on their arms, dressed in their gaudiest because it was Christmas time, and laughing men with sprigs of holly in their caps, and faces as rosy as apples from the potations they had partaken of at the taverns and inns in honor of the festive season. The bad smells of the town had been obliterated by the continual snow showers and the hard frost—it would be a different story when the thaw came, but sufficient unto the day is the evil thereof—and delicious festive scents floated out into the streets from open doors and windows; scents of baked meats and roasting apples, of ale and wine, of spices and perfumes and the fragrant wood-smoke from innumerable fires of apple wood and beech logs and resinous pine branches. And at night the city seemed almost as brilliant as the starry sky above. From sheer good will doors were left ajar and windows uncurtained, so that bright beams of light lay aslant across the shadows, and the gay groups that thronged the streets carried lanterns that bobbed like fireflies over the trampled snow. The bells rang out continuously and the laughter and clear voices of the children made unceasing music. . . . And outside the city walls the fields and the low hills lay silent, shrouded in white. The murmur of the streams was hushed by the ice and the willow trees drooped above them without movement.

2.

On Christmas Eve, after the sun had set, it all seemed a little intensified; the stars shone yet more brilliantly, the bells rang clearer and sweeter, the firelight seemed ruddier and the laughter and gaiety of the townspeople more contagious. Yet Nicolas, as he strolled idly across Carfax into Cornmarket, felt oddly apart from it all. Used as he was to being always at the center of whatever excitement was afoot this unusual loneliness was a little frightening. It was because he was so unhappy, he thought, that he felt so lonely. It seemed that suffering of any sort made one feel lonely. He had not suffered before and so he had not discovered this before. He wondered why it should be so, for one was not alone in suffering; the whole world suffered. Perhaps this loneliness had some purpose in the scheme of things. Joyeuce would know. He would like to talk about it to Joyeuce.

With his thoughts so full of her it did not surprise him that he should find himself outside Saint Michael's at the North Gate. He thought that if left to themselves his feet would always now take him either to where she was, or to some place connected with her, for where she was would now always be home, and it was with a sense of home-coming that he turned into the old porch and sat down on the wooden bench.

But it was a rather desolate home-coming. On Midsummer Eve it had been warm and balmy, with the scent of flowers coming on the wind, and Joyeuce had been in his arms, and now it was midwinter and dark and he sat alone on the bench, huddled in his cloak against the cold. Why was one lonely? Where do the feet of the lonely take them? As the body turns always homeward at evening when the crowds are gone, so perhaps there is a country of the spirit to which the spirit turns in desolation. Perhaps one needed to be desolate to find that country, for if one were always happy one would not bother to look for it. Sitting with his eyes shut he remembered that Joyeuce had said something like that when they were together in the Meadows. What was that country? . . . Heaven. Fairyland. The land beyond the sunset. The land above the stars where the great multitude which no man can number stand before the throne, clothed with white robes and palms in their hands. The land behind the tree trunks where Queen Mab and her fairies leave the track of their passing in flowers upon the grass. Raleigh's land, where birds of white and carnation perch in tall cedar trees, where the stones are of gold and silver and rivers fall down crystal mountains with the noise of a thousand bells clanging together. . . . They gave it so many different names but he supposed it was the same place and that the spirits of some lucky people, saints and little children and dreamers like Raleigh, could follow the road of loneliness until they reached their home. . . . But for him, if he opened his eyes, there would be nothing but the darkness of the musty-smelling old porch.

He opened his eyes and found himself gazing straight at a blazing star. His blood tingled through his veins and he felt himself gripped by a strange excitement. Was this his star, whose face he had thought was turned away from him? Was it at last pointing upon him graciously? It shone so brightly straight into his eyes that for a moment he put up his hand to cover them. It was surely speaking to him. It said, "Come."

He got up and looked at it intently. It was hanging low over a gabled roof and beneath it was a tall chimney like a pointing finger. He knew that roof and that chimney. They belonged to the Crosse Inn, next door to Tattleton's Tavern where he had supped with Joyeuce.... Surely once before upon Christmas Eve a star had hung low above the roof of an inn. ... The young man who stepped out of the porch of Saint Michael's at the North Gate into the clamor of Cornmarket was no longer lonely and unhappy. His cap was set at an angle and his cloak was flung back from his shoulders as though the wind took him. He was Saint Nicolas, the Christmas saint, come down from heaven, or Oberon king of the fays, or a sailor sailing towards the sunset. He was caught in a fairy tale and the glory of it swept him along as though his feet were winged.

Yet he was still sufficiently upon the earth to notice that the crowd in Cornmarket had grown considerably while he sat in the porch of Saint Michael's. And they were all going one way. They were all flowing in under the great archway of the Crosse Inn into its galleried courtyard. They too were bound for the Inn. What was happening at the Inn? "The Players!" cried voices in the crowd. "The Christmas Players! The Players are here!"

Bands of traveling players still journeyed up and down the country, playing the old Morality Plays in the innyards and at the market crosses, and their coming was still one of the events of the year at Oxford. Scholars were strictly forbidden to attend theatrical performances in inn yards, lest they should catch diseases or have their morals contaminated by the crowd, but this prohibition had never been one to which Nicolas thought it necessary to pay any attention; least of all tonight when he felt himself star-led to his destiny.

He was only just in time, for as he flung himself into the crowd that streamed in beneath the archway the clear note of a trumpet told him that the performance was about to begin. The rough wooden stage was set up in the middle of the courtyard, as though at the heart of the world, lighted at each corner by lanterns and decked with holly and evergreens, with the gaily dressed trumpeter standing upon it with his trumpet to his lips; and all round it surged the jolly Christmas crowd, fighting to get up to the best seats in the gallery that ran round the courtyard, or failing that a place on the wooden steps that led up to it, or failing that an inch of room in the packed space below. Aldermen and citizens with their fat wives and rosy children were there, apprentices and pretty girls, rogues and vagabonds and dirty little urchins, all pushing and kicking and scrambling, but brimming over with humor and good will. They knew how to enjoy themselves on Christmas Eve, did these people of Oxford, and they were doing it. Nicolas had hard work to gain the spot which he had marked out as his own, a place against the gallery balustrade where he would get the best possible view of the stage, but he got there at last, wedged himself in between two fat citizens and a horde of apprentices and dirty little boys, and settled down to watch.

They were playing an old Nativity play tonight, followed by the story of Saint Nicolas, and he was no sooner in his place than the trumpeter stepped down, the lights in the gallery were hidden, and in a sudden silence, that fell upon the noisy crowd as though the shadow of an angel's wing passed over them, the first figures of the Christmas story stepped upon the stage.

It was very crude and at some other time Nicolas might have been moved to mirth, but he was not so moved tonight, neither he nor a single man, woman or child in that densely packed throng. It was Christmas Eve, and the same stars shone above them as had shone upon the fields of Palestine some fifteen hundred years ago. They sat in a deep and lovely silence, their eyes riveted upon the rough wooden stage where the figures of shepherds moved, and angels whose dresses had shrunk in the wash and whose wings and haloes had become a little battered by so much packing and unpacking, and a Virgin Mary whose blue cloak was torn and whose voice was that of a young English peasant boy who had not so long ago been taken from the plow.

Wedged against the balustrade of the gallery Nicholas watched and listened in that state of heavenly concentration that leaves the human creature oblivious of himself. He was not conscious any more of the apprentices who pressed upon him, or of the smell of unwashed human bodies, or of his own empty stomach that had been presented with no supper this evening. He was only dimly aware of the crowd as a great multitude that he could not number, watchers in the shadows who had been watching there for fifteen hundred years. The Christmas story itself absorbed him. Though it was so old a story, one that he had known as soon as he was capable of knowing anything, it seemed tonight quite new to him. "Glory to God in the highest. . . . A child is born." The old words that he had heard a hundred times over seemed cried out with the triumph of new and startling news. The figures that moved before him, Mary with the child in her arms, Joseph and the shepherds, Gabriel and the angels, Herod and the Wise Men, that he had seen so many times pictured in stained glass windows and on the leaves of missals, moved now in this tiny space at the heart of the crowd as though they had come there for the first time. . . . The love of God is with man. . . . That, Nicolas knew suddenly, is the news of the far country, the mystery like a nugget of gold that men travel so far to seek, the fact that is stated but not explained by all the pictures that have been painted and by all the music and the poetry that has been written since the dawn of the world. It was as easy as that, and as difficult.

The Nativity play ended with a flash and a bang as the devil in black tights appeared to fetch away Herod to where he belonged. No one considered this an anticlimax; on the contrary they were all suitably impressed; this might happen to them if they were not careful. They groaned and shivered and were glad when the lanterns that had been hidden beneath cloaks were uncovered and the auditorium shone out into brilliance again. This was the interval between the two performances and a roar of voices broke out as though a river in spate had been let loose. Nicolas found that he too was shivering, not with fear but with the very intensity of his feeling, and looked round upon the noisy crowd with sensations that were entirely new. He felt so at one with them. A feeling of superiority had always been one of the most familiar of his pleasures, but now it had entirely gone from him. These burly perspiring

merchants, fat matrons, laughing girls and jolly apprentices, these rogues
and vagabonds that pressed about him, seemed as much a part of him as
his own body. He did not care that a beery citizen was breathing heavily down the back of his neck or that two filthy little boys were holding
themselves steady in a kneeling posture by clinging to his legs. In fact it
was a pleasure. He loved them. All of them together were the men whom
God was with. He wondered vaguely what he would be feeling like in
a few days' time, whether he would be again the old superior skeptical
Nicolas. . . . Perhaps. . . . Yet he would never be able to forget what he had
felt tonight. He prayed God that he would never forget.

The trumpet sounded once more to give warning that the second
part of the performance was about to begin. The lanterns in the galleries
were hidden again and the roaring voices dropped away to an indistinct
murmur, then to silence, and Saint Nicolas stepped upon the stage in
a red robe, a long white beard, and a most genial, fatherly expression.

Nicolas de Worde knew the history of his patron saint well—too
well—for it had been dinned into his ears by every nurse he had ever
had, so it was with a certain detachment that he listened to Saint Nicolas
telling the audience the story of his own early piety; as a new-born baby
plunged into his first bath he had frightened everyone into fits by standing upright in the basin in an attitude of ecstatic adoration. Having thus
early shown his aptitude for spiritual things it was but to be expected, so
he informed the listening audience, that he should now have attained to
his present position of Archbishop of Myra under Constantine the Great.
And now, he said, he was upon this cold winter's night waiting to receive a
visit from three little boys, children of a friend of his, who were traveling
to Athens to school and were to stop at Myra on their way to receive his
blessing; for he loved children and cared for their happiness and their
welfare more than anything else upon earth. Then he hitched up his red
robe, adjusted his white beard, which was slipping a little sideways, waved
a hand to the children in the audience and stepped down from the stage.
His place was taken by a most villainous looking red-headed man, accompanied by the devil bearing a large wooden tub, who announced in flowing couplets that the stage was now an inn and the red-headed villain the

innkeeper, and the rub was intended for the storing of murdered guests to the inn, whom it was the innkeeper's habit to slay for their valuables and later to sell at a profit as pickled pork; children, he said, being juicy and tender, pickled best. A shiver of horror shook the audience, and the children in it squeaked aloud, their squeaks rising to cries of warning as three little boys were seen to he moving out of the shadows towards the lighted stage, two older boys with dark hair and one minute little fair-haired boy clasping a woolly lamb with tin legs in his arms. But the three doomed children took no notice of the warning cries, and failed to see the devil hiding behind the tub. Confidingly they mounted the steps to the stage, and confidingly they piped out, "Innkeeper, Innkeeper, please will you give us lodging for the night? It is too late now to disturb the good Archbishop. Innkeeper, Innkeeper, is there room for us in the inn?"

"Come in, my little dears," cried the innkeeper, rubbing his hands together in horrid glee, and suddenly seizing the foremost boy by the scruff of his neck he whipped out a huge long knife and waved it in the air so that it flashed about his head like lightning. The audience moaned and cowered, and afterwards they were all ready to swear that they had actually seen those three shrieking little boys cut up into small pieces and stowed away in the tub; the fair little boy being cut up last and his lamb pitched in after him as a final tit-bit.

Having thus bestowed the little boys to his satisfaction the innkeeper sprinkled salt over them, stirred them about with a wooden spoon, and then settled himself on the floor with his back propped against one side of the tub, the devil being upon the other, for a well-earned night's rest.

But no sooner were their snores ringing out triumphantly upon the frosty air than Saint Nicolas came hurrying along to the scene of action. He had had a nightmare, so he told the audience in breathless couplets as he climbed the steps to the stage, in which the fate of the little boys had been revealed to him by Almighty God with such a wealth of detail that every separate hair upon his white head had stood completely up on end. At this point he reached the innkeeper, fell upon him and shook him with a violence surprising in one so aged. "Villain!" he shouted. "Awake! Repent! The day of judgment is at hand!" It is a well-known fact that a criminal startled out of sleep will, if charged with his crime, acknowledge it, and the innkeeper was no exception to the rule. He awoke, yelped at finding himself shaken by an Archbishop, fell upon his knees and made a full confession. Seeing him so penitent the saintly Archbishop prayed loudly for his forgiveness, banished the now awakened and peevish devil with a wave of the hand, and concentrated upon the tub. He made the sign of the cross over it, he prayed over it, he wept over it, he stirred its contents with the wooden spoon and prayed again.

Up popped a small dark head. "Oh, I have had a beautiful sleep," it said.

Up popped a second. "So have I," it said.

Then up popped a golden head and a tiny bell-like voice piped, "And as for me, I have been in Paradise."

The audience rocked and roared and cheered, and their cheering did not cease until the opening of the second scene, when the three little boys, dressed now as three little girls, sat at the feet of a sorrowing father—the red-headed villain only thinly disguised by the addition of a black wig—and were told that because of his poverty they could have no dowries.... They would in all probability have to be old maids.... At this awful threat the three little girls wept most pitifully, with their fists thrust into their eyes so that they did not see Saint Nicolas peeping over the edge of the stage, and did not see him take three little parcels from his red robe, throw them in, and then creep away chuckling to himself.... But they heard the thud as the parcels fell at their feet; they opened their eyes and picked them up; and they were three purses of gold.

The crowd cheered again and Saint Nicolas reappeared and came to the front of the stage, his genial white-bearded face beaming like the rising sun and his red robe shining gloriously in the lantern light. "Go home, all you little girls and boys," he said, "and before you go to sleep tonight put out your little shoes beside your beds, and it may be that Saint Nicolas, who loves little children as dearly today as he did all those hundreds of years ago, will come in the night and put presents for you in them." Then Saint Nicolas beamed and bowed again, and the performance was over.

Nicolas thought afterwards that it had been his detachment that had made him so acutely conscious of the little fair-haired boy with the

woolly lamb with the tin legs. He had been one of the principal actors
from the beginning. He had trotted at the heels of the shepherds as a
little shepherd boy, clasping his lamb. He had knelt at the foot of the
manger in Bethlehem as a little cherub, with his halo slipping a little
sideways and the lamb still clasped to his bosom. He had been one of the
innocents slaughtered by Herod and had died beautifully in the middle
of the stage with the lamb still clasped to his chest. And then, with the
lamb still apparently an inseparable part of his person, he had been one
of the little boys saved by Saint Nicolas.

And in this story the other Nicolas had noticed him as a person for
the first time. Before he had been part of the Christmas story, one of
the gleaming facets of this jewel at the heart of the world, but in this he
had been a little boy acting in a play and as such Nicolas had not been
able to take his eyes off him; and was surprised at himself, for as a rule
he took not the slightest interest in children. The little boy's hair was
smooth and fair, and shone in the lantern light as though his shapely
little head were encased in a cap of gold. His face, grave and absorbed
as he performed to the best of his ability the task that had been set him,
was small and delicately heart-shaped, and the little bare feet that pattered so obediently over the hard boards of the stage were shapely and
slender as those of a fairy's child. Nicolas could not see his eyes, but
he was sure that they were blue, a deep violet blue that would turn to
the color of rain when sorrow clouded them. Surely this was no child
of a strolling player. . . . If Joyeuce were to have a son, thought Nicolas,
with a sudden constriction of the throat that hurt him, he would have
just such a smooth fair head, just such a flower-like delicacy and grave
absorption in his duty. . . . To possess such a son, thought Nicolas, the
cares of fatherhood would not seem heavy.

3.

The play had ended and the actors and their stage had disappeared
as though by magic. The lights shone out again and the chattering multi-
colored crowd flowed down the steps from the galleries and out from

the benches beneath them, filling the well of the courtyard as though wine had been poured into a dark cup. The stars were still blazing in the square of sky that rested on the gabled roofs and the Christmas bells were ringing. Nicolas found himself caught up in the singing crowd and carried bodily towards the archway that led back into Cornmarket, and the normal world that he had left behind him when he had stepped into the porch of Saint Michael at the North Gate. He pushed his way towards one of the wooden supports of the gallery, seized it and clung there and let the crowd surge past him, for the time had not come to return to the normal world. His star had not finished with him. He knew that as certainly as he had ever known anything.

"Will you come inside and take a tankard of ale, pretty master?"

The crowd was thinning and Nicolas looked down into the face of a pert little serving wench, with lips as red as holly berries and a snowy apron tied over a flowered gown. Since he had known Joyeuce he had rather lost his taste for serving wenches, but he smiled and chucked her under the chin and followed willingly enough. He was waiting upon events and her invitation seemed the next one in the sequence.

He followed her through a stout oak door into the main room of the inn, where a great fire of Christmas yule logs blazed on the hearth and was reflected in a ruddy glow in the faces of some two score of good citizens who were drinking ale, laughing, shouting and singing in an orgy of good fellowship well befitting the festive season. The air was thick with the fumes of the ale and the smoke from the fire and it was impossible for even the loudest-voiced to make himself heard under a shout. Yet through the haze there loomed the great bulk, and above the tumult there sounded the bellow, of Master Honeybun, mine host of the Crosse Inn, as he heaved himself this way and that refilling tankards, quelling disputes and getting the best of every argument with a playful blow upon the chest and a pat upon the head that were like to be the death of those so favored. But in spite of his multifarious duties he espied Nicolas and greeted him with a roar of welcome like to the roaring of a hundred bulls, for Nicolas was of the quality, and the quality were more likely to be found at the Tavern next door than at the humble Crosse.

Nicolas, his sense of unity with all mankind still powerfully with him, felt himself instantly at home. He seized the proffered tankard and was soon laughing and talking with these ruddy-faced gentlemen as though he had known them all his life. The players were among them, he discovered, no longer angels and shepherds but English vagabonds of the road with weather-tanned faces and worn jerkins. But they showed themselves to be artists, messengers of another country, by little eccentricities of dress and manner that aroused the mockery of the rollicking apprentices drinking beside the fire; one wore a gay yellow sash and his shabby jerkin, one, whose clothes were in rags, brandished a perfumed handkerchief of crimson silk, another wore heavy gold rings in his ears as though he were a seaman, and all of them had deeper voices than ordinary men, more graceful bodies, and gesticulating fingers and sparkling eyes that could convey in half a second the meaning or emotion that an ordinary man could not have expressed in twenty minutes of laborious speech; but Nicolas in his new mood found their unconscious striving for beauty and their lovely ease of communication matter for reverence rather than mirth.

"That is a lovely child of yours who played tonight," he said to him of the rags and the perfumed handkerchief, a slim boy who had played the part of the angel Gabriel.

"Which child, master?" asked Gabriel.

"The fair child. The one with a woolly lamb."

"Oh, that child. He's not one of ours. He's a gypsy's child who is staying at the inn. Our boy is sick and this child took his place. A clever child; it took only a couple of hours to teach him his part." A wicked grin spread over the face of the angel Gabriel and his slim fingers gripped Nicolas's arm. "Come and let me introduce you to his father."

The ruddy apprentices by the fire surrounded a group of older men, rough men from the poorer part of the town, a traveling tinker and a few gypsies, and into this group the angel Gabriel propelled Nicolas. "Here, Sampson," he cried, "here's a gentleman would like to meet the father of the infant prodigy."

Nicolas stared in amazement at the drunken giant of a creature who confronted him. He looked at the great broad shoulders, the dark matted beard, the coarse crimson features and the bloodshot green eyes that twinkled at him rather angrily, and in spite of himself he recoiled a little at the sight of the man's great hairy chest showing through his torn jerkin, and the reek of drink and sweat that assailed his fastidious nose. The recoil and astonishment were momentary, but they were seen, and a huge red hand shot out and gripped Nicolas by the front of his exquisite leaf-green doublet.

"So my young cockerel thinks I can't be the father of that damn child, does he?" bellowed Sampson in maudlin indignation, shaking Nicolas as a terrier a rat. "The little whey-faced puling brat! So I'm not capable of fathering it, eh?"

"I never said so," remarked Nicolas breathlessly but with humor. "I consider your worship capable of fathering any number of brats." His feet slipped on the floor, and his teeth clashed together as he rocked this way and that in the ruffian's grip, but he managed to continue, his eyes merry in his empurpled face. "It is merely that in this case I do not consider the family likeness very remarkable."

A great roar of laughter went up, for it seemed this was not the first time that the paternity of Sampson had been called in question, and it seemed this particular subject was a sore point with him, for he let go of Nicolas and hit out with blind rage at the circle of mocking faces that hedged him in.

"Eh, Sampson!" shouted the Tinker, a great bully of a man almost as vast as Sampson himself. "Can you give a name to the father of that boy? Can you give a name to the father of the child Sara's brought to bed with at this moment! Cuckold! Cuckold!"

Suddenly the affair that had begun as a coarse jest turned ugly. Sampson hit the Tinker and the Tinker hit Sampson. The laughter turned to a tumult of shouts and curses. Mine host bore down upon them and with one huge hand plucked Nicolas out of the hubbub as he would have lifted a chestnut from the fire.

And then somehow the whole crowd of them were out in the courtyard, under the starry sky, and there was a fight on. Sampson and the Tinker, roaring drunk and mad with rage, were fighting each other in the center of a ring of men whose faces were alight with a bestial eagerness to witness blood and suffering that was hideous to see. Now and then they yelled encouragement to the fighters and their cries were animal cries. Lanterns were held aloft that they might see the better, and the stars looked down.

Nicolas, with the boy who had played Gabriel grave-eyed beside him, stood on the outskirts of the crowd, and he felt sick. He had witnessed fights before, and always with keen enjoyment. He had fought himself, and felt the better for it. He had even attended several hangings and derived pleasure from the titillations of horror that ran up and down his spine on those occasions. But tonight he felt sick. Only a short while ago, on the very spot where those two brutes were fighting, the loveliest story in all the world had been enacted. Only a short while ago, in this very place, he had learned so to love the men around him that they had seemed a part of his own body. . . . And now, because he still loved them, he had to stand here and watch the degradation of his body. . . . "Deus, propitius esto mihi peccatori," he murmured. The boy beside him looked at him, uncomprehending, but the sorrow in his eyes was an Amen and the stars seemed to press down a little lower, brighter and more pitiful.

It was soon over. The Tinker was the less drunk of the two, and he got the best of it. A yell came from the crowd as Sampson crashed over backwards, then a sudden silence in which they could hear the voices of the Christmas waits singing far off in the town, and then an outbreak of shocked incredulous murmurings.

"What has happened?" demanded Nicolas, and pressed a little nearer.

Sampson was dead. He had fallen with his head on a projecting cobble stone and his magnificent great body was now as worthless as a heap of rubbish. Nicolas caught one glimpse of him, with his head lying in a pool of blood and his sightless eyes turned towards the stars, and then turned away in misery and horror. . . . For he had done this. . . . With a word spoken in jest he had started the whole tragedy. And somehow he had rather liked that coarse bully. There had been something attractive about him; his rage had been swift and splendid, as elemental as a thunderstorm or the onslaught of a tiger, and his twinkling green eyes had stirred some vague memory in Nicolas that was sweet as it was elusive. He was sorry that the man was dead.

4.

They picked him up and carried him away and gradually the sobered crowd dispersed and went home. Loneliness possessed the innyard. There were no lights but the few that shone from the inn and the stars that glittered overhead, no sounds but the soft chiming of the bells and the far-away singing of the waits. But Nicolas still lingered. There seemed nothing that he could do, but he still lingered, pacing up and down over the soiled and trodden snow, his cloak wrapped tightly about him and his heart heavy.

A touch on his arm made him look round. It was the pretty little serving wench, shivering with the cold, her face white and frightened.

"Yes?" encouraged Nicolas, but she seemed to have nothing to say, and only huddled herself the closer in the shawl she had thrown about her shoulders.

"What ails you, my dear?" asked Nicolas again, and turned up her face to the starlight with one finger beneath her chin.

At this she recovered, and her dimples peeped. "I must tell her," she confided, "and sure as I live, I've not the courage."

"Tell whom?" asked Nicolas.

"Sara. Sampson's wife. Sampson brought her into Oxford two days ago, for she was taken very bad and he wanted to get the physician to her."

"You mean that she is here? At the inn?"

"Yes. She often comes here to amuse the company with her fortune telling, and so she came here in her trouble and Master Honeybun took pity on her. He's a kind man, Master Honeybun. We made a bed for her in a part of the stable that we don't use. The babe died yesterday, and now she's likely to die herself."

"Then need you tell her?" asked Nicolas.

"Master Honeybun said I was to," she said, and looked down, twisting her shawl round her fingers.

"I'll tell her," said Nicolas suddenly. She looked up again, her eyes two round "ohs" of amazement, and Nicolas himself hardly knew what possessed him. Afterwards he thought it was his sense of responsibility for the death in the innyard that drove him to make what amends he could.

The girl was so thankful to have him relieve her of her duty that she allowed him no time to change his mind. She hurried him forthwith across the courtyard to a door on the far side. "In there," she whispered.

Nicolas lifted the latch and walked in. He was at the far end of the great inn stable, in a little space partitioned off from the rest by a rough curtain. A lantern hung from the raftered cobwebby ceiling and a small fire in a brazier brought a little warmth into the bitter air. A broad rough bed spread with old blankets and soft hay stood against the wall and in the glow of the lantern and firelight he could see the outline of a woman lying upon it, with another smaller figure curled up beside her. He stopped, his heart beating, aware that death was here too, not the sudden death that had struck like lightning in the courtyard outside but an invisible brooding spirit whose presence seemed to set this little room at a great distance from the rest of the world. For a moment all memory fell away from Nicolas. He, this woman, the unseen child and the angel of death were alone together, enclosed in a little circle of light that hung like a star between heaven above and the unseen earth far away beneath them. When it was shattered the four of them would go their ways to where they belonged, but for the moment they were alone together in a unity so deep that understanding would need few words.

The hay on the far side of the bed rusted softly and a little gold head popped up. Nicolas, moving forward, found himself looking straight into a pair of blue eyes, a deep violet blue that would turn to the color of rain when sorrow clouded them. . . . Somehow he had thought that this child would have eyes like Joyeuce. . . . He smiled and a merry little answering smile tilted up the corners of the child's mouth and set sparks in his eyes. He seemed to like this visitor and he turned and poked his mother with his toy lamb that she too might wake up and like him.

She stirred and moaned a little, a sound that was half-question and half-plaint, and Nicolas came to her side and stood looking down upon her. He had expected to see a rough-looking woman, the feminine counterpart of the man who had died outside, and he was amazed at what he saw. Sara was dying, and sickness had robbed her of much of her beauty, yet even the remnant of it roused his homage. He bowed his head as he looked at the fine bones of her face, showing like ivory beneath the tightly stretched skin, at the mass of night-dark hair and the deep eyes, clouded with mystery, that looked up into his.

"So it was he who died outside?" she whispered.

"Yes," said Nicolas. As he had thought, few words were needed.

She moved her head a little restlessly on the pillow but she gave no sign of grief. Perhaps, thought Nicolas, she had not loved him, or perhaps she was too near death to have any care now for anything that might happen on earth. But even as he thought this he knew he was wrong, for she turned her head and looked at him as though he himself were of extreme importance to her. She looked at the gallant picture that he made, standing straight and slim in his fine doublet and hose of dark green, the color of holly leaves, with his scarlet-lined cloak flung back from his shoulders. In reverence for her he held his cap in his hands and the lantern light shone upon his crisp dark hair and the face with the mocking eyebrows, smooth girlish skin and strong mouth that in gravity could look so lovely. She looked at him appealingly, hungrily, as though he were not only a man who could help her but a symbol of something that she had intensely desired. She put out a hand and felt the fine stuff of his cloak as he stood beside her. "I wanted him to be like you," she whispered. "That was why I did it."

Nicolas did not understand, but he saw that she had something more to say to him and he bent over her, smiling reassuringly into her eyes. He felt no fear, now, of sorrow and death, only desire to succour. "I will do anything I can to help you," he said, slowly and clearly so that she should understand.

"Where do you come from?" She spoke so low now that her whisper was a mere breath.

"From Christ Church," said Nicolas.

She made a little motion of her head towards the boy beside her. "Then take the child with you. Take him back where he belongs," she said, and sighed in relief and weariness as her eyes closed and her head rolled weakly back into the dented hollow on the pillow.

"Where?" asked Nicolas, but even as he asked he knew it was no use. Her dark lashes, lying on the dark hollows below her eyes, trembled a little and then lay motionless. He knew that they would not lift again. He put his fingers gently on her wrist and felt the tiny flutter of the pulse, and even at his touch it was still.

He straightened himself and held out his arms to the little boy who was kneeling up in the hay staring at him. He had thought there would be tears and protestations, but there were none. Grave-eyed and obedient the child too held out his arms, his lamb clasped by a hind leg in one hand, and let himself be lifted across his mother's body.

As Nicolas with the boy in his arms, lifted the latch of the door, he could have fancied that he heard the flutter of dark wings. The little circle of light in which the four of them had hung above the earth was shattered now and they were going their different ways, two to death and two to life.

The girl was still lingering in the courtyard and Nicolas paused only to send her inside to Sara before he made tracks for home. Now and then, as he strode down Cornmarket and across Carfax into South Street, he looked down at the boy. The little face looked very pallid in the starlight but there was always the flash of an answering smile when Nicolas looked at him, and his golden hair shone like a gallant cap of gold. His bare feet and legs were cold as ice and he was shivering, but he made no complaint. Nicolas, who had thought he did not care for children, held the little body close to his own to warm it and tucked his cloak round more firmly. He had no doubt at all as to where to take this child. . . . To Joyeuce, for a Christmas present.

5.

And meanwhile Joyeuce sat in front of the parlor fire with the children grouped around her, and her father and Great-Aunt in their big chairs one on each side, and listened to Faithful laboriously reading aloud from Foxe's "Book of Martyrs." It was long past the children's bedtime but they had not wanted to go to bed and she had let them stay up. Even the little ones felt the sorrow that hung over the house, this first Christmas after Giles's death, and they shrank from their dark cold bedroom. It was more cheerful in the parlor, where the log fire sparkled and crackled and a most extravagant array of candles shone all round the room.

But even then it was not particularly cheerful, for Great-Aunt, who had the indigestion, kept heaving great sighs, their father sat with his head sunk on his breast, rousing himself heroically now and then to make forced cheerful remarks that were more depressing than silence, and Joyeuce stitched away at her embroidery with a sort of desperation, as though she dared not let herself think. Grace, the boys and the twins stared sadly and a little sullenly into the fire, for they felt that happiness was their right at this season and they could not but feel bitter against the fate that had snatched it away from them. Diccon sat curled up on the floor at Joyeuce's feet, his curly head resting against her knees, and was still a prey to his secret sorrow, his poppy mouth drooping and his green eyes staring mournfully at the tips of his little pointed scarlet shoes. All the rest of the family were in black but he wore elfin green, with the scarlet shoes and a knot of cherry ribbons at the breast. Sitting there in the middle of them, so bright and fair to see, Joyeuce thought he was like the spark of unconquerable hope at the heart of sorrow. It did her good to look at him, even though he was so sorry a little boy.

All the time, muted by the closed windows and the drawn curtains, they could hear the bells ringing and the waits, bands of poor scholars who were allowed by the Vice Chancellor to sing and beg at the houses of the rich, singing as they passed up and down the snowy streets. Sometimes a band of them passing up Fish Street would stop and sing under their window, and then their singing was hard to bear. "Unto us a Child is born. Unto us a Son is given." Tonight the words seemed nothing but a mockery.

6.

It was after one such visitation that Faithful decided he had better read aloud to his adopted family, and fetched his beloved "Book of Martyrs." It had accompanied him through all the many changes and chances of his own life and he had always found it an unspeakable comfort. Not only was the example of the martyrs so uplifting but it was really impossible to think of one's own woes when absorbed in blood-curdling descriptions of other people being burned alive. There is nothing like the troubles of other people to distract one's attention from one's own.

But tonight, knowing Joyeuce to have a squeamish stomach and Great-Aunt's indigestion to be by no means a thing of the past, he concentrated upon the milder stories of Master Foxe. Finally he read them the account of the riot in Saint Mary's church at Oxford in the year 1536, when Bloody Mary sat upon the throne of England and persecution was at its height. A certain poor heretic, a Cambridge M.A., was sent to Oxford that he might recant openly, bearing his faggot in the church of Saint Mary the Virgin upon a Sunday, in front of the whole congregation of Doctors, Divines, Citizens and Scholars. It was felt, apparently, that to make a fool of himself before Oxford University would, for a Cambridge man, be the final humiliation; it was thought, too, that it would give pleasure to Oxford to see him do it, and would be a great warning to such of the scholars as might be heretically inclined. . . . The church was packed to the doors and in the middle stood the Cambridge heretic with his faggot on his shoulder.

But no sooner was Doctor Smith, the preacher, well away into his sermon, denouncing the poor heretic with the full force of his lungs, than from the High Street outside came a cry of "Fire! Fire!" Somebody's chimney was on fire, it afterwards transpired, but the crowded congregation had but one thought; sympathetic heretics and demons had fired the church. "Fire! Fire!" they yelled, and in the space of five minutes, pandemonium had broken out, the panic-stricken congregation fighting like wild beasts to get out of the church. "But," said Master Foxe in his narrative, "such was the press of the multitude, running in heaps together, that the more they labored the less they could get out. I think there was never such a tumultuous hurly-burly, rising so of nothing, heard of before, so that if Democritus the merry philosopher had beholden so great a number, some howling and weeping, running up and down, trembling and quaking, raging and gasping, breathing and sweating, I think he would have laughed the heart out of his body."

Now "in this great maze and garboyle" there were only two who kept their heads, the heretic himself, who hastened to cast his faggot off his shoulder and bring it down hard upon the head of a monk who stood near by, breaking the head to his great satisfaction, and a little boy who had climbed up on top of a door to be out of the way of this seething horde of lunatic grown-ups.

Sitting up there on top of the door the little boy wondered what he should do, for though he was not frightened, he thought that it would be rather nice to go home. Then he saw a great burly monk who was fighting his way to the nearest exit with more success than most. He wore his monk's habit and had a big cowl hanging down his back and he was coming quite close to the little boy. The urchin waited until the monk was right underneath him and then he slithered down from the top of the door and "prettily conveyed himself" into the monk's cowl.

The monk got out and made tracks for home, and being a very burly man, and the little boy being such a very tiny little boy, he did not at first notice anything out of the ordinary. But as he turned from High Street into Cornmarket it struck him that his cowl felt heavier than usual, and he shook his shoulders in some annoyance. . . . Then there came a little whispering voice in his ear. . . . Terror seized him like an ague, and he was more frightened than he had been in the church, for he had a guilty conscience and he had no doubt at all that one of the demons who had fired the church had jumped straight into his cowl. "In the name of God and All Saints," he cried, "I adjure thee, thou wicked spirit, that thou get thee hence."

But there was no crashing of thunder, no searing of blue flame as the demon took his departure, only a little voice that whispered, "I am Bertram's boy. Good master, let me go." And then the long-suffering cowl suddenly gave way at the seams and the little boy fell out and ran away home as fast as his legs would carry him.

7.

It was a cheerful story and everyone felt the better for it except Diccon, and Diccon most unaccountably began to cry. He did not roar and bellow, he just sobbed noiselessly in that devastating way he had when his heart was breaking. Everybody was most upset and gathered round to soothe and comfort, while Joyeuce, pressing his curly head against her knee, implored him to say what ailed him.

"I want that little boy," he whispered at last. "I want that little boy. I want him now."

As it had been with the ruby in the window of the aurifabray so it was with the little boy; he must have what he wanted or he could no longer support life. Why, he seemed to ask, was I born into this cruel world? Whose fault was it that earthly life was given to me? Why was I dragged from the realms of celestial glory, where the angels gave me the comets to play with, to this earth where I stretch out my empty hands in vain for my heart's desire?

"But you can't have the little boy, my poppet," explained Joyeuce. "He's only a little boy in a story."

Diccon knelt up on the floor in front of her, his hands laid on her knees and his tear-stained face raised imploringly to hers. "He's a real little boy," he hiccuped, "and Diccon must have him."

"He was a real little boy years ago, when Master Foxe wrote that story," explained Canon Leigh, "but he is not a little boy now."

Diccon shook his head and choked, the tears running out of his eyes and dripping off his pointed chin on to his cherry ribbons in a positive cascade. "A real boy," he insisted, "just so big." And he stretched out his arms to show his own minute height. "Just so big as me. He has fair hair. Diccon wants him." And again he raised his imploring face to Joyeuce who loved him and always gave him what he wanted.

Joyeuce was near tears herself. Was this his sorrow? Was he so lonely? The twins were older than he and he had no one but Tinker to play with. She had heard that lonely children often invented imaginary playmates to be with them. Perhaps he had imagined his little fair-haired boy and was heartbroken that he could not turn him into flesh and blood. She shook her head helplessly and Diccon, his hands still resting on her knees, shook her lap almost angrily. . . . It was Christmas Eve and seated upon it she should have had for him a little fair-haired boy.

The door opened and they all looked round in astonishment. Standing there smiling at them was the gallant figure of Nicolas de Worde, dressed like Diccon in the Christmas colors of scarlet and green and carrying a little fair-haired boy clasping a woolly lamb with tin legs. He walked across to them and deposited his burden in Joyeuce's lap.

There was a moment's pause of utter astonishment and then a chorus of ecstatic cries.

"It's Baa!" shrieked the twins and Will and Thomas. "The little boy has Baa!"

"It's Joseph!" shouted Faithful.

"It's a little Christmas angel," cried Grace.

"Tilly-vally! Angel indeed!" ejaculated Great-Aunt in some displeasure. "Some filthy child out of the streets!"

Diccon, with the tears still wet on his cheeks, clasped Baa's tail with one hand and Joseph's left foot with the other and laughed and laughed, his dimples peeping and the whole of his pink tongue exposed to view, while Joseph, curled up on Joyeuce's lap as though it were his proper home, seized his foster-brother's dark curls with both hands and laughed too.

As for Joyeuce and Canon Leigh, bewildered, incredulous, yet with a queer new joy struggling through their bewilderment, they found themselves gazing down into a little face that was the exact counterpart of that of the wife and mother they had both adored.

Nicolas leaned against the mantelpiece, his eyes upon Joyeuce. "I was lonely and unhappy," he told her, "and so I went up into the town. And so I found him at the inn." Her eyes fell before his and he said no more, but watched the family group with smiling satisfaction. Without understanding yet what he had done he knew that he had done something good, and something, too, that would bring him into the very heart of this family. Moreover he found the picture of Joyeuce with Joseph in her arms as satisfying as he had expected it to be.

The Christmas bells were still ringing and the waits were singing again under the window. "Unto us a Child is born. Unto us a Son is given." There was no longer any mockery in the Christmas message.

CHAPTER XIII

PROMISE OF SPRING

But in my mind so is her love inclosed,
And is thereof not only the best part,
But into it the essence is disposed.
O love! (the more my woe) to it thou art
Even as the moisture in each plant that grows;
Even as the sun unto the frozen ground;
Even as the sweetness to th'incarnate rose;
Even as the center in each perfect round;
As water to the fish, to men as air,
As heat to fire, as light unto the sun;
O love! it is but vain to say thou were;
Ages and times cannot thy power outrun.

WALTER RALEIGH.

1.

IT was February the fourteenth, and Canon Leigh, on his way home from the lecture he had just given in the Lady Chapel, paused for a moment in the cloisters. The scholars who had clattered out at his heels had gone back to their rooms, for the spring viva voce examinations were not far away and it behooved them to keep their noses well wedged in their books, and he was quite alone. It was a windless day and there was not a sound to be heard except the cawing of a rook, and a faint chiming of bells so muted by distance that it seemed only the echo of some music past or to come. The gray mist that hid the sun, and veiled the roofs and towers so that they lost their hardness of outline and became little more than shadows in the sky, had in it a warmth and fragrance that told of the coming of spring. The smell of the earth was in it, a soft wet earth through which the snowdrops had already driven their green spears, and some elusive scent that was like the ghost of the fragrance of a thousand flowers. It seemed all there behind the mist, the colors of all the springs that had passed and yet would come again, the riotous music of bird song and falling water that would pour over the earth in so short a while. In the darkest days of January one might doubt if it would come again, but on these warm February days one was certain.

They destroyed all sense of time, these days. Past and present and future seemed all one. There were ghosts of the past as well as of the future about on these days, and those who watched and listened could see their gray shapes in the gray shadows and hear again, muffled by the mist, the voices and the laughter that had once rung out in arrogant possession.

In no part of the College did Canon Leigh feel so aware of the passing and re-passing of the ghosts as he did in these cloisters, for here, at the heart of Wolsey's College, the old Priory that had succeeded Frideswide's Nunnery still seemed to have its stronghold. To the north was the monks' Cathedral Church, to the east the Deanery that had once been the Prior's house, and at right angles to it the monks' refectory that was now the library, and in the center of the inclosed square old gray stones, the remains of the monks' washing place, showed through the green grass. This little square, with the cloisters running round it, seemed always a little dark and dim, a little withdrawn from the rest of the College. In it old memories lived on.

But today was February the fourteenth and Canon Leigh, as he stood in this place of memories, saw not the cowled figures of the monks pacing in the cloisters but a packed mob of people, as many as the place would hold, bishops, courtiers, scholars, citizens and riffraff of the town, swaying this way and that in the grip of wild mob excitement, mocking, taunting, and crying out in compassion, anger or horror; and standing before them, the object of their hatred or their pity, was Thomas Cranmer Archbishop of Canterbury, come here that he might be publicly degraded by the people whose shepherd he had been.

That scene had only been a few years ago but so much had happened since then, so much horror had flowed over Oxford, and then again as much joy and thanksgiving, that it seemed that centuries had passed.... And yet it was happening now and Canon Leigh, as he stood with bent head, was watching it.

The Archbishop had been three years in prison, finding himself unable, now that Queen Mary was on the throne, to change at her command the convictions that had been his when her father had made him Archbishop. He had been imprisoned in the Tower of London and then, with Bishop Ridley and Bishop Latimer, in the prison of Bocardo. In the Oxford Divinity School they were tried and condemned to death, they being Cambridge men and it being apparently the policy of the Queen always to humiliate Cambridge men at Oxford. From the top of Bocardo the Archbishop had seen Latimer and Ridley, who were to suffer before him, led out to be burned to death outside the North Gate, and had knelt down and prayed to God to strengthen them.

Then his own turn had come. After the formal excommunication in the Cathedral he had been led out to the cloisters for his degradation. They had put up a mock altar there and upon it were laid copies, made of rough and coarse materials, of an Archbishop's vestments, mitre and pastoral staff, and with these two jeering priests invested him; yet it was said that his dignity was so great that the crowd did not notice that the vestments he wore were only a mockery. Then one by one they were taken off him, the threadbare gown of a yeoman bedel was thrown over his shoulders and a townsman's greasy cap was forced upon his head. He was no longer Archbishop, he was Thomas Cranmer, an old man led away through the crowd to die as his friends had died.

Canon Leigh could never think of the fate of those three "special and singular captains and principal pillars of Christ's Church" without sick rage. It gripped him now as he looked round him at the quiet scene of the Archbishop's humiliation. It hurt him to the heart that it should have taken place within the walls of his own College. He had to remind himself of Latimer's words to Ridley when the fire was kindled at his feet. "Be of good comfort, Master Ridley, and play the man. We shall this day light such a candle, by God's grace, as I trust shall never be put out." He was right; it burned yet; and would do while the stones of this town stood. So many candles had been lit by saints and martyrs in this city that surely the flames had burned up all the cruelties and obscenities that might have tarnished its spirit.

Canon Leigh sighed a little and found himself musing upon the life of cities. As the hands of men had laid their stones one upon another, clumsily or with grace according to the conception of beauty that was in them, so surely the spirit of the city was woven of the spirits of the men who had lived within it, woven coarsely or finely according to the fiber of their spirits, but as vital to the material city as is heat to fire, or light to the sun. It seemed to him that both the body and the spirit of this city had in this sixteenth century an incomparable beauty. He wondered how much the men who lived here today, rejoicing in the beauty of the towers and spires against the sky, of gardens planted with fair flowers, of quiet evenings whose silence seemed to rest upon the foundations of fortitude and peace, were aware of their debt to the creators of the past, how often they paused to watch for the passing of ghosts in the shadows and to listen for their footfall on the stones. . . . Well, the men of today had their work to do. They were busy with their ambitions, their loves and their hates. They too were creators who were building for the men of the future. . . . And he must go home and prepare questions for the coming examinations.

2.

Raising his eyes as he passed under the dim archway that led from the cloisters to the quadrangle he saw, outlined against the brighter light beyond, the glittering figure of that scapegrace Nicolas de Worde. He was dressed at this moment in the sober garments of a scholar, yet nevertheless he glittered. His dark blue doublet and hose fitted his graceful figure with such an elegant neatness that they looked as jaunty as crimson satin studded with sapphires, his ruff, that on most scholars was apt to become a sordid and bedraggled affair, pale gray in color and wavering in outline, was crisp and white, the cap that he held in his hand had in it a curling white feather, his cheeks glowed with health and his eyes with some suppressed excitement, and his whole body was taut and vigorous as a drawn bow. When Canon Leigh, bowing a little distantly and uttering a slightly frigid "Good morning," had brought his own bent and weary body on a level with this radiant vision and was about to pass on, Nicolas, to his consternation, wheeled round and paced alongside. ... He saw that he had been waylaid and trapped, he, a busy man in the midst of the many labors of his arduous morning.

"Can I serve you in any way?" he inquired politely, for though he could never feel himself much attracted by Nicolas de Worde he realized that in spite of all assertions to the contrary it is in this world the old who must serve the young; they are wasted by them, despoiled of their riches and wisdom by them, grateful if they can win their liking and allegiance, thankful at the end to be given, as reward for their sacrifice and labors, a small portion of a warm chimney corner to end their days in.

"Any help as regards your work?" he asked with gloom, for the examinations were upon them and he had no doubt that Nicolas's stock of information was, as ever, low. And Nicolas had the right to ask him for help, for to Nicolas he owed the restoration of his son Joseph, that adorable and happily most intelligent child who had come so miraculously out of the darkness of Christmas Eve to take the place of the son who had gone. ... Certainly Nicolas had claims upon him. ... Though he could wish, at times, that the young man were not so aware of the fact. During the last few weeks Nicolas had impudently inserted himself into the life of the family to a degree that seemed to Canon Leigh unnecessary. He was always there. If one went into the garden he would be there playing with the children and increasing their noise, at any time quite sufficiently severe, tenfold. When one entered the hall he was to be seen sitting up above at Great-Aunt's window—he got on uncommonly well with Great-Aunt—paying the old lady such outrageous compliments that her cackle of laughter rose up to the rafters in the most unseemly way. If one went into the parlor he was there too, holding skeins of yarn for Joyeuce; with Joyeuce looking most unlike herself, her usually pale face feverishly flushed, her eyes bright as though she were happy yet her mouth poignantly drooping. He doubted if the young man had a good effect upon Joyeuce. It would be better if he were to attend to his work.

"It goes well?" he inquired further.

Nicolas shook his head, but showed no signs of that shame that would have been becoming in him. "It is about Mistress Joyeuce," he said, "that I wish to talk to you."

Canon Leigh, as ever when he thought of his daughters in connection with emotional disturbances, with which he knew himself to be quite incompetent to deal, came out in a cold sweat. He had hoped, and believed because he had hoped, that that highly emotional evening which the pair had spent at the Tavern on Midsummer Eve had left no trace. . . . But it seemed it had. . . . He was bereft of words and the glance which he flung at Nicolas was one of deep alarm.

This strengthened Nicolas's hand. Any qualms which he might have felt, and he had felt a few, were a thing of the past. With kindly benevolence he took the older man under his wing.

"I asked her to marry me some time ago," he explained, "but she thought it her duty to devote herself to you and the children."

"But you should have asked for my daughter's hand in marriage from me, not from herself," ejaculated Canon Leigh in some indignation.

"At that time you did not know me well, and I doubted if you cared for me much," explained Nicolas. "While she did."

Canon Leigh was touched by Nicolas's implied certainty that now he did know him he must care for him; even though it augured a certain bump of conceit in the young man there was a child-like confidence about it that warmed him.

"But does Joyeuce love you?" he asked in bewilderment.

"Oh, very deeply indeed," Nicolas hastened to assure him.

"And what," asked Canon Leigh, with a meekness that thinly veiled a suggestion of sarcasm, "do you wish me to do in this matter?"

"Explain to Joyeuce that she is not as indispensable in your household as she thinks she is. Her sister Grace is perfectly capable of taking her place. I have talked the matter over with Faithful Crocker and he agrees that he and Grace together would find it an easy matter to run your household to your entire satisfaction."

"But why should Faithful Crocker concern himself in this?" demanded Canon Leigh in some indignation.

"You forget," said Nicolas gently, "that he has been my servitor since—since—"

"I remember," said Canon Leigh hastily, and with more warmth. Nicolas, with that fine generosity of his that even a prospective father-in-law was bound to admire, had not left Faithful at Giles's death without a rich scholar to share his room with him. He hated having an intellectual servitor whose industry was a perpetual reproach to his lack of it, but he was not going to leave Faithful stranded.

"It is natural," he said, "that we should talk together."

"Quite, quite," said Canon Leigh. "I merely wondered why Faithful should contemplate making himself responsible for the welfare of my household."

"He hopes to marry Grace."

Canon Leigh stopped dead in his walk and put a hand against the wall to steady himself. Grace, that child hardly out of the cradle, in love? Joyeuce, his demure housekeeper, in love? And the young men—mere infants, both of them—coolly arranging the affairs of his family and household between them? And all this behind his back? He did not know what the modern generation was coming to.

"It seems to have been a shock to you," said Nicolas in some surprise.

Canon Leigh removed his hand from the wall and passed it across his forehead. "A slight shock," he murmured. In his young day elders had not been so treated by the young. Their idea was, apparently, that they should arrange things to their liking while their parents footed the bill.

"And on what," he asked, "do you intend to support Joyeuce? And on what does Faithful Crocker intend to support Grace? And are you aware that while you are scholars of this University you are not permitted to marry?"

"I am leaving Christ Church at the end of this summer," said Nicolas. "Then I hope, with your permission, to marry Joyeuce. My father," he added with a touch of arrogance, as though the honor of the de Wordes had been called in question, "is of course able to support his eldest son in the married state."

It was as Canon Leigh had thought; in this generation the parents paid.

"Then you do not mean to take your M.A.?" he questioned mildly.

"I don't think, my intellectual powers being what they are, that it is of the slightest use even to try for it," said Nicolas disarmingly. "Do you?"

"Frankly, no," agreed Canon Leigh. "But Faithful Crocker—I should be sorry to see him throw away his chances of academic distinction."

"He doesn't mean to. Grace must wait the seven years until he takes his M.A. Grace is quite willing to wait, for she will be occupied meanwhile in the bringing up of the little boys and the twins. When Faithful has finished his career at Oxford he will marry Grace."

"And upon what will he support her?" asked Canon Leigh again.

"He will obtain some lucrative post."

"I hope he may, I hope he may," murmured Canon Leigh doubtfully. "Grace, I see, is a party to all these plans, but Joyeuce, if I have understood you aright, is not?"

"No," said Nicolas, and for the first time his confidence seemed to desert him. He made a little helpless gesture with his hands and his bright eyes clouded. "She loves me, but her sense of duty stands in her way. It is almost as though she loved martyrdom. I do not understand. Ever since December I have not dared to speak to her about it again. She holds at arm's length yet all the time her eyes are asking me to come and take her. . . . What can I do?"

Canon Leigh looked at the young man with new attention. There was patience in his voice, humility and suffering, qualities which the older man recognized as being ingredients in a love that time had tested and matured. They were not characteristics that he would have expected to find in Nicolas, either. It might be, he thought, glancing at him keenly, that there was a strength in this boy that he had not suspected. He wondered if perhaps he was inclined to distrust beauty and charm and gaiety as such. . . . In his own sex, that was, for like all men, no matter how saintly, he could not but feel that it was the duty of a woman to be lovely. . . . He feared that he was. He was inclined to be drawn most easily to the man in whom a plain face was transfigured by beauty of soul. But why should not the contrary be sometimes the case? Might not outward beauty sometimes work inwards? The longing of every human creature is for unity and it might be that the beautiful strove, even though unconsciously, to make their minds and souls as fair as their outward seeming. . . . They had reached the further end of the quadrangle and he himself turned that their pacing might be prolonged.

"A lover of martyrdom," he said slowly, his thoughts going to Latimer who had embraced it with such eagerness and Cranmer who had so pitifully shrunk from it. "There are those who have it, those whose loyalty is so confident that they burn to put it to the test. But they are rare who have such confidence, and I do not think that Joyeuce is one of them. She has never been over-confident."

"Then why?" asked Nicolas.

"A conviction she has that what she wants to do must necessarily be wrong. Many of us carry that certainty with us out of childhood, especially those, like Joyeuce, who have had to grow up too soon and have lost that time of happy transition in which old habits of thought quietly leave them and new ones as quietly take their place. They are often very childlike, those men and women who have had to grow up too soon."

"And yet at the same time very old and very wise."

Canon Leigh nodded and glanced at Nicolas with growing appreciation. In a few meetings he seemed to have learned a good deal about Joyeuce.

"Then," pleaded Nicolas, "will you not persuade Joyeuce that it is right she should marry me?"

"But is it right?" smiled Canon Leigh. "Will you make her happy? What do I know about you?"

"It is quite right," said Nicolas, and flung up his head with something of his old arrogance. "I think my love permeates her life, and hers mine. It is to me what light is to the sun and perfume to the rose; I am valueless without it. We have that to give each other which we must give each other. I must have her joy and she needs that I should give her that

transition time, that time of happiness, of which you spoke. . . . I shall
take her to Court."

"What?" gasped Canon Leigh. It seemed to him that Nicolas had
dropped abruptly from insight to childishness. He spoke of capacity for
joy in Joyeuce, of which her father himself had seen no signs, and then
he spoke of taking her to Court, a place in which Canon Leigh had no
doubt at all that she would be perfectly miserable.

"You are wrong," Nicolas said, answering the unspoken criticism.
"I think she is like me. I think that she is not very happy in a humdrum
life. . . . You should have seen her joy on Midsummer Eve when I took
her to that enchanted garden at the Tavern. . . . She wants unordinary
experiences and it is not good for her that she should have them only
in her spirit. She needs to laugh and sing and dance. She needs to wear
a new dress every day and have all the men at Court writing verses to
her eyebrows. She needs to be so very happy for a short while that the
whole of the rest of her life will glow with it. . . . And all that she needs
I will give her."

"To promise that is to shoulder a great responsibility," smiled Canon
Leigh.

"I don't care," said Nicolas. "I used to dodge responsibility, but I
don't now. You can't have anything you want without it."

"And so I am to persuade Joyeuce to marry you."

"Yes," said Nicolas.

"Well, I will do it," said Canon Leigh. "I know next to nothing about
you, but I believe that you are right." He sighed. It seemed odd to him
that it should be the duty of parents to hand over their children to the
care of comparative strangers; even odder that these strangers should
seem to have an instinctive knowledge of the children's needs that the
parents in years of intimacy had not fathomed. But it was the way of life.
By a continual progression to things that are new and strange the world
goes on. He turned and led the way back again towards the Fair Gate.
They parted in silence but courteously, Nicolas's cap with its curling
white feather sweeping the ground as he bowed. They felt respect for
each other and even a dawning of affection.

3.

Nicolas careered joyously up the steps to his room, three at a time, and burst through the door with a noise and speed that seemed to Faithful, immersed in his books, unnecessary. He raised his large head from the hands that propped it and gazed at his fellow scholar more in sorrow than in anger. Then silently he raised a lean forefinger and pointed it at a sealed document that lay on the oak table.

Nicolas's jaws dropped and he felt a prickly sensation up the spine. He had been just about to tell Faithful of the conversation in the quadrangle but the spate of words that had been tumbling up his throat now fell suddenly back again, making him feel slightly sick. He had known that this was coming, of course, but it was his habit never to concentrate upon unpleasant things until they were actually thrust under his nose. He too pointed a finger at the sealed document. "Pass me the damned thing," he groaned. Faithful passed it, holding it cautiously by one corner as though it were filled with gunpowder that might explode at any moment. Nicolas, sighing pitifully, opened it and read words that from past experience he knew only too well, though the detestable missive was written in Latin.

"In Dei nomine, Amen. . . . By this present document let it plainly appear and be known to all that in the fifteenth hundred and sixty-sixth year of the Lord, in the seventh year of the reign of Elizabeth, by the grace of God Queen of England, France and Ireland, defender of the faith and on earth supreme head of the English and Irish Church, there have been summoned by the Subdean, with the consent of the Dean, the learned Censors in the Church of Christ at Oxford to examine the youth of the same Church according to the statute of that house, which orders that at the end of two years each one be examined as to his progress both in learning and in morals. Let all them to whom this present writing comes know that for those whose names are written below such a trial by the Subdean and Censors is to be held."

And Nicolas's name was written below. He tossed the thing to Faithful and fell groaning on to the stool before the desk.

" 'Learning and morals,' " quoted Faithful from the loathsome missive. "Well, anyway, your *morals* are all right." He spoke a little tartly for
he himself, though he dreaded the ordeal that would be his also at the
end of his first two years, was nevertheless already armed at all points.
There was nothing, he was able to assure himself modestly, that they
would be likely to ask him that he would be unable to answer. . . . But
with poor Nicolas he feared it was very much otherwise.

Poor Nicolas arose, dipped a towel in a jug of water, tied it savagely round his forehead, collected an armful of books and once more
dropped groaning upon his stool. "By the mercy of Providence," he
informed Faithful, "I have tackled the old man before instead of after.
He's Subdean this year, you know. If I had left it until after—" He broke
off and shuddered at the thought of Canon Leigh's possible reaction to
the pleading of a prospective son-in-law who had just degraded himself
academically in the eyes of the whole College.

"Left what until after?" asked Faithful.

Nicolas explained and Faithful's eyes widened in horror. "You didn't
mention me and Grace?" he gasped.

"Of course I did. How could I help it? I said you and Grace couldn't
be for years and years, and he seemed to take comfort in that."

Faithful waved his hands in some distress of mind, but then, his
eyes falling on his book, he forgot about his marriage problems. He
loved Grace dearly but, like Saint Edmund before him, his first love was
learning. In a moment he was so absorbed that he was deaf and blind to
everything but the printed words that marched across the page in front
of him, carrying him with them into a country that was his own country,
where he belonged and where he was happy.

So it was Nicolas who heard the sounding of the trumpet and the
clatter under the Fair Gate.

"What's that?" he demanded, casting the wet towel from him, for it
covered his ears and prevented him from hearing things that were really
important.

"What's what?" asked Faithful crossly, for the flung towel had hit
him in the face and brought him back out of the far happy place where

he had been. . . . If Nicholas found it a trial having Faithful for his servitor Faithful found being Nicolas's servitor an even heavier one. . . . The man would neither work himself nor permit others to do so.

Nicolas swept all the books off his desk on to the floor with a gesture of his right arm and leaned across it with his head out of the window. "The Chancellor!" he cried.

At this even Faithful took his nose out of his book and thrust it out of the other window. "Coming this way!" he gasped.

The Chancellor, dressed in puce velvet, with a purple cloak embroidered with silver, it being the season of Lent when a certain soberness of attire was considered seemly, was strolling beneath their windows, attended by Dean Godwin and a couple of conversational and portly merchants dressed in fine furred gowns, with gold chains about their necks and be-ringed fat hands folded upon their stomachs, who strutted in their wake like a couple of gobbling turkey cocks.

"Now what are they up to?" demanded Nicolas of Faithful. "That is Master Wythygge of the Guild of Stoneworkers, and the other is Master Baggs who does house decorating. Is the whole College to be spring-cleaned?"

"They're going to the Leighs'!" ejaculated Faithful.

"By cock and pie, they are!" cried Nicolas, and hung out of the window at infinite peril to life and limb. There came a thundering knock at the Leighs' modest front door, which yielded with the suddenness of complete astonishment, and the four great ones entered and were lost to sight.

"Canon Leigh is in debt," said Nicolas with some satisfaction. . . . His academic inferiority made him take pleasure in a feeling of financial soundness. . . . "In debt to Master Wythygge and Master Baggs."

"The Chancellor wouldn't concern himself with *that,*" said Faithful. "It must be something much more important."

"Then let's go and call casually and find out," said Nicolas, withdrawing his head.

But Faithful was firm. "I have never met anyone," he said bitterly, "who could think of so many other things to do besides work." And he pointed once more to the fatal document. "In Dei nomine, Amen. . . .

Examined as to his progress both in learning and in morals," it said, staring mockingly up from the floor. Sighing, Nicolas searched for his wet towel. "This place would be perfect," he said, "if it were not for the work."

4.

Canon Leigh the Subdean was bent low over his study table, setting searching examination questions upon morals, when Dorothy Goatley, her eyes bulging in her head and her hands clinging to the edge of the door as though she were about to fall to the floor in a fit, ushered in the Chancellor, Dean Godwin, Master Wythygge and Master Baggs. Canon Leigh, more annoyed than honored by the interruption, rose and bowed, exchanged greetings, and swept a litter of papers from the chairs to the floor that his visitors might sit down.

"The Chancellor has come," said Dean Godwin, exchanging an unseen glance of sympathy with his colleague, "to discuss with us matters pertaining to the Queen's proposed visit to Oxford this summer. The Queen's Grace has expressed it as her wish that she should be lodged at Christ Church. She takes a great interest in our College, as you know, because of its connection with Westminster." He did not add because also of its connection with his own good looks, but the knowledge of the connection was in the deep gloom of his eye.

Canon Leigh bowed politely but without enthusiasm. He had already heard of the Queen's proposed visit and feared that, though doubtless an honor, it would nevertheless be a great hindrance to concentrated work on the part of the scholars.

"I have examined the plans of the College," said the Chancellor, "and it seems to me that your house is the best place in which to lodge Her Grace and those more intimate members of her household who will be with her. Other members of the Court will be lodged in other houses and in the rooms of the dons, who will, I am sure, not be slow to appreciate the honor done them."

Another glance of profound sympathy sped from the Dean to Canon Leigh. "Yours is the only house," he explained in a low voice, "which immediately adjoins the great hall. Her Grace must be lodged where she can pass from her place of residence to the hall without exposing herself to the outer elements. It might rain."

"But there is no door from my house to the hall," said Canon Leigh.

"Doors can be made," said the Chancellor, and waved his scented gloves airily.

Canon Leigh now understood the situation, and also the presence of Master Wythygge and Master Baggs. He and his family were to be swept from their home that the Queen might be accommodated. Holes would be knocked in his walls by Master Wythygge. The house would be re-decorated, probably quite regardless of his personal taste, by Master Baggs, who as likely as not would paint naked cupids all round the house and place a portrait of Venus, a woman he detested, over his study mantelpiece. He would be unable to get at his books for a long period of time and his life, what with fuss, excitement, muddle and one thing and another, would for an even longer period be a complete hell. But he did not blench. He knew what was expected of him. He bowed low to the Chancellor and expressed himself as overwhelmed with delight that his poor home was considered worthy to shelter her beloved and sacred majesty Queen Elizabeth of England. . . . Behind the Chancellor's magnificent back Dean Godwin's eyes, once more meeting Canon Leigh's, expressed the woebegone conviction that for him too this affair was going to be no joke.

But they knew themselves to be not alone in their sufferings. The Queen's Royal Progresses, when she traveled with her entire Court from town to town and country house to country house all over her kingdom, were her annual summer holiday, and she enjoyed them every bit as much as did her loyal poor people in town and country who were allowed to come pressing up to her litter to see her and talk to her and bask in her smiles. But for the Court and her hosts it was not all jam. The preparations for the Progresses were arduous for those who went with her, and their sufferings throughout them those of the souls in purgatory. The hundreds of luggage carts going on ahead frequently made the roads almost impassable. Probably they lost their luggage. Only the most important of them could expect comfortable rooms to sleep in at night. The Queen changed her plans every five minutes and snapped their heads off when they disagreed with her. It rained. They caught cold. They did everything they possibly could to persuade the Queen's Grace to curtail her Progresses, but were invariably unsuccessful. "Let the old stay behind," she would say caustically to grumbling noblemen of uncertain age, "and the young and able come with me." Then, of course, they would all have to follow after, cursing volubly. Nor was it all pleasure for the hosts, who found the Queen's visits an expensive honor. A ten days' visit to Lord Burghley cost him over a thousand pounds and my Lord of Leicester himself, after entertaining the Queen at Kenilworth, found himself out of pocket by a small fortune. So the Dean and Canon Leigh were only two more among an army of martyrs who were spread over the length and breadth of England. They submitted with only the breath of a sigh.

"Perhaps I may be permitted to make a tour of the house?" suggested the Chancellor. "Master Wythygge and Master Baggs will then see what work will need to be done."

Master Wythygge and Master Baggs bowed fatly and smiled with delight, their generous curves suggesting to Canon Leigh's tormented mind that they would without doubt think a great deal needed to be done. He opened the door, ushering them and the Chancellor into the hall, himself lingering behind to whisper in distraction to Dean Godwin, "Who pays?"

The Dean made an equally distracted gesture with his hands. "God knows," he whispered. "You—me—the whole College. God help us all."

Outside in the hall Canon Leigh found his whole family, with the exception of Will and Thomas, mercifully absent at school, and Great-Aunt, even more mercifully absent upon one of her rare shopping expeditions, gathered in a row to gape at the Chancellor. They stood in order of height, Joyeuce at one end of the row and the little boys, with the dogs and Tinker, at the other end. The girls in their billowing black frocks sank to the ground in curtseys, like four blackbirds coming to rest upon the earth, Diccon and Joseph, one dressed in scarlet and the other in sky blue, bowed till their heads nearly touched the floor, the dogs

wagged their tails and Tinker sat down suddenly and washed himself.
. . . The whole collection was a pleasing sight and the Chancellor was
touched. He kissed the girls and chucked the little boys under the chin.
He patted the dogs and took trouble not to step upon the tail of Tinker.
Then he turned back to the little boys, the one with the mop of dark curls
in his doublet of poppy red, and the other with the fair head in his suit
of azure. "Pages for the Queen," he said. "Attired as cupids, or what-not,
they would be likely to tickle the fancy of the Queen's Grace exceedingly.
Jog my memory, Master Dean, when the time comes."

The Dean nodded and a gasp of excitement and incredulous questioning went up from all the children. "The Queen, when she visits
Christ Church this summer, will honor our poor home by staying at it,"
Canon Leigh told them gloomily. "Joyeuce, you had better accompany
us round the house to receive directions as to what alterations and deco-
rations will be necessary."

"Lead on, mistress," said the Chancellor gallantly.

Joyeuce stepped bashfully forward, but Grace, to her father's astonishment, stepped forward too, with her chest well thrown out and her
hands clasped importantly upon her stomacher. He had half a mind to
order her back, for he had not commanded her attendance upon this
occasion, but it was his habit never to rebuke his children in front of
strangers, and he let it alone for the moment. He would deal with her
insubordination later.

Yet, as the tour proceeded, he found that it was Grace who was the
most helpful of the two girls. While Joyeuce hesitated she answered
questions with decision and promptitude. She knew what to do and
how it ought to be done. She even went so far as to haggle with Master
Wythygge and Master Baggs; the prices they quoted, she had the temer-
ity to tell them, were far too high. And once, if not twice, she actually
snubbed the Chancellor, whose knowledge of household affairs, she
gave him to understand, was by no means equal to her own. Indeed in
a very short time she had all the males present, helpless as always in the
hands of a woman who is a good manager, completely in subjection. Her
father gazed at her in amazement. How was it that he had not noticed

how she had developed? Her chest was now firmly rounded and her waist compact. Her rosy face was curiously mature for so young a girl and the direct gaze of her blue eyes demanded obedience. The keys at her waist jingled importantly and the sound of her small feet stepping decisively upon the bare boards was louder than one would have expected. . . . Joyeuce, he noticed, wore no keys at her waist, and her step made no more sound than the patter of falling leaves in autumn.

The house was explored from top to bottom and matters soon arranged. The Queen, the Chancellor had no doubt, would wish to occupy Great-Aunt's room. Its central position would please her, for very little could go on, said the Chancellor as he swung in delight from the window commanding the hall to the window opening upon the garden, either in or out of doors that she would not know about; her loving interest in the affairs of her subjects, he hastened to assure his audience, was always unswerving in its devotion. . . . "It's the same with Great-Aunt," said Grace. . . . And then the girls' room leading out of it would serve excellently for her ladies of the bedchamber, and in its far wall could be made the door leading to the hall. "Another door will increase the draughts in this room," objected Canon Leigh. "No matter," was the Chancellor's answer. "The room will merely be occupied by the ladies of the bedchamber." Canon Leigh, sighing, supposed that in future years the door could always be blocked up again at his expense.

They were so occupied in deciding the position of this door that they did not hear a footfall in the next room. It was not until they turned back and were about to re-enter Great-Aunt's room that they saw her standing in the middle of it. She had just returned from her shopping expedition. She wore a voluminous purple satin farthingale over an immense kirtle of purple velvet. Her cloak, also of purple velvet, was flung regally back from her shoulders. One gnarled jeweled old hand was placed upon the head of her stick, the other was laid dramatically upon her bosom. Her eyes and the diamonds in her ears flashed. Her nose was hooked more aggressively than usual and her chin jutted truculently beneath it. "Tilly-vally!" she ejaculated in a deep bass voice. "And what is the meaning of this?"

Canon Leigh presented the Chancellor to her, and explained the reason for his visit, while the Dean hastily suggested that the Leighs would feel themselves deeply honored when their roof sheltered the Queen's Grace.

"I've no objection," said Great-Aunt amiably. "I shall be happy to receive the Queen's Grace. If the children are distributed among our friends there will be plenty of room for the Queen and her personal attendants. ... I should suggest, Gervas," she said, fixing her nephew with a glittering eye, "that you sleep in your study and hand over your room to the Queen's Grace. Her attendants can sleep in the boys' room." Her eye swung round and fixed itself upon the Chancellor. "It is unfortunate that the girls' room is not available, but, as you see, it is only reached through my own."

The Chancellor, his gloves airily brandished, courteously explained to her the arrangements that had already been made. He exerted all his charm of manner. He was not slow to see in her face the remnants of great beauty, and he did homage to it, though there was an edge to his voice. He was to perfection the iron hand in the velvet glove. His voice flowed melodiously on, then ceased. He waited, hand on hip, to receive her submission and apology.

None came. Her eyes, that had been fixed on his face, traveled downwards, noted the cut of his beard, swept over his magnificent clothes, concentrated upon his shoes with their long exaggerated points, closed as though the sight tired her, opened once more and returned to his face, thinking little of it.

"It is entirely out of the question," she said, "that I should relinquish my room. The Queen's Grace, were she to be made acquainted with my age and infirmities, would be the last person to wish such an outrageous step to be taken."

The eyebrows of the Chancellor were raised and his mouth slightly ajar. Such an outrage as this he had not yet experienced. ... Men had been beheaded for less. ... Joyeuce and Grace, mentally seeing Great-Aunt at the block, clung to each other in terror. Master Wythygge and Master Baggs gasped. Canon Leigh and the Dean stood with their hands thrust into the long sleeves of their gowns and their eyes upon the floor. A slight smile played about the lips of the Dean, for he remembered the battle there had been about the making of that window in Great-Aunt's room, and her final victory. Far be it from him to interfere in a battle between such well-matched protagonists. . . . For himself, he backed Great-Aunt.

"I think, madam," said the Chancellor, "that you have not completely understood the situation. Let me explain once more—"

"My Lord," interrupted Great-Aunt, "you have already explained at quite unnecessary length. I retain, I thank God, the use of my hearing and my intelligence."

The Chancellor was about to speak again but her eyes checked him. They appeared to be boring right through his head, noting the quality of his brain and finding it exactly what she had expected, and coming out at the back where he had a slight bald patch that was causing him anxiety. He flushed suddenly and swung round upon Canon Leigh. "Sir," he ejaculated, "cannot you bring this aged gentlewoman to a sense of her duty?"

"That, my Lord," said Canon Leigh, raising his head, "is a task upon which I am ever engaged, but ever unsuccessful."

"Hold your tongue, Gervas!" cried Great-Aunt, striking her stick upon the floor. She was in one of her rages now, one of her magnificent rages that seemed to send unseen thunderbolts hurtling through the air and electric currents throbbing through the bodies of all present. "These Tudors have robbed me of much," she said to the Chancellor, rounding upon him. "King Harry cut off the head of my brother and Queen Mary burned my husband, the worldly goods that should have come to me being appropriated by the throne, and I'll not be robbed of my bedroom by another of 'em; and she a red-headed sharp-nosed young hussy whose flirtations with the gentlemen are enough, from all accounts, to bring a blush to the cheek of every modest gentlewoman; as you should know, my Lord of Leicester, who—"

"Madam, hold your peace!" thundered Canon Leigh suddenly. "I will have no such immodest remarks made in my house. You will relinquish your bedroom to the Queen's Grace, and be thankful that it is not your head also."

"I will do no such thing," said Great-Aunt. "I have slept in that bed for a number of years and I will sleep in it till I die. The Queen may pass through my room, due warning being given beforehand, to reach the door you propose to make into the hall, but a further concession than this should not be expected of me, at my age, with my infirmities, to these Tudors, who have so grossly misused my family and brought me in my old age to be a penniless pensioner upon the grudging charity of my unwilling nephew."

Canon Leigh, remembering her quite considerable wealth and the Christian welcome he had given her in his home, said nothing. The Dean said nothing. The Chancellor, choked by rage tried to speak and failed. It was Grace, lifting her head like a bright little robin, who piped out cheerfully, "Father's bedroom has a very pretty view."

"Extremely pretty," said Great-Aunt, "allow me to conduct you thither that you may behold it for yourself." Her rage had suddenly fallen from her and with a confiding smile she laid a jeweled little hand upon the Chancellor's sleeve. She made play with the fine eyelashes that still were hers, and her eyes were now soft as pansies. She moved forward a little, her silk farthingale whispering upon the floor, and he was obliged to move with her, for though her hand had been laid so gently on his arm the fingers were now fixed upon it like a vice. A faint smell of violets clung to her skirts. It was like the ghost of her beauty, a ghost that could be very potent when she chose. . . . The Chancellor found himself smiling upon her. . . . They all moved forward, out of Great-Aunt's room, across the passage and into Canon Leigh's. As they entered the sun burst suddenly through the mist, illuminating the awakening garden outside the window and the delicate tracery of the trees beyond, touching the soft tapestries on the walls to a riot of blues and greens and shining upon the white linen of the bed—clean sheets today, thank God, thought Grace—so that it shone like driven snow.

"A charming room!" cried my Lord of Leicester. "The best in the house. I did not, when I saw it just now, realize its beauty. Charming! Charming!"

CHAPTER XIV

THE TROUBADOUR

Loving in truth, and fain in vase my love to show,
That she, dear she, might take some pleasure of my pain,
Pleasure might cause her read, reading might make her know,
Knowledge might pity win, and pity grace obtain,
I sought fit words to paint the blackest face of woe;
Studying inventions fine, her wits to entertain,
Oft turning others' leaves to see if thence would flow
Some fresh and fruitful showers upon my sun-burned brain.
But words came halting forth, wanting Invention's stay;
Invention, Nature's child, fled step-dame Study's blows,
And others' feet still seemed but strangers in my way.
Thus, great with child to speak, and helpless in my throes,
Biting my truant pen, beating myself for spite,
"Fool," said my Muse to me, "look in thy heart and write."

PHILIP SIDNEY.

1.

CANON Leigh sat reading in his study, rejoicing in a most unusual peace. The news that the Queen meant to visit Christ Church had lately set the whole College-full of scholars chattering like starlings, and concentration had been impossible for the serious-minded. But now, praise be to God, the imminence of the spring examinations, fixed for the day after tomorrow, had shed abroad a spirit of depression and a subsequent blessed silence. The scholars were all within doors, groaning over their books, and the quadrangle was empty except for two black figures; Tinker the cat basking in the sunshine and the Dean on his way from the Deanery to the scholars' rooms, to inquire into the progress of their studies. . . . These tender visits of inquiry were at that time the custom, and part of his official duty, but they were at a later date discontinued because of their extreme unpopularity both with the visitor and the visited.

Thank God, thought Canon Leigh, turning a page of the great leather-bound book that lay before him, there was no one likely at this moment to visit *him*. Afternoon peace reigned both inside and outside the house, and the window was open to the first real warmth of the year. He allowed himself to lean back in his chair for a moment, enjoying it. Those colors and scents of spring that on that day of the Chancellor's visit, only a short while ago, had been waiting behind the mist, had drawn a little nearer. The sunshine seemed to smell of the primroses that were already out in sheltered corners of the gardens, and snatches of bird-song rang out like carillons of hope in the blue air. It was a day to shelve all problems, domestic, collegiate and national. It was a day to follow the example of Tinker the cat, sleeping in the sun, awaking to blink at it, then stretching himself luxuriously to sleep again. Canon Leigh followed it, closing his eyes that he might think the better, opening them to admire a billowy white cloud floating dreamily across the blue sky, closing them again that thought might deepen into contemplation and contemplation into sleep.

He was awakened, not by any means for the first time in his life, by sounds of domestic disturbance. "Perdition take those two little boys!" was his first unfeeling exclamation, followed instantly, as with full awakening the thoughts of a father superseded the reaction to noise of the natural man, by "the high spirits of the dear little children sorely need the curb of wholesome Christian discipline." He arose to apply it and, sighing, looked round for his cane.

Yet when he had reached the hall, and the sounds of rage and woe from beyond the kitchen door smote like blows upon his ears, he was astonished to find that every member of his household was apparently adding its quota to the general tumult. The roars of Diccon led the van, so to speak, but they were followed by the tearful hiccups of Joseph, the distressing squeaks of the twins, the loud crying of Dorothy Goatley, the voice of Grace raised in most unusual anger, and during a pause in the row he thought he heard the pathetic gasping sobs of Joyeuce herself. Joyeuce crying? Were they bullying her? At the thought of any harm threatening his favorite child the usually gentle scholar became as a primeval savage, upon the warpath. Gathering up his black gown in one hand and brandishing his cane in the other he launched himself upon the kitchen door.

The sight that met his eyes was heartrending in the extreme. In the window stood Dorothy Goatley, her apron flung over her head, weeping loudly, and clinging to her skirts were the twins, squeaking nineteen times to the minute, tears rolling down their far cheeks and dripping on to the floor in heartbreaking cascades. At the table sat Joyeuce, her head buried in her arms, sobbing, and on the floor beside her, burrowing their heads against her in a passion of love, were Diccon and Joseph, roaring and hiccuping their sympathy. Before the fire stood Grace, flushed with anger, demanding indignantly, "Why didn't you do as I told you and leave it to me? Why in the world didn't you leave it to me?" Midway between Joyeuce and Grace, white to the lips, bewildered and unhappy, stood the only man present, Faithful. The room was stiflingly hot, with the fire roaring up the chimney and the warm oppressive smell of ironing hanging heavy in the air. Piles of sheets, pillow cases, towels, quilts, aprons, coifs, shirts and kerchiefs took up every available space, and upon the table before Joyeuce was a lovely lace-trimmed petticoat utterly ruined by the application of too hot an iron. "My *best* petticoat," wailed Grace.

But at the first whiff of that hot ironing smell Canon Leigh had understood the situation, had lowered his cane and regarded his family with an indulgent smile. Until he smelled that smell he had momentarily forgotten that they were in the midst of that terrible infliction of the sixteenth century, the Annual Spring Wash. Yearly, at the first spell of settled sunshine, it fell upon every household like a blight. It always began well, with the females of the family falling upon every washable piece of material in the house in a spirit of inspiring enthusiasm, and the males betaking themselves hastily to the nearest tavern, but as the laborious days went on, the first inspiration was apt to flag a little, giving way to grim determination, and that in turn to a shortness of temper very distressing to all concerned. Looking back, Canon Leigh remembered that all the serious family disturbances of his married life had taken place during the latter period of the Spring Wash; and had sprung, all of them, from accidents so trivial that they would hardly have been noticed at other times. They were, he remembered, well into the latter period of the Spring Wash now. For days the garden had been festooned with washing. The yew hedge had been lost to sight beneath snowy sheets, and Romulus and Remus, the clipped yew peacocks, had been draped with towels as though about to step down to the river to take a dip. The lawn had been white with spread quilts and every species of undergarment had fluttered from lines between the apple trees. . . . Certainly the time was ripe for the Annual Family Disturbance.

With deep sympathy his eyes met those of Faithful. . . . Faithful, poor fellow, was doubtless enduring his first Spring Wash, but, poor fellow, were he to perpetrate matrimony he would doubtless have to endure many more. . . . "These little upsets occur at this time," he told him soothingly. "Have you any idea what started it?"

"It seems that Joyeuce has spoilt Grace's best petticoat," said Faithful miserably. "But something much more dreadful must surely have happened to cause all this terrible lamentation."

"Probably not," said Canon Leigh. "Well, Grace? You have my permission to speak."

Grace would have spoken with or without his permission; she was boiling over with indignant speech. "I *told* Joyeuce to leave the ironing to me," she burst out. "She has no gift for ironing. She is so dreamy, so absent-minded, that she cannot keep her attention upon the matter in hand. She lets the iron get too hot. She neglects to test it. Yet when I came in from the garden with the towels from Romulus and Remus I found that Joyeuce had already embarked upon the ironing and ruined my best petticoat."

"That will do, Grace," said her father sternly. "Come with me to my study. And you, Faithful, may come too."

He led the way back to his study, placed the cane in a corner with a sigh of thankfulness that it had after all not been necessary to apply any Christian discipline, and sat down in his chair, motioning the two to stand before him. He had, as yet, made no effort to deal with the domestic situation revealed to him by Nicolas, but he had been waiting for his opportunity, and now it was here.

Grace was crying now. The words "come to my study," reviving as they did painful memories of early youth, were always enough to start her off. And she was sorry that she had made Joyeuce cry. She loved Joyeuce, even though her incompetence drove her distracted. And she was afraid her father had discovered about her and Faithful and was about to forbid the banns. She drew nearer to Faithful, clutching him with one hand while with the other she tried to stem the cascade of tears that rolled down her rosy cheeks.

What a couple of children, thought Canon Leigh, and yet how mature they had lately become. Faithful was looking at him unflinchingly, his face wearing that strange expression of peace that was his special beauty. Canon Leigh remembered that he had behind him a record of experience and endurance that was not possessed by many men twice his age; he had already been tested and not found wanting. And Grace, though she cried like a child, rubbing her knuckles in her eyes and sniffing dolorously, had already the figure of a woman and the competence of an experienced housewife. What had they found in each other, he wondered, that had made them indispensable each to the other? That was a question, he knew, that could not be answered. Not even lovers themselves can tell you why the one particular person is the only person in the world.

"And so you want to be married?" he asked quietly.

Faithful nodded his huge head like a top-heavy owl and Grace whispered childishly, "Yes, please."

"It grieved me," said Canon Leigh, "to hear of your hopes from Nicolas de Worde and not from yourselves."

Faithful explained. They had been afraid to anger him. They had been afraid he would not realize that they were old enough to contemplate such things.

"I quite realize your maturity," their father assured them solemnly, but with a suppressed twinkle. "You are now fourteen and fifteen, a man and woman grown and of marriageable age; though of course," he added with relief, "it will be many years before you are able to marry. But I gather that you are willing to wait. I gather that Grace feels more than equal to taking Joyeuce's place should she decide to marry and leave us."

But at this Grace showed that she too, beneath her surface confidence, had a portion of the Leigh humility. Her tears, that had been checked by delight at her father's unexpected reasonableness, brimmed over again and she hung her head. "I can never take Joyeuce's place," she whispered. "I can cook and wash and iron better than Joyeuce, but you and the children will never love me as you love her."

Her father stretched out an arm and pulled her upon his knee. "Dear little Grace, we shall," he assured her. "You are your mother's daughter. You have her lovely competence, as Joyeuce has her gift of insight. As the years go on Joyeuce will grow more practical and you will grow in sympathy, until both of you reach the full stature of the perfect woman that your mother was."

But Grace, shaking her head dolefully, had her doubts. One was born a certain sort of person, she thought, and though by ceaseless struggle one might become as nice as that sort of person ever is, one could never become as nice as a nicer sort of person. Never, she knew, would she attain to that sensitiveness of mind and spirit that people loved in Joyeuce, and never, never, she was quite sure, would Joyeuce be the slightest use at ironing.... At the thought of her burned petticoat she wept afresh.

This new outbreak of grief in the beloved was too much for Faithful. Though it was not considered correct to be demonstrative before parents he could not contain himself. He took her hand and kissed it, holding it against his cheek. "No girl has ever been loved as I love you," he told her solemnly. "I don't know how to say it, but if I did know how to say it I should not love you so much."

Grace raised her head from her father's shoulder and looked at her inarticulate lover. Her father intercepted their look, a look of such

profound trust that he was humbled by it. They would be an unde-
monstrative couple, these two, and they would always seem rather comical to others, but he thought they had as great a chance of happiness as
any couple he had ever known. "Kneel down, children," he commanded
them. "I have not yet given you my blessing."

2.

He continued to deal with the havoc created by the Spring Wash.
Having blessed Grace and Faithful he made his way to the kitchen.
Here he found Dorothy Goatley and the twins reviving themselves
with large slices of plum cake and a draught of ale. Their eyes and noses
were still red but they were chartering happily. He perceived that food
for the body had proved so restorative that spiritual comfort was not
now required. . . . In his experience it was often so. . . . He paused but
to inquire the whereabouts of Joyeuce and left them to find her in the
garden.

She was sitting on the grassy bank by the apple trees, the little boys
cuddled up one on each side of her, gazing mournfully at the family
underclothes that still fluttered in the spring wind.

"Still grieving for that petticoat, Joyeuce?" he asked her, sitting
down beside her and lifting Joseph on to his lap.

"Not for the petticoat," said Joyeuce with trembling lips, "Grace has
heaps of petticoats, but that she should treat me so. She is always like
that now. Always trying to push me out."

"Not trying to push you out, Joyeuce," said her father, "but trying to
grow up. She cannot help herself, for her domestic competence seems
to me so excessive that it must surely be a gift of God, and not allowed
full use it is turning sour within her and proving slightly inconvenient to
ourselves." He pointed to the snowdrops at their feet, spearing their way
up through the winter earth. "Look how they are shooting up. Once they
were bulbs hidden in the earth, now they must be leaves and flowers.
They cannot help themselves. Always we must push on."

"But not with unkindness," murmured Joyeuce.

"That cannot always be helped. If one hesitates to pass on the other who comes behind to take her place must knock into her. That's unavoidable. Is it not time, Joyeuce, that you yourself passed on?"

Joyeuce gazed at him with astonished, wide-open eyes that were the color of rain because she was so unhappy. "I—pass on?" she asked stupidly.

"Do you not want a lover, Joyeuce? I loved your mother, and born of love as you were it is natural that you should travel towards love again. You would make a good wife, above all to a gay and prosperous man who needs your perception of invisible things to be, as it were, the unseen life of his happy attributes that will give to them eternal value. What did such a one say to me? 'Her love is to me what light is to the sun and perfume to the rose; I am valueless without it.' I have so often wished, Joyeuce," lied her father blandly, "that you could marry Nicolas de Worde."

Joyeuce looked at him again, and gasped. She perceived that he knew all about it. Then she shyly stroked his sleeve, looking down at little Joseph curled up sleepily in his lap, and at Diccon who had run away from her and was pulling Pippit the unfortunate little greyhound round and round an apple tree by his tail. Her father understood what she would have said had humility not silenced her.

"I shall miss you unspeakably," he told her. "No other daughter can ever take your place, no other sister will ever be to the little boys what you have been. But you will not be lost to us, Joyeuce. You will not be going to the land beyond the sunset; you will only be going to Gloucestershire; I will visit you and you will visit me. I think it right that you should pass on. It is a rule of life."

She gave a shuddering sigh, half of happiness and half of pain, and sat looking down at her hands clasped in her lap. "So it was all for nothing," she whispered.

Canon Leigh looked down at Joseph, who was now asleep in his arms, his fair head fitting into the hollow of his father's shoulder as though it had always been there. "Your sacrifice? I don't think so. I have never yet heard of a death to self that was not followed sooner or later by a re-birth. I seem to remember Nicolas saying, on Christmas Eve, that he had gone to the Crosse Inn because he was unhappy. If you had not made him unhappy would he ever have found Joseph?"

No more words were needed. They sat together in a companionable silence and understanding more satisfying than any they had ever known; until an outbreak of yelps, barks, roars and shrieks down among the apple trees told them that Diccon, this time, had gone a bit too far with Pippit, and they must fly to the rescue before murder was done.

3.

When Canon Leigh returned to his study the Spring Wash was once more in full swing, but progressing this time in a spirit of such amity and politeness that he murmured to himself the wise words of Master Richard Edwardes, "Now have I found the proverb true to prove, the falling out of faithful friends is the renewing of love."

He picked up his book, sank thankfully into his chair and would once more have slipped from literature to peaceful contemplation and repose had not a murmur of voices beyond his window disturbed him. . . . The College this time. . . . "Perdition take the College!" was his unbecoming thought as he opened his eyes and looked out.

The Dean and Nicolas stood together in the sunshine and judging by the tones of their voices, the Dean's sharp with reproof and Nicolas's honey-sweet and pathetic in the frank acknowledgment of guilt, the Dean during a visit of inquiry into Nicolas's intellectual progress had met with very little satisfaction. But Canon Leigh was happy to see that the attitude of his future son in-law was all that could be wished; his comely head was bent in true humility and his broad shoulders drooped under the burden of his shame. . . . But the fingers that held a book behind his back were pattering upon it as though practicing the notes of some merry tune.

The interview ended and the Dean strode back towards the Deanery, the swirl of his black gown expressing outrage and the set of his shoulders registering extreme annoyance. Nicolas remained where he was, but now he held his book in front of him as though it were a musical instrument and performed a difficult trill very diligently with the fingers of his right hand.

Canon Leigh thrust his head out of the window. "Nicolas!" he commanded.

Nicolas swung round, bowed and smiled with the utmost charm, and presented himself beneath the window.

"And for what purpose," demanded Canon Leigh with some asperity, "did you conceive that books were created?"

"They serve so many purposes, sir," said Nicolas with a most disarming grin. "I have been writing a song to sing to Joyeuce and just at that moment I was trying to set it to music."

Canon Leigh was partly mollified. "Well, well," he sighed. "You will now, Nicolas, find your Joyeuce in the right frame of mind to appreciate it." At this such a light of joy broke over Nicolas's face that he was instantly completely mollified. "Come in now, my son," he cried cordially. "You will find her in the kitchen."

"Propose to her in the kitchen, amongst the family wash? By cock and pie, no!" cried Nicolas in powerful indignation. "That would not please Joyeuce at all. She is romantic. I know a better way than that."

"Find your own way," said Canon Leigh. "Doubtless you know best." And he withdrew from the window in that humble frame of mind which, in these days, he was becoming more and more convinced was the right one for age to adopt when confronted with all-conquering youth.

4.

What with emotion and the Spring Wash Joyeuce was utterly worn out by the time she went to bed. Yet when she had slipped into her place in the four-poster, and lain down beside the sleeping little boys, who lay as always curled up together like two puppies, with Baa clasped in Joseph's arms and Tinker festooned over Diccon's feet, she knew that she was not going to sleep. She was too tired—tired as only the

Spring Wash could make her—almost too tired to realize that in just ten minutes' talk with her father the whole direction of her life had been changed. I ought to be gloriously happy, she told herself, turning over on her right side to ease her aching back. Why am I not gloriously happy? So often, she thought, turning over on to her left side because the right one had proved quite unsatisfactory, the moments that we had expected to be joy-giving are not, while those of whom nothing is expected suddenly present us with some heavenly gift. I am going to marry Nicolas, she whispered dolefully, and flopped over on to her back because lying on her side was giving her the stomach-ache. But was she? Did he still love her? Since that day in the Meadows he had been a gay and a good friend to her, as she had asked him to be, but he had said no word of love. Had she done what she had then tried to do, and killed it in him? At the thought that what she had tried to bring about might really have come about desolation swept over her in a sickening flood. Surely it was one of the greatest misfortunes of human nature that what one wanted to happen, by the time it did happen, one didn't want to happen any more. If Nicolas did not now want her after all she thought she would die of grief. She began to sob, the trickling tears making stiff wet tracks from the corners of her eyes to her ears, her hands clasped childishly on the place where the pain was, biting her lips that she might not cry out loud and wake the children. It is nothing but the Spring Wash, she whispered, as she felt herself sucked down and down into an abyss of misery. There is nothing the matter with me but the Spring Wash. It is because I am so tired that I feel so dreadful. In the morning it will all be different.

But faced with a night of pain and sleeplessness, with every problem looming up in the darkness at three times its normal size, it is hard to realize that the dawn will ever come. She turned over again on to her face, lying on the pain to discourage it. When will it be morning? she whispered, and fell to thinking how stupid it was that one had to work so hard just to keep the human body clothed, clean and fed. . . . Sewing. Washing. . . . Cooking. . . . By the time they were finished with, one was too tired to live. It was very silly. She began to sob afresh.

There was a soft rustling of the bushes under her window, those bushes where the buds were already showing faint little tongues of green, thrust forth to taste the air, and then some soft faint notes of music. Whatever bird was that? Surely it was a most peculiar bird. Joyeuce raised her face from her sodden pillow and listened. The faint bird notes sorted themselves and became a tune, sounding for all the world as though a troubadour thrummed very softly on the strings of a viol, and Joyeuce twisted right round and sat bolt upright, her tears stemmed as though a tap had been turned off and her pain as utterly forgotten as though her stomach had vanished into thin air; so prompt and beneficial in its working is the medicine of a stimulated mind.

She crept to the bottom of the bed, parted the curtains and peeped out into the room. There was moonlight and starlight tonight and it lay bathed in a lovely soft radiance. She could see the flowers and trees in the tapestries, that in the moonlight had the mysterious color of flowers blooming in a dream, and the dark floor stretching before her full of shifting lights and inky shadows like a fairy tarn at midnight. Surely it had been the rustling of those flowers and trees, and the lapping of that water, that she had heard, and not the bushes beneath the window? She smiled, because just for the moment the fancy had seemed reality, and like a light flashing suddenly into her tired mind came the thought that the most ordinary things, seen from a new angle, can take on all the colors of romance; they have many facets, and some people have the power to turn them about and see the one that reflects the laughter of God.... As Nicolas could do.

A voice singing drove all thought from her mind and pulled it back into fairyland, where there is no speculation but only a lovely wonder. Who was singing, and was it to her he sang? The lovely voice, not very strong but crystal clear in tone and articulation, reached her effortlessly and seemed to come from the trees in the tapestry. What fairy lover was hiding behind them? She sat back and listened, greedily gathering in every word to store in her memory as though from the trees gold pieces were flung to her to catch.... For never before had a fairy lover sung to her in the moonlight.... Now she was rich indeed.

All day in the hot blue sunshine,
On quivering, tireless wings,
The lark between earth and heaven
Ceaselessly, joyously sings.
But now at last she is sinking
Down to her nest.
So turn to your rest, my lady,
Turn to your rest
And dream.

The scarlet lamps of the tulips
Are fading and burning dim,
Faint as the sun that is sinking
In softness o'er the world's rim,
Draining the world of the color
At night's behest.
So turn to your rest, my lady,
Turn to your rest
And dream.

From somewhere beyond the drawn curtains, that stirred in the breeze from the open window, came a sharp ping, as though a string snapped, and a voice whispered softly but clearly, "Damn!"

This was no fairy lover but one whose mortality was much in evidence. Quick as a flash Joyeuce slipped out of bed, flung her cloak round her and scuttled to the window, thanking her stars as she scuttled that little short of morning or the last trump could wake the children. "Nicolas!" she whispered, slipping behind the window curtains and leaning out to him. . . . How bright the stars were, big stars and little stars, as though every angel and cherub had thrust a fist through the floor of heaven to take a look at her and Nicolas. Surely the stars were auspicious tonight, and every little rustle in the garden was a whisper of friendship. . . . She remembered how once she had dreamed that Nicolas and Dic-con had entered the gates of fairyland while she had been shut out. She was not shut out now. The song of her lover had drawn her inside those gates and they had clanged behind her with the sound of chiming bells. "Oh, Nicolas!" she breathed.

"Good, wasn't it?" said Nicholas, cocking a bright eye at her as he fitted a new string into his viol. He took her ecstasy as a tribute to his musical prowess, and was pleased, for upon the Dean telling him that he lacked concentration in labor he had spent the best part of an hour in work upon his song, and thought highly of it. "I wrote the words *and* music. And there's more to come, too. Amongst other men's songs I could not find one that I liked enough to sing to you, and so I said to myself, 'Fool, write your own.' There are no tulips out yet, of course, but there will be when I sing it to the Queen."

"Will you sing it to the Queen?" whispered Joyeuce with a little tremor of disappointment in her voice. . . . She had hoped this song was all her own.

"Under her window, at night," announced Nicolas. "And she will labor under the delusion that it was written for her, and be so flattered that she will promise me my heart's desire, like a Queen in a fairy tale."

"What desire?" breathed Joyeuce.

He stood up straight under her window, his head tilted back and his bright eyes fixed on hers. "To take you to Court when we are married," he said.

Joyeuce slipped down on to her knees, her elbows propped on the windowsill and her chin in her hands. She could not speak for excitement but her eyes were as bright as two stars.

"And when we are tired of Court life we will go home. You will like my home, Joyeuce. It is built of gray stone, with very tall chimneys that carry the banners of the wood-smoke so far up into the sky that when Mistress Joyeuce de Worde is at home people miles away will know it, and be glad. It has wide windows with diamond panes that let in all the sun by day and catch a star in each pane by night. There is a beech wood behind the house, and a garden full of lilies in front of it, and when you are my wife there will be no Spring Wash."

"But, Nicolas," protested Joyeuce, "one *must* wash."

"The servants will wash," said Nicolas grandly. "But you, Joyeuce, will walk up and down the grass paths between the lilies with your husband and listen to the verses he has written to the brightness of your eyes."

"But there always *must* be domestic tasks," insisted Joyeuce, dazzled but still doubtful.

"Of course there must be," said Nicolas, suddenly serious. "And sickness and accidents and losses and old age. But everything has several sides and I will teach you to see the funny side of them all, and you will show me which way round to turn them to make of them stepping stones to God. . . . Which reminds me," he added inconsequentially, "that I have not proposed to you again. Will you marry me, Mistress Joyeuce Leigh?"

The cloak fell back from her shoulders as she leaned out to him. He jumped upon a garden seat that stood there and his hands came creeping up the wall towards her as they had done at the other window nearly a year ago. They clasped her wrists, and slipped up her bare arms under the sleeves of her white night shift, caressing them. "Now I am only your betrothed who must stand under your window," he whispered, "but soon I shall be your husband. . . . Soon. . . . Soon. . . . Now you must go back to bed, Joyeuce. I will sing you the rest of my song and when I get to the last word you will be asleep. Do you hear? Fast asleep."

His hands slipped down her arms and obediently she turned away from the window and ran back to bed. She jumped in and lay childishly curled up, her cheek resting in her hand upon the pillow. There came again those soft faint notes of music, like a bird talking to itself, and then the voice of the fairy lover singing behind the trees in the tapestry.

The wind that laughed in your garden
Has wearied and dropped asleep,
Leaving the lilies his playmates
His whispered secrets to keep,
The lilies in golden-crowned white
Royally dressed.
So turn to your rest, my lady,
Turn to your rest
And dream.

Wrapped in her mantle of twilight,
Her cloak of silver and gray,
Night the great mother steals downward
To banish the burning day.
Her voice comes clear in the stillness,
"Now sleep is best."
So turn to your rest, my lady,
Turn to your rest
And dream.

Holding out arms of cool comfort
To her children, whispering low
Of that dark, deep, peaceful silence
That only her sleepers know,
The merciful night is holding
Earth to her breast.
So turn to your rest, my lady,
Turn to your rest
And dream.

By the time he had reached the last word she was, as he had told her to be, asleep.

CHAPTER XV

THE QUEEN'S GRACE

Where are all thy beauties now, all hearts enchaining?
Whither are thy flatterers gone with all their feigning?
All fled; and thou alone still here remaining.

Thy rich state of twisted gold to bays is turned.
Cold as thou art are thy loves that so much burned.
Who die in flatterers' arms are seldom mourned.

Yet in spite of envy this be still proclaimed,
That none worthier than thyself thy worth hath blamed;
When their poor names are lost, thou shalt live famed.

When thy story long time hence shall be perused,
Let the blemish of thy rule be thus excused:
"None ever lived more just, none more abused."

   LINES ON QUEEN ELIZABETH. THOMAS CAMPION.

1.

THE summer term was upon them again, lovelier than ever, more vibrant with life, overflowing with happiness. This year every beauty seemed intensified. The shining gold of the kingcups beside the streams was more brilliant, and the fritillaries grew taller than usual, holding their frail bell heads high above the fresh green grass, covering the meadows where they grew with a pale amethyst mist whose beauty caught at the heart. The primroses and violets clustered more thickly in the hedges. The anemone stars alighted in every wood and fluttered delicately poised, tiptoe for flight, silver in the sunshine, snow-white in the dusk, gone like a flight of butterflies almost before there had been time to worship their beauty. When bluebell time came they seemed to pour over the world in a flood, enameling every little knoll and beech-crowned hill with heraldic azure, flowing through the woods in winding rivulets of blue, gathering in every hollow in deep pools, throwing out their intoxicating scent to every breeze that it might be wafted to men's noses and drive them mad with joy. . . . Yet not madder than the birds, who shouted from every bush and tree until it was a marvel that their bunched, vibrating, feathery bodies could hold together with the noise they made.

And, as always, it was gone so soon, this time of the bluebells and the shouting birds to which one looked forward all the year, gone before the bewildered senses, besieged by a thousand scents and sights and sounds of intoxicating beauty, could take firm hold of the miracle and hold on to it in possession. "Next year," sighed tired men and women, still exhausted by the griefs and the hardships of their winter, and sorrowing afresh to see the bluebells faded and the anemones flown clear away, "next year I shall have clearer eyes, and a more awakened spirit. Next year spring will come again and next year it will not catch me sleeping." Yet, if they had bothered to remember, they had said the same thing last year, and would say it again next year. Spring was always so swift, so miraculous, that man was caught forever unaware.

Yet this year there was little time to grieve for vanished anemones, for no sooner had they flown away than the hawthorn was out, piled like snow along the hedges, and then the apple blossom was pink and white in the orchards and the wild cherries were tossing their foam on the hills. And then the wild roses were in bud, and stumpy purple orchids grew sturdily in the fields, and after that no one knew what happened in the country outside the city because they were imprisoned in their own gardens, enslaved by the charms of their own roses and carnations, enraptured by their canterbury bells and purple pansies, bowed to the ground in worship before their lilies.

And the city itself seemed to rejoice more exuberantly than usual in the flower of the year. The towers and spires, that had been so often heavily darkened by winter rain, seemed again light and airy things spun out of mist and sunshine, and the bells had a merry note. There was more talk than usual in the streets and singing and laughter floated out from every window. . . . For the Queen was coming. . . . When? When? asked every voice. Soon, they said. Next month, perhaps. This summer. When she comes there will still be red roses to strew before her, and tall lilies to bow like courtiers beside the garden paths that her feet will tread. The leaves will be still green on the trees and the birds will be singing. There will be tapestries hung from every window and a great shouting in the streets as she passes by. . . . And surely to goodness, they said, becoming slightly irritated as the weeks went by with no date fixed, the Queen's Grace having already changed her mind about it seven times, the woman will come to a decision some time.

But the irritation was only fleeting and the mood of exaltation remained. For she meant so much to them; she was more than a woman, more even than a Queen; she stood to them for all the happiness and inspiration of this new age, for all its release and promise and newborn beauty. The older men and women remembered their country as it had been when she came to the throne: persecuted, humiliated, its only vital life the flame of martyrdom; they remembered how they had turned in despair to a young girl to save them. And she had saved them. She knew how to make herself the inspiration of men and women of good will. She was valiant, and they re-kindled their courage from hers. She was wise, and wisdom seemed to them once more a thing worth striving for. She had shown them how to save themselves and they saw in her the very figure of salvation.

And the young loved her too. She was witty and beautiful, she loved laughter and the singing voice, and all the fair and gracious things, the poetry and music and dancing that had wilted and died, lived again because she loved them. Perhaps the scholars did not understand, as they trooped to their verse readings on Sunday afternoons and learned to thrum the zither and the viol in their rooms, that their new understanding of beauty would not have been theirs had Gloriana not sat upon the throne of England. Perhaps the young girls did not realize, as they put on their farthingales of rose color and azure and buttercup-yellow, and danced the pavane at evening when the moon shone and the candles were lighted in the halls of their homes, that they would not have looked so fair and felt so happy had the Queen's Grace not possessed a hundred dresses and a foot as light as their own. They might not understand, perhaps, but they saw in her all beauty and all grace.

And the Oxford merchants were prosperous under Queen Bess. People were not so occupied with their troubles, these days, that they could not stop and gape in front of a shop window. The amount of gaping that was done now, compared with the gaping that had taken place under the late Queen, was phenomenal. And they did not only gape, they came inside and bought too, for a light heart always makes a heavy spender; it is not content, your light heart, with the unseen glitter of its own merriment, it must show it to the world in the outward symbols of flower-like draperies, dew-drops in the ears, and golden shoes that will tap out the heart's joy in the figures of the dance as radiantly as summer showers beating upon the thirsty earth. Is not the earth arrayed freshly in beauty every year, cry the light hearts, because of the joy that is in her? Then give us your silks and satins and velvets, your gold chains and pearl drops and ruby stomachers, your carpets and perfumes and spices, that we in this new age may be as fine as the old earth in her springtime garment. . . . And the merchants gave, receiving the equivalent in good hard round gold pieces, and saw the Queen's Grace as a veritable Midas who had let loose this sweet rich flood of gold that ran so obligingly into honest men's pockets. . . . And the young men, their sons, who left the city of Oxford to sail under the flag of the Merchant Adventurers that they might bring back from the lands beyond the sea the rubies and pearls, the carpets and perfumes and spices that the light of heart were calling for, may not have realized what an impetus to adventure had been given by the adventurousness, and the covetousness, of the Queen herself; they may not have realized, but when the capstan was manned, and the sea chanties were sung, and the great sails of their ship leaned for a moment against the sunset before she sailed over the rim of the world, their homing thoughts went back to her.

And the University saw in the Queen the patroness of the Guild of Learning. For her visit had a specific purpose. She was coming, so she had said, to assure all scholars of the royal favor. She herself loved learning; she could dispute in Greek or Latin with the best scholars of her day, going on so long that they were finally reduced to coma. She sympathized to the full with the learned men who were trying to bring back to the University its ancient glory. And so they loved her. She was the symbol of their aspirations.

There was something mystical in the quality of the love that awaited the Queen in these summer days. The people of the city were like Joyeuce on the morning of May-Day, standing at her window and wishing that what she so confusedly loved and longed for might take physical form and come to her. They too loved, and were aware that they loved not only learning, adventure, music, laughter and beauty, but the something behind and in all these for which they could find no name. It was an intense relief to pent-up emotion to see a human figure as the symbol of it.

2.

After changing her mind nine times in all the Queen finally chose for her visit the month of August, the month when the University term would be over and the scholars gone home to help with the harvest. The University tore its hair and the city made very little effort to hide its discreet delight in its discomfiture. But there was nothing to be done about it. The Queen's visit was to Oxford as a University, and the whole University must be there. The scholars must stay where they were, every man jack of them, and the harvest must go to the devil.

The scholars made no objection. Very little work was required of them, indeed very little work had been required of them since the beginning of term, for the atmosphere of the whole city was not at this time conducive to work, and they threw themselves into a perfect orgy of ecstatic preparations.

These reached fever-point at Christ Church, where the Queen's Grace and her Court were to be fed, lodged and entertained for six whole days. On her arrival there was to be a great service of thanksgiving. On one night there was to be a Latin play, on another night an English play, on a third night a stag hunt in the quadrangle; and the rest of the time would be spent in eating. As the great day drew near it would have been difficult to say who were busier, the scholars in the great hall feverishly rehearsing their plays or the cooks in the kitchen down below roasting droves of cattle whole before the great fire, baking scores of lark pies and creating a hundred elegant confections crowned with sugar sailing ships, doves and cupids. Upstairs and downstairs alike the sweat poured off earnest faces, for it was August and the weather was hot, and the tumult and the shouting were so severe that no man could make himself heard until he had yelled himself purple in the face and was dripping like a saturated sponge.

Backwards and forwards across the quadrangle there flowed neverending streams of University dignitaries, divines and city fathers attending the discussions that took place all day and most of the night in the Dean's study, driving the Dean so distracted that he had no doubt at all that the great day of the Queen's arrival would find him incarcerated in a hospital for the demented. . . . For the discussions that had to take place between town and University engendered a good deal of heat. . . . At what point was the town to be in charge of proceedings, and at what point the University? At what street corners were civic authorities to deliver English speeches, and at what corners University authorities Greek and Latin ones? And if the Queen's Grace replied to every speech in the language in which it was given, and at very great length—as was her erudite but distressing habit—how long would it take her to get from the North Gate to Christ Church? And if they did not know how long her progress would take, how could they fix the time for the thanksgiving service in the Cathedral? These questions were not settled easily, nor without discreet wrangling, the noise of which was at times so severe that it almost drowned the noise of all the choirs of Oxford practicing together in the Cathedral for the thanksgiving service; and this latter noise was at times very great indeed, tending as it did—authority being for the most part absent in the Deanery—to develop from anthems in

crescendo to pitched battles in the aisle between the choir of Christ
Church on one side and all the other choirs upon the other, refereed by
the choirmasters, who brought prayer-books down upon the heads of
the combatants with very little effect.

Heatherthwayte and Satan also had a good deal of refereeing to do,
for in these last days of preparation, when excitement ran dangerously
high, the battles between the Christ Church scholars and those of other
Colleges were many and invigorating, and the Fair Gate was a bloody
battlefield from early morning until the ringing of the curfew restored
peace at dewy eve. The rest of the University naturally took it hard that
the Queen's Grace had chosen Christ Church as her place of residence.
Why Christ Church, they demanded angrily at the Fair Gate. Other
Colleges were older and the gentlemen resident at them were better
supplied with brains, blue blood, wealth and theatrical talent. Were
these gentlemen to be denied participation in the theatricals and the
stag hunt in the quadrangle? What did Christ Church know about acting, they demanded to be told. Nothing, they shouted, before there was
time for an answer to be forthcoming. Was a Christ Church scholar ever
in at the kill, they yelled. No, they bellowed, and the whole lot of them
were a lousy, stiff-necked, ignorant lot of varlets whose presence upon
God's earth was a weariness unto the eye and a stench unto the nostrils.
. . . But at this point yet another fight would break out, and Heatherthwayte would have the greatest difficulty in cleaving a way through it
for a couple of aldermen on their way to the more genteel battleground
of the Deanery.

Yet in spite of the utmost vigilance on the part of Christ Church one
outsider managed to invade the sacred precincts of the College and in-
sert himself into that holy of holies, the hall, where rehearsals took place
behind locked doors, and the criminal was Walter Raleigh. He came by
the overhead route which led via garden walls to the roof of the Leighs'
house, and from that to a window that opened directly above the dais
in the hall. The window was high, but Walter Raleigh was always a man
of considerable resource; it was an easy matter to remove a few panes of
glass, and to fasten a rope round one of the Leigh chimneys, with its end

dangling through the aperture; and after that he had only to wait until
the actors below him had formed themselves into a group, whose surface
would be more yielding than the bare boards, to let himself down and
fall upon them with a blood-curdling screech.

They were in the middle of a rehearsal of the Latin play "Marcus
Geminus," a dreary piece written by Canon Calfhill, and Philip Sidney,
playing a long part befitting one whose beauty and whose Latin were
alike incomparable, was just working up to the peroration when the
blow fell. He sprawled sideways, hitting his beautiful nose against the
corner of the table. Other gentlemen fell in other directions, Raleigh
spread-eagled on top of them, and there was a wild confusion of arms
and legs, shouts and yells, which continued unabated until Raleigh had
picked them all up, dusted them down, shaken the senses into them and
explained the object of his visit. "I'm going to be in this," he said. "I'm a
better actor than any of you."

They gathered round him in an angry crowd, threatening, infuriated. Even Philip Sidney, always so courteous and gentle, lost his temper
and blazed and spluttered with the best, and Faithful, sitting in a corner with the prompt book, shouted "Shame!" as loudly as any. Raleigh
stood among them, laughing, head thrown back, one hand on his hip
and the other swinging his plumed purple cap. "Well, throw me out!" he
taunted them. "Throw me through the window I dropped from. Unlock
the door and pitch me down the stairs. We're twenty to one, aren't we?"
But somehow they couldn't. He dominated them, even as years later he
dominated the Spaniards at Cadiz when jeweled and plumed he stood
upon the poop of the "Warspite" blowing defiance at them through a
silver trumpet. They might hate him for his impudence, his conceit, and
his courage that was greater than theirs, but they could no more get
rid of him than they could have freed themselves from a wind that had
blown open the door and swooped upon them. He was as invincible as
a force of nature.

Finally he momentarily got rid of himself. "Look at Sidney's nose!"
he exclaimed. "And the Queen's Grace due in four days! An onion, for
the love of God!" And thrusting them away from him he sped down the

hall like lightning. unlocked the door and catapulted down the stairs to the great vaulted kitchen where the perspiring armies of cooks were roasting their oxen and baking their pies. "An onion! An onion!" he shouted as he went. "In the name of all the saints and devils, an onion for Master Sidney's nose!" And seizing it from the hand of the chief cook himself, who was just about to chop it up for use in a lark pie, he was back up the stairs again three steps at a time before anyone had had the presence of mind to lock the door on him, and anointing Sidney's swelling nose and blackening eye with the tender solicitude of a mother for her babe.

They could not but be mollified. Others of them presented their bruises for attention, and presently they found themselves consulting Raleigh about a few minor difficulties in theatrical production that had that morning cropped up. He dealt with them with ease. Then they got on to the topic of the major difficulty, the fact that the boy who was to play Arcite in the English play, "Palemon and Arcite," had got so knocked about in a fight at the Fair Gate that he was no longer fit to be seen. Raleigh dealt with this difficulty easily too. . . . He would be Arcite. . . . After that he took complete charge of everything and for the rest of the day rehearsals went with a swing and a verve that they had not known before. They hated Raleigh when he cursed them for their stupidity, they glowered when his will rode roughly over theirs, but when everything that he touched, the lines of the plays and their own minds and wills, glowed with fire as when a flame runs among stubble, there was nothing to do but yield themselves. Sidney's presence had given to their performance a moonlit beauty, but Raleigh's made of it a conflagration.

3.

In the Leighs' house also things hummed. The Leighs themselves had long since been distributed among the other Canons' households, and only Great-Aunt and Tinker remained, fed from the Deanery table at great inconvenience to everybody. Efforts had been made to dislodge Tinker but to everyone's surprise he refused to go with Diccon, Joseph,

Joyeuce and the dogs to Canon Calfhill's house across the quadrangle; every time he was carried there he slipped with sylphlike obstinacy from the nearest window and stalked back again to his own home, his tail carried in the perpendicular position, with twitching tip, and his paws placed one before the other with a delicate but disdainful precision that seemed to spurn the very ground that separated him from the place where he would be. . . . And they had thought that he loved Diccon. . . . It seemed he did not love Diccon. He had attached himself to Diccon in preference to other members of the household because Diccon's single-minded determination to have what he wanted had given them a spiritual affinity one with the other; but what he loved was the house, that particular city of mice whose lanes and byways he knew. Canon Calfhill's house might have other mice, but they were not his mice, and his lack of knowledge of the geography of their citadel gave to his soul a strange unease. . . . After the sixth return he was let alone. Cats had always been revered at Christ Church, and always would be, for had not Cardinal Wolsey himself adored them? A wrong-headed man in many ways, the great Cardinal, but he loved pussies. He always had a pussy on the Woolsack by his side.

So by night Tinker hunted his own mice in his own house, and by day he sat beside Great-Aunt at her window and watched the things that went on in the hall below. . . . And a great deal went on. . . . Great-Aunt had never been so happy. The infernal din of a door being knocked in the wall of the room next her, the noise made by carpenters and decorators, the smells of paint and unwashed workmen, troubled her not at all, for her nerves were of iron. What she loved was the spectacle of Life flowing past her window. Old as she was it would never be over for her while she had eyes to see and ears to hear. Curiosity was her great gift, and daily she thanked God for it.

The house was ready at last. The polished surface of it shone like glass, meadowsweet strewed the floors, the carved four-poster where the Queen would sleep had been gilded, and hung with peach-colored satin curtains embroidered with forget-me-nots, and upon it were spread fine sheets scented with lavender. Great bowls of flowers stood in shady corners and wherever the eye might turn it met priceless tapestries and pieces of furniture filched from all the finest houses in Oxford. Two days before that fixed for the Queen's arrival the Chancellor himself galloped over from Woodstock, where the Queen and Court were now in residence, to cast his eye over all the final arrangements, and could find no fault with it whatever. He and Great-Aunt met at the hall door, with every appearance of deep mutual respect, and she herself conducted him round the apartments, pointing out every improvement and decoration, and receiving his compliments upon them as though they were all the result of her own inspiration and hard labor. "Do not mention it, my Lord," she demurred with a gracious inclination of the head. "The supervision of these matters has been a great pleasure to me. . . . I shall, of course, myself receive the Queen's Grace upon her arrival at the house; my niece Joyeuce Leigh being too inexperienced a chit to carry off these high matters with becoming grace." Her eye, that had hitherto been of a melting tenderness, became fixed and steely in its regard and the Chancellor hastened to agree with her decision. . . . It seemed to him a thousand pities to defraud the little Mistress Joyeuce of an honor that was surely hers by right, but he had no time to waste in skirmishes with Great-Aunt; nor, remembering the outcome of the last one, did he think unseemly wrangles with elderly gentlewomen compatible with his dignity. . . . He bowed with a flourish and left her somewhat precipitately to attend a meeting at the Deanery, the frantic, heated, desperate, final discussion as to who should take precedence over whom when the great hour was upon them.

"Upon the Day of Judgment," whispered Dean Godwin to the Chancellor, "there will be quarreling as to who is to have the honor of helping the crowned heads to collect their bones."

4.

The great day dawned fine, with a slight August haze that promised a time of cloudless sunshine. As soon as the sun had pierced its way through, and gilded the towers and spires with a most royal beauty, the bells were ringing and the streets were awash with color; garlands of flowers festooned from house to house, bright silks and tapestries fluttering from every window, eager citizens and scholars surging everywhere dressed in their gayest garments, flowers in their arms, smiles on their faces, pent-up excitement bursting from them in jokes and banter and such echoing roars of laughter that it seemed the very cobblestones cried out for joy. The city was drenched in happiness. If there were any sad people in it, if any sick folk, they did not show themselves.... They knew better than to intrude upon this day.... For it was one of those days when everything conspires together to make men forgetful of their fate. With bells ringing, color ebbing and flowing, sunshine pouring upon them and the Queen of England drawing with every moment nearer to their city gates, there could be no thought of past or future. With such strange turbulent joy in their hearts it seemed that they already held in their hands all that they longed for; what they had lost was theirs again and the garlanded flowers and fluttering silks were their dreams come true.

The first great excitement of the day came in the early afternoon, when deputations from University and city rode out to meet the Queen. There was a burst of cheering as the Chancellor, Vice Chancellor and Heads of Houses, most good to look upon in full academic robes, passed up Cornmarket and under the North Gate towards the village of Wolvercote, on the road to Woodstock, where they would greet the Queen with a Latin address of welcome. After them rode the Mayor of Oxford and the city fathers, resplendent in scarlet robes and golden chains of office, who were to post themselves midway between Wolvercote and Oxford and greet Her Grace with three or more English addresses of welcome, according as Her Grace seemed to be fatigued, or not fatigued, by the Latin one that had preceded them. Hard at their heels pounded a horde of apprentices, self-appointed messengers who were to run backwards and forwards between Wolvercote and Oxford reporting the progress of events to those within the city.

When the last shouting urchin had disappeared into the dust and sunshine beyond the gate, there was nothing for the crowds within it to do but wait with what patience they could muster. All the way down Cornmarket, across Carfax and down Fish Street to the Fair Gate, the scholars stood in two long lines keeping the way clear for the Queen's processional passing, and packed behind them were the townspeople in their holiday clothes, swaying backwards and forwards in turbulent excitement, only kept from breaking across the street by the linked arms and the stalwart backs of the laughing scholars. But the time of waiting did not seem long. Every stray dog that ran up the route was cheered, every pretty girl who showed herself at an open window was loudly appraised, jokes flew backwards and forwards, laughter rang in the air, and all the time the bells were pealing that the Queen might hear their welcome as she came upon her way.

Then suddenly the apprentices, all in a glorious perspiration of haste and enthusiasm, came dashing one by one back through North Gate with reports of the progress. News flew through the waiting crowds, and little whispers and cries of excitement broke from them. Yes, she was coming, and the whole Court with her. Oh yes, she was beautiful beyond words, dressed all in white and blazing with jewels, carried in a wonderful litter roofed with cloth of gold. Yes, she had reached Wolvercote and the Provost of Oriel had read the Latin address of welcome. Oh yes, she had replied to it; in Latin, of course, and at very great length. The Court had seemed a little restive but she had taken no notice, working up to her peroration in a way that was a marvel to all present. . . . Now she had reached the Mayor and the city fathers. . . . There had been five speeches and they had pleased her mightily. Had she replied? Oh yes. Five times? No, only once, for the horse of my Lord of Warwick had turned very troublesome, and my Lord had sworn in unseemly fashion, and it had seemed best to all to proceed upon their way. . . . Now she was nearly here. . . . She was passing St. Giles' church. . . . Now she had stopped outside North Gate for Master Dell, a don of New College, to make another oration in Latin. . . . Now she was moving again. . . . She was so close that those inside the city walls could hear, through the pealing bells and the cheers, the trampling of horses and the jingling of their harness. . . . The procession was passing right under North Gate. . . . She

was here. . . . Vivat Regina! Vivat Regina! A great roar went up, a roar
that echoed through the streets like thunder, and all along the length of
the route the scholars fell upon their knees.

The procession passed very slowly, but even so there were so many
eyes blinded by tears, so many pounding hearts and throats choked with
excitement, that they all found it difficult afterwards to describe what
they had seen. The Chancellor, the Vice Chancellor and the Heads of
Houses had come first, they remembered, leading her in. . . . The Chancellor had looked magnificent, but they had hardly noticed him, for their
eyes were straining to see the golden litter that was borne behind him.

She sat upon it as though it were her throne, swaying easily to its
motion, smiling at them, her lovely long pale, hands clasped upon her
lap and her head held high. She looked beautiful, and so young. It was
hard to believe she was thirty-three years old; she was so slender that
she looked a girl still. They gazed in adoration at the face they had heard
described a hundred times but yet had never seen, not even in pictures:
a face of a beautiful oval shape, with a clear olive complexion, aquiline
nose, fine dark eyes under delicately arched eyebrows; a fine, proud,
shrewd face, the face of the woman who had saved England. Their eyes
were suddenly misted and they saw only dimly the jeweled coif set upon
masses of fair reddish piled-up hair, the beautiful ruff that framed her
face like the calyx of a flower, the white satin dress scintillating with
jewels and the slender feet in golden slippers set so firmly upon the
velvet cushion.

Then she had gone on her way and with a jingling of harness, a
breath of many perfumes, in a glimmering kaleidoscope of color, the
Court was passing by. So many lovely ladies, beruffed and jeweled, sitting their horses with lovely ease, their long skirts sweeping almost to
the ground, their laughing faces turned this way and that to greet the
smiling scholars; so many magnificent gentlemen riding by, reining in
spirited horses with a clatter of hoofs upon the cobbles, plumed hats
raised in greeting, bold eyes roving up to the windows to exchange
twinkling glances with the pretty maidens gathered there. A few knowledgeable people in the crowd pointed out one and another, whispering

their names in awed tones. "The Spanish Ambassador. Sir William Cecil. My Lord of Warwick, brother of the Chancellor. My Lord of Oxford, married to Sir William's daughter, though he is but sixteen years of age. My Lord of Rutland." The cavalcade swept by, the Mayor and city fathers bringing up the rear, and the crowd came tumbling at their heels to hear what they could of the Greek oration at Carfax.

This was delivered by Canon Lawrence, the Regius Professor. It was very long and very learned and delighted the Queen greatly; she would have done her poor best to reply to it, she told Canon Lawrence later, but looking about her she saw that the distress of her illiterate Court was by this time very great, and in mercy she forbore. Then on again to the Fair Gate where Master Kingsmill, the University Orator, delivered a speech which it had taken him the best part of two days and nights to prepare and nearly as long to deliver. . . . . But yet, at the end of it, the Queen most unaccountably turned testy. "You would have done well had you had good matter," she said, and turned abruptly away from him that the Chancellor and Dean Godwin might help her from her litter.

But she was all smiles again when she stood beneath the Fair Gate and saw the great quadrangle stretching before her wide and peaceful after the turmoil in the streets, with the spire of the Cathedral splendid against the blue sky and the buildings her father had loved standing beneath it, warm and serene in the sun. Towards her over the green grass came four doctors in their scarlet robes, holding a canopy under which she was to walk to the Cathedral. "It is a fair sight," she said to Dean Godwin. "And it is a fair house, this house of Christ that my father founded. I am glad to be here with you all."

And they were glad to have her. The Christ Church scholars, coming pelting back from their posts in the streets, ran to line the path that led across the quadrangle and through the cloisters to the Cathedral door, and with them stood all the other people of Christ Church, the dons and servitors, the Canons' wives and families. Joyeuce was there in her green frock, with Nicolas beside her, and Grace and Faithful stood together keeping a firm hold of Joseph and Diccon, who pranced and curvetted like puppies on the leash. The twins, in new daffodil-yellow dresses, curtseyed as Joyeuce had taught them, but unfortunately, owing to their weight and excitement, capsized at the critical moment, and Will and Thomas bowed so low that their tow-colored shocks of hair nearly touched the grass. The Queen paused for a moment as she passed this group, laughing at the bows and curtseys, returning with humor the impudent unblinking green stare with which Diccon fixed her. "The greeting of little poppets," she said to one of the scarlet-robed doctors who carried her canopy—it happened to be Canon Leigh—"gives to any arrival the sense of home-coming."

She had unerringly struck the right note for her visit— "Homecoming." The whispered word flew from one to another and was gloated over. This was the house that her father had founded and she had come home to it. They were her very own household. She belonged to them as she did not belong to other, inferior Colleges. When the procession had passed into the cloisters they all came tumbling after, calling out to each other, laughing and exuberant as they would not have dared to be but for that whispered intimate word; and over their heads the bells, Hautclere, Douce, Clement, Austin, Marie, Gabriel and John, rang out in a jubilation greater than any they had known since they had come from Oseney Abbey to live in the tower of Christ Church.

When they had trembled into silence those who could not get into the Cathedral stood outside in the cloisters, listening to the solemn intoning of the long prayers, to the singing of the anthem to the accompaniment of cornets, and then to the intoning of more and longer prayers, until the first gold of evening stole into the sky and the coolness of it fell upon them like a benediction. . . . The first day was over. . . . It had gone well.

5.

Everything continued to go well. The Queen, except for the one regrettable lapse when Master Kingsmill's oration at the Fair Gate had just for the moment turned her testy, was so gracious and so charming that every heart in Christ Church was bound to her in love forever.

Everything seemed to please her. Never, she said, had she tasted such delicious food as that cooked at Christ Church, nor heard such sweet music as was played while she consumed the same, dining in state each day upon the dais in Christ Church hall. She thought her lodgings charming, and expressed herself as much touched that a door should have been made from the house to the hall for her convenience.... She was ravished, so she said, by the song that Nicolas sang beneath her window on the night of her arrival. She would never forget him, she said, looking down at him where he stood below her in the shadows of the garden. He was a comely lad, such as her heart loved, and one day he should ask of her what he wanted. She took a rose from her dress— she always had a flower of a knot of ribbons easily detachable upon the bodice of it, for it was by such little ruses that she bound men to her for life—and tossed it to him before she drew back again behind her curtains, leaving him to slip away through the apple trees to the garden gate in a tremor of ecstasy and excitement.... She even vowed she had taken a fancy to Great-Aunt; and spoke truly, for she found the old lady's gossip highly entertaining and in the evenings would summon her to her presence to hear her malicious comments upon the life and character of those learned men who had that day delivered orations before the Queen.... For the orations continued.... Though she lodged at Christ Church, and spent most of her evenings there, the Queen did not neglect other Colleges. She heard orations at them all, and on three days attended disputations at St. Mary's church, which on the last day went on so long, and aroused the Queen's interest so keenly, that the disputants "tired the sun with talking and sent him down the sky," so that candles had to be set burning round the church.

There, were, of course, as was inevitable, a few minor disappointments and disasters. The scholars found it hard to bear that on the day of the play "Marcus Geminus" the Queen should declare herself too exhausted by Latin orations delivered in the afternoon to attend a Latin play in the evening. But the Court came, and applauded loudly, and the Spanish Ambassador gave such a glowing account of the scholars' acting to the Queen afterwards that she swore with vexation to think what she

had missed, and vowed that she would lose no more sport thereafter. . . .
Nor did she. . . . She attended the performance of the English play, "Pala-
mon and Arcite," in great magnificence, diamonds flashing, silks swirling,
jeweled head held high, and enjoyed it enormously. Nor was she in the
least put out when the stage collapsed, killing three scholars and injur-
ing five more. These little things, she said to the profusely apologizing
Dean, will occur at juvenile performances, and we must not dishearten
the young ones by paying too much attention to slight mishaps.

But nothing went wrong at the miniature stag hunt in the quadrangle, which took place by moonlight, and provided the scholars with
the major thrill of the Queen's visit. The poor stag, captured alive at
Cumnor and conveyed to Oxford with great fatigue to itself and everybody, was let loose at the Fair Gate and fled across the quadrangle like
a stag out of a fairy tale, its great branched antlers shining like silver
and its slender body the color of pearl in the light of the moon. After it
came the hounds, baying wildly, and then a few members of the Court
and the more sporting of the dons, mounted on galloping horses, with
white plumes in their hats and white roses fastened in their doublets. . . .
The scholars, upon this occasion, were severely confined to the upper
stories, where they leaned out of the windows shouting and yelling in
such wild excitement that the Queen, watching with the Chancellor, declared she could scarcely enjoy the scene for fear they should all fall out.
. . . Round and round the quadrangle fled the fairy-tale stag of silver and
pearl, round and round went the shadowy shapes of the baying hounds,
round and round the galloping huntsmen; until the poor stag saw the
thicket of trees at the northern side of the quadrangle, fled to it and met
its death with its silver horns entangled in a hawthorn bush, the huntsmen crashing round it in the undergrowth and the dogs leaping from
the shadows at its throat. . . . The Queen, as she turned away, vowed she
was surprised, though of course deeply thankful to the mercy of God,
to find it was the only casualty.

Such had been the excitement that she was tired that night, and glad
to go to bed in the quiet room looking across the garden to the moonlit
trees of the Meadows.

CHAPTER XVI

PATRIOTISM

There were hills which garnished their proud heights with stately trees: humble vallies, whose base estate seemed comforted with the refreshment of silver rivers: meadows enameled with all sorts of eye-pleasing flowers: thickets, which being lined with most pleasant shade were witnessed so too by the cheerful disposition of many well-tuned birds; each pasture stored with sheep, feeding with sober security, while the pretty lambs with bleating outcry craved the dam's comfort: here a shepherd's boy piping, as though he should never be old: there a young shepherdess knitting, and withal singing; and it seemed that her voice comforted her hands to work and her hands kept time to her voice-music. As for the houses of the country they were built of fair and strong stone, not affecting so much any extraordinary kind of fineness as an honorable representing of a firm stateliness. The backside of the house was a place cunningly set with trees of the most taste-pleasing fruits, and new beds of flowers, which being under the trees, the trees were to them a pavilion, and they to the trees a mosaical floor.

THE ARCADIA.   PHILIP SIDNEY.

1.

THE next afternoon, the last day of her stay in Oxford, the Queen attended archery practice in Beaumont Fields.

Under a blazing blue sky scholars and citizens alike poured out of North Gate, swung to their left along the narrow lane beside the city wall, then to their right into Beaumont Fields. The scholars who carried bows, and who were to shoot before the Queen, were all very eager and excited, and a little strained, for this was a very great occasion. Archery was still tremendously important, even though the hand-gun was now taking the place of the longbow in modern warfare. You were no true Englishman if you could not shoot a straight arrow from your bow, and to be watched by the Queen of England while you tried to do it was enough to turn the hottest blood to water and the stoutest heart to mere pulp. Even Nicolas was flustered as he made his way out of North Gate, with Faithful behind him carrying his bow and arrows, and Philip Sidney and Walter Raleigh, whom they overtook in the crowd at the gate of the Fields, had had their usual gravity and confidence so overturned that they were snapping and snarling at those who got in their way quite like the lesser brethren.

But once in the Fields the beauty of the place quieted them all, for this was a spot of earth that everyone adored, especially on a sunshiny day in summer. Whichever way you looked, as you stood in the Fields, you felt glad to be alive. To the south, crowning a little hill, were the ruins of Beaumont Palace, the royal house built by Henry the First the scholar king, where Henry the Second had lived sometimes when he loved Rosamond, where his son Richard Coeur de Lion had been born, and where later the Carmelites had had their home. The same tempest of destruction that had dispossessed the monks had swept away the old palace too; the walls that had sheltered kings had been pulled down and sold as stone for fresh buildings; there was nothing left of it now but the foundations, and nothing left of the garden but a riot of roses and honey-suckle climbing over the old stones and the fruit trees that the monks had planted. . . . These were now the only fair ladies who inhabited the Fair Mount, and the only musicians who sang there were the singing birds.

But one looked north over the same stretch of country that had de-lighted the eyes of kings and queens and courtiers, a stretch of country that in curve and color was like a piece of music composed by a happy man. Its rhythm was peace and its motif was yet more peace. There was neither grandeur nor the shock of contrast, but lazy curves that rose and fell like a contented sea, and misted colors that melted one into the other imperceptibly. To the west the woods of Rats and Mice Hill were a heavy deep green against the blue of the sky, and to the east the Forest of Shotover echoed their color, while between them a plain of green and tawny meadows and harvest fields stretched away into the distance, clumps of green willows marking the windings of river and streams. Across this plain meandered the highways to Woodstock and Banbury, their peace disturbed by nothing but an occasional lumbering cart or lazily trotting horseman.

But at the butts under the palace wall there was a scene of eager activity. The seats of the spectators stretched the length of the wall, with a raised dais for the Queen in the center, and were already full; dons and scholars, stout merchants and their wives, and apprentices all in their gayest clothes. They were an audience whose comments never lacked ribaldry or point and under their scrutiny the groups of archers, waiting at each end of the butts for the arrival of the Queen, shifted nervously from foot to foot.

As each man's turn came he had to shoot from first one end and then the other, alternately, so that he should not get set in one position. In this continual flying of arrows in different directions there was a certain amount of danger, but according to the regulations if a man cried our "Fast!" before he shot he was not held responsible for the injury or death of anyone he might wound or kill. . . . The accident was unfortunate but quite in order. . . . A really expert English bowman could shoot ten arrows in a minute, with a range of two hundred yards, and Henry the Eighth had ordained that no person who had reached the age of twenty-four should shoot at any mark at less than two hundred and twenty yards distant.

So two hundred and twenty yards was the distance between the two wooden discs set up at either end of the space by the palace wall. Robin Hood, of course, "clave the wand in two" from a distance of four hundred yards, but then Robin was a finer bowman than any man living now in the city of Oxford.

Faithful, having handed his bow and arrows to Nicolas, found a vacant corner at the end of one of the seats and sat there, warm and cozy in the sun, glad to sit still and digest his dinner in peace and quiet while he watched the gay scene, glad for once in a way that his own archery was at present such a danger to the community that it could only be practiced in private, for lookers on, he thought, can sometimes catch more of the thrill of a great occasion than those taking part in it.

In the distance a fanfare of trumpets sounded. The Queen was leaving Saint John's, the beautiful College built in a grove of elm trees outside the city wall, where she had that morning been entertained and feasted by its dons. The sound of the cheering grew louder as she came nearer, growing into a roar as the royal party came into the Fields and mounted the steps to the dais. . . . But the groups of waiting archers did not cheer, for their tongues stuck most distressingly to the roofs of their mouths. They straightened themselves, gripped their bows with tense fingers and swallowed hard.

The dons of Saint John's College had the post of honor today and sat grouped around the Queen. The Chancellor was upon her right and with a thrill of delight Faithful saw her beckon to Edmund Campion, his friend of May Morning, and make him sit upon her left. They had all learned that he was in high favor with her. He had already made two orations before her, in the first one proving to her entire satisfaction that the sea is constantly blown out with vapors, like boiling water in a pot, and in the second speaking extempore on the subject of "Fire" with such eloquence that she vowed he was the finest scholar of them all.

Yet seeing those three radiant figures, the Queen and the courtier and the scholar, laughing and talking together, and remembering the Chapel beneath the Mitre Inn, Faithful felt a sudden pang of apprehensive misery. In the bright sunshine there seemed to be shadows about, as though dark wings swept overhead and brushed those three figures in passing. But they seemed unaware of them. They could not foresee the years ahead, and the room in Leicester's London house where they would meet again; an elderly heart-sick woman with a painted face and a red wig, a grizzled weary courtier and a Jesuit with the filth of the dungeon upon him, brought there on his way from prison to the scaffold that they might plead with him to save himself. They were unaware. They were in the sunshine of life and the darkness of night ahead was not remembered. But Faithful, because at the moment he had no one to talk to, was suddenly aware of it. He was afraid. It was suddenly dreadful to him that we do not know to what we travel; only that the way there is like an increasingly darkening tunnel. At the heart of it the blackness is like pitch. We must pass through it, there is no escape, and there is no one to come back and tell us what it is like in that darkness, or what it is like beyond.

The trumpet sounded again, the murmur of voices died away into silence, and Faithful's sudden depression fell away from him like a black cloak as the figure of a straight young archer stepped forward, brilliant in sunshine, his body laid on his great bow, drawing not with the strength of the arm but with the strength of the body, as Englishmen were taught to do.

As one after the other the figures of the archers took their posts, at the sound of the drawn bowstrings and the sight of the arrows speeding through the air, a queer exultation seized hold of the whole company, consciousness was heightened and imagination took wing. For if it was true that the voice of France could be heard in the sound of the trumpets, that preserved the echoes of the horn of Roland, it was equally true that the voice of England was heard in the music of archery, in the humming of the bowstrings, that was like the sound of a plucked harp, and the singing of the arrows in the air. It was a music that was full of memories: of Crécy and the Black Prince, of Agincourt and Harry the Fifth. And not only their music but the bows and arrows themselves carried one back through time; the bows nearly as tall as a man, made of the wood of English yew trees, the descendants of the sacred yews that the Druids had planted round their holy places before the Romans came, the bowstrings of flax from English fields, and the arrows of birch wood feathered from the wings of gray geese. Over and over again, in battle after battle, had those gray geese, flying out from forests of bent yew, carried death upon their wings. For only Englishmen could use the longbow. Foreigners could never get the knack of it. It was something that Englishmen, yeomen and gentry alike, had to practice from their boyhood up in the butts that stretched behind every village churchyard, sweating over it while the old churchyard yews that had made the bows leaned over the wall to watch, and the gray geese that had feathered the arrows cackled approval up and down the village street. Agincourt had been won by the whole of England, by the yeomen, the yew trees, the gray geese and the fields of flax. The young archer who dazzled Faithful's eyes as he stood in the sunshine was a symbolic figure to the whole of that excited crowd. They thrilled with pride as they looked at him, but they were sad too. He stood for the fast-dying days when a man fighting for his country could feel himself something of an artist and not solely a butcher, and for a voice of England that would soon be stilled.... When the last archer had sped the last arrow to its mark a sigh went up from Beaumont Fields, and then a silence before the trumpets spoke again and the Queen stepped down from her dais.

2.

"Let's get away from here," said Philip Sidney to Faithful; "away from the crowds and out into the country."

The ordeal was over and he had done his part well, but now he was suffering from reaction. He hated the crowds and the shouting. The sound of the trumpets and the music of the longbows had stirred the depths in him. He wanted to get away where it was quiet.

Faithful, as became a good servitor, shouldered Philip's bow good-humoredly, though it was a good deal taller than he was and carrying it gave him a crick in the neck, and lolloped at his friend's heels like an obedient dog. He was, he had noticed, frequently treated as a faithful dog. People who did not exactly want company, but yet wanted that invisible companion who seems to sit enthroned in our minds, and to whom we talk in moments of emotion, to take some visible form would often choose either Faithful or a dog to accompany them on their walks abroad. In both they would find an unobtrusive admiration which helped them to express their thoughts without either fear or shame.

Philip went straight to a place that he knew of, where a lazy stream meandered through meadows where in early summer the grass was as high as little children. It was short now, and had no movement or mur-mur to give back to the wind as it rolled away into the distance to lose it-self in the blue hills and woods that shut in the valley. The afternoon was utterly and completely still. They could see the silver ribbon of the river

winding its way from Oxford past Binsey and the holy well to Godstow.
"Look!" said Philip, pointing to some old gray walls among the trees.
"From here you can see the ruins of Godstow Nunnery. It's odd, isn't
it, to sit here between Beaumont Palace, where Henry the Second lived
sometimes, and Godstow Nunnery where his Rose of the World hid
herself. I wonder how often he sat here, where we are sitting now, after
she had become a nun and he could not see her any more, and looked
at the gray walls that kept him out."

They were silent, thinking of that famous love story, so wrapped
up in legend now that it was hard to disentangle truth from falsehood.

Rosamond had lived at Woodstock, and Henry had met her one day
when he was out riding his white horse in the springtime in the flowery
fields that surrounded his royal palace, fields so lovely that they were like
the fields of heaven. Rosamond came walking towards him through the
buttercups and daisies and cuckoo flowers, and she was so freshly and
radiantly lovely that she seemed to the King the spirit of beauty itself.
The singing of the birds, that rang all about them in the blue air, the
green flames that burned in the beech trees, and the swaying whispering mass of the thousand flowers and grasses that clothed the meadows
seemed to be no more than a garment for the incomparable beauty of
the girl who moved in their midst.

The King was a young man who had been married since his boyhood to Eleanor, the divorced wife of the King of France, a woman so
evil that her husband's life seemed to him to have been poisoned on the
day he married her. She hated him, and taught his children to hate him.
Only in regarding the great beauty of the land that was his kingdom
could he find release from misery.

And now it seemed to him, as he jumped from his horse and gazed
astounded at the girl who came towards him, that this fair land was giving him its very spirit. It was as though the fields and the trees and the
bird song lifted her up and held her towards him, as merciful hands
cup themselves to carry water to a thirsty man. He was bewildered by
the wonder of it. Though he was the King of England he fell upon his
knees before Rosamond, holding her desperately by the skirts of her

long green gown, imploring her to stay as she was, a warm breathing comforting creature who could be touched and held, not a wraith who would float away through the tree trunks when night came on, and the first stars signaled from their watch towers that the sun was set.

What could poor Rosamond do? Held by the compelling hands of a young and comely King, while the birds sang and the flowers shivered in ecstasy under the touch of the spring wind, she seemed to herself drained of all strength. For a moment she shook her head in bewilderment, then put her own hands caressingly over the hands that held her. . . . So he took her home with him, and when the stars signaled warningly, and all good birds and maidens and children hied them home, she did not look at them; she looked only upon her lover.

In the garden of Woodstock Palace there was a labyrinth and at the heart of it the King made a bower all overgrown with roses for his Rose of the World. Only he and one of his friends knew the secret of the labyrinth, but they taught it to Rosamond that she might be able to hide herself there if any danger threatened when Henry was away from her.

He was often away from her, for there was war across the sea and he must be often fighting in France. One summer day Rosamond sat at her embroidery near the entrance to the labyrinth. The sun was warm and the red roses and white lilies were in bloom and she sang as she worked, for she had news that soon her lover would be home again. There was no fear in her heart, only a deep and tranquil happiness that she, of all women in the world, should be the one to bring joy and comfort to the King.

Suddenly from the palace the trumpets sounded, and she lifted her head, for they rang out in that way only when one of royal blood visited the palace. But still she was not afraid, for Queen Eleanor never came to Woodstock, and she was sure that no one could have been so cruel as to betray the King's secret to her. Was it Henry himself? Had he come earlier than he had promised? She jumped up in joy, still holding the end of a long thread of embroidery silk that she had been unwinding from its ball when the trumpets sounded, and she would have started to run to the palace had she not seen the bright figure of a little page coming pelting towards her through the trees, his face as white as the white lilies that grew beside the entrance to the labyrinth.

"Hide, Rosamond!" he gasped. "Someone has betrayed you and the Queen is here!" Then he turned and doubled back again, quick as a darting dragonfly, terrified that someone at the palace had seen the way he came.

Instantly, as quick in her flight as he was, Rosamond ran through the mazes of the labyrinth; but in her terror she still held the end of embroidery silk and the ball unrolled behind her as she ran, showing the windings of the maze.

At the heart of the labyrinth, crouching in the bower of roses, Queen Eleanor found her. That evil lady was not a woman who wasted time. In one hand she carried a bowl of poison and in the other a dagger, and coming instantly to the point without undue expenditure of words she briefly offered Rosamond her choice. Rosamond, also coming to the point after only a brief interval of desperate pleading, chose the poison, and died there, and the roses dropped their petals pitifully upon the maiden who was fairer than they.

That was one version of the story, but there was another, less picturesque but more likely, that related how Rosamond of her own will cut herself adrift from the King.

Wandering among the roses in the Woodstock garden at evening, after the sun had set, she wondered what would be the end of it all. What could be the end of it for Henry, what for her? Could there be any outcome for Henry except dishonor and bewilderment, any for her but shame and torment that her name should have tarnished his? She looked up at the quiet evening sky where the first stars were signaling to the world, "Go home," and then she looked about her at all the myriad of God's creatures who had listened to that command. Most of them were safely home already. There were no butterflies or little birds about now; she could picture them safely asleep in their own particular nooks and crannies, wings folded and heads tucked under wings. Many of the flowers were tightly closed, their golden hearts and amber honey drops safe and inviolate behind the shut doors of their petals. Over in the

village of Woodstock lights sprang out behind windows, telling of labor-
ers home from the fields and little children safely cradled for the night.
Above her head flapped a party of rooks, flying home to the rookery
in the great park beyond the garden. All these creatures had their own
appointed places, and however far they might have wandered through
the day when the stars signaled from their watch towers that the night
had come they turned always homeward.

But Rosamond, with a sickening stab at her heart, remembered that
she had no home. One of the twinkling lights, over there in Woodstock,
shone out from the window of the house where once she had lived;
but its door was shut against her now; though she came only of yeoman stock her people were people who had their honor, and she had
disgraced them. Once before the stars had told her to go home, but she
had not gone. Now it was too late.

What should she do? Standing there in despair on the garden path,
with her knuckles pressed into her eyes, she heard a harsh rhythmical sound, a sound that though ugly always delighted her. The swans!
They came sometimes by day to visit the lake in the park, but at night
they always flew back again to that particular reach of the river that
was their home; it was at Godstow, Henry had told her, at Godstow
where the nunnery was.

She gazed up at them in delight. They were flying in perfect formation, first one alone, then two more, then three, and so high up in the sky
that the last gleam of sunset caught them and bathed their snowy feathers in a light that seemed to shine right out from Paradise. Rosamond
thought that never in her life had she seen a sight so radiantly pure and
lovely; and they were going home to Godstow, where the nunnery was.

Then she knew what she must do. There were more homes in the
world than one. Though the door of an earthly home might be shut
against her there were other doors that never denied the knocking of
the sinner who repented. She did not stop to go indoors and change the
white silk dress that she wore for one more suited for a journey, she did
not even wait to say farewell to those in the palace who had been good
to her, she ran at once to the stableyard and wrenched at the stable door

in a passion of eagerness. It was unlocked, for the grooms were careless when their master was away, and she went in and found her white horse that Henry had given her, the same white horse that he had been riding that day in the meadows when he found her. She saddled him quickly and easily, for Rosamond was no fine lady but a strong country girl who could sweep a room or groom a horse with the best, and then she led him out, mounted him and turned towards Godstow.

She rode quickly through the woods and meadows, for she was fearful that her courage and resolution might falter and she turn back again, but as she rode she looked about her, for she knew she was looking her last upon the world she loved; from henceforth she would see it only through the windows of a nunnery. Though the darkness was gathering she could still see the pale faces of the wild roses scattered over the hedgerows, and the branches of the trees sweeping up against the stars, and she gazed at them as though she were about to be smitten with perpetual blindness. From under her horse's feet there came up to her the scent of wet grass and of those pungent herbal plants that grow near water, and she drew in great breaths of it as though her lungs labored. She pressed her knees tightly against her horse, for this was the last time that she would feel the ripple of horseflesh beneath them.

When she came to the ford, and saw across the gleaming river the gray walls of the nunnery rising out of the reeds and rushes on the other side, her courage nearly failed her. She reined in her horse and sat there trembling, her eyes hot and burning and her heart beating so that it nearly choked her. For, God in heaven, how she loved life! She was not a woman born to kneel all her days upon a cold stone floor, telling the beads of a rosary; she had a gay heart made for laughter and an adventurous spirit that craved its fill of love and danger. In her pride she had felt sometimes that life was not long enough for all she wanted to do, or the world packed full enough of the marvels that she wanted to see before she died. In her dreams she had often pictured herself, Eleanor being dead by some happy mischance, as Queen of England, her passionate love no longer hidden and shamed but crowned with honor in the sight of the world. She had imagined the heaven it would be to be Henry's wife, living with him in his

great house by the river in London town, or over there in the palace of the
Fair Mount at Oxford; or perhaps going with him to France and watching
the English bowmen march out to fight the French, and riding as near as
she dared to the battle to hear the music of the plucked bowstrings and
the singing of the arrows in the air. . . . But Eleanor was not dead, nor
likely to be, for like all nasty people she was bound to live long. . . . And
Rosamond was only a yeoman's daughter. She would never be Queen of
England. She would never, while she lived free in the world, bring Henry
anything but trouble. Why could she not be a man, able to serve her king
and country with her bow and arrows, her strong body laid upon her bow
and her fingers like steel to pluck its music? Why must she be a woman,
her only way of service this of sacrifice and death? In her anguish she
cried out aloud, startling the white swans who were already sleeping in
the rushes by the river, then set her horse at the ford.

The river was running high and the icy water crept up to her knees,
chilling her to the bone. Numbed and silent now she looked stupidly at
the skirts of her white dress floating out around her like the plumage of
a bird, and at the little white water daisies that starred the water. Then
the cold seemed to creep up to her heart and she seemed not to see or
feel anything any more.

The nuns looked at each other, startled, when they heard the knocking at the nunnery door. They were up late that evening, praying in the
cold chapel for that Scarlet Woman, that shameless Woodstock girl who
was the troubler of the King's peace and a disgrace to this fair valley
where they lived. The knocking came so pat upon their thoughts of sin
and shame that it frightened them. They went all together to open the
door, not leaving the round-eyed young portress to face alone the devils
who might be outside.

They opened in fear and trembling, recoiling in astonishment at
sight of the pale-faced girl with the golden hair who stood outside. In her
white dress in the moonlight, one hand holding the mane of her white
horse and the other stretched out to them as though she pleaded for
alms, she looked like a visitant from another world, like a water nymph
risen from the river or the soul of a white swan.

"Or one of the flowers from the heavenly meadows," whispered Sister Ursula the little portress. "She is so white; like one of the lilies of Our Lady."

"Take me in, good sisters," cried Rosamond. "Of your charity give refuge to the sinner that repenteth."

"Who are you, who come knocking here after the night has fallen?" demanded the Abbess sternly. "Riding alone upon horseback with a jeweled circlet on your head and the silks of a queen upon your body. Such behaviour is not seemly in a young woman. Who are you?"

"Rosamond of Woodstock," said Rosamond, but she did not bow her head and she looked at the Abbess calmly and with courage. For suddenly she was proud. They might have left much, these other women who had renounced the world, but they had not sacrificed the love of a king and the silks and jewels of a queen.

The other nuns cried out in horror, but the Abbess did not flinch. "Come in, Rosamond," she said quietly. "We have prayed for you tonight, and God has answered our prayer. Come in, my child, to your home."

Rosamond turned back once, to kiss her white horse on his forehead, then she pushed him gently away into the night, that he might find his way back to Woodstock, and stepped through the doorway into the cold shadows of the nunnery.

But they did not hold her for long. She stayed there for a few years, kneeling hour after hour upon the stone floor of the chapel, telling her beads and praying for King Henry and for the fair land of England that she loved, seeing him more and more as the symbol of it and pleading that her sacrifice of all she loved might by the mercy of God give increase of strength to its beauty; greater courage to the man, a deeper green to the grass and a new sparkle to the winding streams that comforted the valleys; an arrogant prayer, she sometimes feared, but one that was unceasing in her heart and on her lips.

And then she died; died as a wild bird will die who is shut in too small a cage. The nuns mourned for her as though she had been the dearest child of each of them, and buried her in the meadows near the river, those meadows where in the summer the grass was as high as

little children and as full of flowers as the fields of heaven. A gray stone
marked her grave, and the nuns planted roses at the head and the foot
and hung it with silken draperies and embroideries, as though it were
the tomb of a queen.

The years passed, those who had loved Rosamond died, and only
the roses decked the grave. Centuries passed and the gray stone itself
was lost beneath the sea of flowers and grass that flowed over it. Then
no man knew where Rosamond's body lay buried; though perhaps the
swallows knew, as they dipped and darted beside the river, and the white
swans who had once led her home, and the spirit of beauty that lived in
that valley and had absorbed her spirit into its own.

People wondered sometimes if the King had ever seen her again.
They liked to think that the Abbess had allowed him to see her as she lay
dead, dressed in her penitent's dress, with her fair hair hidden under the
nun's coif. Master Samuel Daniel, who lived when Elizabeth was Queen
and Beaumont Palace and Godstow Nunnery were in ruins, wrote in fair
words the thoughts that might have been Henry's as he stood beside the
bier before the altar in the nunnery chapel.

> Pitiful mouth, saith he, that living gavest
> The sweetest comfort that my soul could wish,
> O! be it lawful now, that dead thou havest
> This sorrowing farewell of a dying kiss;
> And you, fair eyes, containers of my bliss,
> Motives of love, born to be matched never,
> Entombed in your sweet circles, sleep forever.
>
> Ah, how methinks I see death dallying seeks
> To entertain itself in love's sweet place;
> Decayed roses of discolored cheeks
> Do yet retain dear notes of former grace;
> And ugly death sits fair within her face,
> Sweet remnants resting of vermilion red,
> That death itself doubts whether she be dead.

Wonder of beauty, O! receive these plaints,
These obsequies, the last that I shall make thee;
For lo! my soul that now already faints
(That loved thee living, dead will not forsake thee)
Hastens her speedy course to overtake thee.
I'll meet my death, and free myself thereby,
For, ah! what can he do that cannot die?

But death did not come to him quite as soon as he wanted it. He governed the country he loved for thirty-five years, one of the best kings and most unhappy men who ever sat upon the throne of England. He was fifty-seven years old before he at last lay dead in the Abbey Church of Fontevraud, deserted by his children and robbed by his servants, his dead body stripped of his royal robes and jewels so that he lay on his bier before the altar as simply and penitentially as Rosamond had done when she lay in the nunnery chapel.

3.

"I expect this bit of earth looked much the same to them as it does to us now," said Philip suddenly, "The same river winding through the valley, with the swallows flying beside it, the same fields and the same blue hills. I expect in the end Henry came to love it as much as he loved the woman shut up in the nunnery; perhaps when she died he felt that her spirit had passed into it; and I expect he found rest for his heartache looking at it. . . . One does find peace looking out on the world and recounting its wonders to oneself. . . . That is if one can find the words."

He broke off in sudden desperation and Faithful inquired with exquisite tact and sympathy, "Is a poem not going well?" He knew these writers—Giles had been another of them—and the absurd importance that they attached to their literary efforts. . . . Should a poem go badly there was no use in living any longer, but the right word chased and caught flung open the gates of heaven.

Yet on the whole he thanked his stars he was no poet. The beauty of the world was to Philip his artist's material; he must always be catching hold of it, re-arranging it, trying to fit the stars and the visiting moon into a lyric and to imprison the glory of the sun in a sonnet. And always the elusiveness of everything seemed to torture him; the sunshine that would not stay in the sonnet, the tail of the comet that got cut off when it was jammed into a lyric, the water that ran away to the sea, the life that escaped from the bodies of birds and butterflies and left behind it a handful of dust to be stamped into the earth. But Faithful, a humble scholar, need not worry either over the uses of beauty or its impermanence. He could just turn it over and over like a picture book and enjoy it.

Philip groaned.

"Perhaps," said Faithful gently, "if you read the poem to me you might see what was wrong with it."

"I might," said Philip doubtfully. "It is about love of England. It seemed all right this morning but now, after archery practice before the Queen, I'm not so sure."

"Try it on me," encouraged Faithful. The phrase "try it on the dog" was not in fashion yet, or he would have felt it to be one that fitted the case.

Philip sighed, fished up his manuscript from down his back, and read.

Who hath his fancy pleased
With fruits of happy sight,
Let here his eyes be raised
On nature's sweetest light;
A light which doth dissever
And yet unite the eyes;
A light which, dying never,
Is cause the looker dies.

She never dies, but lasteth
In life of lover's heart;
He ever dies that wasteth
In love his chiefest part.
Thus is her life still guarded
In never-dying faith;
Thus is his death rewarded,
Since she lives in his death.

Faithful felt a little puzzled. He understood, from the gesture of Philip's hand towards the wide fair landscape in front of them, that the lady of the poem was not Rosamond but the spirit of beauty alive in this country where they lived. . . . But why must they die to keep her alive?

"A country has no life until men see it and love it," said Philip dreamily, sitting with his chin cupped in his hand, "and no soul until they die for it. Without them it is just a beautiful picture. But once love it and die for it and it has an immortal spirit. . . . Look at the river silver under the sun, think of the way the grass ripples in summer as though flames were passing over it; there's something burning there that's been set alight by men's love and kept alight by their death."

Faithful thought this far-fetched, and said so. "Most men don't die for anything particular," he objected. "They die because they are old, or because they catch diseases, or trip over something and fall down."

"Not the lovers in life," said Philip. "What about Christ? What about Socrates? What about the patriots? What about the martyrs? What about Rosamond herself, who died to the world that Henry's honor might live? If you love anything at all you will have to die that it may live."

"Only the great lovers," said Faithful.

"The little lovers too," said Philip. "Even those who don't know they are doing it. How much of the earth of which England is made, and from which the flowers spring, is made up of the dead bodies of men and women who have been buried in it during centuries? If their bodies make her earth doesn't something of their spirits make her spirit? And even while physical life lasts there is the daily death to self of the saints who love God. Love and death are birth and rebirth. When God loved there was creation, when God died there was redemption."

He floated off into a dream, then woke up suddenly to say, "I don't understand men like Walter Raleigh, who want to give their lives to exploring the land beyond the sunset. What do they want with eccentric carnation-colored birds sitting about in gloomy cedar trees, and noisy cataracts tall as church towers? Isn't there beauty enough in this England to love and die for? There are fair hills here, with stately trees on their proud heights, like those over there on Rats and Mice Hill, and many valleys like this one comforted by silver rivers, and meadows and gardens full of flowers that must be the loveliest in the world; and I would rather have one of our little well-tuned brown birds singing of spring in a may-bush than a hundred carnation colored creatures squawking in cedar trees. I tell you I would rather die for this country than live to explore a hundred new ones."

"You're talking like an idiot!" said Faithful, suddenly angry. "Why talk about death on a day like this? Why not talk about life?"

Philip laughed. "It was Rosamond," he said, "who made me think of death and talk like an idiot." He jumped up and stretched his arms above his head. "I mean to live," he shouted. "Live and be famous."

"What for?" asked the literal Faithful.

"For a perfect poem," said Philip promptly. "I would rather be a great poet than anything else on earth." He picked up his bow and fingered it thoughtfully. "They say if you shoot an arrow into the air at random you find your fortune where you find your arrow. Let's tell mine. An arrowhead is in my coat of arms, so it ought to be able to tell me the truth."

He took an arrow from Faithful, fitted it into place, laid his body upon the bow and shot. The arrow went far and fast, gliding through the air and disappearing into the sunshine as though it were a part of it.

"Now we shall never find it," grumbled Faithful. "And we shall be late back trying to find it. And if we do find it how can it possibly tell you anything?"

"If it's sticking in the ground with the barb hidden and only the feathers showing," laughed Philip, "then I shall be what I want to be, a scholar and poet whose only weapon is a quill pen. But if it's lying flat with the barb showing then I shall have to be what my father wants me to be, a soldier as well." And handing his bow to Faithful he ran off along the bank of the stream, following the flight of his arrow towards Oxford.

"Don't you want to be a soldier?" panted Faithful, struggling after with the impedimenta.

"No!" Philip cried vehemently, his voice borne backwards by the wind. "I hate wounds and ugliness and stink and death."

Faithful forbore to point out that he had just been glorifying death. There is always a discrepancy, he had noticed, between what we think when in a moment of vision we have got free from the body and what we think when the body is once more in a position to make life unpleasant for us.

It seemed that the arrow meant to be found. They followed along the bank of the stream, pushing their way through the undergrowth, and came upon it quite suddenly, transfixing the speckled breast of a dead thrush.

"I've shot it!" said Philip in horror. "One of those well-tuned brown birds who sing of spring in a may-bush!"

"And it's a young one!" cried Faithful pitifully.

A cold fear fell upon both boys, making them white to the lips. Philip picked up the thrush, pulled out the arrow and stood holding the limp mass of bloody feathers in his hands.

"A dead singer," he said.

"And a young one," repeated Faithful. His own delight in life was so great that the death of even a young bird seemed to him the greatest of tragedies.

Philip laid the thrush down, wiped the blood off his hand on the grass, broke the arrow in pieces, the cruel gray goose that had killed a singer, and flung it in the stream.

"Anybody would think they feathered arrows from the wings of geese on purpose, just to lay stress upon the idiocy of killing," he said somberly. "Well, now I know. I shall be famous for my death."

"You don't know at all," growled Faithful. "There's nothing in omens. You're talking more like an idiot than ever."

"I am," agreed Philip with sudden cheerfulness. "A sentimental, conceited idiot. All the trumpet blowing and cheering on Beaumont Fields churned me up."

"Look at the sun," said Faithful. "It's late. If we're to be back in time for the feast in hall we must run."

They ran, their resilient spirits leaping up at every bound. At the sight of Oxford, rising grandly before them against the blue sky, and at the thought of the feast that awaited them at Christ Church, they shouted for joy.

"It's a good city," said Philip, "and a good country, this of ours that we will love and die for," and he began triumphantly singing the last verse of his song.

> Look, then, and die; the pleasure
> Doth answer well the pain;
> Small loss of mortal treasure
> Who may immortal gain.
> Immortal be her graces,
> Immortal is her mind;
> They, fit for heavenly places;
> This, heaven in it doth bind.
>
> But who hath fancies pleased
> With fruits of happy sight
> Let here his eyes be raised
> On Nature's sweetest light!

CHAPTER XVII

FAREWELL

Every month hath his flower and every season his contentment.

BESS THROGMORTON.

1.

JOYEUCE remembered that last evening as being the best of all, a never-to-be-forgotten evening that was one of the highlights of her life. There was a great feast in hall at which the Queen and her Court were entertained by the whole College, and afterwards there was music and dancing until the stars paled in the sky, and the birds, twittering under the eaves, made of their morning song a lullaby for sleepy revelers staggering home to bed.

Joyeuce had her own special part to play at this entertainment. She had to arrive as soon as the feasting was over bringing with her Diccon and Joseph attired as cupids, that they might present to the Queen a heart composed of crimson roses as a token of the devotion of the College. It was the Chancellor's idea and he thought it was a pretty conceit. Canon Leigh thought it was outrageous. The little boys, he considered, were far too small to make such an exhibition of themselves at such a late hour of the evening; and the affair was doubly trying as it meant that all the other children had to go too, at a time when they should have been in bed, because neither he nor they considered it fair that they should be excluded from an entertainment at which the babies of the family were to be present. . . . But he was inclined to look upon the whole performance as an invention of the devil and feared the effect upon the children's character was bound to be deleterious.

The children, with no thought at all for their characters, were in wild excitement when Joyeuce and Grace dressed them in Mistress Calfhill's big front bedroom. One of the ladies of the Court, let into the secret, had helped Joyeuce and Grace to make for the little boys exquisite but exceedingly skimpy garments of white feathers sewn upon a shell-pink foundation, worn with little feather wings secured across their chests with crossed golden ribbons, golden fillets round their heads and golden bows and arrows clasped in their hands. Their fat little legs and arms were bare and what their father would say when he saw the scantiness of their attire Joyeuce was sure she didn't know. . . . But they looked adorable.

The twins wore their new dresses of daffodil-yellow. They had pleaded for yellow dresses, real grown-up dresses with the kirtles of a deeper yellow than the farthingales "because the daffodils wear them like that, and when we wear them in Christ Church hall we shall be grown up."

"But you won't," Joyeuce had answered. "Even though you wear grown-up dresses you will still only be little girls, allowed to go and watch a grown-up party for a great treat."

But the twins had only squeaked at this, and shaken their heads very wisely. They knew better. They remembered that day so long ago, the May-Day when Faithful had come, when they had run out into the garden and seen the late daffodils dancing in the wind. They had known then that when the candles were burning in Christ Church hall, and they in their yellow dresses were dancing to the music of the viols, that then they would be grown up. To be grown up, they had thought, would be like being born again.

"We shall be born again," said Meg, as Joyeuce slipped her yellow kirtle over her head. "We shall do no more lessons with Great-Aunt."

"Born again," echoed Joan, and squeaked in joyous anticipation.

"Silly little poppets!" laughed Joyeuce, but the words chimed in her mind as though a merry bell were ringing.

Grace meanwhile was cleaning the nails of Will and Thomas, slapping their hair into something like order with forceful applications of a brush dipped in cold water, seeing that their new green doublets and hose were got into the right way round, and tweaking their starched ruffs into the correct position. "Ow!" they protested, writhing. "Stop it, Grace! It's effeminate to have clean nails. You should have seen my Lord of Rutland's nails; black as ink; we particularly noticed when he passed by in the procession. And my Lord of Oxford—"

"That's enough!" said Grace firmly, and knitting her brows and pursing her lips into a round obstinate rosebud she set to work upon Will's left hand with a deftness and determination that in ten minutes had achieved a result of such striking artistry that Joyeuce gasped when she beheld it.... Her father was right.... Grace's domestic commence was undoubtedly a gift of God.

So it was with a happy but very humble heart that Joyeuce left Grace to keep her eye on the children and dress herself at the same time—a feat that Joyeuce would never even have attempted, let alone accomplished with complete success—and gave all her attention to her own appearance.... For this was her betrothal night.... Before he led her out to dance tonight, so Nicolas had whispered to her, he would give her his ring. Tonight their friends, who had all been told their secret in great confidence, would smile upon them openly and wish them God-speed. Nicolas's career at Christ Church, after a lamentable failure at the spring examinations which had in no way disturbed him, was over now and he was free to marry; in a few weeks they would be husband and wife, riding away from the Fair Gate to an unknown life together, leaving Grace to bear with ease the load that had seemed so heavy to Joyeuce.

Suddenly, as she stood before her glass brushing out her lovely honey-colored hair, her eyes were blinded by tears.... Her heavy load. ... But was it really as heavy as she had thought? In laying it down she would be losing this home that she adored, set in this incomparable city, her father who so tenderly loved her, the little children who had been to her like her own. She put down her brush and pressed her hands over her eyes, fighting her tears. How could she leave them? Until this moment she had not realized how deeply she loved them. Why must sorrow and joy always be twined together like this? She had won her desire, and at the heart of it there was this pain. Why? Why? ... Born again. . . . Once more the twins' words rang in her mind like a little bell to comfort her. Every fresh beginning was a new birth and must have its pain as well as its joy, and without these fresh beginnings there could be no life, without them we should turn sour like stagnant water in a pond. And always, Joyeuce thought, the joy of a fresh beginning lures us on, outweighing the pain, dancing before us like a flame, so that hurrying to catch it the life in us keeps fresh and clear as a running stream. She wiped her eyes and picked up her brush with a smile. . . . In a few minutes now she would be running to meet Nicolas.

She and Grace both had new dresses, made and embroidered by themselves. Joyeuce had a green silk farthingale because Nicolas liked her best in "green sleeves," over a pale-pink kirtle embroidered with rosebuds, and Grace had chosen a very matronly farthingale of lavender color, over a cream-colored kirtle embroidered with purple pansies. They wore coifs of lovely lace on their shining hair and little satin shoes.

"We do look nice," said Grace, surveying herself in the glass with satisfaction. "We shall look as nice as any there. . . . Probably nicer."

Joyeuce flung her arms round the compact, rounded body of her younger sister. "You have such confidence, Grace," she cried, hugging her. "You never find things too much for you, do you?"

"Certainly not," said Grace, with decision. "I don't worry about them beforehand. . . . Now you," she added, with a comically pious expression upon her round rosy face, and plump hands folded at the waist, "cross every bridge before you get there, and in anticipating disasters you entirely fail to remember the powers of endurance that they invariably bring with them."

"You are quite right, Grace," murmured Joyeuce humbly, her eyes cast down that the twinkle in them might be hidden. "But shall I be able to endure it if I don't look as nice as the Court ladies, and Nicolas is ashamed of me?"

"He won't be," said Grace with decision. "I said to Nicolas the other day that the more I saw of other people the more I liked us, and he quite agreed with me."

2.

Joyeuce never forgot the sight that met her eyes when the doors of the hall were flung open by a servitor and she and the children went in. It was dusk now, and hundreds of candles were burning in great sconces set all round the walls, and their lovely light, kinder than sunshine, softer than moonlight, gave to the scene a radiant loveliness that made her gasp. The feast was not yet quite over and at the long table on the great dais at the far end of the hall the Queen was still sitting with the Chancellor, Dean Godwin, the dons of Christ Church and the senior members of her Court. The candlelight shone upon the rich colors of their dresses, upon their sparkling jewels and laughing faces, upon the silver bowls piled with fruit that stood upon the dark shining table, and upon the red wine in the Venetian glasses, held high to drink a toast. At the tables in the lower part of the hall sat the scholars with the younger maids of honor and the Court pages, dressed in their smartest, all on their best behavior but glowing with happiness, their faces as soft as flowers in the candlelight and their eyes like stars as they too held up their tankards of ale—not Venetian glasses and red wine for the smaller fry—waiting in palpitant excitement for the coming toast. . . . From where she stood Joyeuce could see Nicolas dressed in royal blue, his cheeks flushed and his eyes blazing, Faithful beside him in sober dove-gray slashed with lilac, Philip Sidney beautiful and serious in olive green, Walter Raleigh—what was he doing here?—in blazing scarlet, sitting beside a lovely little girl dressed in white like a snowdrop. . . . And then she saw no more, for the Chancellor was on his feet, the whole crowd of them rising with him, and the toast was given.

"The Queen. Vivat Regina!"

Such a roar of cheering and vivats went up that the great rafters of the hall, soaring up into a darkness that the candlelight did not touch, must surely have been shaken by the noise of it. Then silence fell, for the Queen had risen, motioning them all to their seats again with one long pale hand.

She was dressed in pearl-colored satin tonight, slashed with gold, and great rubies burned on her breast and on her shining hair. Joyeuce noticed with surprise that she was shorter than she had thought; her great dignity and splendid carriage made her seem taller than she was. She stood straight as a ramrod, with something almost masculine about the hard clear lines of her face and her stiffly braced shoulders, a something that was echoed in the depth and strength of her voice that carried effortlessly to the furthest corners of the hall. She is indomitable, was the thought in more than one mind. While she lives we are safe.

"Greetings to you, my scholars," she said, "and God's blessing upon you all. This is my last night with you, and my heart would be heavy were it not that you have given to me a memory that will be my possession for always. All my life I have loved learning, and because of my love my thoughts have turned often to this house of learning that my father founded. Often I have thought of it, pictured it, hoped that I should one day stay within its walls, and now that my hope has come true I find, as so seldom in life, that the fulfillment of my wish is sweeter even than the anticipation of it. I have found this house to be all I had hoped it would be, and more. In the quietness of its gardens, and of the rooms where I have lodged, I have found peace, and in the fellowship of learned men who have attained wisdom, and of young scholars who are striving for it, I have found inspiration. And let me tell you, my friends, that peace and inspiration are the two gifts of God that we most need in this our pilgrimage. If we have peace in our hearts the disorder and cruelty of life will not overwhelm us with despair, and if we have even for a short while seen that flash of light from another country that men call inspiration we shall have the courage to attempt, however unsuccessfully, to do our part in quieting the disorder and quelling the cruelty; until we have battled through them and our rest is won. . . . And it is in such houses as this, my scholars, that we find that peace and inspiration. . . . From the days of the good Saint Frideswide onwards holy men and women have lived here before you. Every moment of solace that came to them as they prayed, every fight for knowledge that won for them the quietude of achievement, was as a drop of water filling up the well of peace that stands in all ancient places.

Drink deep of it, and leave behind you for those who come after, as they did, that something of yourselves that is imperishable. And what shall I say of inspiration? You cannot have lived here and not known it. The stuff of those other men's lives is woven with your own, threads of heavenly silver lightening the earth-brown weft. Every pealing of the bells that called them to prayer in years that are past must seem to you a trumpet call, every sight of the spire that they raised to the glory of God must be to you as the sight of a banner in the sky. So go forth into the world, my scholars, to fight and work for your Queen and your country, with these things as imperishable memories in your hearts."

When once she began to speak it was usual for the Queen's Grace to be so carried away by her own eloquence that she went on a great deal longer than was necessary, but tonight she seemed to have upset herself by her own emotion, or else the dramatic sense of a consummate actress made it appear that she had, for she came to an abrupt end and sat down rather suddenly, to a second outbreak of applause even more thunderous than the first.

This was the moment chosen for Diccon and Joseph to do their part. They had been rehearsed in it very carefully, yet it was with a beating heart that Joyeuce launched them forth upon their journey up the space that had been kept clear between the tables, leading directly from the hall door to the foot of the dais. They had done it beautifully when they had practiced in an empty, quiet hall, but now that they had to make their way through a crowd, blinded by the lights and deafened by the cheering, she was afraid that Diccon would roar and Joseph turn tail and fly, or that upon reaching the dais they might drop the heart of roses and fall upon the food, or alternatively Diccon might bite the Queen and Joseph, a nervy child, might be sick.... There seemed no end to the frightful things that might happen.

But she had reckoned without the sense of pattern that there is in children. As swans will fly one behind the other in perfect formation, as little birds will lean their breasts against their nests to make of them a perfect round, so Diccon and Joseph knew instinctively that they were playing their part in something that had design. They must walk in a straight line to a given point, they must make certain movements, or the whole thing would be ruined. So their bare feet padded unflinchingly up the aisle through the cheering scholars, their little heads were held high and the chubby hands that grasped their golden bows were without a tremor. Between them they held the big heart of crimson roses, which they dropped only twice, and retrieved again without a moment's hesitation. They made straight for the gleaming figure of the Queen, like two little moths fluttering to a candle, and she, when she heard the low ripple of laughter that swept up the ball and saw them trotting towards her as though it were a breeze that carried them, left her seat and came to stand at the head of the flight of steps that led up to the dais. They negotiated these steps with some difficulty, but great determination, and collapsed rather suddenly into two little feathery balls at her feet. At this point they should have held up the heart of red roses in their arms and recited, line and line about, a pretty little verse about it being the heart of the College laid at the feet of a Queen; but they forgot it; Joseph propped the heart carefully against her farthingale, as though he were leaning a picture against a wall, and Diccon, gazing up at her with his green eyes as unblinking as a cat's, said, "For you," continuing further, with his fat forefinger pointed at a ruby drop hanging from her necklace, the very image of the one he had seen and howled for in the window of the aurifabray, "Pretty. Diccon wants it."

The Queen was in a good mood tonight and was not offended. She listened laughing as Dean Godwin repeated to her the forgotten rhyme, then took off her necklace and tossed it to the Chancellor. "Detach the ruby," she commanded, and then bent to take Diccon's face in her hands. " 'Tis a bold, bad face," she commented, "but it will belong one day to a bold, bad buccaneer who will sail the high seas and capture much wealth for his Queen. Is that not so, little cupid?" Diccon made no answer, but freeing his face from her hands—mercifully without biting—stretched out his hand for the ruby.

But Joseph's behavior was beyond reproach. When asked if he, too, would not like a pretty trinket, he gave her his lovely grave smile, shook his head and became absorbed in re-propping the heart upside down, because propped right way up it had fallen over. "An intelligent cupid," commented the Queen. "A poppet of much concentration." And feeling in her hanging pocket she produced a little Latin copy of the psalms, bound in crimson velvet, and gave it to him. He took it shyly, smiling at her, and immediately opened and became immersed in it, holding it upside down. . . . Then, at a signal from the Dean, one of the scholars stepped forward and picking up the little cupids removed them one under each arm; and immediately, the thing being over and the pattern completed, Diccon broke into roars of anger and fury that could he heard right out in the quadrangle.

3.

When the little boys had been taken away to bed by Dorothy Goatley, who had been waiting outside the hall door to perform this necessary but arduous office—Diccon being by now in such a rage at his removal that carrying him was like carrying a young earthquake—Joyeuce felt free to enjoy herself. No more anxieties now, only such pleasure as she had not known since that evening at the Tavern.

With lightning speed the servitors had cleared the tables and pushed them back against the walls to leave the hall clear for dancing. The musicians grouped in one of the big oriel windows were tuning their instruments, the soft twanging of the strings sending delicious tremors through Joyeuce as though fingers plucked at her heart; and the Queen, who loved dancing as dearly as any there, was being handed down the steps of the dais by the Chancellor. The candles seemed to burn yet more brightly, and there was a soft swishing of silks and caressing murmur of voices as young and lovely lovers moved towards each other over the gleaming floor. . . . And Joyeuce found Nicolas before her, beautiful as she had never seen him, smiling confidently down at her, lifting her hand and putting his ring upon it with a certain arrogance of possession that gave her such happiness that she gave a little stifled cry of joy, like a child who is lifted out of darkness into safety. He had taken her, and with such complete certainty that her always questioning heart found sudden rest.

"It is an emerald," she heard him saying, "because of that arbor in the Tavern garden. Those green vine leaves seemed then to be showing me how I should love you. . . . Gently. . . . Perhaps I shall grieve you sometimes, Joyeuce, perhaps you will find it hard to be patient with me. But I shall always love you. I shall always be faithful."

"I too," whispered Joyeuce. "I shall be faithful."

Then the lovely music of the pavane floated out into Christ Church hall, and he swung her into the dance.

Faithful and Grace, sitting together on a wooden table beside the great open fireplace, filled now with branches of greenery and bunches of late summer flowers, watched the gay scene in utter contentment. They looked a comical couple as they sat there hand in hand. Their legs, which did not reach the floor, were swinging childishly, but upon their faces was the wise, owl-like look of contemplative grandparents. Faithful could not dance. Grace had tried to teach him, and he had tried hard to learn, but he fell over his feet in such a distressing way that they had given it up as a bad job. "Never mind," Grace had said cheerfully. "It is perhaps just as well. If we do not dance we shall have more leisure to devote our minds to higher things."

The higher things were at this moment criticism of the scene before them, and gossip about the lovely figures of the dancers who bowed and swayed before them like flowers in the wind. . . . For Faithful, like many other learned men, liked a little gossip.

"Surely Master Walter Raleigh has no business to be here?" asked Grace.

"He got in through a window," said Faithful. "No one in authority has noticed him yet."

"They soon will," said Grace, "in that blazing scarlet doublet. Who is the girl he is dancing with? The pale little thing in white?"

"They say she is Mistress Bess Throgmorton, a little orphan girl whom the Queen has taken under her wing. She will be one of the maids of honor as soon as she is old enough."

"Do you think she is pretty?" asked Grace doubtfully.

Faithful regarded the slender figure of the lovely little girl with the kindling eye of admiration, but he answered stoutly, "She is not my style. Too pale."

Grace, happily conscious of her own pink cheeks and plump chest, sighed with satisfaction and turned her attention to two figures, in royal blue and pale green, who were as lovely as any there. "I had no idea," she said in shocked tones, "that Joyeuce was so worldly."

Faithful too turned his attention upon his future sister-in-law, and the sight of her gave him quite a shock. He had not realized that she could look so beautiful. The stiffness that used to mar her slender figure had all gone. She and Nicolas moved together through the stately figures of the dance with such grace that everyone was looking at them. But Joyeuce, usually so shy, seemed not to know that. Her face was flushed, her lips were parted and her eyes shining as though she saw a vision. But Faithful did not think that she looked worldly, he thought she looked the opposite.

"She looks," he said, "as though she were looking through a peep-hole at something."

"At what?" asked Grace.

"Some unchanging landscape," he murmured dreamily, and fell to wondering about love and joy and the connection between them. It is always love of something, he thought, that brings joy; love of some human being, of beauty or of learning. Love is the unchanging landscape, he thought, at which, among the changes and chances of this mortal life, we sometimes look through the peep-hole of joy; the love of God of which human love is a tiny echo. To be lost in it will be to have eternal life. One can know no more than that.

"Good heavens!" cried Grace, "I thought the twins had gone home to bed, but there they are—dancing!"

Will and Thomas, who thought dancing an overrated entertainment, had departed with some like-minded scholars to the kitchen, in the rear of the retreating food, but the twins were still here, dancing in a far corner of the hall with some little noblemen not much older than themselves. And they too, as they gravely pointed their small feet, executed their wobbly curtseys and turned their plump persons this way and that in the figures of the dance, looked as Joyeuce had looked; so happy that they seemed to be seeing a vision; and all the hundreds of candles, burning round Christ Church hall, did not shine so brightly as the yellow frocks they wore. "They look like spring," said Faithful. "They look like love and warmth and sunshine. All the stars must have danced when they were born."

"Did they make you of starlight?" asked Walter Raleigh of Bess Throgmorton, fingering a fold of her white dress, looking down boldly into the bright eyes that twinkled so merrily up at him. The dance had ended and they stood in one of the oriel windows, away from the crowd, well back in the secretive shadows whose black background gave to her whiteness a star-like glimmer. She dropped her eyes shyly before his that were so bold, for she was only a little girl yet, one of the youngest there; and suddenly the moon, coming out from behind a cloud, stained the snowy whiteness of her dress and bowed, white-coifed head with all the colors of the stained-glass window behind her, pink and blue and lilac and palest green. It was like a sudden blooming of flowers in midwinter, it was like the flooding of passion over the whiteness of her virginity, and Raleigh flung his arms round her with such headlong vehemence that she cried out a little, struggling like a young bird that has been snared and caught too soon.

"Why are you frightened?" he asked her. "You love me, don't you?" She was still then, and whispered, "Yes."

"I love you too," he announced, so loudly that she feared the whole hall would hear. "And one day I will have you for my wife."

"I have known you one hour," she whispered sadly, her head still bowed, "and I shall never see you again."

"You will," said Raleigh, still loudly. "I will find a way. I will have you for mine, even if I have to come to Court and steal you from under the Queen's nose."

But she shook her head. The maids of honor might not marry without the Queen's permission; and besides, she already knew something of men and their ways. "You will forget," she murmured.

"I never forget what I want," he said, "and I get it. Look at me. Do you think I look as though I would forget?"

She dared to raise her head, then, and looked at him, seeing afresh the bold penetrating blue eyes, the obstinacy and impetuous strength of the face bent above her. "I think," she said, "that you will always get what you want; or else you will die trying to get it. What else do you want, besides me?"

He pulled her eagerly down on to the windowseat and began to tell her, holding her so close against him that she thrilled to the pulse of excitement beating in his body and to the eager whispering of his warm, vehement voice. "All sorts of things. I want to sail a tall ship into the west to find the land beyond the sunset, so that the Queen may have a better Indies than the King of Spain. That's a wonderful land, Bess. Birds of white and carnation sing in tall cedar trees, and the stones are all made of gold and silver."

"Do you want gold and silver so badly?" asked Bess a little doubtfully; and she shivered, thinking of that tall ship that would carry him away from her.

"I want masses of gold," said Raleigh hotly. "I mean to sail round the world to look for it, and I mean to make it, too, for I shall be alchemist as well as sailor. We shall never do away with poverty and misery, never build a new world, until we have wealth; lots and lots of wealth."

"One can be happy in poverty," whispered Bess.

He snorted in contempt. He never had any use for poverty. "Only the well-off think so," he said. "Do you know what my idea of heaven is? A place that is all shining with jewels. I've made up a verse about it.

> And when. . . . we
> Are filled with immortality,
> Then the holy paths we'll travel,
> Strewed with rubies thick as gravel,
> Ceilings of diamonds, sapphire floors.
> High walls of coral and pearl bowers.

"Dreams! Dreams!" said a woman's low voice, and looking up the two culprits saw three figures standing by them in their shadowy window, splendid figures that even in the dimness gleamed and sparkled. The Queen, the Chancellor and Dean Godwin. Little Bess, as she slipped out of Raleigh's arms and slid to her feet to make her curtsey, was gasping with terror, but Raleigh bowed with the flourish that never deserted him.

"And who is this who has made away with my little Bess?" asked the Queen tartly, and she motioned him towards the light.

"Master Walter Raleigh of Oriel," said Dean Godwin severely. "He very kindly played Arcite in our play, our own Arcite having met with an accident. But what he is doing here tonight I do not know."

"I came through the window," said Raleigh loudly, "that I might feast my eyes upon Her Grace."

"It seems to me," said the Queen with increased tartness, "that it is upon the little Bess, not the big one, that you have been feasting them." But face to face with the future Captain of her Guard she could not but smile; he gave promise of becoming a very fine figure of a man, and she was always as wax in the hands of a handsome man. "And what were these dreams of which you murmured?" she asked him. "These dreams of carnation colored birds and floors of sapphire? Dreams, young man, are useless things that lead you nowhere."

"I venture to disagree with Your Grace," said Raleigh, his head up. "All achievement is born of dreams followed bravely to an unknown destination."

A figure passing between them and the light threw a shadow on his face and the Queen shivered with a sudden icy little premonition. To what destiny would his dreams bring himself and little Bess? To what end of blood and death and agonizing sorrow? He had answered her impudently, and she had meant to rebuke him for it, but now she could not. "You must bring Bess back into the hall," was all she said. "She is only a little girl and she must not be played with."

She turned and went away, followed by the Dean and the Chancellor, but Raleigh, before he obeyed her, turned and flung his arms once more round Bess. "It was not play!" he whispered fiercely. "I have loved you and chosen you in my happiest hour. You must not forget me."

"I'll not forget," said little Bess.

The Queen, with the Chancellor upon her right and Dean Godwin upon her left, passed on down the hall through the lines of scholars, smiling at their eager faces, pausing now and then to ask a question or recognize a familiar face. "Which are my scholars of Westminster?" she asked the Dean, and there was immediately a great commotion in the crowd, Westminster plunging to the fore with Ipswich kicked viciously into the background. . . . But she would not have that. . . . When she had spoken sweet words to her own Westminster she had Ipswich rescued from a sprawling position under the tables and spoke soothing words to it of its founder, the great Cardinal, of his love for this College and the faithful service he gave to his king. "Love this fair house as he did," she bade them, "and serve me as loyally as he served my father." They promised her to do so, gazing at her with eyes full of worship, and hastened, as soon as her back was turned, to retaliate upon Westminster with hard and well-placed kicks.

The Queen passed on down the line, pausing next for Philip Sidney to be presented to her by the Chancellor. "A fair boy," she murmured to the infatuated uncle, as Philip bowed low before her. "A boy of whom we shall both be proud." And again, as Philip straightened himself and his eyes met hers, she felt that stirring of premonition. She remembered her own words, spoken at the end of her speech, "Go forth into the world. Fight and work for your Queen and country." She had said that word "fight" carelessly, hardly stopping to think what she meant by it, but now it seemed to her that beyond the walls enclosing this space of light and laughter she could hear the galloping hoofs of the Rider on the Red Horse. She hated war; above all things she asked for her reign the blessing of peace. Would she ever have to endure the agony of sending these boys and others like them over the seas to meet the Red Horseman? She saw all their fair lives threatened by terror and blood and wounds. She saw herself, an older woman, weary and sick at heart, standing up with a proud face to make bold speeches, doing her best to hearten men for

death as just now she had been heartening boys for life.... Speeches....
Speeches.... How sick of them she would be before the end. She looked
again at Philip Sidney's face and felt a sharp pang of grief, as sharp as any
she would feel in the years to come when she would weep for his death
and refuse to be comforted, vowing that she had lost her mainstay. It was
a terrible thing to be the Queen of England. It was a burden too heavy to
be borne. She turned abruptly away, without speaking another word to
Philip.... The Chancellor, much annoyed at her neglect, followed her
with a heightened color.

But her next encounter cheered her. Joyeuce in her pale green gown
and Nicolas in his royal blue, standing hand in hand, were a couple to
challenge attention. Joyeuce she remembered as a fragile wraith who
had hovered behind Dame Cholmeley on her arrival at her lodgings,
but Nicolas's face puzzled her. She remembered the eyebrows so wickedly tilted at the corners, the laughing black eyes and the strong chin
with the cleft in it, but she could not remember where she had seen
them last. Nicolas, putting his hand into his doublet and bringing it out
with a crumpled red rose lying on the palm, enlightened her. "Ever since
the Queen of England gave it me I have worn it next my heart," he lied
superbly.

"The troubadour!" she laughed. "The young man who sang me a
lullaby under my window. And what can I do for you, good sir?"

Nicolas gripped Joyeuce's hand tightly and eyed his sovereign with
boldness. "With the permission of Your Grace, my bride and I would
like to come to Court."

The Dean broke in here with a neat little memorandum of Nicolas's
family tree, which was well rooted in wealth, well-watered with blue
blood, had been quite satisfactory in growth and gave promise of loyal
foliage in the future. The recitation was well received. "You shall come,"
said the Queen.

And instantly joy, like dawn, broke over the two faces before her in
such a flood of brightness that her late sadness was suddenly lightened.
It was sweet to have it in her power to give such pleasure. It was sweet
to know, as she knew, that her people found in her the fulfillment of all

hope and the inspiration of all action. Beyond the walls that enclosed her, out in the night, she remembered that there stretched the woods and hills and valleys of her country, and the towns and homesteads that sheltered the men and women who were her people; a most fair and lovely country, a people compounded of courage, humor and kindliness. And they seemed to her, as she thought of them, to be invincible. The galloping hoofs of the Rider on the Red Horse might pass over them, but they would still endure. It was not so little a thing to be the Queen of England. It was not so little a thing to say of this country and this people, "They are mine."

4.

The sky was a clear cold green, and in the east the morning star blazed gloriously between bars of flaming cloud, when Nicolas supported the slightly wavering footsteps of Walter Raleigh home to Oriel. Everyone else had gone home long ago. They had lingered behind for a few last drinks with some kindred spirits, and now they seemed to themselves to be quite alone in the lovely silence of the dawn. They walked slowly, drinking in the clear air like great draughts of cold water, feeling its freshness like a benediction on their hot faces. . . . Not that they showed many signs, in the outward man, that this dawn was the climax of a night of revelry. . . . Their two brilliant figures, scarlet and royal blue, were both still unruffled, both of them having that gift for keeping tidy under the most unlikely circumstances shared alike by robbins, buttercups, cats, tigers, and all those dowered with stout hearts, self-confidence, and that beauty that draped over the iron foundation of strong nerves is not easily frayed by contact with the sorrows and entertainments of this exhausting world. Though their faces were flushed they were becomingly flushed, though their hair was tumbled it had fallen into that graceful abandon that is more pleasing to the eye than correctitude. The only noticeable signs of a slight tendency to insobriety were in Raleigh's legs, Nicolas's solemn concern for them, and an exceedingly poetical frame of mind in both. Raleigh, as always when in his cups, was composing scraps and shreds of verse so lovely that they seemed to Nicolas to have floated straight out of that beautiful dawn where the morning star burned between bars of flaming cloud.

> *She is neither white nor brown,*
> *But as the heavens fair,*
> *There is none hath a form so divine*
> *In the earth or the air.*

He sighed heavily, and looked up at the fleecy clouds above his head as though challenging them to form an image lovelier than the one he had in his mind. "Look where you're going," said Nicolas, easing him round the corner of the quadrangle towards Peckwater Inn. "And you can't have met a maiden as lovely as that tonight; there wasn't one there; except Joyeuce." Raleigh rolled upon him an injured and rebuking eye and began again.

> *Such an one did I meet, good Sir,*
> *Such an angelic face,*
> *Who like a queen, like a nymph did appear*
> *By her gait, by her grace.*

They pursued their wavering way to Canterbury College, where he cried out in despair so profound that he nearly lost his footing and sent them both sprawling.

> *Know that Love is a careless child,*
> *And forgets promise past;*
> *He is blind, he is deaf when he list*
> *And in faith never fast.*

"Sometimes," said Nicolas gently, remembering the pledge he had given to Joyeuce, "he remembers."

"Sometimes," murmured Raleigh dolefully, but as they crossed Shidyard Street he seemed to change his mind, for his face lightened, and when they had reached the gate of Oriel he propped himself carefully against it and faced Nicolas with a sudden blaze of triumph.

> *But love is a durable fire*
> *In the mind ever burning;*
> *Never sick, never old, never dead,*
> *From itself never turning.*

Then he turned and disappeared, admitted by a watchful porter who delighted, as did Heatherthwayte for Nicolas, to keep the eccentric hours of his exits and entrances hidden from the eye of Authority.

Nicolas strolled homewards through the lovely morning, that grew with every moment richer in beauty and promise. At the doorway that led to the room he still shared with Faithful, under the carved pomegranate of Catherine of Aragon, he paused to look back at the towers and spires so delicately penciled against the glorious dawn sky that curved above them in the semblance of a great circle. He felt a pang of pain to think that he must so soon leave it all, but yet he had at the same time a glorious feeling of permanence. Raleigh at the last had been quite right. Love was an unchanging thing, not an emotion but an element in which the whole world had its being. All the lovely things upon earth, beauty and truth and courage, were faint pictures of it, even as the puddles of rain water at his feet held a faint picture of the fiery sky bending above the earth. And in the mind of man too the flame was caught and held; in his own mind whose strength and vigor made it possible for his eyes to see this picture of a fair city and a golden sky, for his soul to face life vowed to integrity and courage, for his heart to feel for Joyeuce an affection so strong that he dared to call it by the name of that eternal and embracing love.

> *But love is a durable fire*
> *In the mind ever burning;*
> *Never sick, never old, never dead.*
> *From itself never turning.*

5.

That same day the Queen left Oxford. It was now early September, a calm and lovely day, one of those soft blue days of early autumn when the color of the sky seems to have soaked into the earth. The city itself seemed built of blue air, and the flowers in the gardens, the late roses, the hollyhocks and michaelmas daisies, had drawn a thin blue veil over their bright colors. When evening came again the shadows would be very deep and very blue and the calling of the birds would be very clear in the stillness.

But now, in the morning, the city was full of noise and bustle. The Queen was to ride out of East Gate and up through Shotover Forest on the first stage of her journey to London, and once more scholars lined the route, from the Fair Gate to East Gate, with the townspeople packed behind them. Once more garlands were slung across the street, tapestries hung from every window, and the bells rang out to speed the Queen upon her way. But though all was noise and bustle and excitement there was an undercurrent of sadness about this day; the longed-for visit was over and it might be many years before the Queen's Grace came again. Yet mixed with the sadness there was still rejoicing, for during this time of heightened living, dreams and visions and ideals had glowed more radiantly, and when the Queen had left the city the life she left behind her would burn the more brightly because she had been.

So when the cavalcade left Christ Church it was greeted by another great roar of cheering, and shouts of "Vivat Regina! Vivat Regina!" rolled up Fish Street and down the High Street as the procession wound its way down through the town. The departure was perhaps a lovelier sight than the arrival had been, for the beautiful curves of the High Street lent themselves to a processional passing. It was like a lovely ribbon of color slowly unwinding itself between the cheering crowds and the gabled houses, slipping downwards to coil away forever into the green and silent woods.

The Queen was on horseback today, sitting her white mare superbly, wearing a long blue habit whose skirts nearly swept the cobbles and a tall blue hat with white plumes in it. She was quite alone that all the people might see her, with the Chancellor, Vice Chancellor and heads of houses riding in front and the Court behind, and she took most gracious notice of all that was done to show her love and honor. She missed nothing of the long and polished Latin oration delivered outside the Fair Gate by Master Tobie Matthews, an M.A. of Christ Church, even though she was trying to mount her spirited horse at the time and it was difficult to fix her attention on it, and as she rode down High Street she reined in her horse that she might have read to her the copies of verses bemoaning her departure that were hung upon the walls of All Souls and University College. And all the while she was waving to the people, raising a laughing face to the little children crowded at the windows, smiling when armfuls of flowers were flung upon the cobbles and the sweet smell of bruised September roses came up to her from beneath her horse's feet. When she had passed the people strained forward, leaning perilously from windows, standing on tiptoe to see over each other's heads and shoulders while tears ran down their faces, trying to catch a last glimpse of that dazzling blue and white figure on the white horse, the young and lovely Queen whom they might never see again. Then the cavalcade passed under East Gate and they had lost her. Sadly they turned homeward.

Under Magdalen tower the pealing bells were stilled and the procession was halted that the Mayor and city fathers, gathered there to take their leave, might take it with the customary speeches. But it was noticed that though she smiled and bowed at the correct moment the attention of the Queen's Grace seemed inclined to wander; her eyes were continually leaving the earnest perspiring faces of the city fathers and gazing at Magdalen tower, soaring up into the blue sky above her, its ornamented belfry fretting the sky like wing-tips; and when the speeches were over and the farewells said, and the horses once more curvetting forward, she looked up at it and raised her hand in greeting, as though it stood beside the East Gate like a veritable presence set to guard the city, one whom she would remember and who would remember her.

The Vice-Chancellor and heads of houses, loth to say good-by, rode with the Queen and her Court up the bridle path through the woods and out on to the heights of Shotover, and here they halted for positively the last speech from the Provost of Oriel, for the last farewells, for the last promises that while life went on they would never forget.

Then the Queen abruptly wheeled her horse away from the laughing throng of courtiers and scholars and rode by herself to the brow of the hill where Faithful had stood on May morning. She saw the valley full of green trees that were already touched here and there with the colors of autumn, backed by low blue hills resting against the sky. Her eyes followed the curve of the valley until they reached a certain place that she knew of, where towers rose out of the autumn haze. It looked like a fragile city spun out of dreams, so small that she could have held it on the palm of her hand and blown it away like silver mist. Perhaps she knew at that moment how many years would pass before she visited that city again, years of unceasing work and anxiety that would never break her spirit but would strip her of her beauty and make of her a weary old woman in a red wig. Perhaps it was because she doubted if the shouts of "Vivat Regina!" that had greeted the young Queen would be as full of love when they greeted the old woman, that she wept, or perhaps it was because she knew quite well that the passing of the years would make no difference, but it was reported by those who had followed her that as she raised her hand in farewell to the city her eyes were full of tears.

"Farewell!" she cried. "God bless you and increase your sons in number, holiness and virtue. Farewell, Oxford, Farewell. Farewell."